T0036377

Also by Sara E. Johnson

The Alexa Glock Forensics Mysteries
Molten Mud Murder
The Bones Remember
The Bone Track

THE BONE RIDDLE

THE BONE RIDDLE

AN
ALEXA GLOCK
FORENSICS
MYSTERY

SARA E. JOHNSON

Poisoned Pen
PRESS

Published by Poisoned Pen Press, an imprint of Sourcebooks
P.O. Box 4410, Naperville, Illinois 60567-4410
(630) 961-3900
sourcebooks.com

Library of Congress Cataloging-in-Publication Data

Names: Johnson, Sara E., author.
Title: The bone riddle : an Alexa Glock forensics mystery / Sara E.
   Johnson.
Description: Naperville, Illinois : Poisoned Pen Press, [2023] | Series:
   Alexa Glock Forensics Mysteries ; book 4
Identifiers: LCCN 2022061934 (print) | LCCN 2022061935
(ebook) | (trade paperback) | (epub)
Subjects: LCGFT: Detective and mystery fiction. | Novels.
Classification: LCC PS3610.O37637 B664 2020 (print) | LCC PS3610.O37637
   (ebook) | DDC 813/.6--dc23/eng/20230106
LC record available at https://lccn.loc.gov/2022061934
LC ebook record available at https://lccn.loc.gov/2022061935

Printed and bound in the United States of America.
SB 10 9 8 7 6 5 4 3 2 1

For Beau

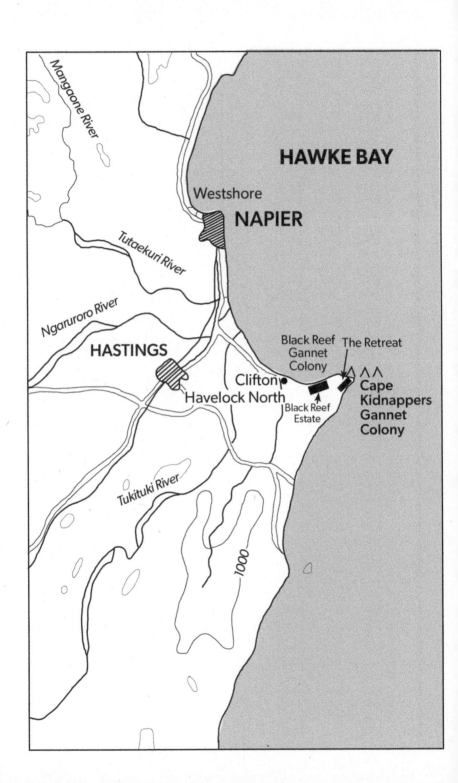

THURSDAY

Chapter One

Alexa Glock had the two things she needed: an Instagram selfie and an X-ray of a skull. She manipulated the two images on the computer screen. The young woman in the selfie—wide, pale eyes, bulbous cheeks, expectant smile—deserved her full concentration.

Three days ago, adult female skeletal remains had been found in a gully in Aoraki/Mount Cook National Park. Her death was probably the result of a rockslide. Alexa had X-rayed the skull yesterday at the morgue.

The selfie was of twenty-year-old Karin Johansson, who had last been active on social media six months ago. Her distraught parents, from the west coast of Sweden, had shared her social media accounts with the New Zealand police after their daughter stopped responding to texts and emails.

The onset of a nightmare.

Alexa ignored her coffee and positioned the two images atop each other as if they were on tracing paper. She moved the X-ray forward and backward, up and down, left and right, orienting the cheekbone without flesh to the cheekbone with flesh. When she had them aligned, the skull was consistent with the selfie face. Not that that was a clincher. Another skull of similar size and contours could be consistent too.

Smiling selfies were valuable postmortem investigative resources when dental records weren't available. Alexa didn't do Instagram, but Karin had been fond of posing and posting. Alexa imagined she was confident and boisterous—having an adventure in a foreign country, on the cusp of adulthood. She zoomed in on a space between the top incisors and clicked Adjust Image Transparency.

A sudden voice made her jiggle the adjustment.

"We have a bunker body."

She looked up from the screen at her bespectacled boss. "A what?"

Dan Goddard, in his signature red Converse tennis shoes, was Alexa's age, thirty-seven, and director of Auckland's Forensic Service Center, where she worked. They had a running Converse versus Keds shtick.

"A bunker body. A dead man in a bolt-hole. Has probably been dead a few days."

She studied Dan's sober face, not grasping the situation.

"A lot of rich Americans have bought up Kiwi land and built compounds with bunkers, I guess for when the apocalypse comes," he explained. "They'll pop into their private jets, fly to the southern hemisphere, and hole up like hobbits."

Alexa wasn't a Tolkien fan.

"This bunker is in Cape Kidnappers," he said.

Her eyes jumped to the map she had tacked to her cubicle wall to become familiar with her home away from home. "Where's that?"

New Zealand is divided into two major islands and many smaller islands. Dan ran his finger along the east coast of the North Island and tapped a spot. "Four hours south."

Alexa squinted; she wondered if she needed to have her eyes checked. The North Island was a bottom-heavy figure eight. Auckland is where the two ovals join together, as fragile a connection as the neck is to the spine. Dan tapped farther below, where the coast indented like a bite mark. "A Silicon Valley CEO named Harlan Quinn owns the estate," Dan said.

She thought of Apple and Facebook and Google.

"The estate has a name: Black Reef."

The name sounded ominous.

"There's a big house and a cottage. Plus the bunker. The housekeeper cleans the bunker once a month. She showed up this morning and the bunker was locked from inside. Her husband, the caretaker, got in through a back door. He found a nasty surprise."

"Jeez. The CEO locked himself in his bunker? You suspect suicide?"

"We don't even know if it's him."

"Has he been reported missing?"

"That hasn't been confirmed." Dan bent over to tie his shoelace. "Facial recognition isn't possible. All that's known is the deceased is an adult male. If it's the billionaire, this will be big international news. We don't want to spare any expense in identifying the deceased."

Alexa's mind cartwheeled. "Are there signs of foul play?"

"I don't know. I told the police you'd be there this afternoon."

She nodded. In suspicious circumstances, a forensic examiner should visit the death scene before the body is removed. This is a critical component in the success of an investigation, and this scene sounded plenty suspicious.

Dan straightened. "The closest police station is thirty minutes away. Hastings is a city of maybe fifty thousand. The DI is Mic Steele. Follow all orders, right? No coloring outside the lines?"

Alexa stiffened. There had been a time or two recently when she'd had to think for herself and do what needed to be done—for the good of the case. Some sergeant or constable must have complained. Not DI Bruce Horne, with whom she occasionally worked and was seeing regularly. She thought of his steady gaze, his honesty, his imperturbability. He would never betray her. She was about to defend herself but bit her tongue. Keeping her job as a traveling forensic investigator allowed her to stay in New Zealand on a work visa. There was no point in returning to North Carolina. No one waited with open or closed arms.

"No scribbling, I promise. Should I drive the Batmobile?"

"No need. The Hastings Police Department has a good lab."

Alexa hid her disappointment. The forensic van had all kinds of cool gadgets she wanted to play with.

When Dan left, she realigned the images and zoomed in on the teeth. Her specialty was odontology, and it was the rotated incisor on both the selfie and X-ray that clenched—well, clinched—the ID. The computer would use objective and numerical data for evaluating matches and confirm Alexa's finding.

Karin's parents' nightmare exploded into reality.

That was the dichotomy of her work. Results could cause heartbreak. *Knowing is better than not knowing,* she reminded herself. She grabbed the phone to report her findings.

When one riddle was solved, another opened wide.

Chapter Two

Alexa sprinted up three flights of stairs, added a side kick at the top—she had started kickboxing classes recently—and entered her apartment. Her cop roommate, Natalie, was folding clothes from a pile on the kitchen table. "I thought you'd be gone by now," Alexa said.

"Yeah nah." She stuffed navy cargo pants into her duffel bag. "You didn't come home last night."

Alexa flushed; she'd spent the night with Bruce. For the first time. "Didn't think I'd see you before I left," Natalie said.

She was leaving for a six-week orientation at the Police Dog Training Center near Wellington and would return with a German shepherd. Alexa skirted a giant dog crate and filled the electric kettle with water for a second cup of coffee. One for the road. She was uneasy around dogs—never having had one—but since her name wasn't on the lease, she kept her mouth shut. The apartment was close to work, and the rent was reasonable.

While she waited for the water to boil, she fetched her to-go bag, prepacked with three days' worth of work outfits and running gear. She stuck her latest copy of *Forensic Science International* and the romance novel she was reading into the outer compartment. Her crime kit was already stowed in her ten-year-old Toyota Vitz hatchback.

Back in the kitchen, she said, "I'm going out of town, too. I've got a new case in Cape Kidnappers."

Natalie tightened the sash on her kimono robe. "Cape Kidnappers is not the original name." She stepped to the dryer wedged next to the refrigerator and reached in. "I grew up near there. Te Matau-a-Māui is the Māori name."

Alexa poured boiling water into the French press, antsy to get going. She practiced a few jabs and crosses; Natalie was the one who got her hooked on kickboxing.

"It translates to Māui's fishhook." Natalie, un-coplike in a shortie robe and pink slippers, shook wrinkles out of a gray polo. "There's a gannet colony there."

"A what colony?"

"Gannet colony. Massive white seabirds with golden heads. Thousands of them around Hawke's Bay. Smell 'em before you see 'em. We used to stand on the cliffs—my cuz, my little sister, and me—and watch them plunge dive. Like missiles, they are." She fished a couple black crew socks out of the laundry basket at her feet, balled them, and stuffed them in the duffel. Alexa suspected they were dirty.

"Captain James Cook sailed into the bay back in 1769, yeah, I think? We studied it in school. The Māori paddled out from shore in *wakas* to do trading."

Alexa knew *wakas* were canoes. She'd been living in New Zealand for ten months now; her Māori and Kiwi vocabulary was accumulating. She poured the coffee into her travel mug, added milk, and secured the lid. She wanted to leave, but Natalie prattled on.

"The crew used a Tahitian cabin boy to hand over the goods. One of the Māori grabbed the boy and paddled back toward shore, the boy packing a sad."

Alexa surmised "packing a sad" meant pitching a fit. She'd add it to her dictionary.

"Captain Cook ordered his sailors to fire their muskets." She tucked strands of brown hair behind her ear and made a gun with her hand. "Pop."

"I have to…"

"One of the paddlers was hit. The boy dove into the water and swam back to the ship. That's why Cook named it Cape Kidnappers." She zipped up the duffel. "Not that it was his to name. The Māori…"

"I have to go."

Natalie flushed as pink as her robe.

Alexa felt bad to interrupt, but the bunker body was waiting. In minutes she had loaded the car and pulled onto Queen Street.

Her driving route would bisect the North Island and take her through Rotorua, where she'd wormed her way into her first New Zealand case. She smiled. It's where she met Bruce. He was living there at the time but had now transferred to Auckland to work in the serious crimes department at Auckland Central Police Department.

And maybe to be closer to her. She fought traffic for several blocks and then merged onto the highway. Bruce was spending this coming weekend in Rotorua with his daughters, Denise and Sammie. Last night, while he was frying steaks, he suggested she come with him. She choked on her beer. Meeting Bruce's daughters reminded her of meeting Rita, her stepmother. She'd been about the same age as Bruce's youngest, thirteen. Alexa hadn't spoken, smiled, or made eye contact with Rita. "Your daughters don't want to meet me."

"Sure they do," he said. "Sammie loves *CSI*."

"That show gets it all wrong," she said.

There was a difference. Bruce's daughters hadn't lost their mom to a brain tumor; they lived with Sharla except for two weekends a month with Bruce. *Sharla*. What kind of name was that? The invitation fluttered unresolved. She'd call Bruce from the road and tell him she was sorry, but duty prevailed.

She reached for her coffee.

Dammit.

She'd left it on the kitchen counter. Once she was free of Auckland's clutches, she spared five minutes to buy a flat white and a pastry at a roadside café. A few heavenly bites and sips in— the road ahead devoid of traffic—she called Bruce. He answered on the first ring. "DI Bruce Horne."

"Hi. It's me."

"What's up? I'm on my way to a meeting."

Jeez. She wasn't calling to tell him she was glad he had pulled her back under the covers this morning. "I have a new travel case. I'm on the way."

"The bunker body?"

No surprise that he had already heard. "Yes."

"Steele just got promoted."

Why was he talking about steel? Then she remembered Steele was the Hastings detective inspector's name.

"I'll check in with you later," he said and disconnected.

Alexa stuffed the phone in the cup holder. Had she overstepped by thinking Bruce would want to know where she was going? Probably. She always messed up relationships, usually by bailing. She fingered the *pounamu* pendant hanging around her neck on a soft leather cord. The spiral shape symbolized new beginnings and tranquility. Rubbing the greenstone calmed her down.

Heat sometimes radiated from the greenstone. When that happened, she figured it was communicating with her. Trying to tell her something or guide her.

She zipped past the turnoff for Rotorua and focused her thoughts on the body. Dan had said a caretaker discovered it, and that the door was locked from the inside. Suicide? If not suicide, had the dead man locked the door to prevent someone from getting in? What if he had accidentally locked himself in and couldn't get out?

She didn't know boo about bunkers.

Anticipating the smell of a decomposing body made her think

of the country farmhouse case she had worked a couple years ago. It had been August, in North Carolina, and odor mortis hit her as soon as she opened her car door. She rolled her window down at the memory. The woman was sprawled on the kitchen floor. Maggots poured out of what was left of her nose and mouth. The same greeting might await her in the bunker. She panicked until she remembered her tube of StinkBalm Odor Blocker. She would smear it under her nose before she masked up. She hadn't ordered the coffee scent, though. She was afraid it would turn her off from her favorite brew. She had settled on evergreen.

A sign announced Cape Kidnappers was twenty-two kilometers away. Alexa converted the distance into miles: thirteen. In the one-horse town of Clifton, she slowed for a parade of four red tractors, each towing an empty trailer. On the side of the trailers, in blue letters, was GANNET TRACTOR TOURS. A black dog rode shotgun in the last tractor.

She laughed.

The little town faded in her rearview mirror as the Toyota climbed for a half mile to a cliff-top plateau, no railings in sight. Out the passenger window, Hawke's Bay stretched in a teal semicircle: the bite mark on her office map. An image of driving off the ledge, catapulting through space—the call of the void—flashed in her head. She gripped the steering wheel until the GPS ordered her to turn, leaving the bay behind.

This road was gravel and single lane. It wound by fields of sheep and cattle, up and down hillocks, past meadows of Golden Tussock. Alexa relaxed. One half-hidden turnoff led to something called The Retreat, and then a canopy of trees thrust her into shade. She pulled off her sunglasses and tightened her grip again, banking a bend too fast.

A dark blur of movement made her brake. An ATV barreled straight at her.

"Move over, idiot!" At the last moment she jerked the car into a ditch, her fender crunching into a rock. Blood pulsed in her ears.

Holy hell.

She checked the rearview mirror. The ATV—a fancy one with a windshield and roof—was swallowed by a curve. There had been a single shadowy occupant. She breathed deeply and unbuckled her seat belt. The car was still running. She turned it off, listened to the engine tick, three times, then silence.

The driver wasn't coming back.

Her right bumper was making out with a boulder. She gritted her teeth, started the car, and put the Toyota in reverse. The wheels churned pebbles. If she rocked it back and forth, it would do more damage. She turned the car off, grabbed her phone, and got out.

She was in the middle of goddamn nowhere. The wop-wops. She checked the GPS on her phone screen and noted two things: it was only a kilometer to Black Reef, and her battery was three percent.

"Dammit."

Someone at the scene would help her out of the ditch. She hiked her crime kit over her shoulder—it weighed twenty pounds—and set off. After so much openness, the tree canopy was claustrophobic. Beech. Oak. Rimu. A towering fern. A motor.

Alexa jumped into the ditch. A Volvo station wagon banked the curve, slowed down, and stopped next to her. A narrow-chinned woman peered out her open window. "Had a little trouble, eh?"

A teenage boy gawked at her from the passenger seat. Alexa stepped closer. A police badge was pinned to the woman's blazer. "I'm Alexa Glock, a forensic examiner. I'm heading to Black Reef." She explained what happened.

"Fancy that. I'm Detective Inspector Micala Steele. Get in."

Alexa had assumed "Mic" Steele was a man; she was surprised and excited to work with a woman DI. She shoved the crime kit next to a bulging backpack, probably the kid's, and climbed in. Why wasn't the kid in school?

"The ATV must have passed you," she said.

"No one passed us." DI Steele put the Volvo in gear and they jerked forward. "It probably turned off to The Retreat. It's a posh inn."

Alexa wanted to ask about the case but kept quiet because of the boy. She studied the back of the DI's long neck; her brown hair was twisted in a knot at the nape. Alexa hoped they'd get along. That was a problem with being a traveling forensic investigator. She had to adjust to a different crop of cops with each case.

They drove past a NO TRESPASSING sign. Alexa searched the trees for cameras. "Are there surveillance cameras on the property?"

The kid turned toward her, his eyes alert.

The DI snorted. "Nah yeah. My sergeant said they're fake."

After a half mile they emerged from the thicket to a parklike setting.

"Take a gawk," the kid said.

DI Steele stopped the car. "This cost the big bucks, alright." Alexa leaned forward. Between the DI and the kid, she saw a sprawling single-story house of stone and timber. It perched above Hawke's Bay. *A million-dollar view*, Alexa thought. No. Make that a billion-dollar view. She had read that one million seconds was about twelve days, and one billion seconds was thirty-one years, but a billion dollars was still an abstract concept.

She squinted. A pool jutted out over the cliff. To its left she spotted a small cream-colored cottage.

As the DI pulled forward, a sculpture of three giant silvery seabirds—wings outstretched—caught Alexa's eye. One bird's wingtip was embedded in the grass as anchor. Alexa searched for the bunker, then realized it wouldn't be visible. A police car, a red-orange-yellow checkered Hastings Volunteer Brigade fire engine, and a hearse were parked on the gravel near the big house. Three people, one a cop with pumpkin-orange hair, huddled together.

DI Steele parked and faced the boy. "You stay put."

He turned away from her and looked out the window.

"Joe? Did you hear me?"

He sank down in the seat and put his big black boots on the dash.

The DI turned to Alexa, her eyes hard. "Excuse us."

Alexa grabbed her kit and hopped out. As far as she was concerned, work and family didn't mix. The orange-haired cop started toward Alexa, who met her halfway.

"I'm Sergeant Allison Atkins."

"I'm Alexa Glock, forensic examiner."

"It's about time."

Chapter Three

The orange-haired sergeant directed Alexa away from the Volvo, toward the two men standing near the fire truck. "I was first on the scene. The bunker is over there." She pointed to a long berm thirty or so yards away. On top of it, a little farther in, Alexa spotted a shed and a silver tree. She blinked. Yep. A silver tree.

Her eyes traveled down the berm. She saw caution tape fluttering. She took deep breaths of sea air and followed Sergeant Atkins past the bird sculpture, a helicopter landing pad, and what looked like a water cistern. "How did you handle it?"

A stiff breeze ruffled the sergeant's choppy hair. She ran a hand through it and checked her notepad. "I received the call just after eight a.m. and arrived at eight forty. I saw the victim was dead." Her gold-flecked brown eyes were rimmed in thick black eyeliner, contrasting with her fair skin. She looked to be around thirty. "I removed the caretaker from the bunker, photographed and sketched the scene, and caution-taped the entrance. Do you want to see the photos?"

"I'd rather see firsthand, thanks." Alexa, on alert for improprieties, thought the sergeant had handled things properly. The wind shifted, carrying something pungent.

The sergeant's nose wiggled as if she smelled it too. "Are you from Nashville?"

"Asheville?"

"No. Nashville."

Why was the sergeant asking where she was from when a body was waiting? "I'm from North Carolina."

"Is that near Tennessee?"

"One state over."

"I'm going to Nashville soon as I accrue enough leave. Country Music Hall of Fame."

Alexa ranked country music with Elton John and the Eagles: avoid at all costs.

"I took statements from the caretaker and housekeeper, a married couple name of Cobb. They live in Clifton."

The tractor town, Alexa thought, relieved to be back on task. "Did they both enter the bunker?"

"Only the caretaker. When the missus couldn't get in the front entrance to clean, she called Mr. Cobb. He went in through that shed." She pointed to an outbuilding atop a small hill.

"He found the body, all leaned forward on the sofa, head almost touching the floor. He straightened the body to check for a pulse. In a panic, he was."

"He moved the body?"

"That's what he said, to check for a pulse. Might have done the same myself."

Alexa pointed at the big house. "Is anyone home?"

"No one answered the door. Mr. Cobb said the owner hasn't been here since January. Can't fathom having this big house and not using it." She scratched her nose stud. "But who else could it be?" She gestured for the men to join them and introduced Alexa. "This is Taika Dean. He's our funeral director."

"G'day," he said.

"And this is Captain Reece Weiner, with Hastings Volunteer Fire Brigade. They're waiting to remove the body."

Alexa nodded. "Did either of you touch him?"

"No need," Dean said. "The state of the body is incompatible with life."

"No question about that," Sergeant Atkins added.

"I'll take a look first before you move him."

"I'll show you the entrance," Sergeant Atkins said.

"Hey," Alexa said to Captain Weiner, "can you get my car out of a ditch? It's just up the road."

"Hit me with the keys."

She did so, literally. Her toss was off.

Her stomach flip-flopped as they crossed browning grass. Reviewing her goal calmed her: Gather information about the circumstances of the person's death. Look for anything that might help identify the deceased. A huge white bird circled above. Alexa stopped. "Is that a gannet?"

The sergeant looked up. "Aye."

A car door slammed, making them both turn. Detective Inspector Steele had gotten out of the Volvo and was talking on her phone.

"That's her nephew in the car," Sergeant Atkins said. She put on a mask. "He's giving her heaps of trouble."

"Has she been in the bunker yet?" Alexa asked.

"She's only now arrived."

"Should I wait for her?"

"Who knows how long she'll be? Go on, then."

Beyond the caution tape a metal staircase descended into darkness. The stench of death strengthened.

The sergeant pulled a flashlight out of her pocket and cast light toward the base of the stairs. A six-foot landing led to a thick metal door, which stood half open. *The gates of hell* pounced in Alexa's head. She didn't like the idea of going underground.

"Do you want me to come with?" Sergeant Atkins asked.

Alexa took a deep breath and regretted it. "It's better that you stay up here. Why is the door open?"

"The caretaker said it would lock automatically if closed. And yeah? Your phone won't work down there. No reception."

Alexa flinched. The last thing she wanted was to be locked in a bunker with no way to call for help. "Where is the body located?"

"In the living area. On the sofa."

The sergeant watched her kit up. That's what the Kiwis called the act of donning protective clothing. Kitting up. Alexa pulled on coveralls and booties. She applied her StinkBalm around and below her nostrils—the evergreen scent a welcome relief—and then readied her camera. Her back scars, from a childhood scalding, throbbed as she adjusted her mask and gloves. She took another deep breath and turned on her Maglite. "Are there lights in the bunker?"

"Nah yeah," Sergeant Atkins assured her. "In the main part. You'll see."

Alexa descended like she was brave and sure. She eyed the vault-like door and fought an impulse to turn back and run. She slipped through it and entered a shadowy corridor, shining her Maglite at the concrete walls, floor, ceiling, straight ahead. The beam illumined another half-opened door at the far end, and an alcove tucked to the right with an open concrete shower stall with a sign:

DECONTAMINATE HERE

Alexa stepped past the alcove toward the second vault door. She wondered if on the other side of this passageway would be another passageway.

A box within a box within a box.

She stepped through and kicked the door stopper in place. The smell of decomp overpowered the StinkBalm.

It appeared to be a combined supply and control room with a generator, an HVAC system, and some other machine with pipes running from it to the wall and ceiling. Three panel boxes were attached above them, each with a label: SOLAR, BATTERY, DIESEL. A built-in computer monitor glowed FLOOR PLAN VIEW.

It displayed a choice of lighting: OFF, SUNRISE, ENTERTAIN, DAY, SUNSET, and NIGHT. She studied the lights above her and wondered what mode they were on. Hopefully Day. She stashed her flashlight in a pocket of her coveralls and studied the floor plan. The bunker was L-shaped, and the rooms were labeled: KITCHEN, DINING, LIVING, MASTER BED, MASTER BATH, BED #1, BED #2, HALL BATH, THEATER, GYM, and WINE.

Wine?

Another monitor controlled temperature, music, video, and security. A final screen was labeled WEBCAM.

The remaining space was shelves of oatmeal, flour and sugar, cans of soup, rice, powdered milk and eggs, protein shakes, sea salt, bags of whole bean Avalanche coffee, beef jerky, granola bars, and freeze-dried meals like backpackers use. Enough supplies for six months, she ventured, with a wine room to boot. Might as well drink yourself silly if the world was ending.

A blast of methane, sulfide, and ammonia overwhelmed the StinkBalm as she approached another open door.

Get a grip, Glock. It's just eau de putrefaction.

She counted to ten and walked into an open-concept kitchen/ dining area from *House Beautiful.* The ceiling was high, and the lighting came from glass pendants and a Sputnik-like chandelier. A picnic basket rested on a marble island. Past the island was a round pedestal table and six upholstered chairs.

Alexa crossed into the living area. The deceased, clad in a dark T-shirt and jeans, sat on a couch, head and shoulders leaned sideways, resting on the cushion. His right hand was between his thighs and his left hand was exposed palm up.

Maggots feasted on his face.

She tore her eyes away. She needed to check other parts of the bunker before she examined the body.

Kitty-corner to the sectional, a recessed fireplace ran the length of the wall. A huge flat-screen TV dominated the wall above it. Drapes hung from an opposite wall. A window in a bunker? Alexa parted them. Movement and sunlight and color made her blink. *What the heck?*

A silent movie of gannets flew past. Rock ledges teemed with speckled birds hopping back and forth, flapping wings. An adult skittered to a landing, scattering a few chicks. Below the rock shelves, the sea licked the cliff base and then retreated. Today's date and time was displayed in the corner. This was a live view of the Black Reef gannet colony.

Crazy rich American, Alexa thought, swishing the drapes closed.

She walked down the hallway to the master bedroom. The spread was thrown back, the linens tousled, but other signs of habitation—a book, reading glasses, discarded clothes, a wallet and phone on the nightstand—were absent. The master bathroom had toiletries in a neat row. No prescription drugs, insulin supplies, or drug paraphernalia. A wrinkled hand towel and wadded tissues in the wastebasket were the only signs of use.

She popped her head into the two remaining bedrooms, the hall bathroom, and then the gym and theater—a row of three red recliners with cup holders and a wall-sized screen—but didn't find personal effects. The room at the end of the hallway, which she guessed opened to the wine cellar, was locked.

The whole place was like a high-end Airbnb rental between guests. Except for the stench.

Cognizant of the fireman and funeral director, Alexa returned to the living area. An open laptop, its screen blank, and a chess set, a few pieces overturned, sat on the ottoman near the body. She scanned for anything to help her determine how the man died. There was no visible gun. No drug paraphernalia. No note.

Alexa took video and still photos of the scene and trusted Sergeant Atkins's sketch would suffice. She set out evidence markers and photographed the computer, chess set, and a single flip-flop—the other was wedged on the man's right foot. She walked to the marble island and parted the picnic basket cloth: red grapes and a sad tangerine, sandwich crusts, moldy cheese, an opened box of crackers, a tiny jar of Te Mata fig relish, and an empty bottle of lemongrass kombucha—whatever that was. Had this been the man's last meal? Had he shared it?

She turned toward the body, speculating.

Had the man been playing chess? That didn't make sense if he'd been alone.

Had he been working on his laptop? That made sense. The laptop was open.

What made him keel forward? She racked her brain for sudden death causes. The likely suspects were myocardial infarction, massive stroke or embolism, and arrhythmia.

Her head hurt thinking about ways to die. Then she got mad at herself. How John Doe died was for the pathologist to determine. She was stalling, pure and simple.

The exposed skin on the man's arms had a greenish sheen. It had no ruptures yet, but it wouldn't be long. Below the taut skin, membranes were rupturing, releasing enzymes to eat the cells from inside out. She lifted his left wrist. Rigor mortis had passed. He'd been dead at least thirty-six hours. The maggots on his face made her suspect longer. She examined the hands and then fingers, wondering if she'd be able to take prints. No go. Not at the scene, anyway. The fingertips were sloughing. A pathologist would probably need to remove the epidermis and put it over her or his gloved fingers to carefully ink and roll it. There were other options, too.

Alexa shook her head to focus on the here and now.

There was no symbol of eternal love on his ring finger. Was this the remains of the billionaire? If so, his money hadn't bought him a long life. Alexa felt smug in her relative poverty, as if needing a roommate and driving an old car would extend her warranty.

Ha.

She photographed his full body, then his upper, mid, and lower parts, first without case markers, and then with. Finally, she zoomed in on his face, alive with wriggling maggots. The caretaker had said the man's head had been hanging between his knees. The increased blood flow had attracted flies. The flies had laid eggs in his mouth and nose. The eggs had hatched into the maggots, feeding and hastening decomp. They'd move on to other body parts soon, maybe already had. The mouth was partly open and a dark liquid—purge fluid—seeped onto the couch. Alexa lowered the camera, aware she had a niggling headache.

She studied the face again, this time without the camera as a shield. She wanted a look at his teeth. There might be an identifier—a gold tooth, a gap, a rotated incisor like the young selfie woman—but she held back. Her dental examination would come after the autopsy.

There might be identifiers on his clothes. The T-shirt was black and blank. She lifted it to examine his jeans button; below two inches of dad-bod paunch, it was gold instead of the usual silver and had an intertwined AP logo. Alexa had never heard of the brand.

Her niggling headache turned into a persistent throb. A trickle of sweat itched her cheek. She thought a bunker would be cool like a cave. Her temperature data collector registered 24.4 C, or 76 F. No wonder she was sweating. The thought of being subterranean much longer made her headache bounce back and forth.

Get out of here.

Time of death. She had the room temperature and maggots to help determine the postmortem time interval.

Cause and manner of death. The difference between cause of death and manner of death confused some of the people she worked with. Cause of death was the specific injury or disease that led to this man dying. Manner of death was natural, accident, suicide, homicide, or undetermined. Or was it the other way around? Suddenly she couldn't think clearly.

Before she made a hasty retreat, she decided to check his jean pockets. Maybe a note or heart medication or wallet. She held her breath and wormed her hand into his front right, wriggled her fingers around. She snagged something small and extracted a wrapped Jolly Rancher. Green Apple. The body was rancid but the candy looked dandy.

She held her breath again and wormed her way into the left pocket. The lights blinked and went out. Alexa froze in darkness, her hand in a dead man's pocket.

Chapter Four

Alexa wrested her hand free from the pocket and straightened, her back scars constricting. She couldn't see a thing. Total darkness. Like a cave.

Predators hunt in the dark.

Fight or flight kicked in, but she couldn't see her hand in front of her face. She took a deep breath and retched from the rotting flesh smell. She backed away from the body into the ottoman, almost stumbled.

She listened. Strained her ears. For footsteps. Someone's breath. A clanking door.

Don't lock me in.

Maybe someone was messing with that FLOOR PLAN monitor. "Turn the lights on," she yelled.

Nothing.

She thought of her phone. Call for help. Then she remembered it didn't work in the bunker.

She waved her hands to see if the lights were sensor-activated and felt like an actress in a horror movie. A nightmare.

Her childhood nightmares had started soon after her mom died. Six and a half years old, she'd been. She kept dreaming mommy was coming to get her. To take her into that dark hole that the casket was lowered into. She wanted to be with her mom.

But not in that hole.

And not with that mom with no hair and bony arms she had backed away from when they opened for a hug.

I'm sorry, Mom.

Dad had let her sleep in her brother's room. Charlie had been two or three and his snuffling sweetness had tamed the nightmares.

Then she remembered the Maglite, her trusty friend, and fumbled it on. The beam landed on the corpse's face. She recoiled at the O-shaped mouth emitting a silent scream. She swerved and directed the beam around the room. Faint light that she hadn't noticed a second ago emanated from behind the drapes where the live cam was probably still recording soaring gannets. The thought of soaring gannets beyond the bunker gave her hope.

She skirted the ottoman and crossed through the kitchen into the storage room where the FLOOR PLAN monitor glowed. She shone her light toward the far door; it was still propped open. Her shoulders released in relief. She walked into the corridor, past the creepy decontamination shower, and was about to bound up the stairs when she remembered the crime kit.

Crap. It was next to the bunker body. Leaving the kit behind felt like leaving a child behind. *Like Mom leaving me behind.*

She walked back purposefully, casting her beam directly ahead, avoiding corners. She hefted the kit onto her shoulder and retraced her steps, reining in the impulse to run.

Outside, she could only see light and movement until she blinked a couple of times.

She ducked under the caution tape, stuck the Maglite under her armpit, and whipped off her mask and gloves. She let the kit slide off her shoulder and focused on gulping clean air. Sergeant Atkins, standing with the fireman and funeral director, waved at her. Alexa stuffed the mask and gloves in her pocket, shoved the Maglite into her other pocket, and started over.

Her Vitz was parked next to the Volvo. The fireman had retrieved it for her.

"All good, then?" he asked as she approached. He must have noticed her face. "Pretty bad in there, eh?"

"The lights went out. It was pitch-black."

"I would have carked it," Sergeant Atkins said. "Your torch is on."

Alexa looked down. Her pocket glowed.

The fireman look mystified. "Maybe a fuse? I'll take a look."

Alexa spotted the DI walking toward them. She was tall and thin, and her trousers matched her navy blazer. "He'll be the death of me, that boy," she said. "He's taking a walk until my partner gets here to fetch him."

The DI had been messing with the kid this whole time. Alexa couldn't believe it.

Sergeant Atkins told DI Steele about the lights.

"A power malfunction, eh? How do lights run in the bunker, anyway? Solar? Or generator?" She turned to Alexa. "What's the report from down under?"

Alexa breathed another lungful of clean air before answering. "The adult male is beginning to bloat. No sign of violence. No suicide note. I didn't see any heart pills or insulin supplies."

Her face looked pinched. "Did you find a phone?"

"I didn't see a phone lying around, and there wasn't one in his front pants pockets." Even though she had been wearing gloves, she wanted to scrub her hands.

DI Steele announced that they'd wait on the porch of the big house. Alexa retrieved her water bottle from her unlocked car—the key was in the ignition—and peeked at her fender. It had a cantaloupe-sized gouge. To fix or not to fix? She had no idea what her New Zealand auto insurance would cover. She gulped water and joined the DI on the steps. "Is there any info about the bunker owner?"

Sergeant Atkins leaned against a railing. The sun had shifted, painting her hair a shade of apricot. "We think the dead bloke is the American CEO, right, Senior?"

Alexa was used to the term "senior," what New Zealand cops call their superiors.

"Harlan Quinn's mobile numbers are unlisted," DI Steele said. "His LinkedIn lists his past and present companies, but the woman who answered my call at his present one—some biotech place—said he is unavailable; did I want to leave a message?" She twisted the black silicon band she wore on her ring finger. "Like what? 'Is your CEO dead in his bolt-hole?'"

Sergeant Atkins laughed and gave her phone to Alexa. "He doesn't do social media—no Facebook or Instagram or Twitter—but I found one picture of him."

The caption said: Harlan Quinn, 46, BioMatic CEO. It was a chest-up photo. Quinn had low-hung eyebrows, a dark buzz cut, and a defiant jut to his chin. Handsome and swarthy, Alexa thought.

"Could he be the bloke in the bunker?" Sergeant Atkins asked.

Alexa gave the phone back. "The hair matches."

Sergeant Atkins laughed. "Matches my boyfriend's and our fireman's hair, too."

"His primary residence is in Palo Alto," DI Steele said. "I'm waiting for the local police department to return my call. They can find out what's what." She stopped twiddling her ring. "Sergeant, call that husband and wife, the Cobbs. They must have Quinn's working contact number, right?"

"On it." Sergeant Atkins stepped off the porch to make the call.

The DI focused on Alexa. "If the deceased is Mr. Quinn, there will be an international media frenzy. We need to be very careful."

Was that a warning? Alexa heard a motor, and watched a blue sports car round the long drive and pull next to the Volvo.

DI Steele sighed. "Kersten—at last."

She left the porch and joined the woman as she climbed out of the car. Alexa overheard bits and pieces of their exchange: "started a fight" and "no time to fetch the veggies." Nothing about a body in the bunker.

Joe sauntered past the porch, his head down. He climbed into the sports car. Sergeant Atkins called, "You be good, eh, Joe?"

There seemed to be family drama going on. Alexa turned her back and decided to update Dan, but the GPS had zapped her phone battery. She didn't like being cut off. She got up and peered through the windows into the house—gleaming wood floors, beams, a sitting room, windows facing the sea.

When she turned, Sergeant Atkins was driving off behind the blue sports car.

"She's on her way to speak with the caretakers," DI Steele said.

The fireman approached and pulled off his mask. "I turned on the exhaust fan to help with the odor, eh. You know that FLOOR PLAN screen? The lights were turned to Night. I switched them back to Daylight and they came right on."

Alexa shivered. *How had the mode changed?*

He cleared his throat. "Can we remove the body?"

Alexa looked at DI Steele. "You want to see him, right?"

"No. I've got the photos. You can take it away."

Him, not "it," Alexa thought. Bruce would never pass up the opportunity to see a body in situ. Until they had evidence of how the man died, the circumstances were suspicious.

A quarter hour later the two men loaded the body bag into the hearse. DI Steele and Alexa watched. "Off to Hawke's Bay Hospital," Mr. Dean called.

"Tell Dr. Li to schedule the autopsy first thing," DI Steele said. She took an index card out of her pocket and glanced at it.

The hearse and fire truck made a sad parade as the women suited up.

DI Steele referred to her index card. "I've got three goals and we're out of here. Establish the path of entry. How did the deceased enter the bunker? How did the caretaker enter? Two different ways, according to Sergeant Atkins."

What was with the index cards? Maybe they were cheat sheets.

Alexa remembered Bruce said that DI Steele had recently been promoted.

"Number two is to photograph and video the scene of death."

They crunched across the grass. Alexa patted the crime kit. "I've done that except for where the body was."

"Right-o. All that's left is to collect personal belongings and anything that can be used in identification."

A gannet soared by, its white wings outstretched, their tips black. "There's a laptop, but not much else," Alexa said. "What about the big house?"

"We aren't touching it. This isn't a crime."

Alexa hoped those weren't famous last words.

DI Steele stopped short of the caution tape. "The bunker entrance is hard to spot if you didn't know to look for it." The thirty-yard-long berm tapered into tall grass and russet flax at either end. Bushy shrubs toward the berm's middle hid the bunker entrance.

"When the shit hits the fan, you don't want visitors. Or marauders," DI Steele said. "Where's the escape-hatch entrance? My sergeant should have taped it off."

Alexa surveyed the landscape beyond the berm: rocks, tall grasses, another sculpture—this one a silver tree—and a shed that supposedly contained the escape hatch, with the door open. She wondered why the DI wasn't more informed. "Sergeant Atkins said it's in that shed."

"Again—hidden from view. Let's enter through the front door like proper guests."

"Doors. There are two of them." Alexa's heart pounded against her ribs as she held the caution tape for the DI. She didn't want to go back down—what if the lights went out again? Their steps down the metal stairs were muffled by their booties. At the bottom Alexa pointed to the propped door. "This is most likely how the deceased entered."

DI Steele leaned close but didn't touch. "They call this a blast door. Looks like about eight inches of steel. Probably can keep out radiation." She gestured to the keypad. "And that didn't work?"

"That's what Sergeant Atkins reported."

They walked down the hallway. DI Steele studied the decontamination shower. "I've heard these are to remove radiation. Wonder if that's possible?"

A wedge of light seeped through the second door, calming some of Alexa's anxiety. The DI led the way into the control room. She surveyed the food supplies. "Enough here for months." She studied a red canister. "BeReady Organic Meat Bucket. I'll pass."

Alexa watched the DI scan the FLOOR PLAN monitor. "Are you telling me this thing has a wine cellar?" she asked.

The whole place was a cellar, Alexa thought. "That door was locked, so I don't know." She pointed to LIVING. "That's where the body was."

It had left Rorschach-like stains on the couch, but the body hadn't hidden a suicide note or any other evidence. Alexa set the crime kit down and retrieved the camera.

"Let's find the escape hatch first," DI Steele said.

They located the drop-down stairs in a walk-in closet of a spare bedroom. Cool air flowed down from the opening.

DI Steele climbed up. "It's the shed. The escape hatch opens into the shed. That's how Tony Cobb got in."

Alexa climbed up next—for a quick look—and felt like a mole, head level with the plank floor, shed door open, bag of potting soil and tools against the wall. Why did the owner need an escape route? Escape from what? Or whom?

Did all bunkers have escape hatches?

DI Steele tried the door at the end of the hall. "Locked. He doesn't want his wine to go walkabout."

Alexa led the way back to the living area. She set up the camera and took photos of where the decedent's body had been, and then pointed to the laptop. "Before we bag it, I want to dust the case and screen for fingerprints. If it belongs to Mr. Quinn, and his fingerprints are on file, this could help us identify him."

"See if it turns on. He might have left a suicide note on it."

Alexa was surprised the DI didn't know better. "That's for the tech people to handle."

DI Steele looked around. "Here's the charger." It coiled on the ottoman near an upended pawn and wasn't connected to the computer.

Alexa dug out her print kit. The surface of the computer was smooth and nonporous, so she had high hopes. She dusted it with powder, used the flashlight on her phone to locate a print, and lifted it with clear tape, which she stuck to a backing card. She did it again with another print. She would do the keyboard and screen at the lab, if necessary. Satisfied, she placed the laptop into a large paper evidence bag.

In the master bedroom, DI Steele examined the tousled sheets. "I see stains. Bag them up."

Alexa stripped the sheets and slid them into a paper bag. She did the same with the hand towel, the remaining flip-flop, and the contents of the kitchen trash can: one Jolly Rancher wrapper and shriveled tangerine peels wrapped in a paper towel.

DI Steele was impatient. "Let's get out of here."

Alexa led the way, anxious to leave the crypt.

Chapter Five

Sergeant Atkins met them at the entrance. "Was hoping I wouldn't have to fetch you down there. The caretaker is waiting for you in front of the shed."

Alexa started to follow DI Steele when the sergeant tapped her shoulder. "Your Blake Shelton is my fave."

"Who?"

"The country singer. 'Honey Bee,' 'Austin,' 'Hell Right.'"

"Hell right?"

The sergeant beamed. "Hell, yeah."

"I didn't know Kiwis liked country music."

The sergeant stared at her in disbelief. "Don't you watch *Brokenwood*? It's my fave TV show. DSS Shepherd loves country music. Helps him solve the crimes."

Alexa was in the dark again. She hurried to catch up with DI Steele. To the right of the shed, the silver tree caught the sunlight and glistened. She wondered what a life-sized silver tree cost and what the point of it was.

In the shed, the caretaker smoothed his pants with his hands and pointed to the hatch. "It's a compression release lock from the inside. But from up here you need a code to open it."

The stink of death was diluted by the potting soil and maybe weed killer. Alexa spotted Weed B-gon on a shelf.

"The keypad is there." Mr. Cobb pointed to a lockbox mounted near the door. "I used the emergency override code to get in."

"When did you see the owner last?" DI Steele asked.

"Never met him. The missus gets the codes by email. A random-number bot sends them, all high-tech."

"Take me through your discovery again," DI Steele said.

Alexa interrupted. "I need to get this evidence to the station."

"Fine." DI Steele told Mr. Cobb she'd be right back and walked Alexa out the door. "My partner and I are having a barbie." She wrote her address on a slip of paper and handed it to Alexa. "Come over at eight."

Alexa perked up. She was starved.

The sun was setting as she approached the glass-and-wood police station. An inscription ran almost the length of the entrance: *E tū ki te kei o te waka, kia pakia koe e ngā ngaru o te wā.*

Alexa recognized the word *waka*, canoe, and wondered what the phrase meant. Inside a three-story atrium lobby, she passed through a metal detector and showed her ID to a desk clerk. "I've got some evidence to drop off."

He shoved a *Living Hawke's Bay* magazine aside and studied her with hound-dog eyes. "The bunker body, eh?" He patted at a cowlick that made a tuft of his short bangs stand up. His ID badge said Constable Tim Gavin. "Our lab tech is gone for the day. I can check the evidence in for you."

Alexa followed him down a flight of stairs. He used a key fob to open the lab. She surveyed the microscopes, a fume chamber, desktop computers, workstations, and a row of evidence lockers. Labs were her happy place.

"Sign in here?" Constable Gavin said.

Alexa did, and then removed the evidence items one by one as Constable Gavin checked that each was sealed. He signed off on the transfer.

"Two lockers will do," Alexa said.

"Load them up." His nose scrunched.

Her clothes smelled foul. She placed everything but the maggots in the lockers; they needed refrigeration. The constable closed the lockers, scanned his fob across a blinking light, and entered the locker numbers. "Brilliant, eh? The computer logs every deposit or removal."

They had the same system in Auckland, but Alexa didn't tell him. "I'll need access tomorrow morning."

Once the maggots were tucked into the fridge, she called her boss, Dan. "It was bad. We don't know who he is or how he died. I'll attend the autopsy in the morning. Hopefully that will tell us COD."

"It's in the news," Dan said.

"What are they saying?"

"That it's an unfortunate incident and identification is pending."

"Sounds right."

Alexa spent forty minutes writing her preliminary report and sent a copy to Dr. Li, the pathologist who would be conducting the autopsy.

She had that to look forward to.

Chapter Six

Her studio at the Apple Motor Lodge faced the pool and cost more than her per diem, but now dinner would be free. She plugged in her phone and sealed her stinky clothes in a plastic bag. Hot jets of water in the shower washed the odor from her hair and body. Afterwards, she tamed her shoulder-length locks with a brush and blow-dryer. She dressed in tomorrow's khakis and button-down, this one striped, and added her new possum fur cardigan.

When the woman in the shop had said the cardie was knit from possum fur, she thought she had misunderstood. "The marsupial?"

"Australian bushtail possum. It will keep you cozy," the saleswoman said. "The fur has hollow fibers similar to polar bear fur."

Alexa held the rose-colored sweater to her cheek, relishing its softness. She knew possums had been purposefully brought to New Zealand, and the results had been calamitous for the birds.

"No worries; we don't have fur farms," the woman added as if Alexa was from PETA. "All the fur comes from trapped or hunted possums. You can read about it." She gave Alexa a pamphlet titled "Millions of Native Birds Eaten Every Year by Introduced Predators."

Alexa bought the cardigan to do her part for the birds. She

had lost her old cardigan a few cases ago. It was at the bottom of Golden Bay Wharf with the sharks.

A bit of lip gloss and she was ready. She checked her phone for a text from Bruce—nada—and wondered what he was doing. Was he thinking of her?

Sometimes she wished she could wash away her longing for Bruce like she'd washed away the stink of death. Her hypothalamus had a mind of its own—*ha!*—up there stimulating hormones and producing dopamine. Her attraction to Bruce boiled down to evolution insisting on reproduction, not that she planned to personally perpetuate the species.

Children? No, thanks. Sex with Bruce? Yes, please.

It was dark when she parked in front of a single-story bungalow on Flax Field Drive. Before she knocked, the front door was opened by a heavyset woman in gray pants and tunic. "*Kia ora.* You must be CSI. Come in, come in." Large silver earrings dangled from beneath her short black hair. "I'm Kersten, Mic's wife."

"I'm Alexa." *Dammit.* She should have brought a bag of pineapple lumps—the chocolate-covered pineapple-flavored marshmallows that Kiwis loved (she did too)—or a bottle of wine as a hostess gift.

Everything inside was cedar wood—ceiling, walls, floor—like a sauna. Kersten led her past a hallway and through a living area. The news flashed on the flat-screen, volume off. She glimpsed an aerial view of Black Reef. A bowl of soggy cereal and a video game controller topped the coffee table. Alexa wondered where the nephew was.

"I'm on drinks duty. What'll you have?" Kersten asked, showing her into the kitchen.

"White wine, please."

A man and woman leaned against a granite island, picking at a charcuterie board. Mic Steele, her damp hair hanging loose, cocked an eyebrow at Alexa. "Trouble finding us?" Her clingy top and skinny jeans showcased her angular body.

"No trouble."

Kersten pulled a bottle of wine from the fridge. "Introduce her to our friends, sweets."

"This is Alexa Glock from the States. She's helping with the bunker body."

"You've come all that way?" the woman asked.

"She came from Auckland," DI Steele said. "These are our neighbors, Patch and Aurora. My brother, John, is on the deek."

Was "on the deek" the same as "on the dole"? Why would the DI broadcast that?

Aurora flicked the bangs out of her eyes. "Maybe your billionaire died doing that sexual strangulation thing. What's it called?"

"Autoerotic asphyxiation," DI Steele said. "We don't know who the dead man is. A spokesperson for the family said it can't be Mr. Quinn because he's in Germany."

This was news to Alexa; she was surprised the DI was sharing it, or any bunker information, in mixed company. Maybe it was a rookie mistake.

"Then who could it be?" Patch asked.

Alexa stared at a square patch of gray hair at the man's temple. Which came first, she mused? The name or the patch?

"Probably someone taking advantage of a free place to stay," Aurora said. "Burrowing in, so to speak."

"Good one." Kersten poured a Marlborough sauvignon blanc in a glass and handed it to Alexa. "Do you have a family in Auckland?"

Alexa sipped appreciatively. "I have a roommate."

"Those Yanks who buy up property hardly ever visit their estates," Aurora announced, raising her narrow nose. "There was a picture on the internet of an American wandering around a sheep field looking for his bunker entrance. What an idiot. He had to call the man who installed it to find it."

He can't be too big an idiot if he can afford to build a bunker in NZ, Alexa thought.

"It's not just Yanks," Kersten said. "There's been a big Chinese land grab, too. Half of Queenstown is empty mansions. Let's head outside."

Alexa, who'd been hoping to snag a cheese and cracker, followed Kersten through sliding glass doors onto a deck. *Deek* was deck, she realized.

The man at the grill said, "Just in time." He waved an oven mitt at Alexa. "I'm John. Hope you're hungry."

Alexa liked John immediately. A picnic table, festive under fairy lights, was set for six. She took an end seat and watched attentively as John placed a platter of kabobs in the middle of the table. DI Steele added a big bowl of salad and a casserole of some sort. "This is Alexa," she said.

"Glad you could make it." John had his sister's narrow chin and wore dark-framed glasses. "Where are Joe and Adam?" he asked.

"Gone to Macca's," DI Steele said. "They'll be along soon."

"I don't know why you let them go out for tea," Kersten said. "Joe is on punishment."

"I'm the good cop," DI Steele said.

Alexa laughed, but then realized maybe she shouldn't have. Kersten's face was stony. She slid two kabobs of steak, greens peppers, tomato, and pineapple onto her plate. "McDonald's over this?"

Aurora sat next to her and took one kabob. "Teenagers have different tastes."

Alexa didn't have experience in feeding teenagers. She heaped what looked like hash brown potatoes next to the kabobs.

"I'm sure you're here legally and all," Aurora continued, "but we're fogged off at foreigners buying up our land. You know about Peter Thiel? He bought up Wanaka."

"Who is Peter Thiel?" Alexa asked.

A dog barked from a couple gardens over.

"Mr. PayPal," Aurora said. "New Zealand is the in place to bug out. Your LinkedIn CEO and a biggie at Google are here too. They call New Zealand 'apocalypse insurance.'"

Alexa hadn't realized she should be so concerned about the state of the States.

Patch guzzled his beer. "There's this California-based company that built a three-hundred-person bunker north of Christchurch," he said. "Their website is all about mass extinction and threat levels. Wish they'd build their bunkers in their own country."

"We need to ban the investment visa," DI Steele said. She rubbed her fingertips together. "Rich people buy their way in."

Alexa hoped DI Steele didn't want to ban work visas as well.

"Get this." Patch looked at Alexa. "Your Silicon Valley blokes can have bunkers made in the U.S. and ship them here. One landed at Waitematā Harbor and there was a picture of it on telly."

"The cost of that?" Kersten said. "I can't even imagine."

"Millions just to get it here. It was all secretive where it was going. It will have an indoor pool and a theater. If you have that in your primary home, you want it in your bolt-hole."

"I wish that dog would stop barking. Can you do something about it, Mic?" Kersten interrupted.

DI Steele ignored her wife. "The one I was in today had a gym, a theater, and a wine cellar. It's obscene." She slid next to her brother and reached for the platter. "What are all the foreigners trying to escape?"

"Climate change, nuclear annihilation, pandemics, greed, and violence," John said.

"It pays to be in the middle of nowhere," DI Steele said. She clinked glasses with her brother.

Alexa buttoned her cardigan and looked beyond the fairy lights at the darkness encircling their bubble. Perils of the world could pierce the bubble any moment. Perhaps the barking dog was a warning.

The glass doors slid open. "I'm home," a boy announced.

"Hi, luv," Kersten said. "How was your tea?"

Adam shrugged one shoulder. He looked like Joe, but smaller. "Hi, Uncle John."

"I made some bikkies. They're in the kitchen," John said.

Alexa perked up. Bikkies was slang for cookies.

"Do you want me to put the cheese and crackers up?" the boy asked.

"No need. Where's your brother?" DI Steele asked.

"Watching telly."

"Tell him to come out to say hello," Kersten said.

Alexa chewed her last bite of casserole as Joe stepped onto the patio. "What?"

"Don't be rude," DI Steele snapped.

"Say hello to our neighbors," Kersten said. "And Ms. Glock. She's from America."

"Hello," he said tonelessly. Then he cheered up. "Your bunker has booby traps and stash vaults."

DI Steele stiffened. "Where did you hear that?"

"Everyone is on about it," he said.

When he closed the sliders, Aurora asked how it was going. "You've had the boys, what, six months now?"

"Five. We're worried about Joe," Kersten said.

"He's heaps of trouble," DI Steele said.

"Ease up, Mic. They've been gutted by Nora and that rotter of hers," John said.

"You try parenting," DI Steele said.

A vehicle with no muffler roared by.

"Hoons," John said.

Alexa knew "hoons" were reckless drivers. Usually male. Usually young.

"I'll take the boys Saturday," John added. "Put 'em to work on the farm."

"Not Adam," Kersten said. "He has a tourney." She sat shoulder-to-shoulder with DI Steele now and smiled at Alexa. "No more family talk. More wine? What are your job duties?"

The corpse's face popped into her head. Alexa covered her glass with her hand. "They vary. This is the first time I've ever been called to a bunker."

Aurora pointed an empty skewer at her. "Bunkers are all about fear. Stockpile food, gather your family unit, and batten down the hatches."

FRIDAY

Chapter Seven

Alexa checked out of the Apple Motor Lodge in the morning, figuring she'd find a cheaper place to stay. Why pay for a swimming pool view when she hated swimming? On second thought, she didn't hate swimming. She hated wearing a bathing suit, her ugly back on view. But her scars didn't bother Bruce.

She smiled. Maybe she'd buy a swimsuit in Auckland.

On the way to the hospital, she listened to a message from DI Steele: "I'm running late. The kid again. God save me. No word on ID. Ask Dr. Li if our bloke had a heart attack."

Alexa rolled her eyes. Telling Dr. Li to look for signs of a heart attack would be like Joe Blow telling Alexa to take photographs at a crime scene. She entered the Hawke's Bay Hospital lobby and asked the receptionist where the morgue was.

"In the basement, dear."

Decomps weren't as rare as people think. Bodies found in warm temperatures, drowning victims, social recluses. Alexa thought of the body in the Raleigh farmhouse again. That woman had died alone, sprawled on the kitchen floor.

That could be me. All alone.

Everyone technically dies alone, Alexa reassured herself.

A body in a bunker, though. That was a first. Alexa took the stairs and hoped the ventilation system worked well in the autopsy room. She filled her lungs while the air was still passable. She pushed open the door at the bottom of the stairwell and entered a long hallway buzzing with fluorescent lights.

She reminded herself that any death classified as unnatural, violent, or suicide must undergo a postmortem. Unless a family member objected.

We don't know who this man's family is, Alexa thought. That was one of the things she hoped the autopsy would help them discover.

She pushed open the door marked MORGUE.

It was an anteroom with cupboards, sinks, and a window view of the dissection room. A petite woman in surgical scrubs, a plastic apron, and white gumboots looked at her quizzically.

"I'm here for the autopsy of the bunker body." Alexa showed her ID badge. "I'm from Auckland Forensic Service Center. I did the initial examination yesterday afternoon."

"I'm Dr. Jennifer Li," the woman said. "I see we have a decomp. Mild to moderate, I'd say from the looks of him. What a way to start the weekend. Are you American?"

"Yes, but I live in Auckland now."

"I've been to California. Hollywood, L.A., Big Sur, Disneyland."

Alexa nodded as if she had been to all those places, too. She'd barely stepped a Ked out of North Carolina before moving to New Zealand.

The doctor pulled on sleeve guards. "It's a possible high-profile case, right?"

Alexa nodded again.

"We're sparing no procedures, then. The deceased has undergone radiographs and scans. No foreign bodies. No pacemaker. No sign of blunt force trauma. No current fractures, but one healed. Left wrist."

That was something.

The pathologist pointed through the window at a lanky man, suited up and blocking the view of the body. "My registrar Dr. Yellin will be assisting. He's doing the external exam."

A registrar was equivalent to a medical resident in the U.S., Alexa had learned. She donned protective gear, using the supplies available on the shelves above the sink. She checked around the room for a shelf of gumboots, mad at herself for not bringing her own. She didn't see any and had to do with booties. "DI Steele is running late," she said.

The doctor shrugged. She pulled down a plastic face shield and backed into the autopsy suite.

Alexa followed. The steel counters, cupboards, portable dishwasher, and large butcher-shop scale resembled an industrial kitchen, she thought, except instead of spatulas and whisks, there were scissors and scalpels. The cutting board, Tupperware, and ladles could go either way. She introduced herself to Dr. Yellin, squared her shoulders, and looked at the body.

He was naked. His skin was mostly greenish with a smattering of mottled purple and gray. The abdomen was slightly distended—gases were at work beneath his epidermis. The face was blackened, the eyes shrunken and recessed, a hint of cheekbone was exposed, and his teeth protruded beyond wizened lips. The more advanced decomp on the face was probably due to the position he'd been found in: head lower than body.

Blood rushed to Alexa's head. She didn't want to faint and stepped back, bumping into the cutting bench, and steadied herself by slipping onto a stool.

"Are you okay?" Dr. Li asked.

"I'm fine, thanks." From her perch she continued her study of the corpse. What could she learn to aid the investigation? The man's dark buzzed hair was growing out. She tucked a strand of her hair behind her ear and corrected herself: the man's hair was not *still* growing out; it was a myth that hair continued growing after death. Cells divide to make hair strands grow longer, and this man's cells were cut off from an energy source.

The color and cut of John Doe's hair matched the photo of Harlan Quinn. But his wife said he was in Germany.

Dr. Li examined the man's fingertips with a magnifying glass. "Note the sloughing. I'll work on getting prints later."

Alexa nodded. "I'll try to identify him by dentals, but it will be good to have a print backup."

Dr. Yellin scribbled John Doe on a whiteboard and added H: 177 cm, W: 85 k. "John Doe's height/weight ratio is within healthy range. Maybe a little stocky."

"What else did you find during your external exam?" Dr. Li asked.

"No tattoos, obvious scars, or punctures. Rigor has passed. Lividity indicates a sitting position."

Lividity was the result of gravity. Since John Doe was found in a sitting position, blood had pooled in his thighs, lower back, and buttocks.

"Color?" Dr. Li asked.

"Reddish purple, mostly."

The ventilation fans rattled. Alexa was glad the smell wasn't as strong as it had been in the bunker. She pondered lividity: it provided clues such as whether a body had been moved after death, whether limbs had been bound, whether the surface under the deceased was soft or hard. Cello music interrupted her musings.

Dr. Li turned from the cabinet where her sound system was. "I like Yo-Yo Ma for company. What was the temperature in the bunker?"

Alexa was ready with her notes. "Twenty-four Celsius."

"Warmish, then."

The higher the temperature, the faster decomposition occurs, Alexa knew.

Dr. Li looked at Dr. Yellin. "Are we ready?"

He nodded, his eyes eager.

Dr. Li bowed her head briefly and then picked up tweezers. She extracted a maggot from the corpse's ear canal, its muscles contracting in wriggling movement. "I don't normally keep our friends here, but since this is potentially a high-profile case, we'll send a few to our entomology lads." She dropped it into a container, labeled it, and did the same with a couple more.

The larva made Alexa scratch her nose, which was hidden under her mask. "I have a few at the police lab."

"You can destroy them," Dr. Li said.

"How are they still alive?" Dr. Yellin asked. "The body has been in cold storage overnight."

"It takes more than twelve hours of refrigeration to kill a maggot," Dr. Li answered. "I'll be the one to open him up."

Alexa took a deep breath and then regretted it.

Dr. Li made a Y-shaped incision from each shoulder joint toward the middle of the chest and then straight down to the pubic bone. She then picked up what looked like pruning shears. Alexa expected her to use a saw to cut through the chest plate, not pruning shears. She wished the cello music would drown out the snip and crack of bone. She studied her booties until the snipping ceased. When she looked up, Dr. Li was lifting the chest plate off like a lid.

Sickly sweet gas escaped, and a small amount of fluid seeped onto the table. She stepped back. "Dr. Yellin, would you remove lungs and heart en bloc?"

The intern confidently cut the organs free and placed them on the cutting board. Dr. Li separated them and placed the heart on the scale. One sign of cardiovascular disease was an enlarged heart. Alexa held her breath to hear the verdict.

"Average for middle-aged male," the doctor announced.

Alexa let her breath go in a whoosh. There was still a chance of cardio abnormality, but less now. The pathologist poked and prodded the heart with her scalpel, checking it for disease or hemorrhage. "The arteries look good," she said. "No narrowing of the blood vessels."

Alexa turned away when the doctor started slicing. After ten minutes, Dr. Li said, "All good. Next."

Dr. Yellin removed the liver. Dr. Li set it on a scale and recorded the weight. She repeated the process she had with the heart. The minutes ticked by. Alexa felt steady on her feet again. From what she could tell, the organs were in good shape. She watched closely but felt useless. How did knowing the weight of the man's spleen solve the riddle of who he was?

The cello music creaked and groaned. Alexa ranked it on par with country. A music-appreciation elective in college might have broadened her tastes. She preferred listening to podcasts. "Just Science" and "Double Loop" were her favorites.

She dreaded what was next.

Dr. Yellin used a small electric saw to cut from the left ear, high across the man's forehead, to the right ear. The grinding and dentist-drill smell made Alexa go clammy. She had to sit on the stool again as he removed the skull cap.

"A beaut," he said, admiring the exposed brain.

Alexa watched as he removed it from the cranial vault and set it on the scale. All the man's experiences and knowledge had been housed in a grayish blob that settled so that the hemispheres flattened somewhat and parted slightly.

"Weighs 1,388 grams," Dr. Yellin said.

Around three pounds, Alexa mused. Average for an adult male brain.

Dr. Li made notations on her pad and then picked up her scalpel again, and Alexa had to look away. When the doctor was finished, she said. "This ends my part. We'll take a look at all the samples, and I'll send off for a tox screening."

Alexa hopped off the stool.

"You can conduct your dental exam now," she said. "Dr. Yellin can assist you."

"How long before we get some results?" Alexa asked.

The pathologist raised her plastic shield. "I have to send a preliminary report to the coroner immediately. Since I didn't see any potentially lethal visible natural disease, I'm going with cause of death pending toxicology and microscopic exam." She turned her music off. "I believe they'll require further investigation, eh?"

Alexa agreed. "What's your best estimate for how long he's been dead?"

"Three or four days, given the temp. The entomologist team will be more accurate."

Maggots, Alexa marveled: the gold standard in evaluating postmortem interval. She scratched her ankle.

Dr. Yellin busied himself placing the organs in a plastic bag, which he placed in the chest cavity. He took care closing the body up. Alexa fiddled with her dental probe.

Finally it was her turn to dance. Metaphorically. She adjusted the deceased's head farther back on the block so his mandible jutted up. "Open wide," she said and pried the jawbone apart.

Dr. Yellin wheeled a portable X-ray machine near the head. "What are you looking for?"

"Anything that could identify him. Gold tooth. Implants. An overbite." She thought of the man's penchant for hard candy and probed for decay. She didn't imagine finding a pink molar.

"Take a look at this," she told Dr. Yellin.

Chapter Eight

Alexa had read a couple of articles about postmortem pink teeth, but had never seen it. "It's called pink tooth phenomenon. PTP."

Dr. Yellin leaned in, his nose inches from the dead man's mouth. "What causes it?"

Alexa set down her probe, changed gloves, and readied her camera. Her heart revved. "Teeth are made of enamel, dentin, and the pulp chamber, right? The pulp chamber is where the blood vessels and nerves are. The color can be caused by the penetration of hemoglobin in the dental tubules."

"You lost me at *dental tubules*," Dr. Yellin said.

"The hollow channels inside your teeth."

"So what does it mean?"

She took several photos of the discolored molar as facts flooded back. "After-death pink teeth sometimes occur from lack of air. Pillow smothering, strangulation, drowning, carbon monoxide poisoning."

It had been stupid to enter the bunker without considering the air quality. She should have asked if it had been checked instead of assuming all was well. Maybe the subterranean headache she'd experienced yesterday had been a symptom of carbon monoxide poisoning.

"We can rule out drowning," Dr. Yellin said. "And the hyoid

bone was intact. Sometimes it's broken during strangulation." He paused, his forehead scrunched. "I didn't notice cherry-red lividity. That's a carbon monoxide indicator. But it isn't always present, and the body has degraded."

Alexa's hand shook as she filled out the dental profile form. She found four amalgam fillings, evidence of a root canal filling in the left lower second molar, and a benign bone growth near the pink molar.

"Will you rush the carbon monoxide testing?"

Dr. Yellin nodded.

———

Alexa found DI Steele in her office at the police station, talking with Sergeant Atkins. "Ms. Glock. Do you have a cause of death?"

Didn't the DI know autopsies rarely resulted in rapid answers? "We do know at some point in his life he had a broken wrist."

The DI snorted and waved away a woman coming at her with a stack of papers.

Alexa set down her crime kit and hoped she didn't stink. "Has anyone checked the air quality in the bunker?"

DI Steele shifted forward. "Why?"

"One of the man's molars was pink. A possible cause of this is oxygen deprivation."

"A pink tooth? Never heard of it," DI Steele said.

Sergeant Atkins dragged her fingers through her tangerine hair. "I didn't have any trouble breathing in there, except for the stench. 'Course I didn't stay down long."

"You left the door open," Alexa reminded her. She counted six earrings in the sergeant's left ear, four in the right.

"Could be like that cave rave in Oslo," Sergeant Atkins said.

"What are you talking about?" DI Steele asked.

"It was all over TikTok. All these ravers broke into this abandoned air raid bunker and partied. In the middle of the night.

Some of them started crawling out all sick, dizzy, headaches, nauseous. Seven people went unconscious. The authorities said it was carbon monoxide poisoning from portable generators. It was a miracle no one carked."

"No one enters our bunker until the air is checked," DI Steele said.

"It's just a theory," Alexa said.

DI Steele told Sergeant Atkins to get the firemen out to Black Reef. "I'll meet them out there."

"Any news on who our dead man is?" Alexa asked.

"It's still a mystery," DI Steele said. "The Palo Alto officer has been in touch with Quinn's personal secretary. She gave him Harlan Quinn's direct phone line, but Mr. Q doesn't answer."

"No one answers their mobile anymore," Sergeant Atkins said. "Did you text?"

DI Steele pushed back from her desk. "The secretary told the officer that Mr. Quinn is in Munich, at some company he does business with, PharmaTex. Since the first of April. She's trying to contact him."

"What about Mrs. Quinn?" Alexa asked.

"Audrey Quinn is supposedly at a yoga retreat," DI Steele said. "She's returning today."

"Tell her about the permission to enter the big house at Black Reef, Senior," Sergeant Atkins said.

"The officer asked the secretary to obtain permission for us to enter. To check it out. See if there are any belongings or whatnot. The secretary said no and threatened litigation."

"Americans are sue-crazy," Sergeant Atkins said.

Alexa opened her mouth to argue but decided against it.

"I've filed for a warrant," DI Steele said.

"I took X-rays of the deceased's teeth at the autopsy," Alexa said. "Did the officer obtain Harlan Quinn's dental records?"

"No way. We did get Mrs. Quinn's private number. I tried earlier. She had it set to some message about focusing on herself, regaining her center, no communication except with nature and her yogi."

"Sign me up, Senior," Sergeant Atkins said.

DI Steele eyes gleamed. "Why don't you call her, Ms. Glock? Maybe she's home now. Maybe she'll release dental X-rays to a fellow Yank. Tell her we want to rule out that our dead man is this blasted billionaire."

"Or confirm," Sergeant Atkins added. She fiddled with her phone and handed it to Alexa. "Ms. Q posted on Instagram."

Harlan Quinn, in a tux, had his arm around a woman several inches taller. Her coppery hair was swept up on top of her head, adding to her stature. Glittery earrings dangled to her bare shoulders. Her smile looked posed rather than natural. Alexa squinted. The photo had been posted in December.

She hadn't ever groveled for dental X-rays before. She figured it was worth a chance. It was eleven a.m. Friday here, so it was midafternoon yesterday in California. "I'll give it a try."

DI Steele read out the numbers as Alexa tapped them into her phone, amazed that a simple 00 and 1, plus the number, could reach the United States. It should be harder to span hemispheres.

On the third ring, a female voice clipped, "I don't recognize this number."

Alexa put her phone on speaker. "Hi. Hello. I'm Alexa Glock with the Hastings Police Department in New Zealand. Is this Mrs. Quinn?"

"This is Audrey Quinn."

Alexa repeated who she was. "But originally I'm from North Carolina. Raleigh."

Silence.

"A Palo Alto police officer contacted your, um, secretary about an unidentified body found in your Cape Kidnappers bunker."

"It's not my bunker," the woman retorted. "I have never been to Australia."

"New Zealand." Why did people lump Australia and New

Zealand together? Of course, before she came to New Zealand, Alexa did the same. "Does your husband own property here?"

"My husband owns property everywhere."

The woman's namaste had worn off. "Is there a possibility that Mr. Quinn is currently in New Zealand?"

"Letitia told that officer last night that he is in Munich."

Alexa figured Letitia was the secretary. "When did you last talk with your husband?"

"I've been at a retreat that bans outside communication. Harlan respected that and hasn't called."

Alexa tried another angle. "Has Mr. Quinn ever broken a wrist?"

"I am certainly not giving out medical information."

This didn't bode well for the dentals. "Mrs. Quinn, a man was found dead. On your husband's property. We want to confirm that it's not him. You can do that by releasing his dental records."

A derisive laugh was her response.

"It's good to be careful," Alexa said. "Your local police can verify who I am."

It took a moment for Alexa to realize Audrey Quinn had hung up. A flare of anger colored her cheeks.

"Bit of a dag, eh?" Sergeant Atkins said.

"She's not worried," DI Steele said. "Evasive, yeah, but not worried. Who knows with these billionaires? All this 'he's in Munich,' but no one in Munich confirms that. I'm acting as if the deceased is Quinn until we rule it out. Constable Gavin is checking the local airports to see if he was on a passenger manifest. He had to fly in, right? Can't swim."

"Private yacht, maybe," Sergeant Atkins said. "There's this reality show called *Below Deck*? You should..."

DI Steele flicked her hand dismissively. "A yacht would take too long. A month to get here from California."

The failure with Mrs. Quinn rankled Alexa. She considered the two birds in hand: dental X-rays of the deceased and fingerprints from the laptop case. "I'll run the fingerprints I lifted. Maybe Harlan Quinn has prints on file. For security reasons, or something. And then I'll submit the dental images to the FBI's National Dental Repository. I'll contact local dentists too."

DI Steele told Alexa to meet her at Black Reef at one o'clock. "Hopefully, the fire lads will give us the all-clear in the bunker. Might be the warrant comes through by then. We might find a phone and wallet in the big house."

When Alexa entered the lab a few minutes later, a curly-haired woman looked up from her computer. "Hiya."

Alexa showed her badge and introduced herself.

"I heard you were here, working on the bunker body. I'm Pamela Amick." She took off strange amber lenses and polished them with her shirt. "Everyone is yakking that it's the American billionaire."

"We don't know yet."

"What can I do?" Pamela asked.

Alexa was trying harder to be a team player. "Can you run the fingerprints I lifted from a laptop case?"

Pamela beamed. "I'll finish this report and get on it."

The amber glasses, Alexa guessed, were to reduce blue light eye strain. "Pam? Make sure to submit the prints to the FBI database too, not just New Zealand's."

"Pamela, not Pam. I was planning to."

Alexa borrowed a work desk and got busy. She completed a postmortem dental form on John Doe, attached the images, and sent them to the U.S. databank and to the ten Hastings dentists she found on the internet, with a note about the unidentified remains.

Her stomach growled. She gave Pamela her business card. "Call me if you get a print match. What's a good café around here?"

Pamela recommended Artisan Café.

Alexa thought about the pink molar on the five-minute drive to the café. During her odontology training she had learned about something called tooth resorption that caused pink discoloration in patients, but mostly pink teeth were associated with postmortem.

The homey decor of the café and tempting array of cabinet food—desserts, pastries, meat pies, wraps, quiches—refocused her attention. She ordered a club sandwich, and in no time, a server delivered her food. Two bites in, her phone buzzed. Bruce's name flashed on the screen.

She swallowed quickly and answered.

"How's the case going?" Bruce asked.

A little foreplay would have been nice. She had just spent the night at his apartment. "I haven't been able to identify the man, and cause of death is pending." She thought of her pink molar theory, but conjecture wasn't science. "The California billionaire is supposedly in Munich, but no one has been able to verify. His wife refuses to release his dental records."

"Those are odd roadblocks," he commented.

Alexa pictured him naked and blushed.

"Your American bloke Fitzgerald said the very rich are different from you and me."

"It's not just rich people who have bunkers." After returning from DI Steele's last night, Alexa had searched bunkers on the internet. In South Dakota, a development company was selling six hundred private bunkers "to regular folk." Each was equipped with blast doors, electrical wiring, a power system, plumbing, and—her jaw had dropped—nine-foot-thick concrete walls. One buyer had said a comet was coming this way and that the government wasn't doing a thing to protect the people.

Her gaze landed on a mom giving bites of a muffin to her toddler. The way the baby opened its mouth, trusting, joyfully, gave her hope for the future.

"Alexa? Are you there? How do you like working with DI Steele?"

"She's not as good as you." True, but she regretted saying it. Bruce might think she was sucking up. Or smitten, which she was.

"This is her first big case. Tell her I'm available if she needs assistance. I'm heading to Rotorua to spend the weekend with the girls. We'll be in Clifton tomorrow afternoon."

Alexa recognized the name of the tractor town.

Bruce cleared his throat. "I want you to meet the girls. Can you join us for a tour to some gannet colony? It's Sammie's idea."

"To meet me?"

"To go on the tractor tour."

Like the girls would want to meet her. Alexa was glad Bruce couldn't see her blush. She liked those birds, she liked Bruce, she liked the thought of being pulled along the sea behind a tractor. But meeting the girls terrified her.

———

A bright red, orange, and yellow-checkered Hastings Volunteer Brigade truck dwarfed DI Steele's Volvo and another car—a clunker—when Alexa arrived at Black Reef. She parked and found the DI and a woman on the porch of the big house. The woman tapped ash from her cigarette over the railing and eyed Alexa with minimal curiosity.

"This is Mrs. Tina Cobb," the DI said. "She's the housekeeper."

The woman took a drag on her cigarette and kept her other hand buried in her smock pocket. "Tony said it was terrible. The man's face was covered in bugs."

"Take me through it again," DI Steele said.

The woman straightened. Alexa pegged her as mid-fifties. "When the code wouldn't work, I called Tony. He went in through the shed. Came out all shaking."

"How do you get the codes?" DI Steele's voice had an edge to it.

Mrs. Cobb took another drag. Through the smoke her pale blue eyes had gone wary.

"I'm not allowed to say."

"What do you mean?" DI Steele asked.

Mrs. Cobb's eyes darted to the berm. "I, we, signed a contract that we wouldn't discuss the estate."

DI Steele's jaw clenched. "This is an emergency. Who made you sign a contract?"

"The property manager. She lives in Auckland and sends us codes. She pays us, too. I called to tell her about the body, but her mailbox was full."

"I'll need her name and contact info," DI Steele said sharply. "Have you seen Mr. Quinn recently?"

"I've never seen him." She stubbed the cigarette on the railing. "Mr. Quinn is keen on his privacy."

"Do you think it was him in the bunker?" Alexa asked.

Mrs. Cobb wrapped the butt in a tissue and stuck it in her smock pocket. "I don't know, do I?"

"Come to the station this afternoon and give a statement," DI Steele said. "Bring a solicitor, if that makes you feel better."

"I can't miss my shift at The Retreat. I'm on at five."

"Tomorrow morning, then. First thing."

They watched Tina Cobb drive away in the clunker car. "I don't like this cloak-and-dagger contract stuff." The DI's voice bordered on shrill. "There's a man in the morgue with no toe tag. The warrant to search the big house is delayed. The Super is on my back."

Alexa sympathized. She wanted answers, too.

"Plus Joe. My boy. He did a runner last night." The DI glanced at her. "He's being recruited by the Curs. I don't know how to stop it. I'm a detective, and I don't know what to do."

"He's being recruited by the what?"

"The Curs. A gang."

"I didn't know New Zealand had gangs."

DI Steele looked incredulous. "There are gangs everywhere."

Alexa thought of her nephews, Benny and Noah. What would she do in the DI's place? Lock them in their rooms? Send them to boarding school?

The fireman from yesterday crossed the grass, waving a gizmo at them. "I tested the air in the bunker," he called. "It's all good. Can't say what it was when the doors were shut tight." He stopped at the bottom of the steps and looked up at them. "Keep the doors open as a precaution."

Alexa ran through the symptoms of carbon monoxide poisoning that she could recall: headache, dizziness, weakness, nausea, seizures and chest pain, loss of consciousness. Death. "If there had been carbon monoxide in the bunker, how long would it take to dissipate?"

"That depends on the fresh airflow." The fireman squinted in the afternoon sun. "With the exhaust fan running and both doors open like they are now, half the CO would leave in five hours, and the other half five hours after that."

It reminded Alexa of the half-life theory for radiocarbon dating. Living things absorb carbon from the atmosphere and food. When they die, they stop absorbing. The carbon they've accumulated during their lifetime decays at measurable rates which can determine how long a person or animal or plant has been dead. Just recently she had read radiocarbon absorption varied depending on whether you were in the northern or southern hemisphere.

The fireman stuck his gizmo in a case. "There's a carbon monoxide detector in the control room, but the battery is dead."

"We check our batteries the same day as we switch clocks back or forward," DI Steele said. "Easy to remember that way."

Alexa had hoped daylight savings was only in the States. No such luck.

"Smart, yeah. A dead battery can mean a life snuffed out," he said in parting.

The thump of rotors beating the air caused Alexa to lean over the railing and search the sky. A helicopter skimmed the cliff line coming at them. Her mouth went dry.

DI Steele looked, too. "Probably a reporter."

In Alexa's last case, a helicopter pilot had tried to kill her. With a bag of rocks. She'd had nightmares about it.

The graphite black copter homed in and circled the landing pad once, twice, and set down.

"Could be our billionaire," the DI yelled.

Chapter Nine

The blades continued to rotate as a door swung open. A uniformed man lowered steps and helped a woman in knee-high boots climb out. Her loose black hair shielded her face as he set a wheelie suitcase next to her. Alexa glimpsed a white leather settee and gleaming wood table in the cabin. Even a vase of flowers.

The man saluted and pulled the door closed.

The woman wheeled the suitcase under the helicopter blades without a flinch. Her long hair went tornado as the copter lifted and veered away.

DI Steele marched up to her. Alexa followed a few feet behind.

The woman whipped off sunglasses. "Who are you? Why is a fire truck leaving the property?"

"I'm Detective Inspector Micala Steele, Hastings Police Department. Who are you?"

She swept her tangled hair up in a bunch and let it fall down her back, blending in with her black turtleneck. "Has something happened?"

"Please identify yourself," DI Steele said.

"I'm Lynn Lockhart, manager of Black Reef estate." She pointed to the guest house on the other side of the infinity pool. "That's my cottage."

DI Steele extended her badge for Ms. Lockhart to inspect. "So you live here?"

"Sometimes."

"The cottage belongs to you?"

"I have use of the cottage. What's going on? Was there a fire?"

"Show me some identification, please," DI Steele said, "and then I'll explain."

Ms. Lockhart huffed as she searched through the satchel hanging from her shoulder. She eventually produced a New Zealand driver's license.

DI Steele studied it. "Auckland, eh? Where's the owner, Mr. Quinn?"

"Mr. Quinn arrives tomorrow." She eyed Alexa. "Who are you?"

Before Alexa could answer, DI Steele said, "Ms. Glock works for me."

With you, not for you.

"Let's find a place to talk, shall we?" DI Steele said.

Ms. Lockhart huffed again and led them across the grass, past the infinity pool, to the cottage. Its railing was entwined with vines, and the small porch fit a bench covered in gingham cushions and a wooden table of shells. Ms. Lockhart punched numbers in the key code box and pulled at the door. It didn't open. She pressed the code again, and again it stayed locked.

"A cock-up," she said. "I'll call the security company." She found her phone and turned her back.

Alexa heard *malfunction* and *Black Reef* and *That's what I pay you for.* "The code didn't work for the housekeeper either," Alexa reminded DI Steele.

Ms. Lockhart twirled around and jabbed at the code box again. This time the lock opened. She marched in, beckoning them to follow.

A sun-streaked foyer led to the living area. Ms. Lockhart looked around, apparently to her satisfaction. Alexa guessed she was late thirties. Her eyes were as dark as her hair. "Let me put my bag up. Have a seat." She clacked down a side hallway.

DI Steele sat on a plush sofa. "Nice digs."

Alexa looked around, *want, want, want* kicking up its heels as she took in the vaulted ceiling, blond wood beams, muted rugs, creamy couch, stone hearth flanked by windows framing the sea. Usually she didn't give a hoot about possessions, but even the large painting of sheep in a field and a fossilized shell on the mantel aroused in her a dormant greed for home and hearth.

Maybe with Bruce.

She dropped onto the other end of the sofa, causing DI Steele to jiggle. Interviewing property managers wasn't in her job description. "What would you like me to do?"

DI Steele looked surprised. "Be a second pair of eyes and ears." She got out a notepad and pen. "We'll be on our way soon. I don't expect the warrant until tomorrow."

Ms. Lockhart returned, hair brushed and lipstick freshened, and stood at the mantel.

DI Steele scooted to the edge of the sofa. "There's been an incident, Ms. Lockhart."

"Please, call me Lynn."

"A death. You may have heard about it on the news?"

Lynn ran a plum fingernail along the spine of the fossilized shell. "I don't bother with news."

"A man's body was discovered in the bunker yesterday."

"A body?" Lynn's eyes flew to the foyer. The berm was visible through the sidelight windows of the front door. "Who is it? How did he get in?"

"The housekeeper, Mrs. Cobb, called to inform you, but your voice mailbox is full. Better fix that. We haven't been able to identify who he is or how he entered. We've spoken to Mrs. Quinn in California. She claimed it can't be the owner, Mr. Quinn."

Consternation flickered across Lynn's face as she lowered into a chair. "Harlan doesn't arrive until tomorrow. I told you."

"Can you call him?" DI Steele asked. "He might shed light on who the deceased is."

Lynn kneaded the base of her right thumb with her left thumb, round and round. "Mr. Quinn calls me."

"This is an emergency. We need to identify who the dead man is."

Round and round. "I have no way to reach him."

"I can give you his number," DI Steele said.

"I can't. It's in..."

"Your contract?" Three wavy lines appeared across the DI's forehead. "When did you last see Mr. Quinn?"

Lynn glanced out the nearest window. "He came to Black Reef for New Year's. We sat on the patio and toasted the rising sun. Cape Kidnappers is the first place in the world to see the sun rise out of the ocean. That's one reason Harlan bought it."

"That hardly sounds like property manager duties, watching the sunrise. Was his wife with you?" DI Steele asked.

Lynn flushed. "Mrs. Quinn never comes to New Zealand."

The DI leaned forward. "What *is* your relationship with Mr. Quinn?"

"That's personal."

"Personal, as in none of my business, or personal, as in intimate?"

Lynn squared her shoulders so that her turtleneck stretched taut. "None of your business."

"Did Mr. Quinn have health issues?"

She looked alarmed. "Why do you ask?"

"There was a dead man in the bunker, that's why."

"It isn't Harlan. Besides, he takes great care of himself." She paused. "Do you have a picture?"

Alexa met DI Steele's eye.

"Facial recognition isn't possible," the DI said.

Alexa held her breath, but Lynn didn't seem fazed.

"Why would someone break into the bunker?" she asked.

Instead of answering, DI Steele said, "There's a locked room in the bunker. What's in it?"

"I don't know. I've never been down there. I don't have access."

"Yet you're the property manager?"

A sharp rapping interrupted Lynn's reply. She jumped up and flew to the door. Alexa heard her open it and Lynn say, "Oh, it's you. What do you want?"

"I'm here to lodge a complaint."

Alexa turned around. A woman in her sixties stood on the threshold, frowning at Lynn. A man close to the same age perched behind her.

DI Steele joined them. "What's the problem? Who are you?"

"They belong to some bird protection group," Lynn said.

"The Royal Forest and Bird Protection Society," the woman said. "I'm vice president."

DI Steele held out her badge. "I'm with the police. Your names, please."

"Linda and Dru Crosby," the woman said. "Has someone already complained?"

"About what?" DI Steele asked.

"About that blasted helicopter," she said. "The gannet chicks are ready to fledge. Loud noises can cause them to fall off the cliff or fail to migrate. Their parents might abandon them. The Quinns should never have been able to build on top of the sanctuary and should never arrive by helicopter."

Yikes, Alexa thought.

Lynn pointed at the woman. "*You* are trespassing."

"We have permission to monitor the sanctuary gannets," the birder woman said.

The man shuffled backwards. Lynn turned to DI Steele. "The Crosbys welcomed Harlan by threatening to sue him. They caused a six-month construction delay."

"This isn't the time to hash out grievances," DI Steele said. "Ms. Lockhart, please wait inside. I'll take the Crosbys' contact information and be back shortly." She shut the door firmly behind her.

Lynn stalked toward Alexa. "Those Crosbys are bird crazies."

"People get riled up about animals." Alexa watched Lynn curiously. "How did you meet Mr. Quinn?"

Lynn's facial muscles relaxed as she surveyed the room. "I was a sales associate for Opulence Realty in Auckland. An acquaintance of his bought an estate near here, and Harlan wanted to do the same. We became very close."

Alexa kept her face neutral.

Lynn ran her finger along the ridges of the shell. "This is from the Jurassic period. Can you believe that? We flew around the North Island, looking at property. Harlan settled on Cape Kidnappers and bought fifty hectares."

A hectare was more than twice the size of an acre.

"Would you like a drink?" Lynn said suddenly.

"A water, thanks." Alexa craned her neck to check on DI Steele. The birder woman flapped her hands. The man had retreated down the steps; all Alexa saw was the top of his head.

Lynn returned with two waters and handed one to Alexa. "Your boss is getting a lecture."

"She's not my boss." Alexa uncapped the bottle and drank. Cold and delicious. She checked the label. Something about icebergs. *What?* She squinted to read the fine print. The water actually came from melted icebergs. *What the hell?* She took another sip. "When did Mr. Quinn buy the land?"

Lynn sank back into an easy chair. "Two and a half years ago. He offered me a job overseeing the building and care of Black Reef, so I left Opulence."

Giving up a career for a man who won't let you call him? Alexa thought that was nuts.

Lynn ran a hand across the nubby fabric. "I did all the decorating and furniture buying. The big house, too."

Alexa conceded that she had good taste. "What about the bunker?"

"I avoid the bunker. I can't believe you found a body in there. It's horrible."

"Whoever it is didn't leave a car. How does Mr. Quinn usually arrive?"

Her dark eyes got big. "What are you implying?"

"I'm just trying to figure out how the man got here. It's weird, right?"

"Maybe he climbed up from the beach, I don't know. Mr. Quinn uses LHT like I do."

"LHT?"

"Luxury Helicopter Taxi."

DI Steele strode into the room. "Your neighbor had some information that doesn't jibe with yours, Ms. Lockhart."

"Those people are not my neighbors. They live in Clifton."

"Close enough," DI Steele said. "Mrs. Crosby saw Mr. Quinn a week ago. Standing at the edge of the cliff."

Lynn's eyes sparked. "That's impossible. Harlan is arriving tomorrow. That's why I'm here. To get things ready. I take care of everything."

"Perhaps *Harlan* came early," DI Steele said.

Lynn squeezed her water bottle so that it squelched. "Mr. Quinn would have told me. I'll check the big house. If he came early, I'll know."

"Do you have written permission to enter his house?" DI Steele asked.

Lynn folded her arms across her chest. "I'm the property manager. I don't need written permission."

Audrey Quinn had threatened to sue if they entered the big house. "Mrs. Quinn told us to keep out of the big house," Alexa said.

"It's none of her business," Lynn snapped.

DI Steele snorted. "We have no way of knowing whether Black

Reef is marital property or separate," she said. "Unless you have written permission? If not, we'll wait for the warrant."

Lynn pressed her lips together.

Alexa reminded herself that this was about an unidentified body. Maybe it was Quinn. Maybe he didn't want his property manager, or whatever she was, to know he came early. Her pulse quickened. "Does Mr. Quinn have a local dentist?"

The question seemed to please Lynn. "Mr. Quinn is obsessed with health. I set him up with a dentist, physician, personal trainer, masseuse, chef, and dietitian."

Alexa checked her watch: four o'clock on a Friday afternoon. The dentist might still be at his clinic. "Can I have the dentist's name and number?"

"Why?" Lynn asked.

"Procedure." "Procedure" was Alexa's stock answer to difficult questions.

"Let's not play games. It's to rule out that Mr. Quinn died in his bunker," DI Steele said.

Lynn's eyes flashed. "He's coming tomorrow. He'll be angry you treated me this way."

"How did he contact you?" DI Steele asked.

"He always texts."

"Show me the correspondence," DI Steele said.

"Correspondence from Harlan self-trashes after ten minutes. Security reasons."

Alexa had never heard of such a thing. "Can I have the name of his dentist?" she said gently.

Lynn scrolled through her contacts. "Dr. Vidyarthi at Bay Best Smiles."

Bay Best Smiles was familiar. Alexa had sent John Doe's X-rays to them before lunch.

As Lynn read out the numbers, Alexa punched them into her phone and escaped to the porch. She pressed Call and was relieved when someone answered.

"Best Bay Smiles. How can I help you?" a woman asked.

"I'm working with the Hastings Police Department. Is Dr. Vidyarthi available?"

"He's out of the office. Are you a patient?"

"This is a police matter. We have an unidentified dead man who *might* have been a patient at Best Bay Smiles." She spoke slowly. Kiwis sometimes had a hard time understanding her accent. "I sent Dr. Vidyarthi an email about it a couple hours ago."

"Call him Dr. V. All his patients do."

Alexa heard a TV in the background. "I need to know if he took X-rays of a Mr. Quinn."

"Is that the dead man?"

Alexa tapped her foot. "That's what I am trying to find out. Can you check the records?"

"I'm not even in the office." She giggled. "I'm in my lounge."

"This is a serious matter," Alexa said.

The voice sobered. "Dr. V has gone tramping. The Cape Brett Track. He left early this morning, and he'll be back Monday. Shall I give you his mobile number?"

Chapter Ten

Alexa poked her head in and motioned for DI Steele to join her on the porch. "No luck. The dentist is off hiking." She thought of her recent tramping trip with her brother and hoped the dentist had better luck. "He doesn't answer his phone."

"Bloody hell. There goes the weekend."

Her response irritated Alexa. The bunker body wasn't something to sweep aside for a Netflix binge. She followed Steele back into the cottage.

Lynn leaned forward from her chair.

"We don't know anything more," DI Steele said.

"So it isn't Harlan?"

"Identification is still unknown." The DI checked her phone, scowled, then shoved it in her pocket. "I need to leave."

Lynn sprang to her feet. "What should I do?"

"Keep out of the main house and bunker. I'm posting someone on premises. Don't want the media nosing about."

Lynn's eyes pinged from DI Steele's to Alexa's and back. "Is it safe here?"

Was it safe anywhere? Alexa felt sorry for Lynn and her strange situation.

DI Steele turned to Alexa. "Where are you staying? In case I need you."

She had checked out of the Apple Motor Lodge. "I'm not sure yet."

Lynn pounced. "Stay here. Please. There's a spare bedroom."

"I can't," Alexa said reflexively.

"I'm dining at The Retreat tonight," Lynn said. "I'll change the reservation to two, my treat. I shouldn't be alone."

Alexa looked to DI Steele for help.

"I don't have a problem with you staying here. Maybe it's a good idea." She gave Alexa a look. "Check in with the constable when you return from dinner. I'll see you in the morning."

Alexa felt ambushed. She followed D.I. Steele outside. "My staying here could be a conflict."

DI Steele hurried toward her car. "No worries. You're not a police officer. There hasn't been a crime." She stopped in her tracks so that Alexa bumped into her. "Kersten has always wanted to eat at The Retreat. *Good Food Guide* rated it the best of the best. Take advantage. Find out more about our"—the DI used air quotes—"'property manager,' eh? What's the scoop with her and the CEO? I'm late for a meeting. Joe again. Always Joe."

Alexa watched the DI's Volvo curve, dip, and crest the one-lane drive until it disappeared in that grove of trees where her car hit the ditch. Had she been thrown to the wolves?

There are no wolves in New Zealand, she reminded herself. Not that it was void of predators though. She checked her phone: no texts, one voicemail. She hoped it would be Dr. V, but it was Pamela-Not-Pam from the lab.

"Thumbs down. No matches with the laptop cover fingerprints."

Alexa was disappointed. The case had stalled and she was in la-la land.

A faint crashing of waves lured her around the back of the cottage, past the infinity pool—its surface agitated by the breeze—to behind the big house, which stretched left and right in two expansive wings. Like gannet wings, she thought.

Strands of her hair whipped her eyes. She tucked them into her ponytail and faced the bay, her back to the house. The vantage point reminded her of a Māori *pa*, or fort, with views in all directions. Hawke's Bay frothed. She thought of her roommate's story about Captain James Cook entering the bay and the Māori paddling to meet it.

The twain shall meet.

Two gannets circled high above the choppy water, on the prowl. One broke loose and plunged, headlong, streamlined, into the sea. Her stomach dropped.

A *krok-krok-krok*king enticed her closer to the cliff. The Black Reef gannets clamored somewhere below. She stepped an inch closer—she hated heights—and peered over. A rock outcrop, strewn with dried seaweed and broken shells, obscured her view of the roosting birds. No way she'd lean farther out.

A funny feeling tickled her neck. She whirled around and canvassed the house. She looked for a flicker at a window, for a shadow of a figure. Nothing. She studied the roofline and a lone Norfolk pine. More nothing. But she couldn't shake the feeling of being watched. She jogged back to her car, the speed refreshing, reassuring, and collected her belongings.

Lynn opened the door as she stepped onto the porch. "I'll show you your room."

Alexa followed her host inside.

"The guest suite is on the other side of the cottage from the master suite so you'll have plenty of privacy." Down a short hallway, Lynn opened a door.

The bedroom was gush-worthy. It had its own fireplace and sitting area. The bed was enormous, with six pillows, a duvet the color of Bruce's eyes, and two stuffed sheep, one black and one white.

Lynn walked across a thick rug of wheat, grass, and sky colors and pressed a button. The shades tilted so that Alexa could see the sea. "I don't know who died in the bunker," Lynn said. She opened the shades at the second window. "I feel violated."

Alexa let go of her suitcase handle. "So Mr. Quinn is arriving tomorrow?"

"That's why I'm here." She walked to the dresser and straightened a pale grayish piece of what Alexa guessed was fossilized driftwood. It balanced delicately on a stand. "This is a meteorite. Can you imagine? I called The Retreat and changed my reservation to two people. It's for seven thirty. Would you like to drive or shall I have them pick us up?"

"I'll drive."

Lynn stared at the meteorite for a moment and then left the room, closing the door.

Alexa scuffed out of her Keds and sat on the bed. Ages ago— but what was just this morning—she'd seen a dead man's heart on a scale and discovered a pink tooth in his mouth. *Who was he?* Lynn was certain it wasn't Harlan Quinn.

She popped up and opened what she thought would be the bathroom door, but it was a walk-in closet. Two fluffy robes hung from the rack with two pairs of UGG slippers waiting below them like faithful pets. Alexa slipped into the closest pair, wiggled her toes, and sighed. Staying here had perks.

The bathroom had an array of bath and body products and a waterfall shower large enough for a flock of sheep. Alexa stripped quickly.

At ten after seven and lavender-scented, she found Lynn staring out a living area window. She had wrapped a colorful scarf around her black turtleneck and traded boots for pointy-toed pumps. Alexa looked down at her clean button-down, khakis, and navy Keds. She wondered if she should update her wardrobe. Her mind flew to Bruce. He didn't care what she wore; the less the better, he had told her Wednesday night. She flushed at the memory.

They walked under a sliver of moon to the Vitz. "It's dark so early now," Lynn commented.

Alexa cleared café trash from the passenger seat. Lynn settled in, not bothering with a seat belt. The Vitz was so old it didn't complain. "An ATV drove me off this road yesterday," Alexa said, "right into a ditch." The lane was pitch dark. Alexa turned on high beams.

"It was probably a guest from The Retreat," Lynn said. "They rent spiffy Can-Ams."

Alexa guessed a Can-Am was an ATV brand. "They didn't even stop." The next curve was almost hairpin. No sign of civilization. "DI Steele said The Retreat has great food."

"Horacio is a master chef. He cooks for Harlan and me on the side."

The dimness made it easy for Alexa to probe. "You and Mr. Quinn sound close."

Lynn took a deep breath. "We are." She peered into the darkness. "Turn here."

Alexa turned onto a side road. It curved past a sign pointing the way to a golf course. The well-lit inn was stone and timber like the main house at Black Reef, but more chalet style than farmhouse. The driveway was circular.

"Drive up front," Lynn directed.

As soon as Alexa stopped the car, a young man dashed down the front steps and opened Lynn's door. "Welcome." He helped her out and started toward Alexa's door.

She left the keys in the ignition as if she was a regular valet user. "Have a most wonderful evening," the valet said and drove off in her dented car.

A vase of orange pom-pom flowers graced a round table in the lobby. Alexa wondered if they were real. A young woman in an emerald kimono-style dress glided toward them, a leather book in her hand. "Welcome. I'm Katrina Flores, manager of The Retreat." She noticed Alexa studying the flowers. "Those are craspedia billy buttons. Aren't they fun? Is this your first time dining with us?"

Lynn stepped forward. "I'm a regular diner. I'm usually here with Mr. Quinn."

Ms. Flores looked stricken. "Of course, Ms. Lockhart. Welcome back." She glanced at her book. A lock of ginger hair escaped from her bun, covering her flushed cheek artfully. "I *do* apologize." She gestured for a server to join them. "This is Blair. She'll show you to your table and take wonderful care of you. Do try the hazelnut cheesecake for dessert. The honey-bourbon drizzle is divine."

Sold, thought Alexa.

They followed Blair across plush rugs into a softly lit dining room, where jazz music drifted from hidden speakers. Alexa counted three candlelit tables of diners: an older couple talking quietly, four laughing men, and what looked like parents with their teen son and daughter.

"I have a lovely table ready," Blair said. She slid back their chairs and whisked Lynn's linen napkin off her plate, snapped it open, presented it like a gift, and did the same for Alexa. "We have a set menu tonight. I'll let you settle and be back to describe it."

A young man replaced Blair and filled their water glasses. Lynn sat rigidly. "Harlan will be furious that the manager didn't recognize me."

Alexa decided to tackle the elephant. "Are you in a relationship with him?"

Lynn's eyes flickered with candlelight. "Harlan is going to leave Audrey for me as soon as their daughter is mature enough to handle it."

And I have a wind farm in Arizona to sell you.

When Alexa had first met Bruce, she had thought he was married and tamped the sparks she'd felt for him. She smiled at the memory of how she'd discovered he was divorced and there-fore—in her book of rules—eligible. They had crashed grocery carts at a Countdown. His was full of cookies and frozen pizza. "For my girls when they come for the weekend," he explained.

Alexa refocused on the present. "What sort of man is Mr. Quinn?" *Besides a cheater?*

"Harlan is charismatic and commanding." Lynn gazed around the room. "He sees any obstacle—like those birder people—as challenges to overcome. His favorite thing to do is to start new companies. The thrill of the hunt, he calls it."

Blair returned and chirped about the menu. "We'll commence with Jerusalem artichoke salad, followed by woodsy mushroom soup. The mushrooms are from Ohau Gourmet Mushroom farm, grown specially *yadda yadda*. The main will be Silver Fern fillet of beef, medium rare..."

Alexa perked up.

"...with ginger miso emulsion, puffed rice *yadda yadda*. If you prefer a meatless..."

Alexa tuned out the vegetarian options.

"Shall I send our sommelier over?" Blair asked when she was finally done.

Lynn flipped her hand. "We'll share a bottle of Col d'Orcia Nastagio from Mr. Quinn's collection."

Alexa thought of the wine room in the bunker as a slender mustached man appeared and presented the bottle for Lynn to inspect. She bobbed her head. He cut through the foil with a flourish and worked the cork out. He laid it by Lynn's glass, but she ignored it. He looked pained as he poured an inch of red velvet into her glass. "The Mediterranean climate and hilly landscape gives..."

"It doesn't matter," Lynn interrupted. She took the bottle straight from the man's hand and poured more into her glass. The sommelier bowed slightly and left Lynn to fill Alexa's glass.

Alexa didn't have words to describe the taste. *Like minutiae on a fingerprint* was all she could come up with. A good quality fingerprint could have twenty-five to eighty minutiae. Wine minutiae tap-danced over her tongue, down her throat, in her belly.

The teenage boy at the family table announced loudly he would drive a Can-Am tomorrow. Maybe he was the hoon who drove her off the road, Alexa thought.

Lynn rearranged her scarf as Alexa watched in amazement.

The result crisscrossed artfully and accentuated her black top. "This whole body-in-the-bunker is horrible."

Alexa nodded. "Did Mr. Quinn ever rent his bunker or house to friends?"

Lynn scoffed. "Rent? You mean like for income? Never."

Blair served their salads. Alexa took a cautious bite. Something nutty overpowered the arugula. She forced herself to swallow and pushed the plate away.

Lynn pushed her salad away, too. "In California Harlan is under constant scrutiny and beholden to his stakeholders. When his start-ups do well, everyone wants a piece of him and his brain work." She ran her finger around the rim of her glass. "That's why he comes here. To get away from the rules and regulations, the"—she used air quotes—"'teamwork culture.' No one bothers him here."

Alexa, content to sip and listen, wasn't that big on teamwork either. She preferred autonomy.

"Harlan confides in me. I'm not going to sue him or steal his ideas."

Blair served Alexa a bowl with a single yellowish mushroom at the bottom of it staring at her like a jaundiced eye. Had the definition of soup changed? Fine dining wasn't panning out. Then another server materialized and poured creamy liquid from a tiny pitcher, drowning the lone mushroom.

"Truffle oil?" Blair asked.

Alexa accepted a golden drizzle.

When Blair evaporated, Alexa dipped her spoon halfway and tasted. Her eyebrows rose. "What's with the bunker?" she asked between spoonfuls.

Lynn poured more wine into each of their glasses. "Bunkers are a thing. Before I left Opulence, I had several international clients purchase estates and add bunkers. I won't mention names, but there's a dystopian mindset in your country. Everyone wants a piece of New Zealand. Isn't that why you're here?"

"I had a professional opportunity."

Lynn raised an eyebrow as if she didn't believe her. "Harlan can get here on his private jet. The bunker makes him feel invincible." She swallowed more wine. "I can't wait to see him."

The beef was tender and succulent. To Alexa's disappointment, Lynn turned down dessert and rose from the table. The ride back was quiet, just the crunch of tires on gravel. A flashlight sliced the night as they drove up to Black Reef.

"Who's that?" Lynn asked.

Alexa spied the patrol car. "It's the police officer DI Steele sent. I'll go check in."

She watched Lynn enter the cottage and then followed the light that now shone in her eyes.

The beam lowered. "Constable Gavin here?"

Alexa remembered him. "You checked in my evidence last night. How's everything?"

"All good. A few stray dogs, eh?"

Was he asking if she'd seen dogs, too? Two and a half glasses of minutiae had her woozy. She thanked him and turned toward the berm, squinting to make out the crime scene tape. The thought of the bunker made her shiver. On the way to the cottage she checked her cell phone. One text, from Bruce: Hope to see you 2:00 tomorrow, Clifton Gannet Tractor Tours, and an address.

No heart emoji. She'd have to settle for *Wild Light of Dawn*, her romance novel.

SATURDAY

Chapter Eleven

Alexa craved open space in the morning—she had dreamed of being trapped in the bunker and woke up clutching the black sheep to her chest—but first she called the tramping dentist again. When he didn't answer, she left another message: "It's an urgent police matter. Call back."

Running helped her think, and she had a lot to think about. She put her phone on vibrate and slipped it in the back pocket of her running tights. There was no sign of Lynn as she tiptoed through the cottage and out the door.

The police car was gone; her Toyota Vitz was all alone.

Murky morning gray merged with the dark bay as she rounded the cottage for the cliffside path she had spotted yesterday. Tremolos of *arrr, arrr, arrr* drowned out the murmur of waves. The gannets were waking, probably stretching their wings. Alexa steered clear of the edge and stretched. Tightness in her calves reminded her that she'd turn thirty-eight next month. She would miss being a prime number. Indivisible. There was always forty-one to look forward to.

The windows of the big house stared blankly. She pushed thoughts of the hidden camera away. The path hugged the cliffs, curving, dipping, veering inland and back outward, past DANGER, STAY BACK signs. In one spot the path had caved in, forcing her onto stubbly tussock. She imagined the sea below, gouging and biting.

It was so open, she could see for miles.

A gannet skimmed by at eye level. Its beauty lifted Alexa's spirits. The low-fifties temp was perfect for running. She flew over a ravine on a pedestrian bridge. On the other side, a fairway edged out the path, empty, glistening, contoured. She remembered The Retreat had a golf course. Its plush grass cushioned her stride. She imagined a lot of golf balls ended up in the bay. A woman crested a dune. At least Alexa guessed it was a woman; she wore a hoodie, so it was hard to tell. Alexa waved, but the woman didn't respond.

In the distance, distinctive rock formations in the scalloped bay caught her eye. They cut the water like shark fins. In front of them, a plateau shimmered with an amalgam of golden white movement. Alexa decided it was the Cape Kidnappers gannet colony. Her roommate had said it was the largest gannet colony in the world.

She turned into the wind, eager for the day ahead. Her greenstone pendant thumped with every stride, like a second heartbeat. She might see Bruce and his girls this afternoon. Take that tractor tour. But only if she could identify the dead man.

Near the big house, a woman's voice mixed with the *krukkruk*king of gannets. Alexa slowed her stride. Something about "setting traps." She jogged in place and looked around. There wasn't a soul in sight. Had it been the wind? The gannets?

Then she heard another voice, male.

"...nose where it doesn't belong."

Alexa moved to the cliff edge.

"Up to no good," the woman answered. "*Something something (indistinguishable)*...deserves to die."

She inched closer and peered down, stretching farther than she had yesterday. She could see ledges salted with snowy gannets and peppered with brown-speckled chicks shimmying back and forth. Below them—to Alexa's amazement—a climber's head. A bead of sweat gathered at the tip of her nose as she stared. The climber turned profile. What the hell? It was that birder woman from yesterday. The one who complained about Lynn's helicopter. Alexa searched for the owner of the male voice. The tiers of rock blocked her view.

What was the woman's name? Cosby, maybe. Alexa almost called out but didn't want the woman to fall.

She backed up. Who deserved to die? Surely she had misunderstood. The whole overheard conversation was too Miss Marple. She was glad to leave. As she rounded the cottage, she heard thumping country music. A patrol car crawled to a stop next to her Vitz. Alexa spotted Sergeant Atkins through the open driver's window and jogged over to meet her.

The sergeant sang, "If I had more money, I'd still be broke" as she got out. Today's nose ring looked like a fishing hook. "Senior tried to call you, but you didn't answer."

Alexa groped for the phone pocket at the small of her back. "I didn't feel it buzz."

"There's a press conference at ten a.m. Senior wants you there."

Alexa checked her watch; it was seven thirty. "Any word on who John Doe is?"

The sergeant shook her head dolefully.

Alexa caught her breath and repeated what she'd just overheard. "It's a woman DI Steele and I met yesterday. I think her husband is with her. They're birders."

"Lots of those about," Sergeant Atkins said.

"She complained about Lynn Lockhart's helicopter disturbing the gannets. She's like Spider-Woman, halfway up the cliff."

"She said someone deserved to die?"

"I think so."

Sergeant Atkins looked skeptical. "Might take a look-see. How's Ms. Lockhart this morning?"

"I haven't seen her. Last night she insisted Mr. Quinn is arriving today."

"Senior sent me here to hang out in case he shows up."

"I'll see you later, then," Alexa said.

There was still no sign of Lynn when she entered the cottage. In the guest room she fished out her phone and saw she had two messages. The first was from DI Steele. She texted back that she would attend the press conference. The next was from the pathologist: "Cardiac pathology was negative, no heart attack. Cause of death remains undetermined. Lab tests are pending."

Okay, Alexa thought. Bunker man hadn't died of a heart attack. She still had the pink molar. Tests for CO_2 would take at least a week. Alexa sank onto her unmade bed and called the tramping dentist one more time.

"Arjun here."

Arjun? She fumbled the phone. "Is this Dr. Vidyarthi?"

"Yes?"

"Good morning. My name is Alexa Glock, and I'm working with the Hastings Police Department."

"Ah, yes, I see you've called a few times. You have an unidentified body, eh?"

Alexa pressed the phone harder to her ear. "That's right. There's a possibility it's Harlan Quinn. He owns the property where the body was found. No one has been able to reach him, and his property manager says he is a patient at Bay Best Smiles."

"I don't recognize the name. I won't be back in Hastings until Monday."

Alexa opened her mouth to tell Dr. V to get back here sooner.

"Eh, Campbell, my receptionist, can get you what you need. I'll call her now. Meet her at, what time, nine o'clock suit you?"

Alexa eagerly agreed. The pink tooth popped into her head. "Have you ever heard of pink tooth phenomenon? I discovered the deceased has a pink molar."

Dr. V was quiet. Alexa thought maybe they'd been disconnected.

"It can happen in multiple or single teeth," he finally said. "Never seen it, but pink teeth have occurred in victims of fire, drowning, suffocation, eh?"

"I'd never seen one either. Thank you for your cooperation."

The day was looking up. Alexa took a quick shower, made the bed—this wasn't a hotel, she reminded herself—and packed up. She arranged the stuffed sheep so they were nose-to-nose. She took a look around the sumptuous bedroom for stray socks and then headed to the living area. The cottage was quiet. She said a silent goodbye to opulence. Driving away, she felt more like herself, unfettered by excess and consumerism.

A Hastings café owner fixed her a flat white and sticky bun, which she scarfed down and still arrived at Bay Best Smiles—a little brick building next to a Unichem Pharmacy—early, prepared to wait. A woman in a white puffy jacket was unlocking the clinic door. Alexa hopped out of the Vitz. "Campbell?"

"Never been here on a Saturday before." The fur encircling the hood hid her face. "Streets are empty. You're the police?"

Most Kiwis acted oblivious to cool temperatures, so Alexa was amused by her attire. "I'm working with the police. I'm an odontologist."

Inside, Campbell swept her hood back, revealing a messy honey-colored updo. Alexa imagined she had rolled out of bed at Dr. V's request, but she seemed cheery. She disappeared around a partition and reappeared at the reception window. "I'd die for a coffee," she said, booting her computer.

Colorful dental posters hung on either side of the window: We Want To Make You Smile and Five Tips For Healthy Teeth. Alexa considered tip #5: limiting sugary foods. She shifted uncomfortably; caramelized sugar gummed her molars.

Campbell asked, "What's the bloke's name?"

"Harlan Quinn."

"Ah, yeah, sure, here he is." Campbell studied the screen. "He came in once, for a cleaning. Six months ago. I just sent him a reminder. Shall I pull up his X-rays?" She tapped on the keyboard and then turned her computer screen.

Alexa squinted. The shadowy tendrils of a repaired root in the left lower second molar gave her an adrenaline rush. It matched the X-rays she'd taken of the corpse. *Slow down*, she told herself. Harlan Quinn wasn't the only person in the world to have a root canal on that particular tooth.

"Can you email the radiographs to me?"

"Nah, yeah."

Alexa ran to her car, retrieved her laptop, returned to the office, and sat in the waiting area. Within minutes she had positioned the postmortem and antemortem panoramic radiographs side-by-side. Campbell turned on music, but the sound faded as Alexa compared tooth positions, cavities, the root canal treatment, and a benign bone growth. She was sure of the results, but entered the data into the automatic dental code-matching system to let it determine one of four outcomes—Positive, Possible, Insufficient, or Exclusion.

Chapter Twelve

Campbell stared as Alexa did a jab, a few crosses, and an upper-cut. Her job was done. The automatic system had determined a Positive result: the dead man was Harlan Quinn. All that "he's coming tomorrow" and "he's in Germany" was crap. She thanked Campbell and headed to the car. The station was six minutes away.

DI Steele and a stocky uniformed woman with a silver bob were in the atrium when she rushed in. She interrupted their discussion. "I've got important news."

"This is Superintendent Kate Parker," DI Steele said. To the superintendent, she said, "This is Ms. Glock, our forensic expert from Auckland."

Superintendent Parker had an upturned nose and recessed eyes. "What's your news?" she asked.

"I've identified the bunker body. It's Harlan Quinn. I just found out."

"The man in the bunker is the California billionaire?" Superintendent Parker asked.

DI Steele's brow furrowed. "Are you sure?"

"Teeth don't lie." Uttering those three words thrilled Alexa.

"So that's why no one in Germany had seen him and he hadn't FaceTimed his family. He's been dead. What's the cause of death?" DI Steele asked.

Alexa was annoyed that her big news was pushed aside so quickly. "Dr. Li ruled out heart attack. But we still don't know how he died."

"We'll have to delay the press conference so you can notify Quinn's next of kin," Superintendent Parker said. "I'll grant you an extra hour."

DI Steele watched Superintendent Parker rush away. "Progress, finally. Let's go."

Alexa followed her up a flight of stairs into a briefing room. One wall was glass, a New Zealand flagpole stood in a corner, the flag a blue and red wilt, and three long tables were arranged U-shaped.

"I'll make some calls, get the team together," DI Steele said.

Alexa went up to the whiteboard. Harlan Quinn's photo was tacked on one side and a photo of the body—taken from a distance—was tacked on the other. Each had a list scribbled below. Alexa read under Quinn's photo:

46 years old male, dark hair, H: 177 cm, W: 81 k.
    married: Audrey Quinn, 40, one daughter
    home address: Silverspring Drive, Palo Alto, CA
    last seen by family: 31 March
    NZ Address: Black Reef (big house, cottage, bunker)
    business: BioMatic
    Palo Alto liaison: Chief Andrew Petrie
    In Germany on biz (?)
        - denied by company rep
    Property manager: Lynn Lockhart, Auckland (?)

Under John Doe it said:

adult male, middle-aged, dark hair, T-shirt, jeans, jandles
    H: 177 cm, W: 85 k.
    found: Black Reef bunker

dead several days, COD ?
no phone, wallet
no obs foul play, suicide note, drug paraphernalia
computer encrypted
air quality in bunker ???
   – CO2 detector dead battery

Alexa matched the two lists now that she knew they were one and the same person. The weights of John Doe and Harlan Quinn were off, but everyone lied about their weight, Alexa believed. She sucked in her stomach. She might have to add crunches to her kickboxing routine.

An enlarged sketch of the bunker, with a star marking where the body had been found and the two entrances circled in red, was tacked to the side.

"That's that, then," DI Steele announced. "Sergeant Atkins and Constable Gavin are on their way. I told Atkins not to tell the property manager, eh? The wife deserves to know first. How was your dinner? What did you find out?"

"She admitted she and Quinn were lovers. She said he planned to marry her."

"No chance of that now. I'm calling my Palo Alto liaison officer now. Notifying next of kin should be in person, and I want to listen in. What time is it in California?"

Alexa did the mental arithmetic and came up with noon, yesterday.

"Where are you on that pink tooth thing?"

"The test will take a while."

"I'll put a rush on it, get this thing wrapped up." She looked at Alexa. "You'll be free to go after the press conference."

No "Job well done." No "Thanks for your service." Alexa was ambivalent about being dismissed. She hated not knowing how Quinn died, but she'd be free to see Bruce. And the girls.

She headed to the lab to finish reports. As with all cases, she'd need to be prepared to justify her conclusions in court. She carefully completed the dental identification forms and sent them to DI Steele and her boss. When she finished, she located a pink teeth article in an online forensic journal.

The man in the case study had been kidnapped and murdered. His body was in advanced decomp. The examiner discovered three pink teeth, the color deeper at the neck of each tooth.

Alexa liked the term *neck of the tooth*. It referred to the area near the gumline.

The coroner listed the cause of the man's death as asphyxia. In the Discussion section of the article, the authors concluded that pink teeth alone weren't reliable indicators for determining cause of death, but PTP sometimes occurred in cases related to asphyxia.

Had Harlan Quinn run out of air in the bunker?

Sergeant Atkins popped her head through the door, making her jump. "Thought you might want to hear the convo with Mrs. Quinn. Plus Senior needs to see you."

Constable Gavin put his finger to his lips when the two of them walked into the incident room. DI Steele looked surprised to see Alexa and motioned for them to stand closer to her phone, which she had propped up. "It's on speaker," she whispered.

A man identified himself as Chief Andrew Petrie of the Palo Alto Police Department and stated the time and date. Alexa thought she heard music in the background and then maybe a door shut.

You spoke with my secretary yesterday. What is it this time? a woman said.

Alexa recognized Mrs. Quinn's voice.

I am sorry to tell you I have bad news. It has been confirmed that your husband is dead. In New Zealand.

"Doesn't beat around the bush, does he?" Sergeant Atkins whispered.

DI Steele put her finger to her lips.

Harlan is not in New Zealand.

His body was found in the bunker on his estate. Is there someone you can call to be with you? the officer asked.

Harlan is in Germany.

Dental X-rays confirm that the deceased is Mr. Harlan Quinn, the chief said. *I know this news is distressing. Is there someone who can come be with you?*

I did not release any of Harlan's health records.

Her voice sounded worried, Alexa thought.

A dentist in New Zealand had records of Mr. Quinn.

You are mistaken.

Chief Petrie's voice stayed patient. *Mrs. Quinn, when did you last see Mr. Quinn?*

Letitia. Come in here. Mrs. Quinn's voice was shrill now, maybe on the verge of panic. *This man, this* police officer, *has some story about Harlan being dead. Tell him where he is.*

A new voice chimed in. *I'm Letitia, Mrs. Quinn's personal secretary. We talked on the phone yesterday. As I said, Mr. Quinn left for Germany on April first.*

April Fool's Day, Alexa reflected.

That's a week ago. Where in Germany was he going? Chief Petrie asked.

Munich, the secretary answered. *To PharmaTex.*

I checked yesterday, ma'am. His voice was tight. *The spokesperson said they weren't expecting Mr. Quinn and hadn't seen him.*

Harlan doesn't always announce his arrival, Mrs. Quinn said. *Dropping in is more productive.*

Have you heard from him since he left, Mrs. Quinn? FaceTime? Texts? Phone calls?

No. As Letitia told you, I've been at a retreat where contact with the outside was restricted.

Chief Petrie cleared his throat. *Mr. Quinn must have left Germany and flown to New Zealand. Did he have any medical conditions? Was he seeing a therapist or counselor?*

I don't know what you are getting at. Mrs. Quinn's voice quivered. *I need to pick up my daughter.*

The Chief repeated how sorry he was. Alexa heard a door slam. The secretary said, *Is it true?*

There was silence.

Oh poor Chloe, Letitia said.

The Chief said thank you, gave the time, and terminated the recording.

DI Steele's eyes jumped to the whiteboard. "The wife denies he's dead."

"I think it was sinking in, though," Constable Gavin said. "The shock and all."

DI Steele adjusted her cap and stared at Alexa. "Superintendent Parker dropped by. She wanted to know how certain you are that the body in the morgue is Quinn's. Our legal affairs department doesn't like that we have no contextual evidence except location."

Alexa didn't appreciate her professional integrity being questioned, but she understood. They'd just told the wife Harlan Quinn was dead and were about to announce the billionaire's death to the rest of the world. She sucked in air. "Comparative dental analysis is one of the most reliable means of positive scientific identification."

"Is that yeah nah or nah yeah?" Constable Gavin asked.

"Nah yeah, you idjit," Sergeant Atkins said.

"Let's meet the press, then," DI Steele said.

Chapter Thirteen

The atrium bustled with reporters and townsfolk. Four police officers stood near the back, arms crossed against their chests. They parted for DI Steele, Sergeant Atkins, and Alexa to walk through. Superintendent Parker was already at the dais, speaking to a cluster of reporters.

"Our Organized Crime Unit will target illegal activity of any crime group," she said.

"You mean gangs?" a reporter asked.

"Any organized group that causes harm to our community," the Super emphasized.

Alexa was surprised they were talking about gangs and not the dead man in the bunker.

"Is it true a Hastings school is closing for two days so a funeral can be held there and Curs are arriving from all over?" the reporter continued. "Are citizens safe?"

"Citizens have nothing to fear."

"Excuse me?" a *Hawke's Bay Today* reporter asked. "I'm gob-smacked. Kids losing two days of education for an event that should be held at a church or marae?"

The superintendent spotted DI Steele with apparent relief. "Ladies and gentlemen. Let's get started. Detective Inspector Micala Steele is ready to update us on the tragic accident at Cape

Kidnappers. That's the reason we're here instead of having a Saturday morning lie-in."

DI Steele straightened the lapels of her blazer and made opening remarks. A head shot of Harlan Quinn appeared on a drop-down screen behind her. Alexa studied his face. His heavily lidded eyes scrutinized the crowd, his generous lips gave no hint of a smile.

DI Steele explained who found the body and when. She cleared her throat and gestured to Alexa. "Ms. Glock from Auckland Service Center has only this morning identified the deceased as the owner of the property, billionaire Mr. Harlan Quinn. Ms. Glock, would you give the details?"

Alexa hadn't realized she would be called to the front of the class. She blinked as a camera flashed. "Mr. Quinn had a local dentist who took X-rays six months ago. I compared them to X-rays I took of the deceased's teeth at the morgue. There was a positive match."

"Why was he identified by his teeth?" The *Hawke's Bay Today* reporter asked. "Why not facial recognition?"

"The condition of the body made facial identification impossible." There was a moment of silence and then chatter as Alexa stepped back.

"How did he die?" a man with a TVNZ camera asked.

Superintendent Parker held up her hand. "Save questions until Detective Inspector Steele finishes."

"Wait," the *Hawke's Bay Today* reporter shouted. "Are you confident the new DI is capable of handling a high-profile case? Shouldn't a more veteran...?"

Superintendent Parker cut him off. "I have full confidence in Detective Inspector Steele."

DI Steele straightened her cap. "Mr. Quinn's wife, Audrey Quinn, is in California and she has been notified."

"Is she on her way here?" a reporter asked.

"We don't know what arrangements are being made at this time."

"How did Quinn die?" a reporter repeated.

"Cause of death is pending," DI Steele said. "We'll update you as soon as we know."

"Any sign of foul play?" called the *Hawke's Bay Today* reporter.

"None," DI Steele said.

"Drugs?"

"Blood tests are pending," DI Steele said.

"Christie Barber, *NZ Herald*," a woman yelled. "Was Mr. Quinn alone in the bunker?"

"When his body was found, he was alone."

Alexa thought of the picnic basket remains and mussed-up sheets. She suspected somebody else had been in the bunker at some point.

"Kenau Foster, Radio One. How large is the estate?"

DI Steele looked at Sergeant Atkins.

"Fifty hectares, Senior."

"It's built on top of the Black Reef gannet sanctuary," a woman called from the back. "The birds need protection."

"That's not a question," DI Steele snapped.

"How did Mr. Quinn make his money?" another reporter asked.

"It's on the information sheet we've prepared for you," DI Steele said.

"Why are all these doomsday nuts allowed to buy up our land?" the same reporter asked.

Superintendent Parker broke in. "Must be our natural beauty and well-run police force, eh?"

She garnered a few laughs.

"It's that Investor Plus Visa," the Hawke's Bay Today reporter said. "The rich buy their way in."

The New Zealand government allows it, Alexa wanted to point out.

"I expect that the billionaire's death will bring our area international attention," Superintendent Parker said. "Let's be beacons of responsible news coverage and keep Mr. Quinn's family in mind.

He has a young daughter. Detective Inspector Steele has time for a few more questions."

The reporters parted to let a man with a full facial tattoo through. "I'm speaking for the Campaign Against Foreign Control of Aotearoa. We oppose sales to foreigners. Under what circumstances did Quinn buy that land?"

DI Steele blinked as a flash went off. "I don't have that information."

"In the last six months, Overseas Investment Office has approved the sale of 7,474 hectares of rural land to foreigners," the man said.

"Mr. Quinn bought his land over two years ago and what's done is done," DI Steele said.

A woman's voice from the back yelled, "What are you doing to stop the End of the Worlders from invading our island?"

"The what?" DI Steele asked.

"The End of the World as We Know It. We need to keep those nuts out."

Alexa craned her neck to see who spoke, but her view was blocked.

DI Steele was about to reply when Superintendent Parker stepped in front. "Our purpose this morning was to update you about the death in the bunker. That's what we've done. Thank you for coming."

The reporters grumbled but backed away, letting DI Steele and Superintendent Parker leave the atrium. Alexa snaked past Sergeant Atkins. The *NZ Herald* reporter cornered her by the stairs. "Is there a chance your comparisons are flawed?"

"Slim to nil."

She replayed the conference in her mind as she hustled down the stairs and opened the lab. The animosity had surprised her. Locals were angry for a variety of reasons—gangs, land purchases by foreigners, bird protection—and the conference had given them a platform. They'd been given the facts about the bunker body: A rich American bought land and built a compound. He died in the bunker. He'd been identified.

What was left under wrap were the juicier details. Mr. Quinn had arrived unbeknownst to his wife and mistress. Both thought he'd been elsewhere. Would Alexa ever find out why?

She set up her laptop and updated Dan.

Her part in the strange case was over. Her mind jumped to Bruce. In less than two hours she'd see him—a good thing—and his girls—a bad thing. Teenagers terrified her. What would she say to them? Research calmed her down, so she typed "How to Talk to Teenagers" in the search box.

The results were geared to parents talking to their children: listen, validate feelings, don't judge, yadda yadda.

She refined her search: "How to Meet Your Boyfriend's Children for the First Time."

1. Introduce as "Dad's friend" not "girlfriend." Check.
2. Neutral environment. Check: beach, tractor, gannets.
3. Keep it short. No Check. The tractor tour lasts three hours.
4. No public displays of affection. Check.
5. Ask questions. Check.
6. Keep expectations low. Check.

She took notes and made a list of questions as per #5: Favorite subject? Favorite teacher? Favorite tooth fact? Favorite fingerprint pattern? She felt better.

Her last police station to-do was to check out with Steele. She found the DI in her office with Sergeant Atkins. Before she opened her mouth, DI Steele said, "Just on my way to find *you*. I need you to accompany Sergeant Atkins to Black Reef. Help her break the news about Quinn's death to Lynn Lockhart. She should find out from us, not the media."

Alexa blinked. "You said I was free to go after the press conference."

"You spent the night with her, right? Enjoyed a fancy meal. Having you there will soften the blow. Always in person and always by two, eh? " The DI refused to meet Alexa's eyes. "I can't go. Joe's been in a scruff-up. You can leave from Black Reef."

Alexa let this news percolate. Her boss, Dan, had said to follow orders. Black Reef was close to the tractor town, and she'd still be on time to meet Bruce.

"By the way," DI Steele said. "Mrs. Quinn's secretary called. They're sending a colleague of Mr. Quinn's to represent the family. A Mr. Amit Gupta."

"That's good," Alexa said.

She followed Sergeant Atkins's patrol car until she couldn't stand the pace and passed her on a straightaway outside of Hastings.

The route to Black Reef was familiar now. The only thing that stopped her forward momentum was a flock of sheep crossing Haumoana Road. She lowered her window; baas and bleats and *meh*s and a musky lanolin scent filled the car. One ewe made a break for it. Alexa rooted for her, but a mutty border collie nipped her into cooperation, like DI Steele had corralled Alexa.

She checked her rearview mirror. Sergeant Atkins was nowhere to be seen.

She measured: Black Reef Lane was six kilometers, with one turn off to The Retreat. She didn't pass a soul and no ATV hurtled toward her. She parked near the cottage. The caution tape was visible on the berm. Lynn or Mrs. Quinn or the caretakers would have to hire one of those bio-cleaning companies like Aftermath or Death-Be-Gone to clean the bunker.

It was nasty, but Alexa had witnessed far worse.

Alexa got out and leaned against her car. There was no sign of Lynn Lockhart. She wondered again why a professional woman would give up her career to become a beck-and-call property manager and mistress.

Money and sex. Two powerful motivators.

Sergeant Atkins finally drove up. She got out and wagged a finger at Alexa. "Breaking a few speed limits, eh? We don't have a threshold. I should fine you."

Was she joking? Alexa couldn't tell.

The sergeant kicked a boot into the grass. Her boots were black leather with two-inch stomper heels. "Want to take the lead with Ms. Lockhart?"

"No." Alexa didn't even want to be here.

The sergeant took off her cap and ruffled her orange hair. "See, the thing is, I've never done a DN before."

How did you get to be a sergeant and not have made a death notification? Of course, this was New Zealand. Alexa gave her an encouraging smile. "You'll be fine."

Lynn opened the cottage door as they stepped on the porch.

"G'day, ma'am. I'm Sergeant Allison Atkins, Hastings Police." She held out her badge.

Lynn ignored it and cocked an eyebrow at Alexa.

"Thanks for your hospitality last night," Alexa said. "Can we come in?"

Lynn's face was pale as she stepped aside. "Do you know whose body it is? Is that why you're back?"

"Let's sit down," Alexa said.

Lynn claimed her spot in front of the mantel. "Tell me whatever it is."

Alexa sat on the ottoman and motioned for Sergeant Atkins to sit on the couch. She waited for the sergeant to start and, when she didn't, said, "I'm sorry. We've got bad news. The person who died in the bunker is Harlan Quinn."

Lynn shook her head. "Harlan would have called me if he had come early."

"The dentist you found for him—at Bay Best Smiles—I talked to him. He took X-rays when he saw Mr. Quinn six months ago. They match the postmortem X-rays."

"Postmortem?"

"It's true," Sergeant Atkins added.

Lynn grabbed the mantel with her right hand as if she needed support. "Harlan? Dead? But how?"

Alexa shifted on the ottoman. "We don't know."

She squeezed her eyes shut. "I want to see him."

"It wouldn't be proper," Sergeant Atkins said.

Lynn's eyes popped open wide.

"His wife is next of kin," Alexa said gently. "Is there someone you can call? To come be with you?"

Lynn looked around the room. "There must have been a threat in the States. He had to come and hide out."

Alexa's mind flickered to her brother Charlie and his family. Were they okay? "We'll leave you then." She realized Lynn was stranded out here. "Or maybe Sergeant Atkins could give you a ride to town?"

Lynn didn't answer.

Chapter Fourteen

It was ten kilometers from the main road to Clifton. With each passing one, Harlan Quinn, the bunker, DI Steele, and Lynn Lockhart faded in import. Ahead: Bruce.

And his girls.

Alexa reviewed her list of questions: subject, teacher, tooth, fingerprints. She wondered what they would ask her.

She stopped at a café in Clifton for a bacon butty and used the Ladies' room to change into running gear and a pullover, which seemed more appropriate for a tractor ride than khakis and a blouse.

A block from the beach, she pulled into the Gannet Tractor Tours lot. She parked two cars from Bruce's Ford Ranger and spied him in front of a barn, laughing at a black lab wriggling chest-up on the grass.

She turned off the car, keeping her eyes on Bruce. His arm was slung around the shorter of two girls. Her dark ponytail sprouted from a ball cap. Alexa figured she was Sammie. The taller girl, honey-blond hair, was probably Diane. No, wait. That didn't sound right. Alexa couldn't think of the older girl's name.

Crap.

She checked her hair in the rearview mirror; it had gone haywire. She fished a scrunchie out of the cupholder and fashioned a ponytail, then used the mirror to dab on SPF 50; she didn't need more freckles. She got some in her eye and had to blink until it cleared.

Denise. That was her name. Relieved, she stuffed her floppy fishing hat—she'd "borrowed" it from Dad as she left home for college—into her backpack, along with a water bottle, sunglasses, and keys. She slipped her phone, still on vibrate, into the pocket of her leggings.

Her heart revved as she joined Bruce, sexy in shorts of a reasonable length (she'd seen a lot of Kiwi men in short shorts) and T-shirt. He smiled from under a ball cap. "You made it." He reached out a finger toward her and then retracted it. "I've already checked us in. All you need to do is sign the risk acknowledgment."

The dog tried to jump on her. Alexa turned her back.

"Is this her?" the taller girl asked. She studied Alexa with moody brown eyes. "You've got sun gel on your cheek."

Alexa rubbed it in.

"These are my girls, Denise and Sammie. Girls, this is Ms. Glock."

"Call me Alexa. What's your favorite…?"

Denise broke in. "Alexa, tell me a joke."

Alexa wasn't prepared for Amazon Alexa to butt in.

Sammie jumped up and down. "Why don't sharks eat clown-fish? Because they taste funny!" She laughed at her own punchline. Alexa thought she looked younger than thirteen, all skinny with big feet. Did kids grow into their feet?

Sammie scrutinized her. "Alexa, did you know teeth are made of bone?"

Was this another Amazon Alexa question? Or was Sammie a budding odontologist? "Teeth are stronger than bone. Enamel is composed of more than ninety-five percent mineral, whereas bones are only sixty percent or so mineralized. Also teeth…"

Sammie turned to her dad. "Can I get a Coke?"

"Don't interrupt," Bruce said.

Sammie's eyes widened from under her All Blacks cap. They were replicas of her dad's eyes.

"It's okay," Alexa said. "I'll send you an article about it."

Bruce tossed Sammie the keys. "Go fetch your water bottle." The girls ran off.

Alexa felt whiplashed. "I'm not sure that went well."

Bruce pulled her close and brushed her cheek with a kiss. "I saw you on the news. You looked hot."

She jerked away. The article had said no displays of affection.

Bruce pulled out his phone and scrolled. "Here's the latest."

She took his phone and skimmed an article:

Bunker Debacle

American billionaire Harlan Quinn, 46, was found dead in his exclusive Cape Kidnappers doomsday bunker by caretaker Tony Cobb, a Clifton resident. "I took a squiz and nearly chundered," Mr. Cobb said.

According to Hastings Detective Inspector Micala Steele, Mr. Quinn had been dead for several days. "Cause of death is unknown," she said at an a.m. press conference. "He was last seen by his wife on 1 April."

Quinn acquired the property two years ago.

Alexa Glock, forensic odontologist from Auckland, identified the deceased by comparing antemortem and postmortem dental X-rays.

She felt a flush of pride.

Sammie galloped up. "It's coming!"

A shiny red-orange tractor chugged toward them like a vestige of the past, towing a trailer with two back-to-back benches.

Alexa handed Bruce his phone. "I'll go sign away my rights." In the barn/office, a man behind a rinky-dink school desk handed her a two-page form. Her eyes jumped to the highlighted part: *The Department of Conservation and GNS Science rate the risk of Cape Kidnappers Gannet Tour as higher than whitewater rafting and jet boating or visiting Fox or Franz Josef glaciers.*

"Jeez," she said. "I didn't know the tractor tour was dangerous."

"Like anything in life, there's a wee bit of risk," the man said. "We've never lost a passenger yet."

"What's the risk from?"

"A couple years ago there was a landslip, is all."

She felt better and signed. Bruce, Sammie, and Denise had already climbed aboard the trailer. Bruce patted the spot next to him. Alexa gave him her backpack and scrambled up. The guide sat sidesaddle on the tractor seat, counting passengers. A family of four speaking German climbed on and sat on the opposite bench. "You're last," the guide told them. "Welcome aboard."

"*Guten tag,*" the woman said.

The man to Alexa's right inched closer to his companion to make more room for her. She dug out her sunglasses and hat and stowed the backpack behind her. Denise stared as she pulled on the hat.

"G'day," the driver said. "I'm Bob, your tour guide and master of this beaut." He gestured to the tractor. "A 1949 Minneapolis-Moline."

Weird, Alexa thought. *Tractors from Minneapolis?*

"We've a fleet of six, but it's just us going out today." Bob gestured toward the bay. "The whole area used to be the bottom of the sea. I'll point out the different rock layers as we pass: mudstone, sandstone, volcanic pumice. We've some spectacular fault lines, evidence of several earthquakes..."

Alexa thought of her brother as Bob yakked about the geological formation of the area. Charlie, a geo-engineer, would love Bob's rock talk. He'd come to New Zealand two months earlier for a visit, and they'd hiked the Milford Track. It had been rough going. She probably should have taken him on a tractor tour instead.

"We'll hug the tide line, but the beach is narrow and rocky in many places," Bob said. He surveyed his passengers—fifteen, Alexa counted, plus herself. "Most of the risk is that you'll get wet, eh, or jostled."

A bar bit into Alexa's back scars. She shifted on the plank bench. Bruce's thigh, inches away, distracted her. She caught his eye, and he raised his right eyebrow.

"Hold on to your hats and we're off," Bob said.

When they turned onto the beach, Alexa was glad her side of the trailer faced the water. She pressed her feet against the footrest and decided this was a perfect way to meet Bruce's girls. They didn't have to look at each other or talk.

They joggled past a campground and a few modest houses, some on the beach and a few perched on the hills. *Baches*, the Kiwis call them. The beach narrowed to a sandy strip with sea on one side and cliff on the other.

Bob steered into the lapping surf to avoid a trio of boulders. Sammie and Denise squealed. Alexa raised her running shoes above the sloshing. Bruce nudged her shoulder and pointed at a helicopter buzzing above. "Probably headed to Black Reef," he whispered in her ear.

His warm breath made her think of the guest bedroom in the cottage, those lovely sheets, and what it would have been like to slip between them together.

Bob pointed out birds and rock layers. Two men on dirt bikes zipped around them. Otherwise, the beach was empty. Once, Bob stopped the tractor, hopped off, and pointed out a fossilized whale rib. He told the tourists to stay in the trailer. "Don't want you buried in a slip."

They trundled and bumped. At one point Alexa dozed off and woke with a start, her head on Bruce's shoulder. She hoped the girls hadn't seen.

The tractor headed for the waterline and increased speed. Bob pointed up at the cliff. "That's where the slide happened. Two hikers were pushed into the sea. The Department of Conservation closed us down for over a year."

Sand, boulders, and debris piled up at the base.

"Did they die?" Denise asked.

"They survived their injuries, but let's keep going, eh? Black Reef, the smaller of our two gannetries, is around the next bend."

An ammonia scent mixed with eau de dead fish carried in the breeze. The boy on the opposite bench said, "*Es stinkt!*"

Bob pulled the trailer through two narrow stacks of boulders and around a bend. The beach was full of mesa-like rock formations, some encircled by water, and all full of gannets.

"This colony has roughly two thousand breeding pairs," Bob said.

Alexa surveyed the cliff, which looked like a multistory condo for the birds.

"Hop out," Bob said. "You can get close to the birds; they aren't bothered."

Harlan Quinn's house was barely visible, just the rooftop. The cottage was hidden from view, but Alexa saw the Norfolk pine and swimming pool. She wondered what would happen to Lynn Lockhart and why that crazy lady had scaled the cliff.

"The gannets are members of the booby family," Bob announced.

Sammie laughed. "You're a booby," she told Bruce and started running.

"You are," Bruce said and took off after her. Alexa laughed. She had never seen a playful Bruce. Denise, her nose scrunched in the whiffy air, looked wistful. Alexa felt sympathy for her. Fifteen was an in-between stage of life.

"The chicks are three and a half months old now," Bob continued. "They weigh as much as Mum and Dad. They'll leave soon. Maybe tonight. Maybe tomorrow."

"Where are zey going?" a woman asked. She stood two feet from a row of chicks.

"Off on their OE," Bob said.

Alexa knew OE stood for the overseas experience that lots of Kiwis took before or after college, like a gap year in America. The German woman looked confused.

"They fly across the Tasman to Australia and don't come back for three or four years," Bob explained.

"This is dangerous, yah?" the German woman asked.

"Only twenty-five to thirty percent make it back."

Alexa singled out a chick lifting its head and krokking, and hoped he would make it.

Bob explained that the Māori word for a gannet breeding ground was *tākapu*, and that gannet bones had been used to apply *moko*, or facial tattoos. She thought briefly of a Māori cop she'd worked with in her first New Zealand case. Constable Cooper's lip and chin had dusky blue *moko*.

Two gannets sparred with their silvery beaks and then intertwined their sinewy necks. They reminded her of her relationship with Bruce. She watched him run back, a bright smile on his face. He caught her eye, causing her heart to dance.

Three chicks shuffled back and forth on their rock ledge, beating their wings. "They're doing the cha cha slide," Sammie shouted.

Bruce flapped his elbows. "Right wing, left wing, y'all," he sang.

She laughed at Bruce saying "y'all" and flapped an elbow.

"Let's get back to the trailer," Bob said. "We've twenty minutes to the bigger gannetry. You can cha cha up there."

Alexa's phone vibrated. She fumbled for it and checked the screen: DI Steele. *What now?*

She was tempted to thrust it back in her pocket. Instead she stepped away from the group and answered. "Yes?"

"Someone tampered with the bunker's ventilation system," the DI said. "Get back here."

Chapter Fifteen

Alexa waved her phone in Bruce's face. "I need to leave."

He stopped in his tracks. "What's happened?"

"Harlan Quinn's death isn't an accident." She repeated what DI Steele had said: "The ventilation system in the bunker was tampered with. I need to process the scene."

Bruce's eyes darkened. "Is she thinking homicide?"

Alexa shrugged.

"Let's go, folks," Bob called.

Sammie and Denise raced to the trailer.

Alexa looked up at the Black Reef estate. Could she scale the cliff like that birder woman? It looked forty, maybe fifty feet high. The ledges, dotted with gannets, looked like stairsteps with uneven risers—some for giants, some for toddlers. The thought of climbing up made her stomach roil.

She ran up to Bob. "I need to leave. Is there some shortcut back?"

He looked concerned. "Unless you have wings, the only way is along the sea. Are you ill? Do I need to radio for help?"

"I'm fine. It's a work emergency." She looked down at her running shoes. "How far have we come?"

"Six kilometers."

"How much longer is the tour?"

"Ninety minutes or thereabout."

The thought of riding behind a slow tractor for ninety more minutes was torture. If she pushed, she could run six kilometers in thirty minutes. Then it was a fifteen-minute drive to Black Reef. "I'm heading back," she told Bob.

Bruce touched her shoulder. "Alexa, the scene will keep."

She frowned at him. "People will mess things up. They'll contaminate something. I'll just run back."

Without checking Bruce's reaction, she retrieved her backpack from the trailer, stuffed her pullover into it, and worked her arms through the straps. "Gotta go," she told Sammie and Denise.

"Wait," Sammie said. "Where?"

"To work. Um, it was nice to meet you." She could feel Bruce watching, but refused to meet his eyes. She didn't want him to talk her out of this. She waved at the girls and took off.

"Keep to the waterline," Bob called. "Not under the cliffs, eh?"

It was difficult advice to follow. The tide-line sand was wet. Her feet sank, slowing her to a slog. Nearer the cliff, the sand was loose and deep, also a slog, and she didn't like the way the rock face breathed down her back. She zigged and zagged for an elusive sweet spot. Her backpack got heavier.

She concentrated on what DI Steele had said: someone messed with the ventilation system. What did that mean? She put effort into her stride. A frothy wave submerged her foot. She sidled left and stumbled over a rock, landing on her knees. "Dammit!"

She hopped up, brushed off, and took a swig of water, keeping a wary eye on the cliff. This jaunt was taking longer than she'd anticipated. The sound of motors made her squint into the distance. Two ATVs throttled toward her. She waved her arms. The first flew by, its tires whipping up sand. The second one braked.

Alexa spit sand out of her mouth and ran up to the driver, a girl around Denise's age, her hair in a long dark braid. "Can you give me a ride to Clifton? It's an emergency."

The girl revved the motor instead of answering. A blue cooler was strapped to the seat behind her. The second ATV circled back and maneuvered so that Alexa was trapped between two quad bikes. The driver was male, also young, also not wearing a helmet. He stared at her.

"What's happening?" he called.

A twinge of fear made her scan the beach. It was empty in both directions. "There's been an accident. I need to get back to Clifton. Can you give me a ride?"

"How did you get here?" the boy asked.

"I was on one of those tractor tours."

"You a doc?" the girl asked.

Alexa nodded. Anything to get to the parking lot, she reasoned. The kids looked at each other. "You take her, cuzzie," the girl ordered, revving her motor again. "Catch up with me later."

She zoomed off.

The boy scowled, but jerked his chin to indicate she should hop on. The ATV was a one-seater with no windshield, nothing fancy like the one that ran her into a ditch near Black Reef. Alexa kept her backpack on and straddled the seat behind him. They flew along the water's edge, dodging boulders and tidal pools. Spray and sand coated Alexa's calves. A swirling tattoo of turtles and ferns seeped up the boy's neck and spilled out his left T-shirt sleeve. He drove her all the way to the parking lot. When she climbed off, her body vibrated. "Let me pay you."

"*Takaro whakamua,*" the boy answered.

"What?"

He smiled. "Pay it forward."

She ran to her car on shaky legs and sped to Black Reef.

DI Steele and Sergeant Atkins stood in front of a white van. A tall, thickset man gestured toward the bunker. A police car was parked near the big house. The cottage porch was empty—no sign of Lynn Lockhart.

Alexa grabbed her crime kit and hurried over. Sergeant Atkins ushered her close. "This is Duncan Weber. He's from Texas."

The man extended a beefy hand.

Alexa made a fist and bumped his fingers. "Alexa Glock, forensics investigator."

DI Steele scanned her running attire. "Mr. Weber installed the bunker. He was working another job and drove over when he heard the news about Mr. Quinn. He's the one who made the discovery."

The brim of his Texas Rangers ball cap shaded his eyes. "Stopped in my tracks when I heard the news. A dead man in a Lone Star bunker is bad for business."

Alexa looked up at him. "You're from Texas and you install bunkers in New Zealand?"

"We make 'em in Texas, then ship 'em here. Our clients believe self-protection is worth the price. And they want the best, goes without saying."

"How much does this self-protection cost?" DI Steele asked.

"It depends on your needs." He swiped his cap off and studied the DI. "I could put you in a ten-by-ten Plan B for as little as thirty thousand." He put the cap back on and extracted a card from his back pocket. "You and yer family could retreat from catastrophe."

DI Steele laughed. "Living in a ten-by-ten with my family? *That* would be a catastrophe."

"Funny, Senior," Sergeant Atkins said.

Alexa looked over Steele's shoulder at the card.

LONE STAR BUNKERS

Made in the USA

The Prepared Will Prevail

Mr. Duncan Weber, Site Installer

"'Course we're back-ordered now. You'll have to wait a year. Business is boomin'."

The prepared will prevail? Alexa didn't know whether to be worried about looming disaster or to laugh at the absurdity of burrowing in for safety. It hadn't worked for Quinn.

"Show Ms. Glock what you discovered," DI Steele said. "Sergeant, wait here."

Alexa thought they'd head for the bunker, but Mr. Weber and DI Steele climbed the berm and walked past the shed. "Where you from?" he asked over his shoulder.

She jogged to catch up. A breeze blew strands of her hair across her eyes. "Raleigh, North Carolina."

"One of our guys did an installation in Charlotte, near Lake Norman. For a banker."

"Are there a lot of bunkers in North Carolina?"

"You've got one hundred counties, and we've installed bunkers in almost half. 'Course New Zealand makes a better contingency plan if you can afford it."

"Lucky us," DI Steele said.

The Texan pointed to the second large sculpture on the property, a ten-foot silvery metal tree of barren branches. Its tubular roots crisscrossed a concrete base and draped over the sides, into the earth. "We recommend bunker owners hide their pipes."

"Why?" Alexa asked.

"To keep the location a secret. When the shit hits the fan, you don't want everyone and their Aunt Madge clawing to get in."

The image was disturbing. Who to let in? Who to keep out?

Mr. Weber surveyed the rolling land around them. "Pipes poking out of the ground are a dead giveaway. We provide a list of ways to camouflage 'em. Stick it in a doghouse or mailbox, hide 'em in a lamppost, fence post, or your swing set. One client hid his in a derelict car."

A rusting LeBaron would look out of place here, Alexa thought.

"In bunker parlance," Mr. Weber said, "if a dude messes with your pipes, you mess with his windpipe."

Alexa swallowed. Was this guy nuts?

"So we hid Mr. Quinn's pipes in this here yard art. It's the out-take pipe that's clogged. Big bunkers need two pipes." He pointed to the other end of the base. "Fresh air goes in that there one. It's connected to the air filtration system down below."

At the far end of the eight-foot concrete base, a hooded pipe stuck out of the roots.

The Texan rocked on the heels of his work boots. "But this here one, the exhaust, has been tampered with." He pointed to a pipe crisscrossed with duct tape. "If the generator was running, carbon monoxide would have built up and had nowhere to escape."

"Asphyxiation," Alexa whispered. That pink molar had pointed them in the right direction. She bent close to inspect the four-inch round pipe. Dull gray duct tape formed a seal over the top. Now that she'd seen it with her own eyes, frisson akin to the endorphins she felt after a run flowed through her limbs. The world had changed. Harlan Quinn's death was now a crime or suicide.

"Don't know why the power would be set to generator with all this sunshine around. Solar is better. The generator shoulda been for backup," Mr. Weber said. "I'll tell you this, though. Lone Star didn't have nothin' to do with this." He reached out a finger to touch the tape.

"Don't," Alexa said.

He jerked it back. "I already poked at it."

Alexa looked at him closely: ruddy and sun-wrinkled, fifty-ish. "I'll need to take your fingerprints."

"Fine by me. Whoever did it removed the rain guard."

"What's that?" DI Steele asked.

"Obviously it keeps the rain out, but it also has a screen to keep out insects and debris." He sidled over to the other pipe and pointed. The intake pipe had a metal hood. "Had a snake crawl down an uncovered pipe in Tennessee last summer."

Alexa did not want to think about that.

"Did Mr. Quinn know where these pipes were?" DI Steele asked.

"I take clients on a walk-through when we're finished installing. Explain the ins and outs. I checked my records. Mr. Quinn sent his property manager instead. Gal named Lockhart."

Alexa looked toward the cottage.

"How many people does it take to install a bunker?" DI Steele asked.

Alexa's mind hopped to a light bulb joke, but there was nothing funny about this.

"My work crew is eight, counting me. This here took two weeks. Sometimes we work by night, to keep locations on the hush-hush, but out here, no one was around."

"So your crew and all their mates know where these pipes are," DI Steele pointed out.

"My crew comes from the States." No more Texan friendliness. "They keep their mouths shut."

DI Steele stared at him impassively. "I'll need their names and addresses."

Alexa fished out her ink pad and stock cards and took Mr. Weber's fingerprints. One day soon she'd be carrying around a mobile fingerprint scanner, but she preferred the old-fashioned way. As Mr. Weber cleaned his fingers with a wet wipe, DI Steele said, "This could be a suicide by carbon monoxide poisoning. Instead of a car and a garage, Mr. Quinn used his bolt-hole."

Mr. Weber's jaw clenched. "That don't make sense. Mr. Quinn spent eight million dollars to survive, not die."

Spouting premature theories was unprofessional. Alexa knew Harlan Quinn's death should be assumed homicide until facts proved otherwise.

Alexa asked the DI to send the lab tech, Pamela, to help her process the scene. She watched the DI and Mr. Weber walk down the hill.

She took a few deep breaths as she remembered a case that had gotten a Wake County sheriff's deputy fired. The deputy had responded to a suicide-in-residence call. A distraught husband answered the door. He said his wife shot herself in the bathroom. The deputy heard "suicide" and went on autopilot. He didn't document the scene or speak to anyone other than the husband. He contaminated evidence that Alexa later received at the lab.

A coroner classified the woman's death as homicide. It turned out the husband hadn't wanted a divorce and shot her.

She'd be damned sure not to take shortcuts here. Her job right now was to free herself of preconceived ideas about Harlan Quinn's death and let science be her guide.

Motion caught her eye. A seagull landed on a top branch of the metal tree. Its beady black eyes stared at her. *Get to work*, it squawked.

She kitted up, glad for a thin layer of paper to cover her bare arms, and formed a plan. Tape off the scene. Search the area and sculpture base for evidence. Dust the duct tape for prints and then remove it to transfer to the lab.

She measured a ten-foot diameter around the sculpture base and scanned the trampled grass for discarded tape, a rain guard, or anything out of the ordinary. At first pass, the area was windswept and clean. She used rocks to weigh down the caution tape around the sculpture and wondered who cut the grass. They might have found something. She would have Pamela comb the taped-off area when she arrived.

Alexa readied her camera and took a series of wide-angle, midrange, and then close-up photos of the tree sculpture and tampered pipe. She zoomed in on the tape and studied the photo on her viewer. The top layer, probably polythene, was in good shape despite being exposed to the elements. It sagged slightly and was sprinkled with soil or maybe ocean salt. She set the camera aside and took a swab of the sprinkles to analyze in the lab. Then she focused on what fingerprints the tape might yield.

The tape overhung the pipe by six inches all the way around. She used her magnifying glass to study the edges: they were uniform and scissor-cut, not torn by hand, leaving stringy ends, or serrated from a dispenser. Cutting by scissors made her think premeditation. Who didn't carry duct tape in their trunk? But scissors? Had the snipper worn gloves? Cutting duct tape while wearing gloves must have been challenging.

Black powder would provide contrast against the gray tape. She readied her brush and unscrewed the lid of the powder. Wind blew the particles into a mini-tornado.

"Crap."

Alexa capped the jar. She hoped Pamela would bring a wind shield, but she was too impatient to wait. It was time to remove the entire duct tape cap and examine it at the lab. She took a deep breath of briny air and assessed the edges of the tape. There were no gaps or puckers. It wouldn't give up its hold without a fight.

A couple of years ago she'd attended a workshop on duct tape with the Raleigh Police Department and had learned the three ways to encourage the adhesive to release: steam, liquid nitrogen, or solvent. No steam, no dry ice, but she rummaged through her crime kit for a bottle of Un-Stick Adhesive Remover. The cap of the solvent was sealed. Her heart skipped a beat as she broke it; she loved this job.

The directions said to apply drops to the edges of the tape. Then she could use a scraping tool—she got her dental probe ready—to pry it loose.

Easy peasy. *Not.*

Gravity was stronger than her "Stop dripping!" commands. She gave up wasting drops and saturated a paper towel, which she pressed to the edges of the tape. She waited ten seconds, then wedged her dental probe in, wiggled, and steadily separated the tape from the pipe. An inch at a time. Wet. Wait. Probe. Her lips were dry, and her back hurt. Wet. Wait. Probe. In twenty minutes, the tape lifted off like a shower cap.

Ta-da!

Where was that lab technician? She needed an extra pair of hands. She debated how to transfer her prize to the lab; the tape could adhere to a paper evidence bag. She lined a paper bag with a sheet of acetate and set the duct tape cap in it. She'd have to separate it again at the lab, but that was better than risking contamination.

She peeked down the pipe. Something was stuffed in there.

She took several photographs and then stretched two fingers down the pipe and hooked the object.

Motion caught her eye. From her bird's-eye view atop the berm, she saw Bruce's Ford Ranger drive into the parking area.

Chapter Sixteen

Alexa reeled in her catch. She held it by a corner. It draped stiffly. A few yellow-brown stains and one hole made her guess it was a cleaning rag. She stowed it in another evidence bag, labeled it, and checked inside the pipe again.

No more surprises.

Bruce was out of his truck now. Sergeant Atkins, her hair orange as a Popsicle, hurried toward him. Bruce held out what was probably his badge. The sergeant nodded, gestured toward the berm.

Alexa squinted. She could see the girls in the truck cab. She stepped out of her paper jumpsuit, collected her kit and evidence bags, and walked down the berm. Bruce met her halfway. "You made it back okay." She had expected him to be angry she'd run off down the beach, but instead he'd been worried. Her heart fluttered.

"Your sergeant wouldn't give me the what's up," he said.

Alexa, who had no qualms about sharing information with Bruce, pointed up the berm. "See that tree statue? The bunker ventilation pipes are hidden in it, and the outtake pipe was clogged with a rag and then duct-taped over." She held up her two bags. "I've got the evidence right here."

Bruce was quiet for a moment. "Is Mic opening up a homicide investigation?"

"She didn't say."

Bruce lifted the crime kit off her shoulder and followed her to the Vitz. "The lab tech was supposed to join me out here, but she hasn't shown up." Alexa unlocked the hatch and set the bags in. Bruce set the crime kit next to them.

Denise stuck her head out the truck window. "Dad! Come on."

"I won't be long," Bruce called.

Sammie thrust her head in front of Denise's. "What is Alexa wearing?"

Alexa was confused until she noticed white booties covered her running shoes. She pulled them off and dangled them so Sammie could see.

Bruce pointed to the bunker entrance. "There's Mic. I'll go offer my assistance."

She walked with him. There was a comfort in being by his side. But could she love a man with two teen daughters? The verdict was out.

DI Steele frowned. "Who are you?" She stepped closer. "DI Horne? What are you doing here? Have you been called in?"

His smile was disarming. "No, nothing like that. I was in the area with my daughters. Ms. Glock and I have worked together. How are you, Mic? Congratulations on your promotion."

The DI's eyes flickered to Alexa and then back to Bruce. "I heard you transferred to Auckland. Serious Crime, right? Where did we see each other last? Was it that Prevention First seminar?"

"'Victims at the center,'" Bruce said, using air quotes.

Alexa thought of Harlan Quinn.

"So the situation here has changed?" he asked.

DI Steele twisted her wedding band. "Have you heard the latest?"

"Ms. Glock told me Mr. Quinn's death is no longer considered accidental or natural."

"I think he offed himself," DI Steele said.

Bruce's left eyebrow went up. He turned to watch a mobile locksmith van pull next to his truck.

"Finally," the DI said. "We can get into that locked room in the bunker. Check it out."

Bruce looked at Alexa. "Give me a moment with DI Steele, please."

"I'm leaving," Alexa said. "I need to get the evidence to the lab."

DI Steele frowned. "I need you here. The constable keeping the press out can drop whatever it is at the lab. Ms. Amick is waiting."

"Who is Ms. Amick?"

"Pamela. The lab technician. You said you needed her."

"I asked you to send her here," Alexa said.

"No, you didn't. I told her to be at the lab."

Anger colored Alexa's cheeks. She stalked to her car. The girls stared at her, but she couldn't make herself go over to chat. She realized there was a slim possibility she hadn't made her request for assistance clearly. She shouldn't be so quick to anger. After five minutes, Bruce joined her.

"What did you say to her?" Alexa asked.

"We had a little talk. I offered my services, told her I was staying in Rotorua through Monday." He pressed a finger to her bare shoulder. "You're pink."

His finger left a hot spot. She retrieved her pullover and slipped it on.

"Dad," one of the girls called.

"Keep me posted," Bruce said. "I need to get the girls home."

A patrol car passed Bruce's truck as he drove away. It pulled up beside her, and a uniformed cop leaned out the window. "DI Steele said I needed to courier some evidence."

Alexa reluctantly retrieved her treasures. She grabbed her Sharpie and wrote This End Up on the duct tape bag. "Don't let this get smashed. I'll let the lab technician know you're on the way."

The officer's eyes got big. "Yes, sir." He gulped. "I mean, ma'am."

So she was a "ma'am" now. Yikes.

"Senior said for you to meet her in the bunker."

She called the lab technician and explained what was coming in. "Process the trace on top of the duct tape cap and then wait for me to get there. We'll examine the tape together." She kept talking so Pamela couldn't interrupt. "As for the rag, focus on trace. Look for hair, soil…"

"I'm on it," Pamela said icily.

Her instructions were unnecessary, which might be a reason she didn't have many—well, any—friends. Alexa took a deep breath. "I know you'll do a good job. I'll check in with you later."

Her shadow had lengthened. She checked the time: five thirty. She scanned the cottage porch as she walked by. No Lynn sighting. As far as Alexa was concerned, Lynn was a suspect. DI Steele better not let her slip away.

In front of the bunker, Alexa suited up and forced herself under the caution tape and down the stairs. Her heart thumped in her ears; she did not like the bunker. The thick metal door at the end of the passageway was wide open. Alexa knew the CO had dissipated, but she propped the door open another inch. She stopped in the control/supply room and studied the squat HVAC system. A pipe snaked from it and disappeared into the ceiling. Alexa assumed it was the intake valve. Air would get sucked in, filtered, and released. She searched the area for the exhaust pipe, but couldn't find it.

She hurried through the next door, into the kitchen and living area. She glanced at the couch where Quinn's body had been. She imagined him there, alive. What had he been doing? She remembered the chess set with fallen pieces. Had he been playing? With whom? Had he noticed his head hurt? Had he felt lethargic or confused? Sometimes with CO poisoning, motor function is impaired. Quinn might have wanted to get up, to go outside, but couldn't make his legs move. For a moment Alexa felt impaired.

DI Steele's voice from the hallway revived her.

The drapes across the fake window were closed. She whooshed them open and blinked at the live-cam view. The outdoor light was dimming, but she could still see down stairstep ledges of equally distanced nests and hundreds of chicks and adult gannets. A sliver of beach was at the bottom and a slice of cliff at the top.

The camera must be hidden in the tall Norfolk pine she'd seen. It was the only place high enough to capture the angle.

"Never been in a bunker before," a man's voice boomed. "A doomsayer, eh?"

DI Steele stood in the hallway, scowling as the locksmith examined a square black box mounted by the knob of the purported wine room. She nodded curtly at Alexa, who noticed she wore gloves, booties, and a mask.

"Smells like someone died in here," the locksmith commented from behind his mask. He tapped the black box. It had a fingerprint scanner in the middle and numbered buttons around it. He pressed one with a gloved finger and a green light flashed. "It's a deadbolt replacer."

"Can you open it?" DI Steele said.

"It opens six different ways." He caught Alexa's eye and nodded. "A code, an app on your phone, by fingerprint..."

DI Steele huffed. "All I need is one friggin' way."

He tugged the black box toward him. It opened on a hinge, revealing an old-fashioned key lock. "This is how I'll get in." He opened his case, found the right tool, and began to pick.

"Have you always been a locksmith?" Alexa asked.

He gave her a half smile. "Do you mean did I pick locks in another life?"

She laughed, but that's what she was wondering.

DI Steele turned her back on the locksmith and lowered her voice. "So you've worked with DI Horne before?"

"A couple times."

"I read how he handled a big case in Rotorua. He solved a

couple murders and ended a black market ring. International, mind you."

The greenstone pendant pressed to her chest throbbed. "I worked that case with him."

"Was he in the area or has he been called in?" she demanded.

DI Steele was insecure. "No. His daughters live in the area, like he said."

"Bob's your uncle," the locksmith said and turned the knob. The door opened a crack. Alexa braced for an alarm, but the bunker stayed tomb-quiet.

DI Steele thrust herself in front of the man. "I'll take it from here."

Mr. Pick looked disappointed. As soon as he collected his tools and left, DI Steele pushed the door open.

"Bloody hell," she said.

Alexa peered over her shoulder. There would be no wine tasting. Racked and shelved weapons gleamed under soft yellow light. Guns. Knives. Shotguns. Tasers. She took a step forward. Her eyes jumped from an assault rifle to a sawed-off shotgun to three handguns to a row of knives.

Her favorite idiom—*armed to the teeth*—jumped into her mind. It originated from days when guns were primitive and could only shoot once before needing to be reloaded. She had a sudden vision of Harlan Quinn, a gun in each hand and a knife between his teeth, lunging at her.

"It's a bloody walk-in vault. Look here." DI Steele pointed to a vicious collection of knives. One had a six-inch serrated blade; another looked like a skinning knife, its blade honed to a piercing tip. The DI pointed to a small fixed-blade knife on a cord. "It's a neck knife."

Alexa's hand went to her throat.

"It's worn like a necklace. Tucked under a shirt, easy to conceal," the DI said. "Don't touch anything."

As if.

The air was stale and cold; Alexa heard the blood pumping through her arteries. She stared at the handguns: a Glock, a Sig Sauer, and a Smith & Wesson, each possessing a cold, indifferent beauty. Below them, a shelf held four ammo lockers. She looked around, unsure of DI Steele's position after her chat with Bruce, but Alexa believed if Harlan Quinn had meant to kill himself, he would have used one of these guns.

DI Steele whipped out her phone. "Bloody hell. No bars. Stay here. I'm calling the OCU."

Alexa didn't want to be alone in the underground while the DI summoned the Organized Crime Unit. "I'll come with you."

"No. Guard the weapons."

Being ordered around pissed Alexa off. She took deep breaths to calm down as she photographed the weapons. Funny. She couldn't smell the lingering putrefaction that permeated the other rooms in the bunker. The gun vault must be hermetically sealed. She panicked, afraid she'd be locked in. She finished up the photos and moved to the threshold. She knew all about weapons now. At her request, Dan Goddard had sent her to a three-day Firearms Safe Handling course. The main takeaway popped into her head: assume all weapons are loaded.

At least now she could unload a shotgun. She thought of the ranger on Stewart Island—a man who loved whales—and of the shotgun she had taken from him a couple cases ago. She hadn't known how to handle it.

Ted, a cohort in the Firearms Safe Handling course, had had a big time with her last name. "See you at eight o'Glock," he said each afternoon. On the last day, they'd gone for lunch at a tequila bar. Ted asked if she wanted Glockamole with her tacos.

Quinn had illegal weapons locked in his bunker. Why? Was he afraid for his life?

She decided to wait at the live-cam window, even though it meant being in the same room where Quinn died. She avoided looking at the sofa. The gannets made her feel less claustrophobic.

One of the brown-speckled chicks hopped back and forth, antsy. She worried it might fall off its ledge.

"They mate for life."

Constable Gavin's voice made her jump. She turned to find him staring at the screen. Mating for life sounded like a fairy tale. Bruce had divorced. Her brother, Charlie, almost divorced. If Mom had lived, would she and Dad still be together? "Are you married?"

"Yeah, nah," he stuttered. "Don't even have a girlfriend? My flatties are blokes?"

His upward inflection annoyed her.

"I'm to guard the weapons until OCU arrives, eh? And take inventory?"

She showed him the vault. He whistled flatly, his eyes bulging. He pointed to the sawed-off shotgun. "The weapon of choice of the Curs."

A chill crawled up Alexa's spine. Did Harlan Quinn have connections with the local gang?

Chapter Seventeen

A kitted-up DI Steele waved Alexa over to the porch of the big house. "I'm looking at this as a possible homicide now, so we don't need to wait on that warrant to get inside the house."

Bruce had worked his magic.

The DI waved a slip of paper. "The housekeeper, Tina Cobb, gave me the code, all reluctant like, but I told her a dead bloke can't sue her for breach of contract. I need you in case there's anything we need to tag and bag."

Alexa *was* curious to see what the big house held.

Sergeant Atkins looked up from her phone. "The OCU lads are at a stakeout, Senior. It might be a while before they can get to the bunker."

"They're going to wet their nappies when they see what's down there," DI Steele said.

Night swept the last remnants of light from the sky as Alexa retrieved her crime kit from the Vitz and followed DI Steele and the sergeant. As soon as she set foot in the foyer she sniffed, alert for putrefaction, the metallic scent of blood, maybe the chemical reaction of bleach breaking down. Even fear or neglect had distinctive odors.

The house smelled lemony clean.

A double-sided stone fireplace separated two sitting areas,

the far one with a bank of naked windows facing the sea. Timber beams crossed a vaulted ceiling and matched the dark floor planks. The aesthetic was like the cottage bulked up on steroids. Everything was too big, too modern, too cold for Alexa's taste.

She followed the officers past a contemporary dining table and six yellow chairs into the large kitchen.

"Take a gawk," Sergeant Atkins said.

Shiny mottled stone crept up the walls, covered the counters, and spilled over the sides. The cabinetry was flat-gray panels. The sink was big enough to bathe a baby elephant. The coiled spray handle looked like the one Dr. Li had used in the autopsy suite.

"Where's the refrigerator?" DI Steele asked.

Sergeant Atkins patted the wall panels until she located the fridge. "Blends right in."

It was empty except for bottled water. Alexa recognized the brand. "It comes from icebergs."

"Sweet as," Sergeant Atkins said. "But where's the grub? If Quinn had been staying here, surely there would be grub."

"Ms. Lockhart said that the chef at The Retreat cooks for Quinn," Alexa said.

"Head over there now, Sergeant," DI Steele said. She opened a cabinet, revealing ceramic bowls. "Find out when Quinn placed his last order."

"And ask if they delivered that picnic basket," Alexa added.

Sergeant Atkins took another gawk at the kitchen and left.

The study had a large wood-slab desk and a mesh ergonomic chair that Alexa wanted to try out. No drawers or filing cabinets. "No paper trace anywhere," DI Steele said.

The single object on the desk was mounted on a pedestal. Alexa stepped closer to the gleaming brown-black object. Another fossil. This one was banana-shaped and had tiny serrations along the edges. "Oh, my gosh."

"What? What is it?" DI Steele said.

"I think this is a T. rex tooth." Her palm itched to hold it, to peer into the pulp chamber, to run her fingers along the edge and imagine the serrations at work—ripping apart a duckbill or triceratops. From what she remembered, the front teeth gripped and pulled, the side teeth tore and cleaved, the back teeth diced and sliced. "I think it's a first or second maxillary tooth."

"How much is it worth?" DI Steele asked.

Her question was jarring. "It ought to be in a museum," Alexa said.

The four bedrooms off a wide corridor mirrored the guest bedroom in the cottage, Alexa thought. Closets held robes and UGGs, bathrooms offered spa-like toiletries and pristine towels. Lynn Lockhart had waved her magic wand here, too. The whole house was a stage, and the play hadn't started.

The king bed in the master suite was neatly made. A muted rug and large painting of an androgynous swimmer sitting on a diving board provided the only color. DI Steele pushed a button on the wall and the shades silently lifted. She pushed again and they lowered.

Final curtain popped into Alexa's head.

"There's got to be a passport or wallet somewhere," DI Steele said. She walked to the cube-like nightstand and opened the drawer. "Not even a pair of readers," she said.

The closet was a warren of wall-to-wall cabinets, shelves, and neatly spaced hanging shirts and pants. The first drawer Alexa opened housed quick-dry briefs. Pristine white T-shirts were in the next drawer, colored T-shirts in the third.

DI Steele lifted a polo shirt from the rack. "Still has the price tag." She inspected it. "Can't afford it on my wages."

Shoes nested like birds on ledges. There were tennis shoe brands Alexa had never heard of. Leather loafers and lace-ups had their own ledges. So did flip-flops like Quinn had been wearing in the bunker. They weren't from the Dollar Store. "He didn't need to pack a suitcase when he came," Alexa said. "Everything was waiting here."

"The jeans have tags on them too. Eight hundred dollars, for these," DI Steele murmured. "Here's another pair. Brand new. And another. Kersten won't believe me."

Alexa thought of how she'd agonized over purchasing her possum cardigan. It had been expensive. Would she treasure it as much if she owned thirty possum cardigans?

The cottage had sparked envy and lust in Alexa, but this over-indulgence was repugnant.

They couldn't find a medicine cabinet in the palatial bathroom until Alexa touched the mirror over the dark stone counter. Lights came on and the mirror slid into a wall pocket. Toiletries and toothpaste lined the shelves. In the middle shelf, between Advil and a multivitamin, stood a prescription bottle. Alexa took photos. "It's Propecia. Made out to Harlan Quinn. One milligram, once per day, one refill."

"What's it for?" DI Steele asked.

"I don't know. It was filled four weeks ago." Alexa set the camera aside and retrieved her phone to search *Propecia*. "It's a medication for the treatment of androgenetic alopecia. Male pattern baldness."

DI Steele snorted. "All the money in the world and he was balding. The prescription is proof he was here. So where are his wallet and phone?"

The sliding mirror and hidden fridge in the kitchen gave Alexa an idea. She went around the bedroom, pressing the walls.

"What are you doing?" DI Steele asked.

"Looking for a safe." No panels magically slid open.

"Can't be behind the painting," DI Steele said. "Too obvious."

That's where they found it. They removed the painting. The safe had a fingerprint pad and key code.

"Brill," said DI Steele. "I'll get the locksmith back out here. We're done for now."

Alexa thought of the T. rex tooth, left behind for no one to appreciate. Like being buried.

On the porch they stepped out of the jumpsuits and booties. Alexa bunched the discards in a ball to stuff in her trunk. DI Steele straightened her uniform collar and brushed lint off one sleeve. She still wore the full uniform she'd had on at the press conference.

"Let's go visit Ms. Lockhart," she said.

"I need to get to the lab," Alexa said. "It's important to know whether the duct tape had fingerprints on it."

"Ms. Amick can do that. Sergeant Atkins has run off to The Retreat to speak with the chef. I need someone with me."

"You're not going to tell Ms. Lockhart about the duct tape, are you?" Alexa asked.

The DI jerked her chin up, maybe insulted.

Alexa reminded herself to not overstep her boundaries. Plus, if Harlan Quinn had been murdered, the mistress was a suspect. She stashed the disposables in the Vitz and joined the DI for the short walk to the cottage. The wind was still. A waft of sea and guano from the gannetry reassured Alexa that life without trappings was bountiful and beautiful.

DI Steele was mumbling. "I've got Sergeant Atkins at The Retreat. Check. Constable Gavin is waiting with the weapons. Check. OCU are on their way. Check. You're coming with me to question Ms. Lockhart. Check. Ms. Amick is working in the lab. Check." She looked over at Alexa. "This case is bigger than our tiny team."

"DI Horne said he was available to help," Alexa reminded her.

No one answered the door when DI Steele banged. "Done a runner, maybe," she said.

"Let's go around back," Alexa said. "There's a patio."

Lynn, glass of wine in her hand, stood staring out to sea. A distant crash of waves was the only sound in the still air.

"Ms. Lockhart," DI Steele said.

Lynn sloshed wine as she twirled. "You scared me."

"I have a few questions," DI Steele said.

"I didn't hear you coming." She gestured to the rattan chairs, but remained standing, her back to the night sky. "Why are you here?" she asked Alexa.

"She's here at my request," DI Steele said and took out a notepad. "I'm gathering more information about Mr. Quinn. Tell me again when you last saw him."

Alexa took the other chair and watched Lynn's face under the fairy lights; it was pinched, her cheekbones more gaunt than when she and Sergeant Atkins had stopped by earlier to tell her the bad news that Harlan Quinn was dead.

"He came for the New Year. We sat here and watched the sun rise."

"How was his state of mind?" DI Steele asked.

"Fine. Healthy." She had changed from that silky white blouse to a blowzy jumpsuit. "Excited about his drug trials."

"What do you know about the ventilation system in the bunker?" DI Steele asked.

Lynn shook her head. "I don't know anything about the bunker."

"Are you sure?" Steele's tone switched from cordial to aggressive. "I spoke to Mr. Duncan Weber who installed the bunker. Ring a bell?"

"No. Should it?"

DI Steele huffed. "When the installation was complete, Mr. Weber gave you a tour and explained the ventilation system."

Lynn pushed hair from her face with her free hand. "How could I remember? The estate was completed several years ago. There were all sorts of inspections and walk-throughs and deliveries and arrangements. I was up to my chin. Harlan left it all for me to do while he was back in California. Why does it matter?"

DI Steele didn't answer the question. In the distance a dog howled.

"I didn't even know he was here," Lynn said.

"Did you know he had a stash of weapons?" DI Steele asked.

"Weapons? What for?"

"That's what we're wondering. Why do you think? Was someone threatening Mr. Quinn?"

"I don't know." She sipped the last of her wine and looked toward the open bottle near Alexa. Their eyes met. "In the States, Harlan was threatened a couple times. People jealous of his companies and wealth." She dropped her eyes. "Some competitor accused him of stealing some idea that Harlan helped develop. All sour grapes. That's why he liked coming here and being with me."

The DI leaned forward. "There was a picnic basket in the bunker. From the wrappers, it looked like two people enjoyed the meal. Who was Mr. Quinn picnicking with?"

"Maybe he ordered it for himself."

"There's evidence of sexual activity on the bunker linens," DI Steele said.

Lynn stiffened. "Harlan wouldn't cheat."

Alexa suppressed a snort.

Lynn turned her back to them, stalked to the cliff edge, and hurled her wineglass into the abyss.

Chapter Eighteen

They turned at the sound of tires crunching gravel. A car door slammed. The reverberation carried in the still air.

Lynn lunged from the edge of the sea and tore around the cottage with such vigor that Alexa, following, figured the woman believed Harlan Quinn had arrived to surprise them all.

She half-believed it herself. A silverish SUV was parked at an angle in front of the big house. A slim man headed for the steps.

"Stop where you are," DI Steele called.

The man pivoted.

The DI marched over. "Who are you?"

"My name is Amit Gupta. I've been sent to represent Harlan Quinn's family. You must be the local police?"

Alexa remembered DI Steele said a representative was on his way. She saw Lynn's shoulders wilt.

DI Steele produced her badge. "I'm heading the investigation into Mr. Quinn's death."

Mr. Gupta pushed his small oval glasses back up his nose. "I'm straight from the airport. Flying first class from Auckland to Hastings is a waste of money. It was like cattle."

Alexa had never flown first class. She instantly disliked the guy for complaining about it.

"I'd like to see identification, please," DI Steele said.

Mr. Gupta patted his pockets and pulled out his wallet. He handed over his ID. "I have a letter of introduction from the Quinns' attorney. I'm here to confirm Quinn is dead."

Under the porch light, Alexa saw he was older than she'd thought from his slim build and casual tennis shoes. Maybe early fifties.

DI Steele took her time reading the ID. "Amit Gupta. San Jose, California. Is that another Silicon Valley burb? What made you come straight here and not to the police station?"

"I'm acting on Mrs. Quinn's behalf," he said.

That wasn't really an answer, Alexa thought.

"Mr. Quinn's body is at the Hawke's Bay Hospital morgue." DI Steele motioned for Alexa to join them. "There's no question that he's dead, right, Ms. Glock?"

That was an understatement. "I'm a forensic investigator. Mr. Quinn's body is, well, it's in bad shape. Facial recognition isn't possible."

Mr. Gupta's forehead was shiny under the light. Stubble darkened his cheeks. "I insist on viewing the body. To assure the family."

"I can arrange that," Alexa said. It wouldn't be like TV where someone whipped back a sheet. Most likely Dr. Li would present a photograph of Quinn and explain the condition. If Mr. Gupta still insisted on seeing the body, she would acquiesce then.

"I will accompany the body home," he added.

Alexa got sidetracked. There were laws involved with international transport of a body. Namely, the deceased would need to be embalmed first.

DI Steele shook her head. "Mr. Quinn's body isn't going anywhere until we figure out what happened."

Mr. Gupta stilled.

"Please bring that letter to the police station first thing in the morning. Did you know Mr. Quinn well?"

"Better than most." He noticed Lynn hanging back. "Who are you?"

"This is Ms. Lockhart, Mr. Quinn's property manager," DI Steele said. "She is staying in Mr. Quinn's cottage."

Lynn shifted out of the shadows. "Mr. Quinn gave the cottage to me."

Mr. Gupta just stared.

"I suppose there is a will," DI Steele said. "Ownership of the cottage will be hashed out that way, eh?"

Lynn's jumpsuit billowed in a fresh wind. "Would you like to come to the cottage for a drink? I'm sure Harlan would have wanted me to ask you."

The guy is acting on Mrs. Quinn's behalf, and the mistress is inviting him in for drinks? Alexa felt like she was watching a soap opera.

Mr. Gupta hesitated. "It's been a long day, but thank you. I'll accept."

"I need your number," Alexa said. "To let you know when to meet at the hospital."

He gave it to her.

They watched Mr. Gupta and Lynn walk toward the cottage. "Wouldn't mind being a bug on the wall," the DI said.

Chapter Nineteen

Alexa left the DI at Black Reef waiting for Sergeant Atkins and headed to Hastings. At the curve above the sea—where there were no guardrails—she slowed the Vitz to a crawl. She could see nothing but blackness. Driving off a cliff like this would be a quick way to die. Airborne, then lights out. Where had that thought come from, she wondered.

She believed Quinn had been murdered, though suicide remained a slim possibility. As soon as the road straightened, she pulled onto the grassy shoulder, turned off the car, and called Dr. Li. The pathologist answered.

"Good evening. This is Alexa Glock, the forensic investigator who…"

"Yes. What can I do for you?"

Alexa quickly prioritized. "We've discovered that the ventilation system in the bunker where Mr. Quinn was found has been tampered with. Are there further steps you can take to see if CO poisoning was COD?"

"Carbon monoxide—the silent killer. That pink tooth of yours come to mind, eh? Never seen it before. I'll have further tests conducted."

"Do you have Mr. Quinn's fingerprints ready?"

The doctor sighed. "I'll have them for you in the morning."

"One more thing." Alexa explained that a representative of Harlan Quinn's family wanted to view the remains. "He insists."

"I suppose you tried to dissuade him?"

An animal skittered across her headlamps. Maybe a stoat or possum. Alexa shuddered.

"I'll arrange it for nine a.m.," Dr. Li said.

Alexa peered out the window at what was most likely a farmer's field. She squinted at dark shapes. Bushes? Sheep? She called Mr. Gupta. He didn't answer. This was strange, since she'd just seen him walk off with Lynn Lockhart fifteen minutes ago. She left a message for him to meet her at the hospital in the morning. Finally, she called the Apple Motor Lodge and reserved a room. When she had checked out this morning, she thought she was leaving town. So much had happened since then.

It was eight p.m. when she walked into the lab. Pamela-Not-Pam looked up from a microscope and gave a perfunctory smile. "Your trace sample from the duct tape cap consisted of soil and a hair. A short black hair. Maybe dog."

Without waiting for a reply, Pamela put her eye to the microscope. "The soil is a combination of clay, salt, and silt. I'll take a site sample in the morning to see if it matches."

"What about the duct tape?"

"I was waiting for you."

Alexa was relieved. They pulled on gloves. Pamela set the duct tape cap on a clean work top and stepped back. Alexa appreciated the gesture to her seniority and thought out loud as she lifted the cap. "There are six crisscrossed strips. Whoever did this pulled each strip from a roll, placed it on the pipe, patted the ends into place, and then cut the edge with scissors. See how even they are? Maybe we're dealing with a perfectionist personality. The big question is whether or not he or she wore gloves."

Pamela interrupted. "Let's use orange fluorescent powder. We'll get a nice contrast against the gray tape."

It was what Alexa would have picked. "You go ahead," she said generously.

Pamela returned with a feather duster and a small jar of fine orange powder. "Near the edges, I think." She opened the jar, fanned out her brush, and swirled it around in the cap.

Less powder, more detail, Alexa thought.

Then Pamela swished the brush across the side of the duct tape cap, lightly, expertly.

When she was finished she said, "Ready."

They made a good team. She shone an ultraviolet beam across the powder. Even with the lab lights on, ridge detail in two separate prints jumped out. The little remnants of human touch—invisible only a minute ago—thrilled Alexa.

Pamela photographed the results and then lifted the prints onto a backing card. If only they had Quinn's fingerprints right now.

The Automated Fingerprint Identification System took six minutes to let them know there were no possible matches in the system. They were not dealing with a schoolteacher, police officer, or anyone else with prints on file, including criminals.

"I've got to get home to my squirt," Pamela said.

Partner, child, or pet? Alexa didn't know.

Pamela documented the evidence and returned everything to the locker. "I'll stop by the site and get that soil sample first thing, eh?"

"And I'll get Quinn's fingerprints from the pathologist."

The sky opened in a fit of rain as Alexa stopped at Twisted Noodle for takeout pad thai and spring rolls. The clerk at the Apple Motor Lodge welcomed her back. "Have you in the same room so you'll feel at home."

Home. Alexa seized upon a new motto: home is where the case is.

She was torn between the shower and the noodles. The shower won because she was wet. Finally, in her red NC State T-shirt and jammie shorts, freshly washed hair combed behind her ears, she dove in with chopsticks. Slurp by slurp, as her energy returned, she recounted the day: the bird woman scaling the cliff and talking about how someone (Quinn?) deserved to die, identifying the bunker body, listening to Audrey Quinn learn her husband was dead, the press conference, the tractor tour with Bruce and his girls, and discovering the ventilation system was deliberately clogged. And then meeting Amit Gupta. Who exactly was he?

Alexa stared at the ceiling, attempting to arrange all the information into something coherent. Her phone rang. She answered without checking the screen.

"The girls are back with their mother, and I'm back in Hastings."

Her heart jumped at Bruce's voice. "Why?"

"DI Steele has requested my assistance," he said. "She's treating the case as a homicide."

Bruce paused. "Where are you?"

"At my motel. In bed."

"That's the nicest thing I've heard all day. I haven't checked in anywhere. Mind if I join you?"

She shoved *The Wild Light of Dawn* under her forensic journal and jumped out of bed to tame her hair with the dryer and brush her teeth. Discussing the case was not the first item she planned for their agenda.

———

Alexa leaned against the headboard, nude and disheveled. Her greenstone pendant rested against her damp sternum, pulsing.

Bruce lay on his side, facing her. A sheet covered him from the waist down. Covered too much of him, Alexa decided, and tugged it down a couple inches. Her hypothalamus was busy releasing après-sex oxytocin, and she didn't care. "Those gannets were beautiful," she said.

"You're beautiful," Bruce replied.

The pendant heated up. It was sending her a message. *Open*

your heart to this man. She took Bruce's finger and pressed it to the spiral. "Do you feel that?"

"Feel what?" His fingers moved off the pendant to her nipple.

Alexa shifted to give him full access. "Do you think the chicks are fledging right now? In the dead of night?"

"Probably not in the rain." Bruce's fingers circled her areola, distracting her. "Sammie asked me about your job. She still thinks teeth are made of bone."

At the mention of his daughter, Alexa shifted from Bruce's touch. "I'll send her an article."

He fingered a lock of her hair. "Don't send her one with disturbing pictures."

She looked down at him. "That was fun today, taking that tractor tour, watching you do the Funky Chicken."

"The Cha Cha Slide."

"You have a good relationship with your girls." She plunged ahead. "What did they, um, did they say anything about me?"

Bruce pulled himself up and sat shoulder-to-shoulder with her. She detected a hesitancy and braced herself.

"You running off like that? Denise thought it was strange, but Sammie said you were Supergirl to the rescue."

Alexa relaxed.

"Sammie screamed at me when I dropped her off at her mother's. Sharla thinks she's acting out because I've moved away."

Alexa reached for her T-shirt and slipped it on. "Well, nobody has died."

Bruce stared at her.

"I grew up with only one parent, that's all. Sammie and Denise are lucky, even if, well, you don't live with their mom." Screaming girls and ex-wives were out of her comfort zone. She changed the subject and told him about the fingerprints on the duct tape. Then she blathered about Lynn Lockhart and the fancy cottage. "I don't understand why she gave up her job and independence to basically become a kept woman."

"The lure of money?" He put his arm around her and pulled her closer.

"I guess. Get this, she didn't even have a way to contact Quinn. He called her. And he was married, with a kid, and she knew and put up with it."

He massaged the back of her neck, the spot where she stored tension. "She was looking for something."

"What do you mean?"

"She was lonely or empty. Quinn filled a void."

"But he was married."

"You said that already. Infidelity happens."

She thought of how Charlie's wife had cheated on him and how hurt he'd been, crying into a pool of glowworms on their hiking trip. "You sound like you're defending her."

"I'm stating facts." He pushed her forward so that he could use both hands to knead her muscles. "Infidelity happens and there are reasons for it. It's not my place to judge. Yours either. The only thing that matters is if their relationship had bearing on Quinn's death."

His hands glided below her T-shirt to her upper back. Her muscles recoiled. She didn't like it when he touched her ugly back scars. She jerked away, but he pulled her back and kneaded a tight spot. His hands were warm, safe. She felt a finger trace a jagged indentation. "This is a new scar, right? From the case we worked on Stewart Island?"

A couple of cases earlier, a fisherman had attacked her with a gaff. Her wound had become infected, and now she had a permanent reminder. She took a deep breath and let her muscles uncoil. "Insult to injury," she said. His hands continued their exploration.

"I can't believe how tough you are." His touch was light, teasing, then hard. "Swimming with sharks. Netting bad guys. Facing my daughters."

SUNDAY

Chapter Twenty

"Stay in bed," Bruce whispered in her ear. "I'll find us coffee."

Alexa avoided the "*L*" word, but "coffee" whispered first thing in her ear? How could she avoid it?

She dressed in her last clean work outfit and sat at the dinette to check the news on her laptop. The headlines belonged on tabloids: "Riddle in Luxury Bunker." "Mysterious Death of American CEO." "Doomsday Bolt-hole Didn't Save Billionaire."

There was no mention of the ventilation system.

Bruce returned with two cappuccinos and a Mama's Donuts bag. His blue eyes dimmed as he scanned her attire. "I was hoping you'd still be in bed."

She reached for the donut bag. He held it ransom until she kissed him. Between bites of custard cream donut, she told Bruce about Amit Gupta. "I'm meeting him at the morgue. He wants to see the body."

"Who is he?" Bruce asked.

"Audrey Quinn's secretary called him a family representative." Alexa wiped her hands and did a search on her laptop. "Here he is."

Amit K. Gupta, formerly Chief Operating Officer of Q&G Biologics, a biopharmaceutical start-up headquartered in Silicon Valley, has been promoted by the Board to CEO. Mr. Gupta, an accomplished scientist from San Jose, replaces his former partner Harlan Quinn. Mr. Gupta announced a new name and outlook: "The biosimilars landscape is expanding and AKG Biologics leads the way in cutting-edge technologies."

"Bio this, bio that," Alexa said. She liked the guy better knowing he was an accomplished scientist. "So he and Quinn used to work together. Quinn left to start another company. Gupta got promoted."

"Something to look into," Bruce said.

"Lynn Lockhart said Quinn liked starting new companies."

"Serial CEO-ism," Bruce said.

"What happens to companies when the CEO dies?"

"The board of directors will have a contingency plan. If the company isn't public, his wife might inherit it. Could be a motive for murder. What else do I need to know before I head in?" Bruce asked. "Who's been in the bunker?"

The cappuccino was heavenly. Alexa sipped and thought about it. "The tech team found out the codes to enter the bunker, house, and cottage come from Ultraloq, some remote management company. Lynn Lockhart gets the codes. The caretakers, too." Another sip. "There's a possibility Quinn was entertaining someone in the bunker. There were remains of a picnic lunch and messy sheets. I'll check them out today. If he cheated on his wife, he probably cheated on his mistress, too."

Bruce opened his mouth to speak when his phone rang.

Alexa cleaned up their breakfast trash and listened.

"Good morning, Mic." Pause. "I understand. I have two of my own." Pause. "I'm on my way." He hung up and said, "Mic is going to be late. Something about her nephew."

"Again? That kid is causing her trouble."

They performed a choreographed dance in the tiny bathroom as they brushed their teeth and glanced at each other in the mirror. It felt more intimate than making love.

The Apple Motor Lodge desk clerk was happy to do her laundry. "I'll toss them in with the towels and sheets."

"Maybe rinse them twice."

She was excited to get to the hospital. Dr. Li had promised Quinn's fingerprints would be ready. On the drive, she pictured Quinn's body in cold storage. In New Zealand, a body ends up in the fridge for three reasons: if you die in the hospital and are waiting to be moved to a funeral parlor, if a doctor doesn't sign off on cause of death, or if the death is suspicious. Harlan Quinn was two for three.

Mr. Gupta waved at her from a corner of the lobby.

Alexa appreciated his promptness. She dodged a man holding a bouquet of balloons and joined him. "Good morning."

He bowed his head slightly. He looked smart in a tailored dress shirt tucked into black jeans. The dark circles under his eyes were half-hidden by his glasses. Jet lag, she figured.

"Mr. Quinn's body is in a bad state," she warned. The body wouldn't look much different from yesterday morning—refrigeration slowed the decay process—but the sight of Quinn's face was not for the unprepared. "The pathologist will talk to you first."

The viewing room consisted of a vinyl floor, a sticky conference table with hand sanitizer and tissue box, and a closed curtain. Alexa knew that on the other side of the curtain would be the room where the body would be wheeled in. She pulled out a chair and sat, but Mr. Gupta paced. "So you used to work with Mr. Quinn?"

"We've worked together for several years. I am pleased to assist his family in this matter."

"It's a long way to come." She looked at his hands; he didn't wear a ring. It wasn't any of her business, but she asked anyway. "Are you married? Do you have children?"

"My work is my family," he answered. "My biosimilars are my children."

Weird philosophy. Alexa loved her work but had never thought of it as family.

Dr. Yellin, the registrar, opened the door. "Dr. Li sent me. She's busy." He introduced himself to Mr. Gupta. "Please have a seat. A social worker will be joining us."

The chair screeched as Mr. Gupta pulled it out. "That is not necessary."

Dr. Yellin glanced at Alexa. She nodded.

He opened a folder and slid the top photo, facedown, toward Mr. Gupta, who turned it over and stared. Alexa saw his fingers tremble.

"You can see Mr. Quinn is slumped on a sofa," Dr. Yellin said. "The fireman moved the body to that position."

Mr. Gupta stayed mute.

The registrar fingered the next photo but didn't hand it over. "This one is of the facial area."

Mr. Gupta clasped one hand with the other and squeezed.

"The body was originally found slumped forward with his head almost touching the floor," Dr. Yellin said. He slid the photo over. "That's why his face is in a more advanced stage of decomposition."

Mr. Gupta swiped the photo right side up. He brought a hand to his mouth. "This is Quinn? How do you know?"

"Dr. Glock was able..."

"Ms. Glock," Alexa corrected. "I was able to identify Mr. Quinn by comparing his before-death and after-death dental X-rays. I have them on my laptop if you want to see them. I've sent a copy to the Palo Alto police to share with Mrs. Quinn."

"How do you know it's him?" Mr. Gupta repeated.

"Ms. Glock just explained she was able to confirm identity by matching Mr. Quinn's dental records," Dr. Yellin said.

Mr. Gupta shoved the photos back. "I am ready to view the body, please." He rose and pulled the curtain back, as if expecting Harlan Quinn's body to be waiting on the other side of the glass. The small room was empty.

"As you wish," Dr. Yellin said.

Alexa didn't understand what Mr. Gupta would gain by viewing the body. Was he fulfilling a promise he had made to Quinn's wife?

Dr. Yellin reappeared pushing a covered cadaver trolley. Mr. Gupta stood, feet apart, hands clasped behind his back, face inches from the glass. Dr. Yellin lowered the covering to Quinn's clavicles.

Mr. Gupta gasped.

Alexa studied his profile; his cheek twitched.

"As you have planted," he said softly.

Alexa thought maybe it was the beginning of a poem or psalm but Gupta didn't say anything more. She turned to give him privacy and studied Quinn's ravaged face. The sight whisked her back inside the bunker, alone with the decaying corpse, her hand in his pocket. The eclipse of light. The fear.

"Namaste, Quinn."

Gupta's "namaste" broke Alexa's trance. In addition to her new kickboxing routine, she had a regular date night with her Down Dog app. Yoga kept her back scars from tightening. That's why she had started practicing as a teen. Now she posed, planked, and plowed out of habit. She ended each session by pressing her palms together at her heart, bowing her head, and saying, "Namaste." She thought it meant "I bow to you," so she supposed Mr. Gupta was paying respect to Quinn.

She closed the curtain.

Mr. Gupta plucked a tissue from the box and blotted at the moist gleam on his forehead. His dark eyes bounced from Alexa's to the curtain. "When will the body and personal effects be released?"

"DI Steele can answer that. She's expecting you at the police station this morning. You can follow me."

"I'll find my way." Mr. Gupta glanced at the curtain and left the room.

Dr. Yellin found her in the hallway. "I've got a set of fingerprints for you." She followed him into a room much like a forensic lab. Dr. Yellin skirted a work table and settled at a desk where he rummaged through another folder. He extracted a backing card with inked fingerprints and gave it to her. "Dr. Li used glycerinated gelatin to normalize the skin. Then she used a cadaver spoon to stabilize his fingers."

Alexa wished she had been there. She clutched the card like it was Dr. Henry Faulds's autograph. Dr. Faulds had helped establish a statistical model of fingerprint analysis in the 1880s. "What's the latest on the toxicology screenings?"

"Nothing yet." Dr. Yellin logged in to his computer. "But I heard from the bug guys." He printed a report and handed it to Alexa. She remembered the maggots on Quinn's face; insects colonized cadavers in a predictable sequence and could be used to estimate time since death.

She scanned the report. "Give me the highlights."

"Within ten minutes of death, flies arrive and lay eggs."

"Even in a bunker?"

"If a door has opened, flies get in."

The cleaner. Quinn. His paramour. Unbeknownst to them, they'd invited party crashers.

"Twelve to eighteen hours later, the eggs hatch into maggots. You know that, right?" He didn't wait for Alexa to answer. "People don't realize flies lay eggs that hatch into maggots."

She nodded.

"Maggots have a five-stage life cycle."

In stage five, they'd turn into flies and the cycle would continue. Alexa could see the chart in her mind.

"John Doe's maggots were stage three."

"His name is Harlan Quinn," Alexa said. "It's important to name victims."

"Given stage three and the bunker temperature, Mr. Quinn had been dead four days."

Alexa had guessed three to four days, so the news was anticlimactic. But the report would be helpful if the case ever went to court.

She was surprised Mr. Gupta waited in the lobby.

"May I walk you to your car?" he asked.

She hugged her laptop case to her side and nodded.

Once outside he asked, "You are American, right?"

"Yes. From North Carolina."

He removed his oval glasses. His face was sharply angled without them. "Are you bugging-in?"

Her mind flew to the entomology report. "What are you referring to?"

"Sheltering in place. Did you come to New Zealand for self-protection?"

"Protection from what?" What was with these people? "I came here for a job."

He gave her a tight smile. "A home in New Zealand is a popular safety investment for lots of people in the Valley, Harlan Quinn included. They brag about it at dinner parties."

"Not many people have the means to do it," Alexa said.

He replaced his glasses. "What can I do to expedite the release of Quinn's body? I need to get back to California. To my work."

"I can't help you with that."

"What about the personal effects?"

"Such as?"

"Quinn's phone, wallet, and computer. Mrs. Quinn wants them protected and returned."

She was about to say they hadn't even found his wallet or phone, but caught herself. "Detective Inspector Steele can answer your questions."

"Thank you for your time," he said.

Alexa expected to see Mr. Gupta's silver SUV follow her to the station, but he wasn't in her rearview mirror.

She spotted that reporter who'd asked her about the reliability of dentals after the press conference, stalking the station lobby. She dodged him and headed to the lab. Pamela wasn't in yet. She entered Quinn's fingerprints into the scanner and held her breath. It could take anywhere from twenty seconds to twenty minutes for results. She checked her phone: no messages. She did a sweep, a squat, and a kick, careful not to hit the chair. Her calves were tight from yesterday's beach jog. She was about to check her email when the screen lit up.

Harlan Quinn's fingerprints were not compatible with the prints lifted from the duct tape. Her heart skipped a beat. This result gave more credence to the case being a homicide.

They did match the prints from the laptop found near Quinn's body. Not that the laptop was any help with the investigation. Harlan Quinn had advanced encryption tools in place.

Alexa ran upstairs to share the news.

She found DI Steele in a small interview room, staring through two-way glass. "Sergeant Atkins is interviewing Tina Cobb, the housekeeper," she whispered.

"I've got news," Alexa said.

"Hold it." DI Steele turned up the speaker volume.

The housekeeper looked nervous, like she had when Alexa had met her on the porch of the big house. But who wouldn't be? She probably craved a cigarette.

"Do you clean the bunker, too?" Sergeant Atkins was asking. Her fishhook had been replaced with a bull ring. Alexa didn't like the image that swept into her head: the sergeant being led around by a septum lead.

"Once a month, like I told you. I don't like going down there. Feels like I can't breathe. I get the shakes. But I do it. Jobs are hard to come by."

"When were you in the bunker last?"

Mrs. Cobb pulled her phone out of a large beaded handbag. "My last cleaning was seven March. It was time again. That's why I tried the code, but it didn't work. I called Tony."

"When did you last see Mr. Quinn?"

Mrs. Cobb kneaded the handbag. "I never met him face-to-face. Told you lot that already. Real private, Mr. Quinn was."

DI Steele turned the volume off. "What did you want to tell me?"

Alexa repeated her news.

"Let's get to the team meeting," DI Steele said.

Chapter Twenty-One

Alexa recognized Constable Gavin's upward inflection—always talking in questions—as she followed DI Steele into the briefing room. He was talking to a stocky female in uniform. Bruce stood in front of the whiteboard. He gave her a sliver of a smile.

The stocky female turned around. Her lips and chin were tattooed dusky blue in the Māori tradition to represent her tribe and culture.

Constable Wynne Cooper returned Alexa's stare impassively.

What the hell? Alexa had worked with Constable Cooper in Rotorua. Her colleagues called her Coop. Alexa had been suspicious she had been involved in the murder of a city councilman, and her suspicions hadn't gone over well with the constable, naturally, or with Bruce, who had defended his protégé. That had been the subject of their first disagreement.

Alexa ate crow. Or *tui*, this being New Zealand. Constable Cooper had had nothing to do with the murder. Why hadn't Bruce mentioned she was coming?

DI Steele clapped her hands like a schoolteacher. "Let's get started."

Everyone took a seat except Bruce. Sergeant Atkins rushed in and sat next to Alexa.

"In light of the ventilation system tampering, we now believe that Harlan Quinn's death is a suicide or homicide," DI Steele said.

A helicopter buzzed the station. Alexa felt vibrations through the soles of her Keds.

"The press," DI Steele said. "They're everywhere. Watch what you say. I've asked Detective Inspector Bruce Horne, Auckland Serious Crimes, to aid in our investigation. DI Horne was visiting in the area, lucky him, eh? Would you introduce your colleague, please?"

"Good morning," Bruce said. "I'm honored to assist in any way I can. I called in Constable Wynne Cooper, formerly of the Rotorua Police Department and now in Auckland. Constable Cooper has *whānau* in the area and will be an asset."

Whānau was family, Alexa knew.

Sergeant Atkins said, "Hiya," and Constable Gavin rubbed his chin and then blushed. Constable Cooper sat at the end of the table. Bruce took a seat next to her.

DI Steele pointed to the before-death and after-death photos of Harlan Quinn tacked side-by-side on the whiteboard. The John Doe information Alexa had seen yesterday had been erased. "Case update time."

Alexa saw her glance at a note card on the table.

"We are in the initial investigative stage. Sergeant Atkins, fill DI Horne and Constable Cooper in on the discovery of the body."

The sergeant flipped open her pad and read out the particulars.

Alexa had heard this before. She scanned the faces gathered around the table, wondering how this hodgepodge team of Sergeant Atkins, Constables Cooper and Gavin, Bruce, and DI Steele would meld. One thing she knew: murders were solved by manpower. She almost snickered. Women outnumbered the men in the room. She studied Bruce, his eyes on Sergeant Atkins. She felt better about the investigation now that he was here.

When the sergeant finished, DI Steele turned to Alexa. "Tell them about the state of the deceased and how you identified him."

Alexa recapped the decomp stage and dental identification. "I have two new pieces of information."

DI Steele opened her mouth, but Alexa kept going.

"This morning I talked with the registrar, Dr. Yellin, from the autopsy. He gave me an entomology report. The maggot stage supports that the time interval between Quinn's death and the discovery was four days."

"That confirms our timeline," DI Steele pointed out.

"I also received Harlan Quinn's fingerprints this morning." The pocket loop whorls popped into her head. "Last night Ms. Amick and I lifted two prints from the duct tape. We ran them through AFIS and didn't receive any possible matches. I just compared Quinn's prints to those on the duct tape." She paused; her audience was captive. "They don't match."

After a moment, Constable Gavin asked, "What's it mean?"

"That Quinn didn't tape the vent, eejit," Sergeant Atkins said.

"Or he wore gloves," Constable Cooper said.

"The test that measures carbon monoxide in Quinn's blood is still pending," Alexa said. "Ms. Amick and I will examine the linens today. There's indication of sexual activity."

"Funk in the bunk," Constable Gavin said.

DI Steele looked at Bruce. "If someone was with Quinn in the bunker, that might be the same person who tampered with the vent. Anything to add, DI Horne?"

"All good," he said.

"Moving on, yesterday we discovered a cache of weapons in the bunker," DI Steele said. "I called in the Organized Crime Unit to handle them. Mr. Weber, the man who installed the bunker, said it's common for people to keep weapons in their bunker. He didn't supply them and doesn't know where Quinn got them. The OCU team will let us know what permits Quinn had."

"There are no permits for semiautomatics," Constable Gavin said.

DI Steele turned to Sergeant Atkins again. "What did you find out about that picnic basket? Did someone from The Retreat deliver it?"

"Chef—a bloke named Horacio Ramirez—said he fills the baskets but doesn't know who gets them. The manager, Ms. Katrina Flores, keeps track of that. She wasn't available last night."

Alexa remembered meeting the manager two nights ago. Lynn Lockhart had been insulted that Ms. Flores hadn't recognized her.

"Go talk to her," DI Steele said. "I've arranged to Zoom with Harlan Quinn's wife at four p.m. Our Palo Alto liaison will join us. We need to know where she was when Quinn died. Last night Ms. Glock and I met the representative she sent. His name is Omar Gupta."

Alexa sat straighter. "*Amit* Gupta. He viewed the body this morning. He wanted to know when Quinn's body would be released and asked about his personal effects."

"Mr. Gupta used to work as Quinn's COO at Q & G Biologics," Bruce said. "Quinn left that company five months ago to start another company, BioMatic. I'm wondering why they parted ways, and if it was cordial."

"He should be in the station now. I'll let you talk with him," DI Steele said. "Where are we on Quinn's laptop?"

Sergeant Atkins pulled at her collar. "Nowhere, Senior. The laptop has gone to the Electronic Crime Lab. The bloke said the encryption is almost impossible to break."

DI Steele looked personally insulted. "What about Quinn's flights and arrival dates? What do you have, Constable Gavin?"

A knock interrupted his answer. A woman stuck her head into the room. "Urgent call for you, DI Steele."

Her face drained of color. "Joe again?"

"It's the OCU. There's been a break-in at your bunker."

"Bloody hell." She stood and glared at Constable Gavin. "Didn't we secure it?"

The constable's Adam's apple went up and down. "You said to leave it open as a safety precaution. The air and all."

Her eyes had a wild look. "That was before we knew the bloody bunker was loaded with weapons."

Chapter Twenty-Two

No one said anything after the DI stalked out. Alexa heard Sergeant Atkins's nasal breathing, a pull and then a wheezy release. Maybe the nose ring was obstructing her airflow.

"Who knew about the weapons?" Bruce asked.

Constable Gavin patted his cowlick. "The team. The OCU lads. Maybe Lynn Lockhart? Maybe the Cobbs? We had a grave-yard shift officer out there patrolling."

"Lot of good it did," Sergeant Atkins said.

Alexa looked to Constable Cooper to see her reaction. She was impassive as a carving.

Bruce stood. "Let's create a timeline of the case while DI Steele sorts things out. It will help Constable Cooper and me get the big picture." He wrote HQ last seen by wife on the board and waited.

"First of April, sir," Sergeant Atkins said.

"When did he arrive in New Zealand?"

"I've been working on that, see?" Constable Gavin said. "He wasn't on any passenger manifests in Auckland? Don't know when or how he arrived."

Bruce's eyes darkened. "A billionaire probably has a private jet. Have you checked the smaller airports?"

"Good idea, sir."

DI Steele rushed in. "The weapons are gone." She turned to Alexa. "Get your kit. You'll ride with me to Black Reef."

They left the station quickly and pulled out onto Eastbourne Street West. DI Steele gunned the Volvo through a yellow light. "I'm fucking toast."

Alexa gripped the seat, glad the Sunday morning traffic was sparse. She tried to think who would steal the weapons, but came up blank.

"I should have removed them last night instead of waiting for the OCU to get their asses out there."

Alexa silently agreed.

The DI leaned forward in the driver's seat, her sharp chin inches from the wheel, as if that would get them to their destination quicker. "It's my first big case. Eyes are on me, waiting for me to fuck up. Now this. Guns stolen under the nose of Hastings's new female detective inspector. You know how it is, eh?" She looked Alexa's way. "A woman in a male-dominated field?"

Alexa's forensics program at NC State had comprised seventy percent women, but DI Steele didn't give her a chance to respond.

"All this, plus what's going on with Joe." She braked for a turning car. "I got home past eleven last night. Kersten was asleep. Went to check on the boys. They bunk together. Joe was gone." She exited a roundabout. "He came home at three a.m. We had a row. His hand was bloody. Wouldn't say what happened or let me look."

Alexa had no idea what she would do in the DI's place.

"I can't handle him. Do you have children? How do you do it?"

"No kids," Alexa said. "I have two nephews. Benny and Noah."

DI Steele banked a curve, thrusting Alexa into the passenger door. "That's me, six months ago. Two nephews, no kids of my own, not that Kersten and I aren't trying. Sperm donation, two failed intrauterine inseminations. You know."

Alexa did not know.

"We've stopped all that now, since the boys. If it weren't for Kersten, I'd have turned in my badge."

Alexa had never juggled family life with work. "What happened to their mother?"

DI Steele didn't answer until they were on the outskirts of Hastings. "My kid sister, Nora?" Her hands tightened on the wheel. She pressed the gas pedal and overtook a farm truck. "Died of an overdose a year ago. Chronic pain from a car accident got her started on opioids and then her partner, Frank, turned her on to the other stuff. Heroin cut with Apache. King Ivory. Murder 8. "

Alexa knew those were street names for fentanyl. "I'm sorry."

"Frank did a runner. It's devo, sure, especially for the boys. Joe is angry, and Adam, well, he wants to please everyone to make up for Joe's behavior. He's always tidying their room or doing the wash up. He's deathly afraid we'll leave him too."

The story sat in Alexa's throat, large and raw. She couldn't swallow.

"Last I checked, Frank is in jail. Joe expects he'll be back any day, wants him back. That's normal, I know, but Frank supplied Nora. Sold everything they had for drugs. Neglected the boys. As far as I'm concerned, he killed Nora. Kersten and I quake at the thought of him getting out and turning up. It's a mess."

Alexa shifted in the seat. She'd been judging the DI without knowing what she was going through. They passed a sheep pasture and then turned onto the long winding drive to Black Reef.

There were two cars and a police cruiser where they parked. The driver's door of the cruiser opened and a uniformed man got out.

DI Steele muttered under her breath as she marched toward him. "Constable Karu. Tell me about your night."

Alexa wrestled the crime kit onto her shoulder and followed.

Constable Karu pulled a notebook out of his pocket. "My shift started at ten p.m., eh? At twenty-two forty, I heard voices on the porch of the cottage." He pointed as if they might not know where the cottage was. "Ms. Lockhart was speaking to a man on the porch." He hitched his pants up and kept reading. "At twenty-two forty-five, the man got into a silver Range Rover and drove off."

"Must have been Mr. Gupta," DI Steele said to Alexa. "He stayed long enough to have more than one drink."

"I spoke to the lady in the cottage, let her know I was on the grounds." He was young, early twenties, and maybe Pacific Islander or Māori. "Didn't want her to think she was all alone, like." He stood straighter. "She was grateful. Made me a cuppa."

"Did you enter the cottage for a tea party?"

"No, Senior. I wouldn't have done that."

"What next?" DI Steele asked.

"Did my rounds."

"Which were?"

"A big circle. Up by the bunker, around the shed and that metal tree, down the far side, along the back of the big house and the cottage along the sea, to here again, and so forth. Nothing but bush sounds. Crashing of the waves. Birds screeching." He rubbed his eyes. "A couple times dogs barked. Never a sound of a motor after that man left."

"Did you fall asleep?"

"No, on my honor, Senior." He looked past them, to the woods. "They must have tramped through bush, on foot like."

"And tiptoed back with all the weapons? Can't see how that happened. When did you discover the break-in?"

He looked sheepish. "I didn't. It was the Organized Crime Unit fellas. They got here an hour ago. They discovered it."

"Go home, Constable."

Give him a tail to tuck between his legs, Alexa thought, as the constable got in his cruiser and drove away.

Alexa and DI Steele suited up quickly and silently, ducked under the caution tape, and clanked down the stairs of the main entrance. The outer and inner doors were open. The foul odor lingered.

A bald man in a mask and booties stood guard by the vault room. He looked up from a sheet of paper he was holding as DI Steele squared her shoulders and marched toward him. "OCU Festinger, what do you have?" she asked.

A gold police crest was on the breast of his polo. "According to your inventory here, all that's left is a Taser, one ax, and a canister of capsicum spray."

Another man stuck his head out the vault door. A scraggly beard draped below his mask. "Your dead bloke had an AK-47 in his bolt-hole, and you left it unsecured? After Christchurch? What kind of fucktard policing is that?"

He was referring to the terrorist massacre at the mosques that happened a few years before Alexa arrived in New Zealand.

"I had an officer on the grounds overnight." DI Steele lifted her pointy chin. "I called OCU as soon as I found the stash. Where were you?"

"We were engaged," the other guy, OCU Festinger, said. "Hundreds of gang members are gathering in the area for the *tangi* of a senior member."

Steele's eyes widened. "We've got a dead billionaire and now a gang funeral? The force is going to be stretched to the limit."

OCU Festinger consulted his paper. "I just talked with a clerk at the California Registry of Firearms Transactions. The deceased had two registered guns: a Glock G19 and a Ket-Tec Sub-2000 semiautomatic rifle. The Glock is listed on this inventory, but not the Ket-Tec."

"Did he have permission to bring the Glock into New Zealand?" Alexa blurted.

"Who are you?"

"I'm Alexa Glock, the..."

"Glock?" Scraggly Beard said.

"Like the gun. I'm the forensic investigator."

Scraggly Beard shook his head. "A Glock asking about a Glock."

"I need to process the room," she said.

His hands flew up. "I stood right here, didn't touch a thing." He stepped closer to an empty shelf. "Looky here."

Alexa leaned in. Three dime-sized blotches—dark brown at the periphery and crimson in the middle—jump-started her heart. She backed up and searched the floor for more droplets. It looked clean. She scanned the hallway. No blood trail.

"What was there?" Scraggly Beard asked.

Alexa retrieved her camera and scrolled for the right picture. She held the camera so the Organized Crime Unit guys could see the shelf of knives.

"Quite the collection," OCU Festinger said. "The stiletto is a bad boy, designed to reduce friction. Cuts clean."

DI Steele snorted. "Idiot thief probably cut himself."

Alexa took a swab from one droplet as they watched.

"To answer your question, Quinn didn't have a visitor's fire-arm license or an import permit," OCU Festinger said. "As for all these other weapons," he shook the paper, "he probably had a local source. We know who that is."

The other guy barked like a dog.

Alexa eyed Scraggly Beard warily.

He noticed her reaction. "The Curs. That's their signal. They bark."

The hair on the back of her neck stood. Alexa recalled hearing a dog bark while staying at the cottage.

Had it been canine or human?

"You think there's a connection between Quinn and the Curs?" DI Steele asked.

"How else would he have furnished this room?" OCU Festinger asked.

The OCU duo and DI Steele left Alexa to process the scene. She readied her camera and stood in the threshold of the vault. She didn't look for what was missing; that had already been done. Instead she zoomed in on what was left behind: the droplets, possible fingerprints, dirt, a hair or fiber or wrapper. Her eyes landed on a small pink object—maybe a jelly bean?—left on the shelf. She crossed the vault and leaned in.

It wasn't a jelly bean.

Chapter Twenty-Three

Whatever happened to the finger a colleague, Heidi, at the State Bureau of Investigation in Raleigh had shown her? She had returned from lunch, and Heidi motioned her over, excited. An air-conditioning technician had discovered a pinkie finger ensnared in a spool of copper wire he'd left at a construction site. He'd called the police, and they had delivered the digit to the forensics laboratory.

Copper theft was common. The police officer suspected the finger's owner had been trying to snag the spool. Instead the spool had sliced off a part of him.

"No more drinking tea the fancy way," Heidi said, wiggling her pinkie.

Together, they had obtained a print from the amputated digit that pointed—ha ha—to the suspect.

In this case, the thief had left what she was fairly sure was the fleshy nub of a fingertip. No nail, just a clean slice of oozy pad.

Her fingertips throbbed in sympathy.

Whether she'd be able to get a print from it, she didn't know, but she was excited to try. She wrapped the tip in gauze and slipped it into an evidence bag.

She collected two other prints and a couple partials from the knife shelf and the inside doorjamb. Satisfied, she left the underworld in search of ice. Ice would keep her specimen fresh until she got to the lab. She located DI Steele and the OCU guys in the shed and interrupted their conversation. "One of our visitors left something behind." She told them about the fingertip.

"Why wasn't there more blood?" DI Steele asked.

"He must have stanched it immediately. Probably wrapped it in his shirt."

"Hard to carry weapons with a bloody finger," Scraggly Beard said. "That indicates we had more than one visitor."

"An armed and injured perp," OCU Festinger said, shaking his large head. "I'll call the hospital and walk-in clinics."

"Waste of time. A Cur will tough it out," Scraggly Beard said.

"We believe they accessed the bunker through the shed," DI Steele told Alexa.

The trap door was wide open.

"Every fucking thing unlocked. Might as well have had an 'Enter Here' banner," Scraggly snarled.

DI Steele stiffened. "Whoever did it knew the weapons were here. I'm calling the caretaker back in. His name is Tony Cobb. Maybe he's been running his mouth."

"The name sounds familiar," OCU Festinger said. "We'll handle the interview."

DI Steele opened her mouth and then shut it.

Alexa dangled her finger bag. "I'm heading over to the cottage to get some ice."

"I'll come with you," DI Steele said. "Maybe Ms. Lockhart heard or saw something last night."

As they walked down the berm, a gust of wind carried the scent of guano. Alexa wondered if the gangling speckled chicks would fledge today. The tractor guide had said it would be any day. The chicks faced open ocean and an uncertain future.

"OCU Scylla is a drongo," the DI said.

Alexa assumed that meant Scraggly Beard was a dumbass.

"He'll tell everyone at the station that I messed up. I wouldn't put it past him to leak the break-in to the media."

The crime kit bumped against Alexa's hip. The best the DI could do to redeem herself was solve the case. "Mr. Gupta was here last night, remember? He accepted Lynn's invitation for a drink."

"Your point?"

"Just throwing it out there. Another person on the estate. He might have seen something as he drove away."

The DI nodded grimly.

Lynn Lockhart rounded the cottage as they climbed the cottage steps. She wore shorts and a jog bra that revealed her toned midriff. Her dark hair was in a ponytail. "Have you been looking for me? I took a walk to clear my head."

"I'd like a word," DI Steele said.

Lynn opened the cottage door. "I spoke with my lawyer," she said over her shoulder. "He assured me that a verbal agreement is legally binding. The cottage is mine. I feel much better."

Alexa was pretty sure verbal agreements transferring property weren't binding.

"That's for the will or the courts to decide," DI Steele said.

They followed Lynn into the foyer. "When did you last enter the bunker?" DI Steele asked.

Lynn frowned. "I told you last night that I don't go down there."

"I'll pop into the kitchen," Alexa said. "I need some ice." She skirted the women, but they followed her. Lynn opened the fridge and grabbed a bottle of water.

"Someone broke into the bunker last night," the DI said. "Do you know anything about that?"

Lynn dropped the bottle. "What do you mean broke in? What's going on?"

DI Steele picked up the bottle and handed it to her. "Did you hear anything?"

Alexa pulled two baggies from the kit: one large and one

small. She turned her back to Lynn and sealed the gauze-wrapped fingertip in the smaller bag.

DI Steele repeated her question. "Did you hear or see anything last night?"

Alexa moved two dirty wineglasses out of the sink and added water to the larger baggie.

"Why are all these bad things happening in the bunker?" Lynn asked.

"Answer my question," DI Steele snapped.

She uncapped the bottle but didn't drink. "After you lot left, Amit Gupta and I had a drink, a tribute to Harlan. Amit said Harlan always talked about New Zealand. How great it was. About the house and bunker. I didn't hear anything after he left."

Alexa added ice cubes to the larger bag, floated the smaller baggie inside, and sealed the deal. There: a fingertip on ice. It would be preserved until she got it to the lab. "Was Mr. Quinn close to Mr. Gupta?" she asked.

Lynn's laugh was harsh. "Harlan didn't have close friends. Except for me. That's why he needed me. Everyone was out to get him."

Alexa looked at DI Steele.

"Why did Mr. Quinn have a vault of weapons in the bunker?" DI Steele asked.

"He did?" Lynn sipped the water. "Harlan had a saying: 'Survival of the richest.' He wanted to be ready. I guess that's why he had guns."

Survival of the richest? Alexa's dislike for Harlan Quinn grew three notches.

"Did you buy them for him?" DI Steele asked. "Like you bought the furniture and art?"

Lynn's nostril's flared. "I did not. I wouldn't, either."

"Was he planning to bring his wife and daughter when the shit hit the fan in California?" DI Steele asked.

Lynn studied her tennis shoes—beige canvas with red treads—and shrugged.

"Ms. Glock will take your fingerprints now."

"What for?"

"You said you didn't know anything about that picnic basket in the bunker," DI Steele said. "This will prove it's not your prints on the handle."

Lynn looked at her fingers. "I don't have anything to hide."

When Alexa was through, DI Steele told Lynn to stay in the area.

"I'm not budging," she said.

Chapter Twenty-Four

DI Steele spun her wheels as she backed out of the parking area. "Gupta came straight from the airport last night, right? So he wasn't here when Quinn died."

Alexa fastened her seat belt. If Bruce had taught her anything, it was to never make assumptions. "Better check it out."

The DI's phone rang. She zagged on the narrow lane as she fished it out. "Hi, love."

They passed under the fake surveillance cameras. Why would a high-tech bazillionaire not pay for real cameras?

"I can't. I'm going flat-out today," DI Steele said into the phone. She tapped impatiently on the steering wheel. "Does he need a doctor?"

Alexa hoped they wouldn't meet a car coming at them.

"Tell him it's his last chance," DI Steele said and hung up.

They drove in silence, the DI worrying about her kid, Alexa guessed. She saw the turn to The Retreat coming up. "Should we stop and talk to the manager now? About the picnic basket?"

"What about your fingertip?" DI Steele asked.

"It will be okay for a couple hours."

The Retreat lobby was quiet as a church. They checked the restaurant. One couple lingered over coffee. A yeasty aroma made Alexa's stomach growl.

Blair, the young woman who had waited on Alexa and Lynn, discreetly checked her watch and slid out from behind a bar to greet them. "Good afternoon. Were you here for lunch? We're closing up; I'm sorry."

"We're here to speak with the manager," DI Steele said.

Blair's eyes flickered to the lingering diners. "Just a moment, please. Why don't you wait in the lobby?"

Alexa inhaled the yeasty nirvana and returned to the lobby. She had been curious about how much it cost to stay at The Retreat and poked around its website before Bruce had shown up last night. She'd almost choked on her Apple Motor Lodge complimentary biscuit. All meals included, it was 1,800 U.S. dollars a night. She inspected the fresh vase of flowers on the grand round table—orange again and more delicate than the pom poms.

"Those are poppies," DI Steele said. "I should order some for Kersten."

"Her birthday?" Alexa asked.

"She's borne the brunt of Joe. I don't know what I'd do without her."

Alexa thought of Bruce. Were hard times easier when shared?

The manager, alluring in a knee-length green skirt and silky blouse, strode toward them. "*Kia ora.* I'm Katrina Flores." Her eyes skipped from DI Steele's to Alexa's. "Welcome back. I believe you dined with us Friday night?"

"Yes. It was delicious."

"How can I help you?"

DI Steele introduced herself. "We're investigating the death of Harlan Quinn, the man who owned Black Reef."

Ms. Flores's eyes, the same color as Alexa's greenstone pendant, widened. "I've heard about it. We are most upset. What happened to him?"

"We're working to find out," DI Steele said. "Where can we talk?"

Furrows formed between Ms. Flores's brows. She beckoned for Blair. "We'll take three waters in my office, please."

They followed Ms. Flores down a hallway. Her office was a stark contrast to the elegant lobby: a metal desk, a couple of chairs, a printer, and a filing cabinet. A bulletin board hung behind the desk. Alexa squinted. It displayed work schedules. A map of the grounds was tacked above it.

Ms. Flores stood in front of her desk and didn't offer them seats. DI Steele sat anyway and took out her phone. "I'll just record our convo, eh?"

"I don't give you permission."

"Why is that?" the DI asked.

Ms. Flores tucked an errant lock of hair back into her bun. Alexa realized the manager was younger than her hairstyle and demeanor suggested. Mid to late twenties, she guessed.

"Mr. V says it's our duty to protect the reputation of The Retreat and its clientele."

"I hardly see how answering questions would besmirch a reputation." DI Steele pocketed her phone and dug a pad and pen out of her pocket. She looked up at Katrina. "Who is Mr. V?"

"Mr. Kyle Vanderveer owns The Retreat and several other luxury accommodations."

"Lives in New Zealand, does he?"

Ms. Flores eyed Alexa. "Mr. Vanderveer is American."

"We've got a theme going," DI Steele said. "Rich Americans, buying up Kiwi land, jacking up the prices for the locals."

The DI's remark irritated Alexa. Americans bought the land because the Kiwis let them.

Ms. Flores walked behind her desk and sat. "How can I assist you?"

"Tell me about your inn. How many rooms do you have?"

Ms. Flores's eyes relaxed a tad. "We have guests from all over the world. The Retreat has six spacious suites, each with stunning views and decorated in rustic-luxe..."

DI Steele broke in. "The manager of Black Reef said your chef cooked for Mr. Quinn on the side. Is that true?"

"There was an arrangement."

DI Steele huffed. "Elaborate, would you?"

"Harlan was a valued guest who dined here when he visited. Sometimes he asked for a private chef on his premises or to have food delivered." She straightened a stack of brochures. "We accommodated those requests."

"When did you last see him?"

Ms. Flores's cheeks colored. "I'm not sure. Every guest is important, but they come and go. Almost every day."

The DI's eyes narrowed. "Do you know Lynn Lockhart?"

"Ms. Lockhart occasionally dined with Mr. Quinn." She gestured toward Alexa. "Ms. Lockhart dined with you."

"She wasn't happy you didn't recognize her," Alexa said.

Her flush deepened. "I didn't see her at first. I apologize."

"A picnic basket was found in the bunker where Mr. Quinn died." DI peered at Ms. Flores. "It must be missing from your inventory because now it's in the forensics lab. Who delivered it and when?"

Her green eyes darted back and forth as if looking for escape. "I don't know."

Blair tapped at the door. "The waters?"

Ms. Flores nodded as the server handed out three bottles, more melted icebergs like Lynn had at the cottage. Alexa twisted off the cap and sipped.

After the server left, DI Steele said, "You must know who delivered that basket. No doubt you—or your staff—keep records."

"I'll check with our solicitor to see if I can provide that information," Ms. Flores said. "Privacy is important to our guests."

"Mr. Quinn is past caring about privacy," DI Steele said.

Ms. Flores's eyes widened. "Please check back later."

DI Steele slapped her notebook closed—making Ms. Flores flinch—and set the unopened bottle on the desk. "I'll expect to hear from you by this evening."

In the parking area she complained to Alexa. "Got her pretty lips buttoned tight. She makes me suspicious."

They heard footsteps and turned. Blair, the server, scurried after them. They watched her cross the lot. "I was hoping to catch you." Her pale blue eyes darted from Alexa's to DI Steele's. "I overheard? As I delivered the waters? Ms. Flores wasn't being honest."

"What are you talking about?" DI Steele said.

The server's sandy-colored hair framed her heart-shaped face. "About what Ms. Flores said. In her office. The picnic basket? She delivered it." The server pulled a key fob from her purse and bleeped it toward a car across the lot. "Mr. Quinn was found dead in his bunker, right? That's so sad. He was nice."

"How do you know Ms. Flores delivered the basket?" DI Steele asked.

"Ms. Flores likes riding around in the Can-Ams. She makes the deliveries."

"Did you see her make that particular delivery?" DI Steele demanded.

"I brought it out of the kitchen, and she drove off with it."

"When did you last see Mr. Quinn?" Alexa asked.

"In person?" Blair dug her phone out of her bag and checked something on it. "He and his girlfriend dined in the restaurant. He left me an enormous tip, even though his girlfriend told him not to. She's the lady you were with the other night," she told Alexa. "She said it wasn't customary, right in front of me like I wasn't standing there, but he did anyway. Smiled and put it in my hand. A hundred-dollar bill."

DI Steele gritted her teeth. "When? What was the date?"

"See I don't know. Maybe first of the year? Early January? I haven't seen him since, but it was me who took his recent order for the picnic basket. We call it Romantic Picnic For Two. I recognized his accent. American, like yours," she said to Alexa.

"What date did he place the order?" DI Steele asked.

She checked her phone. "Last Saturday." Then she looked toward the inn. Alexa followed her eyes.

Katrina Flores stared at them from the porch.

Chapter Twenty-Five

"Mr. Quinn was using his bunker as a pied-à-terre," DI Steele said in the car. "Do you think Ms. Flores was his guest?"

Alexa gathered her thoughts. "It's possible. Could be Blair, too, for that matter." *Once a cheater, always a cheater* popped into her head.

DI Steele's phone rang. "What now?"

Alexa heard Sergeant Atkins's nasal voice. Something about a safe and passport.

"Brill. Get them to the station ASAP." The DI hung up. "Our locksmith struck again. Mr. Q's phone, wallet, and passport were in the safe in the big house. Guess he didn't need them in the bunker, eh? They'll hold all the answers."

That was overly optimistic. A flash of green wings out the side window—a parrot, maybe—reminded Alexa of Linda Crosby climbing the Black Reef cliff yesterday morning. The talk about traps and how someone deserved to die. She cleared her throat. "Remember that conversation I overheard? Of that birder woman? She might have been angry enough to kill Quinn."

"Over birds? Doubtful, but I don't like that she was able to access the property from the beach."

"We go right by Clifton, where she lives."

"I have her address on my phone." DI Steele accelerated. "Doesn't hurt to stop by unannounced, eh?"

The A-frame house was hidden amid fern and palm trees, halfway up a cliff like a gannet's nest, and not far from Gannet Tractor Tours. The two flights of stairs leading to the front deck were slippery with leaves. Alexa clutched the weathered railing and led the way.

DI Steele breathed heavy at the top. "Look at the view."

Alexa shaded her eyes. The sea spread like liquid sky. She scanned the cliffs, which gouged inward like a bite mark. "You can see Black Reef."

"There goes a chopper, right over the estate," the DI said.

The Crosby house was modest, but the view was breathtaking. Past Black Reef, Alexa spotted the shark fin–shaped rocks that marked Cape Kidnappers.

A wooden box next to the front door served as a catchall. Alexa spotted nets, a shovel, gloves, shells, and an almost empty bag of cat litter. Fancy binoculars rested next to the box. Alexa was about to pick them up when the door opened.

Linda Crosby's wiry gray hair stood on end as if she'd been cartoon shocked. Her pajama pants featured Garfield the cat. She stepped onto the porch and closed the door, her short-sleeved T-shirt exposing thin muscular arms. "I was out late," she said. "Just getting my bearings."

"Hello, Mrs. Crosby. I'm Detective Inspector Mic Steele. We met at Black Reef."

"Call me Linda, aye? It's all over the news, what happened to the American. Can't say I'm gutted. I've spotted three helicopters over the cliffs today." She frowned and stepped toward the rail. "Four."

"It's the press. As soon as we figure out what happened to Mr. Quinn, the buzz will die down," DI Steele said. "Maybe you can help. May we come in?"

The lines on Linda's face deepened. "The chicks. They might

fall off a ledge what with the racket and vibrations. This has got to stop."

Alexa wondered how far the woman would go to protect the birds.

"Is your husband at home?" the DI asked.

"Dru is doing the groceries." Linda turned toward the door and gestured for them to follow. "Hurry now."

Three was two too many in the foyer. The air was cloying, like cheap lavender air freshener mixed with something gross. Alexa wrinkled her nose.

Linda moved into a galley kitchen. "I know what you're thinking."

Alexa worried Linda had read her mind.

"They kill billions of birds a year, but she's a wonderful friend and we don't let her roam."

Alexa was confused. Who wasn't allowed to roam?

"Sasha?" Linda clapped her hands briskly. "Come say hello."

A giant ball of orange fur careened around the corner. Alexa stepped sideways to get out of the cat's path. Her former boyfriend Jeb in Raleigh had had a cat, Nutmeg, who was more refined than this cat. Nutmeg never responded to commands, and Alexa had admired her independence.

"She's a lovely color," DI Steele said. She bypassed the kitchen and entered the den, choosing the closer of two wicker chairs. "I have a few questions, and then we'll be on our way."

Alexa sat in the matching chair. Its faded cushion was flat, and the chair crackled under her weight. She shifted; it crackled more. A TV was on, set to mute. Harlan Quinn filled the screen. Alexa was struck by his handsome, smug face. Even in stillness he had a swagger. How could he value anything if he had everything?

She let the cat sniff her Keds. She scratched behind its ear. Hair flew everywhere.

"Coffee? Biscuits?" Linda called.

"No, thank you," DI Steele answered.

"Yes, thank you," Alexa said.

DI Steele huffed. "Had you ever met Mr. Quinn?" she called.

There was racket in the kitchen but no answer. Linda came out after a few minutes with a pot of coffee and three mugs, which she filled and passed out. "Milk? Sugar?"

"Milk, thanks," Alexa said.

Linda popped back into the kitchen.

"Had you ever met Mr. Quinn?" DI Steele repeated.

"Eh? Every time I see that helicopter skim the cliffs, I drive right over to complain." She returned with a plate of cookies but no milk. "Someone has to speak for the gannets. Noise disturbance tests on Chatham Island showed that when exposed to blasts and explosives, adult seabirds abandon their nests."

Who could blame them? Alexa studied a harness contraption and a coil of rope that dangled from the A-frame wall. Maybe they were cat toys.

DI Steele declined a cookie and opened her notepad. "When did you last see Mr. Quinn?"

"His partner—that Lockhart woman—ran interference most of the time, but I met him a year ago when he was putting in that swimming pool. One of those infinity types. Right over the cliff, it is. The gannets aren't the only birds that use those cliffs. We've reintroduced the grey-faced petrel. The cliff is full of their burrows."

She finally offered the cookie plate. Alexa took two.

"I set traps in the nooks and crannies of the cliff," Linda said.

Alexa choked on her bite. "Traps for what?"

"Stoats. I'm doing my part for Predator Free 2050. The stoats crawl in for the bait and the trap snaps their spinal cord. Kills them instantly." She said this with glee. "Did you know they climb cliffs?" She picked up a book, turned to a photograph, and held the book six inches from Alexa's face.

Alexa recoiled. A fuzzy ferret-like creature stared at her, a baby bird dangling from its pointy-toothed mouth.

Linda showed the photo to DI Steele. "I've heard stoats referred to as the sharks of the bush," DI Steele said.

"People don't know how bad stoat predation is for seabirds. Kiwis—the birds, that is—get all the attention. Gannets only lay one egg per nest. The stoats gobble it up. Shorebirds have been devastated too. I set the traps to catch the bloody buggers."

That explained the conversation Alexa overheard. She was foolish suspecting the bird lady of killing Quinn and didn't meet DI Steele's gaze. "Isn't it dangerous to climb those cliffs?"

"We'll have a land without birds if we don't do our part." She glared at the stoat picture and closed the book. "The cliff is like stairsteps. You can climb without ropes."

Alexa's stomach lurched.

Linda sat on a wicker couch and whistled. Sasha jumped up next to her. "Back to your question," she said to DI Steele, "I saw the concrete truck, too close to the cliff, and drove right over. I told the operator to stop. Mr. Quinn came outside and asked who I was. Had a lovely accent."

Alexa sipped her black coffee and grimaced. She disguised the bitterness with a bite of cookie, which was ruined by a cat hair.

"He acted interested in the birds and promised he would reduce disturbances," Linda continued. "He did no such thing."

"So that was the last time you saw him?" DI Steele asked.

"Oh, no, I saw him a week ago, standing on the edge of the cliff. Told you that, remember? He was talking into his phone. Couldn't hear, of course."

DI Steele leaned forward. "Where were you?"

"On my porch. Saw him through my binocs."

"It's important that you remember the date," DI Steele said.

"Wrote it down in my bird journal," Linda said. She rummaged through the stack of books and opened her journal. "The second of April, it was."

Alexa thought of the picnic basket. "Was he alone?"

"He was alone on the cliff, but later I saw one of those fancy utes from The Retreat. That man should never have been able to build where he did."

Chapter Twenty-Six

Alexa held her crime kit with one hand and the fingertip bag with the other. She had an hour to lift a print from the nub before the team meeting DI Steele had ordered her to attend. Pamela was already in the lab and beckoned her over. "This is the bottom sheet from the bunker. I used an alternate light. The stains glowed."

No surprise. Nearly all body fluids were fluorescent when dried.

"Then I did an AP." She was referring to an acid phosphatase rapid test for the presence of semen. "It was positive."

"Too bad there's no rapid test for vaginal fluid," Alexa said. Vaginal fluid lacked the proteins necessary for easy identification.

"But there's more." Pamela polished her glasses with her lab coat. "I found two hairs on the pillow cases, and they aren't from the same source. One is short and dark."

A single hair from anywhere on the body can be used to identify the person. "Harlan Quinn had short dark hair," Alexa said.

"The other is from a ranga."

Alexa thought of an orangutan. "What's a ranga?"

Pamela laughed. "Someone with ginger hair."

Alexa licked her chapped lips. She thought of Katrina Flores tucking a strand of red hair into her bun. Then she thought of Sasha the orange-haired cat. "How long is the ginger one?"

Pamela patted her short black curls. "It measured nine inches. The color is consistent throughout, so probably not dyed."

Human scalp hairs are usually longer than animal hairs. You didn't see dogs and cats roaming around with buns or braids, Alexa thought. "What do you suggest we do with the hairs?"

Pamela puffed up. "We can get DNA from both. That will take a week or more. We can also do a comparison to see if they might match another sample. That means sending it to your place in Auckland, where they have a comparison microscope. Like I did with the hair from the duct tape."

With a start, Alexa realized she had forgotten about that hair; too much was happening. The benefits of teaming with Pamela were clear. If the duct tape hair matched the ginger hair from the sheets, it would indicate that whoever had been sharing the bed with Harlan Quinn had been near the duct tape.

Pamela must have read her thoughts. "That hair was short and dark."

"So it could have been Quinn's." Or Bruce's. Or Mr. Weber's. Or a million other people with short dark hair. But not Katrina Flores's. "Send them off," Alexa said.

Pamela finally noticed the fingertip bag and listened raptly as Alexa explained where it was from and what she proposed.

"I've never seen it done," Pamela said.

This time Alexa puffed up. "You roll it, just like a normal attached finger." She slipped on fresh gloves, removed the tip from the baggie and dried the friction side. She allowed Pamela to take measurements while she readied her camera.

The nub measured 1.2 cm by 0.6 cm—about half an inch by a quarter inch, Alexa estimated—and was oval. When they finished, Alexa flipped the nub over and told Pamela to press her gloved index finger into it. Pamela did, and was able to lift the nub. They stared at it.

"Fits like a glove," Pamela said.

Alexa took photographs as backup and then instructed Pamela

to press the nub into the ink and then onto the backing card. She fetched her magnifying glass and studied the result. "A loop," she said. "Most common type of fingerprint."

Pamela twirled her index finger. "It's impossible to differentiate between an ulna loop or radial loop without the rest of the hand."

Radial right hand, ulna left. Alexa remembered this from graduate school.

They ran the fingerprint through AFIS. There were no matches. Alexa reminded herself that much of forensics was a process of elimination. No answer was an answer.

Chapter Twenty-Seven

At five p.m. Alexa slipped into a chair next to Constable Wynne Cooper, who ignored her. She was still miffed that Bruce hadn't mentioned he was bringing Constable Cooper with him. He and DI Steele conferred by the whiteboard in low tones. The burly OCU guy, Festinger, plonked down next to her and ripped open a pack of salt and vinegar potato chips. Alexa salivated.

DI Steele tapped the whiteboard as Bruce took a seat. "I'll start with the good news. We have Quinn's phone. It will hold all the answers."

Alexa almost rolled her eyes.

"Texts, a record of his calls, voicemail, GPS coordinates, photographs, and downloads. But it will take twenty-four hours to get a report in my hands, and our tech team said there is a possibility Mr. Q's data is secured. Let's move on." She gestured to the TV set mounted to the wall. "We'll start by watching the video of our Palo Alto Police liaison interviewing Mrs. Audrey Quinn. Zoom didn't cooperate, so I wasn't able to"—she made air quotes—"'meet' her. Constable Gavin, get that started."

Alexa would have to wait to share her nub news.

Superintendent Kate Parker barged in with a stack of papers. "Sorry to interrupt. I have a press release to hand out."

Constable Gavin backed up against the wall as the super joined the DI at the whiteboard. "Welcome to HPD, Detective Inspector Horne."

Bruce smiled. "I'm happy to assist, Superintendent."

The super had a bulldog's flat face. "Our press team are being inundated with calls. If you are approached, refer them to our office. This is an updated press release that reflects yesterday's discovery of the tampering." She gave one to each person. "Take a moment to read."

FOR IMMEDIATE RELEASE

CONTACT: Detective Inspector Micala Steele
INCIDENT: Death Investigation

On 7 April, at 8:22 a.m., the Hastings Police Department entered the Cape Kidnappers bunker of Harlan Quinn and found a deceased adult male inside.

The deceased was later identified as the owner of Black Reef Estate, Harlan Quinn, age 46, of Palo Alto, CA. *Forbes* magazine ranks Quinn as America's 86th richest CEO with a net worth of $9.2 billion.

It is unclear how Mr. Quinn died, but carbon monoxide poisoning is suspected and tests are pending.

Based on a review of the circumstances, Detective Inspector Micala Steele has opened a suspicious death investigation. DI Steele is using every available resource to bring closure to the case.

Anyone with information regarding Quinn's death or whereabouts in the days prior to his death is asked to call the Hastings Police Department or the anonymous tip line.

Calling the death suspicious would cast ripples across the land and sea, Alexa knew.

Sergeant Atkins raised her hand. "What about the weapons?"

The superintendent's eyes narrowed. "No one says anything about the weapons or their disappearance." Before anyone could ask another question, she turned on her heels and left the room.

"You heard the super," DI Steele said. "No one says a word about the break-in. Let's watch this video before any more interruptions. We need to decide how to proceed with Quinn's wife. Is she a suspect or not?" She cast an eye toward Bruce; he nodded encouragement.

Constable Gavin pushed the button. After five seconds of static, the screen cleared. A man with Netflix-crime-drama looks straightened his tie.

"Full of himself," Sergeant Atkins said.

The man smiled at an auburn-haired woman sitting stiffly on an overstuffed couch. Alexa remembered her phone call with Mrs. Quinn; she'd been taciturn and refused to share Mr. Quinn's dental records.

The man gave the time and date and sat back. "Are you ready, Mrs. Quinn? Officer Kowalski has turned on the camera."

Mrs. Quinn lifted her chin. "I'm not speaking until my lawyer arrives."

The video cut off.

"Lawsuit-happy Yank," OCU Festinger said.

Alexa frowned at him.

The camera cut back on. A deeply tanned woman in a navy pantsuit perched on the edge of the couch next to Mrs. Quinn.

"Thank you for being here, Mrs. Quinn and Ms. Goldberg. For the record, Ms. Goldberg is Mrs. Quinn's attorney. I'm Chief Andrew Petrie of the Palo Alto Police Department."

"My client is aware who you are," Ms. Goldberg said.

Chief Petrie ignored this and looked at Mrs. Quinn. "I am sorry for your loss."

"It's traumatic," Mrs. Quinn said. "And ironic."

"How so?" Chief Petrie asked.

"You don't have to answer that," the lawyer said.

Mrs. Quinn whisked something off the shoulder of her silvery sweater. "It's ironic that my husband died in that bunker. His Eden killed him."

"She's accepted that Quinn is dead," DI Steele murmured. "That's progress."

"When did you last see your husband?" Chief Petrie asked.

The lawyer answered. "Mrs. Quinn last saw Mr. Quinn on March thirtieth at six a.m. He was leaving for a business trip to Munich. To the PharmaTex plant."

"Thank you, Ms. Goldberg. Did he arrive in Germany?"

"There was no record of Mr. Quinn arriving in Germany," Ms. Goldberg said.

Chief Petrie made eye contact with Audrey Quinn. "That must have been a shock."

Alexa noticed a slight twitch in Mrs. Quinn's right eye.

"What do you know about your husband's New Zealand estate?"

"Black Reef was Harlan's contingency plan," Mrs. Quinn said.

"Against what?" Chief Petrie asked.

"He *said* it was against another pandemic or war escalation, maybe electromagnetic pulses, fires and earthquakes, malware, the general collapse of society as we know it. Pick your poison."

Alexa worried things had gotten worse since she left the States.

Chief Petrie stayed quiet.

Audrey Quinn raised her shoulders and let them fall. "We argued about it. Running off isn't a solution; it's elite escapism. I told Harlan he should throw his brain into fixing things here. For our daughter. For her future. Be more Melinda Gates than Larry Page."

"That's the Google bloke," Sergeant Atkins said. "He's been granted New Zed residency."

"A noble idea," Chief Petrie said.

"I don't think Harlan cared about the state of the world; he just used it as an excuse to build an ivory tower." Mrs. Quinn shook her head. "He did what he wanted, like always."

"You have to invest one million NZ dollars to qualify for New Zealand residency," Sergeant Atkins said.

"Hush," DI Steele said.

Alexa thought she wouldn't like Quinn's wife, but she did. A crashing sound off-camera caused Mrs. Quinn to jerk.

"Your mother is busy," a woman said.

A girl in a drooping sweater ran into the room and planted herself in front of Chief Petrie. "Have you found my daddy?"

Mrs. Quinn jumped up. "Candide! What are you wearing?"

"Daddy's sweater." The child, maybe seven or eight, didn't take her eyes off the chief. "Where is he? When is my Daddy coming home?"

The Chief looked stricken.

"Daddy said he'd be here for my birthday and that's in," she stuck her hand in the chief's face, fingers spread, "five days."

The child was a small, fierce animal, Alexa thought.

"Letitia, come get Candide," Mrs. Quinn called.

The camera cut off.

A lump lodged in Alexa's throat. She hadn't thought of how Quinn's daughter had lost her dad. Losing Mom when she'd been around the same age as Candide had left a hole in her heart to this day.

Bruce caught her eye. She was unsure what he was conveying: sorrow for the child? Sorrow for her that she had lost her mom? She looked away.

The camera flickered on. Chief Petrie restated the time and date. "We have family specialists who can help you break the news to her."

"Candide's life coach will help her through this," Mrs. Quinn said.

Sergeant Atkins raked her fingers through her candy-corn-colored hair. "Did she say *life coach*?"

"She's acting cool as a cuke," DI Steele commented.

The chief looked at his notes. "Where were you between April first and fourth?"

Ms. Goldberg opened a leather planner and tapped a page.

"Mrs. Quinn was home on April first. She had two meetings: ten a.m. at Life Moves Opportunity Center and noon at the American Diabetes Association. At three she attended Candide's soccer match. On April second, she drove to a yoga retreat at Redwood Ridge, and returned April fifth."

"A yoga retreat?"

Mrs. Quinn lifted her shapely chin. "In Portola Valley. Meditation, yoga, massage. That sort of thing."

"Easily verified, thank you. What type of succession plan does your husband have for his companies?"

"You'll have to speak with Mr. Quinn's corporate lawyers," Ms. Goldberg answered.

"Who is Amit Gupta? He's in New Zealand on your behalf, is that correct?" Chief Petrie asked.

"Mr. Gupta is one of Mr. Quinn's associates," the lawyer said.

Chief Petrie cleared his throat. "Mrs. Quinn? Did you know your husband was involved with a woman in New Zealand? A Ms. Lynn Lockhart?"

"You don't have to answer that," the lawyer said.

Mrs. Quinn looked toward the door, perhaps making sure it was closed tight so Candide couldn't hear. She swallowed and stayed silent.

"She's probably got a lover-boy on the side, too," OCU Festinger said.

"My client wasn't aware of any relationship with a Ms. Lockhart," the lawyer declared.

"Someone tampered with the ventilation system in the bunker. This might have killed your husband," Chief Petrie said. "Who would want to harm him?"

Alexa leaned forward to hear what Audrey Quinn had to say.

"Besides me?" she answered.

"We are terminating the interview," Ms. Goldberg said.

The screen went blank.

"Came right out with it, she did," Sergeant Atkins said.

"Don't blame her for being hacked off," Constable Gavin said.

OCU Festinger wadded up his empty crisp bag.

DI Steele looked toward Bruce. He nodded, implying this was her show. She straightened her shoulders. "Mrs. Quinn had motive to kill her husband. Jealousy can and does lead to violence. But did she have opportunity? Sergeant Atkins, find out if Mrs. Quinn was actually at that retreat."

"Hand me the credit card, Senior. I'll pack my yoga mat."

DI Steele's mouth twitched irritably. "Since Chief Petrie mentioned Mr. Gupta, I'll let Detective Inspector Horne update us about their interview."

Bruce opened his notebook and stood. "The letter from the Quinns' attorney gives Mr. Gupta the right to transport the body and personal effects. To clarify, Mr. Gupta is not in New Zealand at Mrs. Quinn's request. He offered to come and Mrs. Quinn accepted."

"Your point?" DI Steele said.

"There's a difference, don't you think? I conducted the interview at eleven a.m. Constable Cooper joined us," Bruce said. "A rundown: Amit Gupta is fifty years old, unmarried, and lives in San Jose. He flew Air New Zealand from LA to Auckland and then to Hawke's Bay Aerodrome. He arrived at nineteen hundred hours, April ninth, rented a Range Rover—I verified this—and arrived at Black Reef when you met him."

"What? No private jet like Quinn?" Sergeant Atkins commented.

"Three years ago Gupta started Q&G Biologics with Quinn," Bruce continued. "He was chief operating officer. Gupta said Quinn was the money man—excelled at raising capital—and he was the brains."

"Quinn might have a different slant if he could speak," DI Steele said.

Bruce nodded. "Six months ago Quinn left Q&G to start another company and Gupta moved into his place. Gupta said he and Quinn parted on good terms, but he wouldn't give any more detail. I'm looking into it. He saw Harlan Quinn on March fifteenth, at a dinner party in the Valley. Anything to add, Constable?"

Constable Cooper pushed her chair back a couple inches. "Where was he when Quinn died?"

"Check out Mr. Gupta's whereabouts during our timeline," DI Steele ordered and turned to Alexa. "You met with him at the morgue this morning. Anything to add?"

Harlan Quinn's eroded face flickered in Alexa's mind. "Mr. Gupta was stoic about seeing the body and asked when it, and Quinn's personal effects, would be released." A thought startled her. "He never asked the pathologist how Quinn died."

A desk clerk barged into the room. "Urgent call for you, Senior."

DI Steele and Bruce jumped up.

Chapter Twenty-Eight

The receptionist clarified. "It's for DI Steele."

"Carry on," she said flatly and marched out.

What now? Alexa wondered.

Bruce continued standing. "Let's do as DI Steele suggests." He honed in on the Organized Crime Unit guy. "OCU Festinger, right? Fill us in on the weapons."

OCU Festinger passed out a list of the weapons stolen from the bunker. "Between eight thirty p.m. and eight a.m., the bunker was raided. The only weapon on the list that was registered was the Glock. Quinn did not have a New Zealand permit for it. The other guns are unregistered. Constable Gavin reported that the serial numbers on several had been defaced."

"Nah yeah," Constable Gavin said.

"I would say the acquisition and consequent theft of the weapons is gang-related." OCU Festinger looked toward the closed door. "The weapons should have been removed from the premises and placed in a secure location. Now they're back in circulation. That's on Steele. She's tarnished the whole bloody force."

Bruce's face went rigid.

"We called OCU right away," Sergeant Atkins said. "Where were you?"

A staring contest between the burly man and the punkish woman ensued.

"Move on," Bruce said.

OCU Festinger broke contact first. "The likeliest scenario is that Quinn, or an associate of Quinn's, purchased the guns via the black market. I'm bringing in the Black Reef groundsman, Tony Cobb. He's got possession of class B drugs and drunk-driving on his record. He could be associated with the Curs."

One of Bruce's eyebrows rose. "He's the person who found the body, right?"

"That's him. A couple of my undercover guys are attending the *tangi* for the senior gang leader tomorrow. It's at the school on Te Hute Road."

"At a school? That's bung," Constable Gavin said.

"Bung?" Alexa asked.

"Messed up," Constable Gavin said.

"The dead guy has *whānau* in the area, and the Ministry of Education approved it," OCU Festinger said. "Curs are coming in from all over."

Hell's Angels down under, Alexa thought.

"My guys are already in place," OCU Festinger said. "They'll ask around, find out how Quinn got the weapons. Maybe who has them now."

"That's assuming the weapons were procured locally," Bruce said. "They could have been imported on a container ship by Quinn. Look into other angles. What about the constable placed on the premises overnight?"

OCU Festinger scratched his chin. "Didn't see or hear anything after speaking with Ms. Lockhart at eleven forty. Except dogs barking. The Curs were sniffing around, watching."

The hair on Alexa's neck prickled; she'd heard a dog bark, too, when she'd spent the night in the cottage. Had that been prowling Curs?

"Is there a possibility Ms. Lockhart or Mr. Gupta entered the bunker?" Bruce asked.

OCU Festinger scoffed. "Why not? Place was wide open."

"Because of the carbon monoxide," Constable Gavin said.

"Ra, ra, ra," OCU Festinger said.

Bruce nodded at Alexa. "Ms. Glock, do you have anything to report?"

"I'll report backwards." That didn't make sense. Her cheeks heated as she stood. "I mean I'll start with the latest. Someone left a fingertip in the bunker vault; most likely one of the thieves cut himself stealing a knife."

"Say again?" Constable Gavin interrupted.

Alexa held up her left index finger and wiggled it. "Ms. Amick and I were able to extract a fingerprint from it."

"Like a spook story kids tell," Constable Atkins said. "Bloody fingers."

"There were no possible matches on AFIS. I lifted a couple other prints from the bunker. They could be from the same person who left his fingertip or someone else. Ms. Amick is running them." Again she thought backwards, but kept this to herself. "We lifted fingerprints from the duct tape and picnic basket handle. They do not match Harlan Quinn's, and there are no matches in AFIS."

She looked at the team, expecting rapt attention, but saw blank stares. Maybe sex would revive them. "We've detected semen on the bunker linens found in the master bedroom. There's possible vaginal material as well, but there is no quick test for that. Also on the linens were two distinct hairs. Probably human. One was dark, and one was long and ginger."

"The billionaire was having sex parties in the bunker, like they do in California," Constable Gavin said.

"There was no evidence of sex parties," Alexa clarified.

Sergeant Atkins tugged a tuft of her hair. "Can't be me, but it could be Mrs. Quinn."

Alexa also thought of the manager of The Retreat, Katrina Flores. "After leaving the estate at two o'clock, DI Steele and I stopped by the home of Linda Crosby in Clifton. She and her husband are birders."

"Why?" Bruce asked.

For a second Alexa thought he was asking why the Crosbys were birders. She came to her senses and explained that they had stopped because she'd overheard Linda Crosby talking about setting traps and how someone deserved to die. "She's angry that Quinn built his house right over the gannetry." She took a breath. "It turned out she was talking about stoat traps."

Even Constable Cooper laughed.

Alexa raised her voice. "We found out something important." When the laughter faded, she said, "Linda Crosby saw Harlan Quinn on April second."

"Where?" Sergeant Atkins asked.

"Standing at the edge of the cliff. Mrs. Crosby has a view of Black Reef right from her porch. She let me look through her binoculars." It had been amazing how the cliff came into focus, down to blades of grass and gannet feathers. "She also saw an ATV leaving the property. The Retreat has similar ATVs."

DI Steele stuck her head into the room and motioned for Bruce. Everyone quieted when the door shut behind them.

Alexa added her information onto the whiteboard and sat down. Constable Cooper pushed back from the table, separating herself from the others. OCU Festinger made a phone call and blasted someone out. "Get back in there. Don't fuckin' believe him."

Bruce returned alone and waited for Festinger to finish. "The DI has a family emergency. I'm taking temporary command."

Alexa wondered what Joe had done now. What would it be like to be torn between family and work? She worried that for her, work would win. That's why she didn't have a kid or spouse.

"If Steele can't handle the jandle, she needs to step aside," OCU Festinger said.

Bruce widened his stance. "That's what the Detective Inspector has done, but it isn't because she can't handle the case. Is that clear?"

OCU Festinger shrugged.

"We're going to make a list of suspects and then get a good night's rest." Bruce moved to the whiteboard, uncapped a marker, and scrawled: sus... The marker was dry. He uncapped another and had the same result. "Someone find me a marker that works."

When Constable Gavin returned with a new marker, Bruce said, "Ta," and finished writing suspects. He turned, his face calm. "Who wanted Harlan Quinn dead?"

"His wife, for cheating," Sergeant Atkins said. "Maybe she wasn't at that yoga retreat."

Bruce wrote Audrey Quinn.

"Lynn Lockhart might have found out Quinn was cheating on her," Alexa offered.

"With whom was he cheating?" Bruce asked.

"DI Steele and I spoke with the manager of The Retreat, Katrina Flores. She wouldn't divulge who delivered that picnic basket to the bunker. A server we spoke with said Ms. Flores delivered it." Alexa thought of the long ginger hair found on the linens. "Her hair is red."

Bruce scrawled Lynn Lockhart and Katrina Flores.

"There's that Amit Gupta," Sergeant Atkins said. "Maybe over money when Quinn left his company?"

"Could be a gang member killed Quinn," OCU Festinger said.

Bruce added Amit Gupta and cur member.

"Tony Cobb, the caretaker, too," OCU Festinger added. "Has a criminal record." He checked the time on his phone. "He's stopping by the station in ten minutes. We done?"

Bruce scribbled Tony Cobb and CAFC. "Superintendent Parker said someone from the Campaign Against Foreign Control lodged a complaint about Quinn stealing land from the locals. I'm meeting with the director first thing." He capped the marker. His steady gaze lingered on each individual in the room. "I want alibis for each person on the list by noon tomorrow. That's all for now."

The team started divvying up the list as Alexa walked to the door. Constable Cooper blocked her path. "Ms. Glock? Why don't we go talk to that Flores woman? You can do the introductions."

Alexa looked at Bruce; he was speaking to Constable Gavin. Would the new acting DI—and her bedmate—want her help beyond the lab?

Constable Cooper waited.

"I'm game. Call me Alexa."

Chapter Twenty-Nine

They walked out the front door of the station. Alexa shifted the crime kit to her other shoulder and looked up at the etching, the one she had noticed when she'd first arrived: *E tū ki te kei o te waka, kia pakia koe e ngā ngaru o te wā.*

"I know *waka* is canoe," she said shyly. "What does the rest mean?"

Constable Cooper's dusky lips mouthed the words. She adjusted her police cap and turned her dark eyes to Alexa. "'Stand at the stern of the canoe, and feel the spray of the future biting at your face.'"

Alexa shivered. The inscription felt portentous. During her first case in New Zealand, she and Constable Cooper rode in a small motorboat to a forbidden island. The constable had stood at the bow, where there was even more spray than the stern, where the wind had bitten her face. Alexa's, too. She could almost feel the bracing air, the spray, the turbulent waves under her Keds. In retrospect, she understood Cooper's presence on the island had protected her.

She felt shame that she had ever suspected the constable of murder.

"I'll drive," Constable Cooper said. She strode toward a white station wagon, jazzed up with blue and yellow police checks and the word *pirihimana*, Māori for *police*, and unplugged it from a charging station.

Alexa opened the car door.

Constable Cooper put her hands on her hips. "I said I'll drive."

Alexa sometimes forgot the seasons and the steering wheels were backwards in New Zealand. "My bad." She jogged to the other side and slipped in. She sniffed appreciatively. New car smell was something she'd never experienced personally. "Nice car."

Constable Cooper buckled up and placed her cap on the dash. Her hair, a blunt black pixie, was tucked behind her ears. "It's a Škoda Superb hybrid. Has a range of nine hundred kilometers." She backed out of the parking spot. "If I keep it charged."

A couple blocks from the station Alexa spotted Taj Spice Indian takeout. She had hoped for a cozy dinner with Bruce so they could talk shop, but she knew that wasn't happening, especially since DI Steele was MIA. "I'm starved."

The constable turned into the lot.

They ordered at a window and settled at a picnic table with their fragrant paper bags and drinks—an L&P for Alexa and a Diet Coke for the constable. Alexa zipped her jacket against the cool evening and surveyed the other customers: parents with identical twin preschoolers more interested in their soccer ball than the naan clutched in their fists, and three teenagers—two girls and a boy—eyeballing Constable Cooper. Alexa scooped chicken tikka masala up with her naan and chewed happily. She gulped the fizzy lemon soda to tame the heat. "How are things in Rotorua?"

Constable Cooper wiped her mouth with a napkin. "I don't live there anymore."

"That's right. You've moved to Auckland with Bruce." That came out wrong. "I mean, DI Horne recruited you to Auckland. He thinks highly of you."

She shrugged and took tiny bites, avoiding Alexa's gaze. Her short-sleeved police shirt stretched tightly over her muscular arms. An awkwardness lodged between them.

One of the teens laughed. "You're a crack-up," her friend squealed.

Sated by tikka masala, Alexa blabbed out the story her roommate told her about how Cape Kidnappers got its name. "But it probably already had a name, right?"

Constable Cooper's eyes gleamed topaz in the dim light. "You didn't believe that the Māori kidnapped Captain Cook's cabin boy, did you?"

Alexa hadn't had an opinion. She'd been in a hurry to hit the road. "Of course not."

"Te Kauwae-a-Māui is the rightful name, the fishhook of Māui. The local *iwi* chief and his son believed the cabin boy to be Māori and held against his will. They tried to rescue him. Several were killed for it."

Roaring bombarded Alexa's ears. Four motorcycles pulled into the parking area and surrounded Coop's patrol car—two on one side, two on the other. The riders—all in black and red—revved their engines until Alexa covered her ears. Their helmets and Darth Vader–like visors scared her. One by one they cut their engines.

Alexa held her breath as they lifted the helmets, releasing beards and braids and flattened mullets. Two looked *Pākehā*, or White, and two looked Māori or Pacific Islander. Alexa squinted: one man had a crude *C-U-R* tattooed across his forehead.

A pickup pulled in. Two guys got out and joined the others.

The couple gathered their twins, scowled at Constable Cooper as if she were responsible for the infiltration, and hustled to their car.

"What should we do?" Alexa whispered.

Constable Cooper stood, her face impassive. "Don't worry. They aren't interested in you."

The last biker to dismount pulled a red bandanna from his pocket and wiped his face. Fangs were tattooed on the corners of his mouth. He touched forehead and nose with one of the guys from the pickup truck and then turned and strutted toward their picnic table. Alexa, paralyzed, watched the man stop in front of Constable Cooper. He curled his lip and snarled. Constable Cooper didn't flinch.

The hair on Alexa's neck stood. She focused on the man's steel-capped boots. He walked away, trailing the scent of weed.

Alexa tried to stand, but her knees refused to lock. Constable Cooper glided over to the table of silent teens and said loudly, "*Kia ora*. Do you need a lift?"

One girl's mouth dropped as shook her head. The other two kept their eyes on the Curs.

Constable Cooper whispered to them. They gathered their food and scrambled into an old car. She stood, arms akimbo, as they drove away, the bikers watching her watch the kids.

Alexa rose slowly, careful not to make eye contact with the men. She wanted to sprint to the patrol car, but followed woodenly behind Constable Cooper, who paused in front of one of the motorcycles. "Nice bike," she said. When she finally unlocked the Škoda, Alexa jumped in.

Constable Cooper placed her cap on the dash and checked her mirrors. "I told the kids to go straight home. The gangs like to recruit 'em young. They aren't interested in someone old, well, middle-aged, like you."

Alexa had never thought of herself as middle-aged. She willed Constable Cooper to mash the accelerator and get them out of Dodge. "I can't believe you stood up to that guy."

"That was a senior member, Rikki Griffin. I've met him a few times." She started the quiet motor and pulled onto the street. The last gasp of twilight had faded. "He's here for the *tangi*."

"Whose funeral is being held?"

"Sonny Brown, a former president of the Curs."

Alexa looked over her shoulder. The bikes gleamed under a streetlight. "Why are they allowing a motorcycle gang to hold a funeral at a school? That's crazy."

"The Curs aren't a motorcycle gang. They're a patch gang."

"What's the difference?"

"They're a street gang. You don't have to have a motorcycle to join."

"Why are they allowed to hold the funeral?"

Constable Cooper's jaw clenched. "Everyone has a right to a funeral. Sonny has three grandchildren at that school. His family needs to express their love. A lot of Māori knowledge is passed down to children at funerals. Words to traditional songs, customs. All that's being lost."

Alexa took a deep breath, relieved her heart rate was no longer in the red zone. "Do you think there's a connection between Harlan Quinn's death and the Curs, Constable Cooper?"

"You can call me Coop."

Alexa was honored.

"The pack probably has the weapons, but I don't think they killed him."

Alexa looked out the window, quiet, until they passed through the sleepy town of Clifton. Then she filled "Coop" in on all she knew about Katrina Flores. "She's uptight about privacy. She refused to give any info about who ordered the picnic basket. Then there's a server, Blair. She said Ms. Flores delivers the picnic baskets."

They turned onto the serpentine lane that led to The Retreat and Black Reef. "The first time I drove this road—on Thursday—a fancy ATV forced me into a ditch. The server said Ms. Flores likes driving them."

"Might have been her, but Mr. Quinn was dead by then."

"I lifted a fingerprint from the picnic basket. I'll mention that. See how she reacts." Alexa peered into the dark, remembering how DI Steele had shared her personal problems as they drove this same stretch earlier in the day. She thought of her nephews Benny and Noah. She'd do anything to protect them. Would the DI be back on the case in the morning, another kid episode done and dusted?

Coop parked next to the inn steps. Golden light from the windows and double front doors bathed the wide porch. The valet hustled toward them but stopped a few feet shy of Coop's door.

She stepped out. "I'll leave the car here."

The valet gave the Škoda Superb a once-over and nodded. Alexa shouldered her crime kit and followed Coop into the lobby. The clink of glassware and animated conversation carried from the dining room, as did enticing aromas.

Katrina Flores glided toward them. She had changed from the silk blouse and green skirt to a clingy knit dress. Her coppery hair was gathered into some complicated updo—a little less tame than the bun she'd worn earlier. Her green eyes skimmed Constable Cooper's face and uniform and landed on Alexa. "You're back. What can I do for you?"

"DI Steele sent us for the information she requested, and we have a few more questions."

"I can't answer them now." She gestured to the dining room. "We're busy."

Constable Cooper showed her badge. "Make the time, please."

Alexa heard a familiar voice and craned her head past the vase of orange poppies for a view of the bar. Amit Gupta leaned against it, talking loudly to the bartender. He had struck her as reserved, and she wondered if he'd had too much to drink.

A middle-aged couple entered the lobby. Their smiles faded at the sight of Constable Cooper. Ms. Flores excused herself and greeted them, giving a mouth-watering description of the menu and summoning a server. Then she beckoned Alexa and Coop to follow her down the hallway and into her office. She stood in front of her desk. "How can I help you?"

"Is Mr. Gupta staying here?" Alexa asked.

She shook her head slightly. "I told your boss our guests have a right to privacy."

Alexa let the "boss" comment slide. "This is a suspicious death investigation. Is he a guest?"

"Suspicious death? Why is Mr. Quinn's death suspicious? Wasn't it a heart attack?"

"There have been updates. It's very important that you help us. Is Mr. Gupta a guest at The Retreat?"

She nodded. "He's staying in the Harmony suite."

Coop wasn't speaking, so Alexa forged ahead. "DI Steele asked that you find out who delivered the picnic basket to Black Reef. The menu refers to it as a Romantic Picnic for Two."

Ms. Flores studied her shoes: tiny high heels with straps that made Alexa's feet ache.

"Have you found out who delivered it?" Alexa repeated.

"I haven't had time."

Maybe being on a first-name basis with the manager might melt her reserve. "May I call you Katrina?"

Ms. Flores met her eyes and shrugged.

"A source told us it was you who delivered the basket, Katrina. Is that true?"

She stiffened. "Who told you that?"

Alexa knew to shield Blair. "Did you know Mr. Quinn was married?"

"I don't ask our guests about their private lives."

"Mr. Quinn also had a mistress. You met Lynn Lockhart. He set her up with a cottage."

Katrina's chin quivered.

Alexa glanced at Coop to see if she noticed. Her face was unrevealing. "We believe Mr. Quinn was seeing someone else, besides Ms. Lockhart." She paused. Katrina studied her shoes again, her face flushed. "Earlier when I was here, you referred to Mr. Quinn as 'Harlan.' That's a little familiar for a manager/guest relationship." In for a penny, in for a New Zealand dollar. Alexa plunged ahead. "Were you in a relationship with him?"

Katrina walked behind her desk and gripped the back of the chair. "That would be unprofessional. Mr. V would fire me. I need this job."

Coop finally spoke. "Ms. Glock here is a forensic expert. She lifted prints from the picnic basket handle. She'd like to take your fingerprints."

Alexa raised her kit. "It was a good print. There's sufficient detail to make a comparison."

Katrina pulled the chair out and sat heavily. "I didn't mean for it to happen." Her eyes were fearful. "How did he die?"

Constable Cooper pulled a chair close to Katrina and sat. She took out her notebook and pen. "Cause of death is pending," she said. "How did your relationship with Mr. Quinn start?"

Katrina swallowed. "This January, around the New Year. Mr. Quinn invited me in when I delivered some food. He said he needed a chess partner."

"Did he invite you into the big house or bunker?" Coop asked.

"The big house. It was between meals, so I had time." Katrina found a pen on her desk and clicked it repeatedly. "I'm a decent player. My father taught me."

"I play too," Coop said. "Whatever move you make, the consequences are difficult to determine."

Katrina nodded. "The second time he invited me in, we had wine while we played. We met all that week." A lock of her coppery hair escaped its binds and she twirled it contemplatively. "I got caught up in his charisma."

Alexa felt anger at Harlan Quinn for luring Katrina into his den.

"What about Lynn Lockhart?" Coop asked. "Didn't she catch on?"

"I only saw him in the afternoons. Ms. Lockhart was too busy buying more art, more clothes, more stuff, to notice. He had dinner with her every night."

What a double-crossing double-crosser, Alexa thought.

"You were okay with all that?" Constable Cooper asked.

"I sound horrible, even to myself. I didn't know what I was doing, and then all of sudden there was excitement in my life. He texted me and said he was coming early this time, before Ms.

Lockhart expected him. To see me. He thought we should meet in the bunker so the housekeeper wouldn't get nosy."

Coop took notes. "How many times did you meet in the bunker?"

"Only once. Last Saturday, when I delivered the picnic basket. We shared it. He was supposed to text me Sunday, but never did. Or the day after." She rubbed under her eyes. "I thought he didn't want to see me again. Or that he'd left. Maybe he had an emergency. When I heard the siren on Thursday, I drove over to see what was going on. I saw the hearse and knew it was something terrible."

"You drove me off the road," Alexa said.

Katrina looked at her blankly.

"I need your phone," Coop said.

She wiped her eyes, smearing her mascara. "Am I under arrest?"

"No."

"Do I have to give you my phone?"

Coop didn't hesitate. "You have the right to refuse."

"I refuse," Katrina said in a small voice.

"Come to the station at nine a.m. to make a statement," Coop said. "Bring the phone. Ms. Glock will take your fingerprints now."

Katrina jerked. "I need to contact a solicitor before I consent."

Coop closed her notepad. "He or she can come with you in the morning."

"Here's my card," Alexa said, sliding it across the desk. "Call if you think of anything that might help us find out what happened to him."

Chapter Thirty

Coop dodged two press vans in the police station lot and dropped Alexa off by the Vitz. "I'll report to DI Horne. Give him the lowdown."

"Okay," Alexa said. She wondered whether Constable Cooper knew she was dating Bruce. Staying with him, too. He had texted her to say he'd be late.

Her clean clothes hung in her room at the Apple Motor Lodge. Bruce's suitcase on the luggage rack made her smile. She kicked her Keds into a corner and shed her dirty clothes item by item on the way to the shower. She mulled over the case until the water turned cold. She bet on one of Quinn's jilted women. But when she thought about the weapons and the gang, she felt uncertain. *Concentrate on the science,* she told herself. Science is always true. Her job was to interpret it correctly.

As she dried her hair, a hint of auburn made her think of her mother. She wiped the foggy mirror and mouthed, "Ellen."

Every once in a while she said her mother's name out loud, to pay homage. She fetched one of the few memories she had: Mom taking her back-to-school shoe shopping when she was entering first grade. Just the two of them, no Dad or Charlie.

Blue Keds. Alexa had picked out blue Keds, and her mother said they were perfect.

Before her first grade year was complete, Mom died of a brain tumor. A glioblastoma. Blasted their little family apart. Harlan Quinn's fierce little daughter's world had been blasted apart, too.

As she pulled her sleep shirt on, she pondered the trajectory of her life. Had a well-adjusted Alexa died along with Mom? She'd researched the impact of losing a parent at a young age. Outcomes included depression, anxiety, and poor appetite.

None applied.

The one she hadn't escaped was trouble forming relationships. She was almost thirty-eight and had no husband. No kid. No pet. No friends to speak of. She severed ties without looking back.

She was terrified she'd do the same to Bruce. Mess things up. Hurt him. She uncapped his aftershave and let the woodsy scent calm her down. She could change. She left the bathroom and flopped onto the bed, running her hand across Bruce's pillow, and then reaching for her book. She liked romances because they were predictable. They ended happily. They made her think of Bruce. Her phone woke her an hour later. She checked the screen: Unknown Caller. A knock at the door made her drop it.

"Alexa? It's me."

She left the phone between the bed and nightstand and opened the door. Bruce held up a bag in one hand and two beers in the other. Still they managed to kiss.

The salty scent of fried fish made her taste buds dance as if they had been deprived. She and Bruce ate at the little table, knee to knee. Between bites of blue cod and sips of Speight's, Bruce said, "I've taken another room. Down the street at the Fairmont."

Her heart sank. "Why?"

"I'm taking over the case. Mic won't be back." He wiped his mouth, leaned across the table, and kissed her salty lips. "I'm your boss now."

Not technically, she thought, but she knew what he meant. It wouldn't be proper to shack up with the active DI. Still, she was sad. "Why won't DI Steele be coming back?"

His eyes, sapphire in the dim light, were serious. "It's confidential."

She was about to argue, but tacked in a different direction. "Why didn't you mention Constable Cooper was joining the case?"

"Did I not? Most likely because you distract me." His knee nudged her into forgiveness. "She's an asset. Her *whānau* extends into this area."

"We had an encounter with some gang members and she stood up to them. She was so brave." Alexa told him what happened. "After the guy with the tatted fangs left our table, the others barked. Coop, I mean Constable Cooper, made sure a table of teenagers left safely."

Bruce nodded. "Doesn't surprise me."

"Did she fill you in on what we learned about Katrina Flores?"

He wiped his fingers with a napkin and cleaned up the table. "She did. I look forward to interviewing Ms. Flores in the morning. I find it interesting that she admitted an affair but wouldn't consent to be fingerprinted."

"First Quinn cheated on his wife. Then he cheated on his girlfriend. What a sleaze."

Bruce's eyes darkened. "In our last case together, you cautioned the team against demeaning the victim."

A doctor had been killed, and Alexa hadn't like the way the team had made comments about her sex life. "She wasn't married," Alexa pointed out. "Why get married if you're going to cheat?" When he didn't respond, Alexa said, "Amit Gupta is staying at The Retreat. I saw him in the bar tonight."

"I've talked with Chief Petrie in San Jose. He's digging into both Quinn and Gupta's histories. We know they cofounded Q&G Biologics. They worked together three years, mostly conducting drug trials. Quinn left to start another company, BioMatic. He took along several employees."

"Gupta probably didn't like that. Maybe he came here to exact revenge."

Bruce laughed, surprising her. "Sometimes I forget you're a CSI and not a police officer. Your instincts are helpful. I think I'll swear you in."

Alexa preened. "I've been writing a paper on how crime scene investigators should be incorporated into the criminal justice…"

Bruce leaned over to kiss her quiet. "You know what's happening between us, don't you?"

Alexa stilled.

He saw her face and backed off. "Early start tomorrow. Lock the door behind me."

She did, and then fished for her phone and checked her messages. Katrina Flores had left a voicemail: *"I've remembered something important. Call me."*

There was no answer when Alexa called back.

MONDAY

Chapter Thirty-One

Alexa wanted to review her lab findings before the team meeting, so she drove into the station parking lot early. As she got out of the Vitz, she spotted DI Steele ushering Joe toward the entrance. What were they doing here? Alexa hustled to catch up, but a reporter blocked her way.

"Detective Inspector Steele, what's the latest on the bunker body? Is it true Harlan Quinn was murdered?"

DI Steele didn't alter course. Joe, head down, stuffed his hands into his pockets.

"What about the weapons?" the reporter called out.

"Christ," DI Steele said. She pushed Joe through the doors and had disappeared by the time Alexa passed through security, the reporter's question about weapons ringing in her ears. Maybe Scraggly Beard had let the cat out of the bag. However it happened, the news was loose.

Her phone rang as she entered the lab. Maybe it was Katrina. She dropped the crime kit and fished her phone from her tote, careful not to spill the take-out coffee she'd picked up. "Hello?"

"This is Dr. Li. I have results for you regarding Mr. Quinn."

"Great," Alexa said.

"There are three ways to measure CO postmortem," Dr. Li said with no preamble. "I went with the quickest: automated spectrophotometry. There was a slight problem since the sample wasn't fresh. I told the technician to filter it with a reducing agent to remove debris."

Alexa wanted Dr. Li as a BFF.

"Carbon monoxide reduces oxygen supply and becomes severe at numbers thirty percent or higher."

Alexa remembered the headache she'd had in the bunker.

"Fatality generally occurs at fifty percent or higher." The pathologist paused. "Mr. Quinn's was seventy-one percent. Cause of death is carbon monoxide poisoning."

Her pink tooth suspicion was right. Alexa couldn't wait to study the phenomenon more closely, maybe write a paper. "Thank you, Dr. Li."

She would make the announcement at the team meeting. She heard footsteps in the hall and figured it was Pamela. Instead, Bruce and DI Steele stepped into the lab.

"Can we interrupt?" Bruce said.

Alexa nodded; she was confused again at seeing DI Steele. And where was Joe?

Bruce handed her a tenprint—a complete set of fingerprints on a single sheet. "We need you to compare these to the one you took from that fingertip left in the bunker."

"Now?"

Bruce nodded.

Alexa glanced at DI Steele, who averted her gaze. She scanned the new prints onto the computer and focused on the left ring finger. She suspected the finger nub was left ring as well. She adjusted for better contrast and found a right slope loop with a clear core. She zoomed in and used the computer pencil tool to mark an upward ridge and then a bifurcation. It faced upward and was followed by a downward bifurcation. She methodically counted features, barely aware of Bruce and DI Steele hovering close by.

Satisfied, she brought up the fingertip print, which she had scanned yesterday. Now the two prints were side-by-side. Did they match? She took a deep breath, aware her analysis was subjective. Match or no match, she would have Pamela or another examiner verify her findings.

The first thing she noticed on the comparison print was a right slope loop with a clear core. She realized she was holding her breath. She let it go as she marked ridges and bifurcations, and then compared them to the first print. She felt like there were enough matching features. She looked up.

"I believe they are made by the same finger."

"Bloody hell," DI Steele said.

"Another examiner will need to verify," Alexa said.

Bruce made sure the lab door was closed and said, "Mic, how old is your lad?"

"Joe is only fifteen," she said. "I had no idea he had left the house."

Alexa looked at the two prints. Jeez. The fingertip belonged to the kid. He'd been in the bunker. But the set Bruce had given her included clean prints of ten fingers—no lopped-off tip. "Where did you get the comparison set?" she asked.

DI Steele scoffed. "I had the police education officer finger-print Joe and Adam when they came to live with us. As a safety precaution. We were worried the lads' father might abduct them. I keep the prints at home." Her eyes got bigger. "Now I've implicated my own sister's boy."

"We'll have to hold him," Bruce said gently. "You know that, right? I'll get someone from Youth Court to sit with him during the interviews." He paused. "You'll want to contact a solicitor."

DI Steele sank into a desk chair and pulled out her phone. "I need to call Kersten."

Bruce stepped toward her. "Is there a chance the weapons are at your house? In Joe's room? Do you have a garage?"

"Joe wouldn't bring weapons to our house. Not with Adam around."

Alexa hung her head. That poor younger brother, as if he hadn't experienced a lifetime of loss already. His mother. His father. Now he might lose his brother.

"It will look better to a judge if Joe tells us where the weapons are," Bruce said.

DI Steele looked at her phone screen; it was a picture of Joe and Adam, arms around each other. "I don't know why he was out there, in the bunker."

Alexa suspected she did know. DI Steele had said she thought Joe was being recruited by the Curs. The bunker could have been an initiation challenge.

DI Steele started tapping on her phone.

Bruce held up a hand. "Hold off calling Kersten until we send someone out there to search the premises."

DI Steele dropped the phone to her lap. "So you don't trust me now?"

Chapter Thirty-Two

The knowledge of Joe's participation in the burglary sat like a rock in Alexa's stomach. *Don't some birds swallow rocks to grind their food?* She wondered how Sergeant Atkins and Constable Gavin, their heads together looking through a stack of papers, would react to the news. Coop met her eyes. Alexa figured she knew something was up. Ten minutes later, Superintendent Parker and Bruce entered.

"Sorry for the delay," Bruce said. "There's been a development."

"Is DI Steele coming back?" Sergeant Atkins asked. "I saw her earlier."

Bruce looked at Superintendent Parker. She gestured with her hand. "All yours."

Here it comes, Alexa thought.

"We've learned DI Steele's nephew is involved in the break-in at the bunker," Bruce said. "She's off the case permanently."

Constable Gavin's mouth dropped open.

"Senior's boy?" Sergeant Atkins said. "He's but a kid."

"He's old enough to be charged with a serious crime." Superintendent Parker's face was rigid. "No one. Says anything. To the press."

"But what happened?" Constable Gavin asked. "How do you know?"

Bruce nodded to Alexa.

"Fingerprints," she explained. "The DI's nephew left a print in the bunker." Nubby and bloody.

"Was Joe alone?" Constable Gavin asked.

"I lifted a couple partial prints," Alexa said. "They're inadmissible as evidence but indicate Joe wasn't alone."

"Detective Inspector Horne is now in charge," Superintendent Parker said. "Is this clear?"

Constable Gavin frowned. "Does Joe have the weapons?"

"The weapons are still missing," Bruce said. "The Organized Crime Unit is on their way to search DI Steele's house, with her permission."

"So that's why Festinger ran out of here," Sergeant Atkins said.

"OCU Festinger is leading the search," Bruce said.

"God forbid assault weapons are found at the DI's crib." The superintendent glared at the officers. "If this leaks, there will be a media scrum. We'll look bad all over the globe. Our public's trust will be nil."

Alexa expected steam to spout from her ears.

"There will be no leaks from this room," Bruce assured her. "DI Steele has declared a conflict of interest."

"To say the least." The super turned to leave.

Alexa half-rose. "I've just learned Quinn's cause of death is carbon monoxide poisoning."

"Remind me to never set foot in a bunker," the super said. Even the clack of her heels sounded angry as she left.

Bruce looked from Constable Gavin to Sergeant Atkins. "DI Steele is following all procedures."

Constable Gavin shook his head. "Super will can her."

"DI Horne said she's cooperating," Sergeant Atkins said. "It's not her fault Joe is a muppet."

"She's hardly been right, ever since Joe," Constable Gavin said.

"Not true." Sergeant Atkins's voice was as spiky as her hair.

Bruce wrote COD: CO poisoning next to Quinn's photo on the

whiteboard and kept his back turned. Alexa suspected he was giving DI Steele's officers time to assimilate the news.

"Yeah nah. What about when she left in the middle of that hit-and-run because the school called her?" Constable Gavin said. "Did a runner herself."

"I took care of it," Sergeant Atkins said. "Didn't need a DI to take witness reports, did I?"

"And bringing the kid to Black Reef. That's probably when he cased the bunker."

Was it? Alexa wondered. Had it been Joe who turned off the lights, leaving her, terrified, in the dark?

Bruce turned and hung his blazer on a chair. A whiff of his woodsy aftershave distracted her; there was a reason office romances were detrimental to productivity. He cleared his throat. "I'm in charge now. Everyone clear on that?"

Alexa nodded, as did the three others.

"Here is how I look at a murder case." His blue eyes roamed the room. "A murder investigation is a road trip. DI Steele drove the first leg, now I'm taking the wheel. A direct route is quickest. There's a problem, though. We don't have Navman, right?"

Alexa's car didn't have GPS. She could relate.

"If we work smart, if we keep each other informed—that's key—if we pay attention to detail, we'll encounter fewer wrong turns, judder bars, dead ends. Are you with me?"

The road trip metaphor worked for Alexa. Except judder bars. That sounded like a honky-tonk.

Bruce uncapped a marker and circled CURS on the suspect list. "The big funeral is today."

"A *tangihanga*," Constable Cooper said.

"Thank you. The *tangihanga* is today. OCU Festinger has two plainclothes working the field. I doubt a full-fledged gang member would let a kid take possession of those weapons. Steal them, yes, but store them?"

"They won't find anything at Senior's house," Sergeant Atkins said.

"The undercovers will ask around." He tapped the list of suspects. "Yesterday I asked for alibi verifications. Anything to report?"

Sergeant Atkins stood. "I have an update on Audrey Quinn and her yoga retreat. I spoke with the manager of Portola Valley Spa." The sergeant pulled out her phone and read from the screen. "Her name is Elantra Lorde."

Figures, Alexa thought.

"Ms. Lorde confirmed that Mrs. Quinn checked in on April first and departed April fifth. She said…hold on…'Mrs. Quinn left with rejuvenation in body and clarification in spirit.'"

"Ommm," Constable Gavin chanted.

Sergeant Atkins rolled her eyes. "I'll verify with two more people."

Constable Gavin stood. "I'm working arrivals. First, Mr. Quinn. Good thing you suggested I look into the private airports, DI Horne. Should have thought of that myself? I've got a statement from Immigration NZ and Customs, real helpful lads. They found record of a Gulfstream G700 owned by Harlan Quinn landing at Hawke's Bay Aerodrome on April first." He patted his cowlick.

"Did Quinn fly himself?" Bruce asked.

"No. He had a pilot and copilot. I tracked the pilot down in Auckland. Gary Fitch. He said—get this, eh?—a lady with ginger hair picked Quinn up from the aerodrome."

Alexa met Coop's eyes. Katrina Flores had ginger hair.

Bruce added the info to the board.

"I'm not done, sir? There's Ms. Lockhart's transportation trail? I called Luxury Helicopter Taxi in Auck. They spouted privacy this, privacy that, but once they heard it was about the bunker body? They confirmed her flight on Friday, April eighth, arrival time at Black Reef one forty p.m." He bowed his head and sat.

Alexa remembered Lynn's dramatic entrance, her hair flying as her "taxi" departed.

Bruce underlined Lynn Lockhart. "Where was she April second through April fourth? It's only a four-hour drive between here and Auckland."

"On it, sir," Constable Gavin said.

Bruce pointed to Katrina Flores's name. "Constable Cooper and Ms. Glock spoke with The Retreat's manager, Ms. Flores. She admitted she was seeing Quinn."

Constable Gavin whooped. "How many girlfriends did the bloke have?"

"That's motive for murder, all these women gaga over the billionaire," the sergeant said.

"She wouldn't consent to be fingerprinted," Coop said. "She's arriving at nine a.m. to make a statement. She might have a solicitor with her."

Alexa checked the time: Katrina was due in five minutes.

"I'll meet with her," Bruce said. "Ms. Glock, you'll come with me. Maybe she'll consent to fingerprints now."

Alexa nodded. "Ms. Flores left me a message on my phone last night." She avoided Bruce's eyes. "When I called back, she didn't answer." She didn't mention an hour—spent with Bruce—passed before she returned the call.

"What did it say?" Constable Gavin asked.

Alexa grappled with her phone and played the message on speaker: *"I've remembered something important. Call me."*

Chapter Thirty-Three

Bruce paced in the police station lobby. "You have Ms. Flores's number. Call."

Alexa set down her kit and dug out her phone. The call went to voicemail. "This is Alexa Glock, the forensic investigator. We expected you at the station thirty minutes ago."

Bruce frowned. "That's probably her personal number. What about the business number for The Retreat?" He fiddled with his phone, located the number, and called. When someone answered, he said, "I'd like to speak to the manager, Ms. Flores."

Alexa heard a young woman's voice but not what she said.

"This is Detective Inspector Bruce Horne. It's important that I speak to Ms. Flores."

He listened, cocked an eyebrow at Alexa, and switched his phone to speaker. "When did you see her last?"

"At seven, when I arrived. She was headed out for her morning walk. She goes most mornings."

Alexa recognized Blair's voice.

"There's a guest wanting to check out. Ms. Flores always handles that. It's not like her to not be here."

"Could she have driven somewhere?" Bruce asked.

"I checked. Her car is in the parking lot."

"When she shows up, have her call the Hastings police station."

Two reporters showed their press cards to the desk clerk and then looked their way. Bruce turned his back to them and said, "I don't like the sound of Ms. Flores not returning from her walk. Let's head out there."

Alexa was happy to be recruited to Team Bruce. Professionally and privately.

He drove fast and efficiently until traffic slowed on the ribbon highway outside the city limits. The car ahead of them pulled over and so did the one ahead of it. Alexa heard the deafening roar before she saw a cascade of motorcycles, three abreast, gunning toward them.

Bruce jerked the truck off the road. "It's funeral traffic."

Helmet visors obscured the drivers' faces as they passed in a stream of Cur jackets, black boots, flashes of red, chains, and beards. Most drove one-handed, the other hand pumping a fist. Alexa covered her ears. The vibrations shook her skull.

They kept coming. The stench of burning rubber assaulted her nose. A few cars and trucks were interspersed among the bikes, men hanging out the windows.

Alexa pressed her hands harder to her ears. She'd seen a study that said exposure to noises over 100 decibels caused hearing damage in as little as fifteen minutes. "I don't understand why this is allowed," she shouted. She could tell Bruce couldn't hear her.

Two Hastings Police Department cars, following at a respectful distance, brought up the rear.

Alexa turned to Bruce. "Why didn't the cops do something?"

Bruce released the steering wheel and shook out his fingers. She hadn't noticed how tense he'd been. "That was a Cur strut." He eased the truck back on the road. "We have laws guaranteeing the right to assembly and movement. We can't withdraw them because we don't like a certain group."

Alexa never minded pulling over for a funeral procession back home, but she hadn't been afraid of the mourners. She took a deep breath, held it, and let it go.

Bruce checked the rearview mirror. "The problem is, gangs are growing. We've got new ones coming in from Australia looking to recruit."

Alexa turned around. The traffic had thinned to a few cars. "Who joins them?"

"Who joins gangs in the States?" Bruce countered.

She had been a part of a forensic investigation of a Bloods gang member in Raleigh for cocaine and crack distribution. He'd only been nineteen when he was sentenced to ten years in prison. "Kids mixed up with drugs. Kids who don't have options. Dropouts. Jail recruits."

"Same here. Family connections, too. Mic's nephew, Joe? His father is a Cur."

The kid lost his mother and was recruited by his father. DI Steele and Kersten were up against insurmountable forces. "What will happen to Joe?"

"That's for the courts to decide."

"Do you think there's a connection between Quinn's death and the gang?"

Bruce, tapping the steering wheel, sped up. "Most gang violence is between gangs."

It took miles of pastoral landscape to lull her thoughts from gang activity and back to Katrina. Where was she?

Outside of Clifton a moving cloud of sheep cutting across the road forced them to pull off again. Bruce cut the engine. "I never begrudge a sheep crossing."

"It bleats stopping for gangs." Alexa laughed out loud at her pun, but she knew her laugh was more a release of stress. All those rich CEOs scarfing up land in New Zealand because they thought it was a beacon of safety. It wasn't. Nowhere was safe. "We don't have sheep crossings back home."

Bruce leaned forward and searched the sky. "Some herders are using drone pups."

"What are drone pups?"

"Drones that herd sheep. They even make barking sounds."

Alexa searched the cloudy sky for a flying robot. Crimes involving drones were increasing. On the flip side, forensic investigators used drones to combat crime. She imagined two drones in an aerial standoff.

Bruce shifted his torso and studied her with his Carolina blue eyes. For a moment Alexa thought he was going to kiss her, muddying the boundaries between work and romance. But he didn't.

"What's Raleigh like?" he asked.

She looked back at the sheep. They all vied for the middle of the moving huddle. People were similar: the human brain evolved to seek safety in numbers. But there always seemed to be one sheep on the outskirts. Alexa located the loner, feeling a kinship. She rolled down her window and breathed in the scent of damp wool sweaters. "The SBI, where I worked, is headquartered there, and NC State has a first-rate forensics science institute. Chapel Hill, one town over, has a great dental school. It's where I did my master's in odontology…"

Bruce's laugh cut her off. "But where did you live? Who did you spend time with?"

The last sheep cast a baleful eye at Alexa. Bruce took off with a jerk before she answered.

Blair stood on the porch of The Retreat. She studied them as they pulled into the circle.

"She's the person you talked to on the phone," Alexa said.

A young man drove a golf cart into the circle. He waved to Blair and entered the inn. Alexa recognized him as the valet who had driven off in her Vitz Friday night when she had dined with Lynn Lockhart. She and Bruce skirted the cart and climbed the steps.

"Good morning," Bruce said, showing his ID. "I'm DI Horne. We spoke on the phone. Has the manager returned?"

Blair scrunched her nose. "No. She's been gone over three hours. This isn't like her."

Uneasiness swarmed around Alexa like a cloud of gnats. She

stepped aside to make room for a man and woman leaving the inn. They walked down the steps and slid into the golf cart. The valet followed them with two golf bags swung over his shoulders and loaded them in the cart.

"When will we see the ocean?" the woman asked.

"Between holes four and five," the valet said. "Mind now, hole four is a blind tee."

The couple waved and zipped off.

Missing woman, carefree golf outing. The juxtaposition jarred Alexa.

"Have you seen Ms. Flores, Trippy?" Blair asked the valet.

"I haven't seen her today." He folded his arms across his chest and studied Bruce and Alexa. "What's this about?"

"She hasn't come back from her walk," Blair said. "These are the police."

The valet's eyes got big.

"Who's in charge in her absence?" Bruce asked.

"Chef is. He's in a tither. He's threatening to call the owner."

"Is there a chance she's inside the inn?" Bruce asked.

"I've checked everywhere but the six guest suites."

Bruce looked to the parking area. "Where is her car?"

Blair pointed to a white Mazda compact.

"What about your Can-Ams?" Alexa asked. "Could she be riding around in one?"

"They're all accounted for," the valet said. "Same with the carts. I can take one out and look for her."

Bruce seemed to consider the situation. "I need a map and one of those Can-Ams."

"All good," the valet said. "I've trail maps. Come with me."

Bruce asked Blair to search the guest rooms. He handed her a card. "Call if you find her. Can you describe what she was wearing?"

"A pink jacket," Blair said.

Bruce stopped by the Mazda and looked through each window.

He must not have seen anything amiss because he quickly rejoined the valet. "What's your name?" he asked.

"Kyle Tripp. I handle rental and valet services."

Alexa tagged behind as they passed through the parking area and entered the shadowy woods. A cream-colored building with a corrugated metal roof, stable-like, housed the rental office. Tripp pointed at the two wings flanking the building. To the right were golf carts. To the left, four Can-Ams peeked out of their stalls. Alexa wondered which one had run her into the ditch. "That's the fleet," Tripp said proudly. He led them inside and handed them each a map.

The blurb across the top read: ENJOY 250 HECTARES OF ROLLING HILLS, RUGGED CLIFFS, AND OUR 18-HOLE PREMIER GOLF COURSE. VAST SEA VIEWS AND GLIMPSES OF THE GANNET COLONIES WILL INSPIRE YOU. The legend color-coded the grounds into CLIFFSIDE TRACK, GOLF COURSE, and CAN-AM TRAILS.

Alexa studied it, noticing how the grounds bordered the Black Reef property.

"You can take the Can-Ams everywhere but along the cliffs," Tripp said. "They're too fragile. And the cart-path-only on the golf course, eh?"

Bruce called the officer assigned to guard the bunker at Black Reef and apprised him of the situation. "I need you here."

"I can jog along the cliff path," Alexa offered.

Bruce nodded. "You do that. When Constable Dobbs gets here, he can take the golf course." He turned to the valet. "You and I can take the trails."

She patted her pocket to make sure she had her phone, and in ten minutes she faced the moody gray sea. She scanned the trail in both directions and didn't see a human form. The golf course preened in a palette of forest to mint to green-eyed envy.

Why had she thought of envy? Didn't envy kindle hostility, deprivation, inferiority? Who had been envious of Harlan Quinn?

A golf cart crested a dune. Alexa swatted a fly and squinted to spot a pink jacket. No luck. Maybe it was that couple Blair had spoken to. The waves crashed below. She got as close as she could make herself and looked down. Maybe twelve meters to the beach, with ledges and outcroppings. There was no sign of Katrina. What had her message meant: *I've remembered something important*? Guilt rode like a jockey on Alexa's back. She turned toward Black Reef and began a slow jog. It was then she remembered Lynn Lockhart liked to walk along the cliffs as well. Had she and Katrina met? Maybe they were having a discussion at the cottage.

The track curved in. She ran across a footbridge but then backtracked and looked down the narrow ravine it spanned. Nothing pink caught her eye. When she and Charlie had hiked the Milford Track, it had been Charlie who spotted the body of a missing hiker. No way that could happen twice in one family.

She felt every pebble through the soles of her Keds. She felt exposed and thought enviously of the sheep herd, glued together in safety, protected from predators.

White gulls circled above, calling raucously. A gannet hovered over them. She dodged a spot that crumbled into the sea, but then forced herself to backtrack, thinking the path might have caved under Katrina's feet. Looking down made her dizzy. She caught a glimpse of something red, slow moving. She laughed. The tractor tour was chugging back from the Cape Kidnappers colony.

Ahead, the Norfolk pine stood sentinel. She wondered if the webcam was still recording. The rankness of the gannetry carried in the wind. *Something foul this way comes*, Alexa thought. The big house perched along the cliff like a behemoth.

She checked her phone. It had taken twenty minutes to get here. She'd pop in on Lynn Lockhart and see if she'd seen Katrina. Before veering off, she checked over the side again. Five feet below was a ledge, and below it—on the next ledge—a gannet chick, speckled and homely, opened its beak and krokked. Below it: more ledges, more chicks, a sprinkling of adults.

Pink caught her eye.

She hopped back instinctively, but then looked again.

A person wearing a pink jacket and black leggings lay sprawled on the beach. A seagull had landed on the jacket. When it hopped toward the face, Alexa screamed.

Chapter Thirty-Four

She called Bruce. It rang and rang. "Dammit. Answer!"

It went to voicemail. Alexa screamed, "Katrina fell from the cliff. At Black Reef. She might be alive."

Then she pressed 111 and shouted the same information. "Send an ambulance."

She stuffed the phone in her pocket and scanned the body for movement. The bird lady had said scaling the cliff wasn't hard. She sat on her butt, scooched forward, and hung her legs over, praying the edge wouldn't collapse. She stretched until her toe hit the topmost shelf and lowered herself.

The next ledge was harder to reach and full of chicks. They squabbled and shrieked and flapped their wings, but shuffled over to make room as if she were a giant bird come to roost. Her left hand landed in a fresh pile of guano. She wiped it on her khakis.

Katrina had called last night, and she had ignored her to be with Bruce.

This time she faced the rock and lowered herself down. There. Terra firma. She stood in a nest of dried seaweed, guano, and fish bones. The odor was akin to smelling salts, which utilized ammonia to stimulate the membranes of the nostrils. She wiped sweat from her brow and tried not to gag. Her heart tried to escape the confines of her rib cage as she shuffled over for a better perch. The beach looked farther away than when she started. She lowered herself down to the next shelf. Three large chicks trilled and krokked.

They didn't seem afraid.

She risked another look, horrified to spy two gulls circling above Katrina. Her heart raced as if she were sprinting. She wiped her palms on her pants, crouched, and crabbed right. She stretched down one leg, then the other, and lowered herself. One Ked landed in something slippery.

A chick popped its head over a ledge above her to watch. An adult swooped by so close she could see its blue-rimmed eyes.

Her descent was taking forever. She peered over the edge again, knocking a pebble off. It bounced on a gannet who exploded in wide white wings. She recoiled and pressed against cold rock. More sweat popped out on her forehead. Was she having a panic attack?

Krok, krok, krok. Arr. Arr. Clack.

The gannet chicks couldn't fly. They were trapped like she was.

Katrina needed her. She waited a full minute, and then another, until she could fill her lungs, then faced the cliff and started lowering herself. Her hand slipped. She crashed to the next outcrop, taking the impact on her left knee, and thrust herself forward onto her chest.

Chicks krokked and whirred.

Her phone buzzed.

She hauled herself up and over, facing the sea. Her hands cramped; she couldn't answer the phone. It buzzed and buzzed. Two nearby chicks looked alarmed at the sound. She pushed against the rock wall and dug her fingers into terra damn firma. Time was slipping away.

I can do this.

She searched for the next shelf; it was too far down. She was stuck. Like a boa constrictor, panic squeezed her chest. Sudden noise drew her eyes up. An enormous yellow bird appeared from over the cliff, its blades cutting the air in chops, whipping her hair in a frenzy. She pressed against solid rock and felt the constriction of her lungs ease. The cavalry was here to rescue Katrina.

She craned forward and watched the rescue helicopter land on the strip of beach. Two people in orange jumpsuits climbed out with a rescue stretcher and ran to Katrina.

Please be alive, she thought. She dug her nails into grit and guano as the rescue team loaded Katrina into the belly of the bird and lifted. She squeezed her eyes tight against the downdraft and kept them closed, first in thanks, and then to visualize her climb back up. If she got down, she could get back up, right? Something jabbed her hand. Twice. Her eyes flew open. A damn seagull, topaz eyes rimmed with red, had pecked her.

She jerked her hand back.

The gull burst into flight, screaming. She lifted her hand and studied two jewels of crimson.

"Alexa!"

Was that Bruce?

"Coming down," another voice called.

A man in an orange jumpsuit rappelled to her ledge, kicking stones over the side. Alexa stood up, legs shaky. The four chicks on the ledge flapped their wings and shuffled sideways.

"I'm Graham," the man said. "Stay where you are."

Alexa winced; her left knee hurt. She tested it, glad it could bear her weight.

Graham wore a helmet and harness contraption. He jingled with excess equipment and tugged a rope. "Off belay," he called to the sky.

"Is she okay?" Bruce called.

"I'm okay," she yelled.

"Looks to me like you've had a wee panic attack," Graham said. He glanced at the rocks and water below. "You did right to sit it out. What's your name?"

"I didn't have a panic attack. I was just figuring out my next move."

He smiled kindly, but looked unconvinced.

"I'm Alexa Glock. Like the gun. I was trying to help Katrina. The woman who fell. Is she alive?"

Graham looked toward the sky. "I don't know. They've medevaced her to hospital. My job is to help you."

"Thanks, but I don't need help."

She let Graham have his way, just to be safe, and when he deemed she was properly harnessed, she climbed up.

Bruce was waiting. He hugged her so tight that their heartbeats synchronized.

Chapter Thirty-Five

He lit into her on the way to the hospital. "Why would you risk your life to climb down that cliff?"

Alexa's stomach churned. "She might be alive, right? I could have stanched her bleeding or immobilized her spine until help came. What if the tide came in?"

He turned; his eyes ablaze. "Were you going to stop the tide?"

She looked down at her khakis. One knee was torn and the left thigh was smeared with guano. "I called. You didn't answer."

He ignored her last comment. "You could have died."

"Wouldn't you have done the same?" She sipped the last of the water that guy Graham had given her.

Bruce cleared his throat. "I put you in danger, letting you search along the sea track. You're not a trained police officer. It's just that"—he took a breath—"sometimes you act before thinking."

Action is better than standing there doing nothing, she thought. She turned to the window, watching the blur of fields and a far-off hump of mountain.

"As soon as you called, I radioed for an air ambulance." He accelerated on a straightaway, thrusting her into the seat back. His radio cackled.

"Senior?"

Alexa recognized Sergeant Atkins's voice.

"What?" Bruce said.

"Hospital called. Ms. Flores was DOA."

Bruce slowed down. They were silent the rest of the drive.

Dr. Li was examining Katrina's body when Bruce and Alexa entered the autopsy suite. She nodded to Alexa through her Plexiglas visor and looked at Bruce. "Why are *you* here?"

One of his eyebrows rose. "I'm Detective Inspector Horne, Auckland PD."

"I know who you are. We met at that three-day biological evidence seminar last year. I was with my colleague Dr. Rachel Hill."

That name rang a bell, but Alexa couldn't place it.

"I'm here because I've taken DI Steele's place as head investigator of Operation Bunker." He looked at the body. "Ms. Flores was a part of the investigation."

Katrina Flores had gotten tangled in Harlan Quinn's net and now she was dead. Alexa stepped closer to the body, tuning out Bruce and Dr. Li's terse reunion. The right side of Katrina's face was bashed in, but the left cheek—where bone peeked through raw strands of flesh—disturbed her more. The seagull she'd witnessed hopping toward the face had begun scavenging.

She breathed deeply until she felt okay.

Ms. Flores's right shoulder and arm bore abrasions and cuts. Alexa imagined them glancing off rock ledges. She suspected broken bones and internal bleeding lurked below the supple skin.

Dr. Li stepped next to her. "Injuries sustained by falls are due to the absorbed energy at impact."

Alexa's knee throbbed.

"Mortality depends on the height of the fall, of course, but the EMT said the cliff was close to twelve meters."

"Did the fall kill her instantly?" Alexa was glad her voice sounded normal.

"I suspect she died on impact."

Bruce, on the other side of the table, his face grave, gave Alexa a look. She suspected it meant *You'd have died in vain.*

"Can you tell whether she jumped?" he asked.

"The main cause of falls from heights is suicide." Dr. Li kept her eyes on the body. "Accident is next, followed by homicide. Do you suspect suicide?"

"We don't have information or evidence to make that assumption."

"Her injuries alone are not sufficient to assess mode of death," Dr. Li said.

Her tone was flat. *Maybe she was trying to keep her emotions in check,* Alexa thought.

Katrina's splayed hair reminded Alexa of who that Dr. Rachel Hill was. She was a pathologist in Rotorua. Alexa had met her during her first case in New Zealand. Dr. Hill's hair was coppery like Katrina's. She had a lovely Scottish brogue.

Alexa thought of the prints on the duct tape. "I need her fingerprints, and then I'd like to get Ms. Flores's clothes and personal effects to the lab."

"Shouldn't be hard. Rigor is minimum. I've already scraped under her nails."

Alexa got her ink and pad ready. She checked that Katrina's hands and fingers were clean. One by one, she pressed the pliant digits above the knuckles to straighten them out, applied a thin coat of ink at the tip, and rolled them onto the card Dr. Li held.

Bruce watched as she cleaned each fingertip with a wet wipe.

Dr. Li said, "Come with me. I'll get the personal effects for you before I proceed."

Alexa followed Dr. Li to the same lab Dr. Yellin had taken her to. "You did a great job getting Harlan Quinn's fingerprints," Alexa told the pathologist.

Dr. Li raised her visor and smiled modestly, but it didn't reach her eyes. "I wasn't expecting to see that DI in my autopsy suite."

That DI? Alexa was confused. "I've worked several cases with him. DI Horne is a good detective."

Dr. Li unlocked an evidence locker and pointed to two plastic bags. The larger one held Katrina's clothes and shoes. The smaller held a cracked phone, an earbud, and a ring. She filled out the transfer forms and had Alexa sign off. "Maybe he's a good detective, but he's not a good man."

Alexa figured she'd heard wrong.

"I'd watch out if I were you. He slept with my friend and didn't bother to mention he was married."

"Bruce wouldn't do that."

Dr. Li scoffed. "If Rachel said it happened, it happened."

Chapter Thirty-Six

The police station, where her car was parked, was seven blocks from the hospital. Alexa, clutching the evidence bags and the crime kit, walked in what she thought was the right direction, oblivious to the shops, traffic, and pedestrians.

Slept with my friend. Didn't say he was married.

The phrases blared on repeat in her head.

The throaty growl of a motorcycle didn't penetrate her numbness. She stopped at a town square and sank onto a bench. A sign next to the trashcan said, DON'T BE A CHEEKY CHUCKER; DISPOSE OF YOUR RUBBISH PROPERLY. No wonder Bruce was divorced. His wife—that Sharla person—hadn't put up with infidelity like Harlan Quinn's harem had.

Her phone buzzed. She ignored it. It was probably Bruce, wondering where she was. She'd never asked him why he had divorced. She had trusted it was for mutual, mature reasons and not because he was a cheater from one of Sergeant Atkins's country songs.

She'd broken a cardinal rule of policing: never make assumptions.

Bruce was rubbish; she'd dispose of him properly.

She thought of the lab and the evidence she had to process. Science was something she could count on. In her mind she pulled Bruce out of the rubbish and pushed him off a cliff.

A thought broke loose, swam to her brain like a clot. Katrina might have been pushed off the cliff. Maybe by a jealous Lynn Lockhart. She had a temper; Alexa and DI Steele had witnessed her chucking a wineglass over the abyss.

Despite her throbbing knee, Alexa jogged the last blocks to the station and found the electronic crime lab. She gave the officer the phone bag. "It was recovered from Katrina Flores, the woman who fell at Black Reef. It's part of Operation Bunker." Her own recorded message might be on the phone. "I don't know if it still works."

"Heard of a phone that survived a forty-two-story plunge," the officer said.

They filled out the chain of custody transfer and then Alexa hurried to the lab.

She wondered where Pamela-Not-Pam was as she washed her hands. The soapsuds stung. Cuts and scrapes from her rock-climbing speckled her palms. The back of her right hand had two ruby punctures. That seagull had pecked to see if she was dead. The image of the gull hopping toward Katrina's face blossomed in her mind. She shuddered.

After logging in the remaining evidence, she extracted Katrina's prints and scanned them in to the computer. Then she pulled up the prints from the duct tape, adjusted the scale, and compared them.

No match.

Next she compared them to the picnic basket prints.

She detected enough corresponding minutiae to determine that Katrina's fingerprint and the fingerprint from the handle represented the same finger. But Katrina had admitted she'd delivered it, so it wasn't breaking news.

She cleaned up, slipped on gloves, and turned to Katrina's black leggings and the pink jacket. At first she thought the jacket was thin leather, but the label said viscose/poly with poly lining. Faux leather. It was shortish and maybe stylish—Alexa lacked the fashion sense to know—and featured lace-up sides, a narrow collar, and shallow pockets that Alexa double-checked. They were empty. The right elbow and sleeve had tears. The left shoulder had what looked like a smear of blood on it.

If someone had pushed Katrina off the cliff, they might have left a palm print. Palm prints were as unique as fingerprints and common at crime scenes. The FBI even had a palm print registry. But where on the jacket would a palm print be?

Alexa imagined different scenarios: a sneak attack from behind or, if Katrina had known the person, a shove on the front of the jacket.

Lifting prints from fabric was difficult because of fiber distribution, weave patterns, and porosity. But it wasn't impossible. She thought of the forensic gurus at Abertay University in Scotland. Alexa planned to make a pilgrimage there. Maybe sooner rather than later. She might see if any jobs were available and leave New Zealand behind. *Good riddance, Bruce.*

The Scottish team—the ones who figured how to lift fingerprints from bird feathers—discovered how to do the same from fabric. They used vacuum metal deposition. In technician slang, *vacuum metal dep*, and Alexa thought the process was hella cool. They hang the sample—say a work shirt—in a vacuum chamber. Then minuscule gold particles are inserted in the machine and turned to vapor.

She thought of someone she wanted to vaporize.

The gold particles are sprayed into the chamber where they adhere to the ridge-free surface of a fingerprint or palm print. Then the process was repeated with zinc…

"What's up?"

She hadn't even heard Pamela enter. The lab tech's mouth dropped as Alexa filled her in on this morning's events.

"Quinn's girlfriend is dead?"

"The second girlfriend. The one who worked at The Retreat. There's a chance she was pushed," Alexa said. "I was thinking about the possibility of palm prints on her jacket."

Pamela studied the garment. "You'll want the vacuum chamber, then. Do you know VMD develops latent prints better than superglue fuming?"

Alexa beamed. "I know. And it doesn't mess up DNA."

"Not even! In one case, VMD worked on a garbage bag fished out of water."

Alexa looked around the lab. The chambers were extremely expensive. "Do you have one?"

Pamela pointed to a squat machine taking up half a work counter. It was roughly three by two and a half feet with a viewing window. The one at Auckland Service Center sat on the floor and was three times larger. "I didn't know they made a smaller one."

"It's the compact unit. Otherwise, we wouldn't have one, given the price tag."

Alexa rubbed her palms together. Her phone buzzed as Pamela gloved up. She ignored the call. "If I came at you from behind, I'd aim for the middle of your shoulder blades and use both hands. Let's hang it so we can watch the back side."

Pamela hung the jacket from wires in the vacuum chamber as Alexa watched, rapt.

"It's fully automated." She nudged Alexa to the side and pushed a button on the touch screen. The chamber lit up so they could watch the process. "It won't take long. Ten minutes max."

Particle by particle, as the sprayed metal settled, a palm print emerged on the back of the pink jacket.

Chapter Thirty-Seven

Alexa avoided eye contact with Bruce as she rushed into the briefing room bursting with her news. She felt the energy a second death had infused in the gathered team of Bruce, Constables Gavin and Cooper, and Sergeant Atkins.

A photo of Katrina Flores's crushed and maimed face was taped to the whiteboard next to Harlan Quinn's photo. Bruce tapped it. "I just left this woman in the morgue."

Her tote waited on a chair. Alexa had forgotten she had left it in Bruce's truck. She moved it to the floor and sat next to Coop.

"Twenty-nine-year-old manager of The Retreat, found below the cliff of the Black Reef property." He tapped another photo—an aerial view of the estate—and circled a spot along the cliff, behind the big house. "She fell from here. Cause of death is blunt force trauma from a fall. Because of her relationship with Quinn, I am treating her death as suspicious."

"Might be a selfie death?" Constable Gavin said. "People taking pictures of themselves, walking backwards, falling?"

"It's not like she was on vacation," Sergeant Atkins said.

Constable Gavin patted his cowlick. "Don't like to think about some bloke out there on a killing spree."

"Might not be a bloke," Sergeant Atkins said.

Alexa broke in. "Ms. Amick and I just finished examining Ms. Flores's jacket. There's a palm print on the back."

"Palm print?" Sergeant Atkins examined her own with what looked like wonder.

Alexa nodded. "It suggests Ms. Flores was pushed."

"Blimey," Constable Gavin said.

"We checked the automated palm print registry," Alexa said. "There were no matches."

"Well done, Ms. Glock," Bruce said.

His praise was like a magnet. Was it possible she was overreacting to Dr. Li's story? Was it even true? She met his eyes and kept her voice neutral. "I fingerprinted Ms. Flores at the morgue. The prints don't match the ones from the duct tape, but they do match those from the picnic basket handle."

"There's your proof she was in the bunker," Constable Gavin said.

"It indicates Ms. Flores touched the picnic basket. We don't know where she was when she did," Alexa clarified.

"What have you dug up on Ms. Flores?" Bruce asked Sergeant Atkins.

"The owner of The Retreat had her emergency info. Her parents live in Brisbane. She has one sib, a brother, in Christchurch. Thad Flores, he's called. He's gutted. He's on his way, thinks she had an accident." Sergeant Atkins checked her notes. "She was working off debt, sir."

"Debt for what?" Bruce asked.

"Credit card. Student loans. Car. Made loads of mistakes just out of uni, Thad said, but she was fixing things. The housing that came with the job was allowing her to dig out."

Had Katrina hoped Quinn might help her financially? Alexa wondered.

"If Ms. Flores was murdered by the same person who tampered with the duct tape, who are we looking for?" Bruce demanded.

"Crime of passion, sir? Audrey Quinn or Lynn Lockhart," Constable Gavin said. "Hell hath no fury."

"Scratch Mrs. Quinn," Sergeant Atkins said. "I corroborated her yoga retreat alibi with two more people."

"Get Ms. Lockhart into the station," Bruce said.

Constable Gavin leapt out of his chair.

"Hold on." Bruce said. "What more did you find out about Amit Gupta? Ms. Glock saw him last night at The Retreat. The proximity to Flores and the bunker concerns me."

Constable Gavin sat back down and whipped opened his folder. "I found an article on Forbes.com." He jabbed his pile. "The headline is "Did Quinn Quit or Was He Fired?'" Constable Gavin looked up at Bruce.

"Go on," he said impatiently.

"Quinn had been CEO of Q and G Biologics for three years when, quote, *'his second banana, Amit Gupta, went apes.'* Sounds gossipy like? Listen to this: *'Was it monkey business that caused COO Gupta to show Quinn the door?'* It goes on to speculate. Like why would Quinn leave a company he cofounded that was on the verge of some breakthrough?"

"What was the breakthrough?" Bruce asked.

Constable Gavin ran his finger slowly along the words, moving his lips like a new reader. "Nah yeah. Advancements in diabetes treatment. My gran has it."

"Where are we with Gupta's whereabouts during D-Days?"

Sergeant Atkins waved her hand. "Good news, sir. I talked with the senior manager at his company. After Quinn left, Gupta changed the name to AKG Biologics. She said Mr. Gupta has been working remotely, but called a company meeting at the office on April fifth. That's one of our D-Days, so it rules him out, right?"

"Plus, he wouldn't have killed Quinn, left the country, and then come back, eh?" Constable Gavin added.

Bruce frowned. "He misled us by saying he was asked by Quinn's family to represent them, when in fact he volunteered. Keep digging. Who saw him a day or two earlier? What about his travel records?"

"They pan out," Sergeant Atkins said. "He arrived on Air New Zealand on April ninth."

Bruce turned to Constable Cooper. "What did you learn at the *tangi*?"

Alexa remembered Coop had met with the OCU undercover agents who had attended the funeral.

"The Curs supplied the weapons for the vault, and the caretaker, Tony Cobb, was the go-between. The *whakataratara* is that Quinn didn't pay in full," Coop said. "The gang decided to take back what was theirs."

One of Bruce's eyebrows shot up. "Do you believe Quinn didn't pay?"

The corners of Coop's blue lips twitched. "The Curs wouldn't turn over the weapons on a payment plan. When they heard Quinn was dead, they took advantage. Double the profits."

"Got any names?" Bruce asked.

Coop shook her head.

"Arrange a meeting with Joe and his Youth Court representative. A little time in custody might have softened him up enough to spill."

"His father, Senior. His name is Franklin Rotman." Coop folded her arms across her chest. "He's out of jail and attended the *tangi*. Joe won't rat on his *pāpā*."

"Did this Rotman use his own son to steal the weapons?"

Coop shrugged.

Bruce turned to Alexa. "What about the other prints you lifted from the vault?"

"One matched Joe's. The other two were smudged. They indicate someone was with Joe in the vault, but because of the low quality, they're inadmissible."

"Let the press know that we have those prints. Don't mention the quality. Let's see what the fallout is." He stared at each of them in turn. "It's dangerous out there."

Chapter Thirty-Eight

Bruce hurled orders like a short order cook. Alexa was to accompany Sergeant Atkins to The Retreat to search Katrina's room. "I'll be out there as soon as I interrogate Lockhart," he said. "Don't let anyone leave."

"Placing my wager on that Ms. Lockhart," Sergeant Atkins said as they buckled up in her squad car. "She had motive and opportunity to kill both of them. Her Shanghai crumbling and all."

"Do you mean Shangri-La?" Alexa asked.

She signaled to turn out of the lot. "Nah yeah."

Had everything Alexa invested in Bruce crumbled, too? She focused on Katrina. What had she wanted to tell her? She was angry at herself for not returning the call right away.

Sergeant Atkins pulled into a gas station. "I know what we need."

Alexa thought maybe they needed gas, but the sergeant fiddled with her phone. "Take a listen. It's Joan Osborne." She slowly pulled back onto the street.

Alexa steeled herself for country music torture. She wasn't sure, once the woman's husky voice filled the squad car, what the genre was, but the lyrics tugged on her heart. Maybe that's why she wasn't a music lover. Lyrics made her feel things she'd rather not feel. Want what she didn't have. She looked out the side window as tears welled up. She had opened her heart to Bruce. Had he cheated on his wife? And daughters? Can you cheat on your kids? She owed it to Bruce to ask for an explanation, but what if he said it was true? Then what? Would she be able to trust him? She'd better look into Abertay University in Scotland as soon as the case was over. Have a contingency plan. She could start fresh. Feel the spray on her face. Not have to deal with Sammie and Denise, who would probably hate her anyway.

But could she still send Sammie "The Tooth: Its Structure and Properties," an article she'd found?

The next song was something about looking for real love. "Can you turn off the music?"

"Not your taste, eh? Gav and Constable Karu are behind us. On their way to haul Ms. Lockhart in."

Alexa found the car in the side mirror. Constable Gavin seemed to want to pass the sergeant, who drove at glacial-melt speed. "Who looked into Lynn Lockhart's whereabouts when Quinn was killed?"

"Guilty," Sergeant Atkins said. "She has an apartment overlooking the harbor in Auck. The tech guys are looking at the CCTV for those days. No report yet."

Constable Gavin kept straight as they turned off to The Retreat. Sergeant Atkins honked the horn.

Would Lynn put up a fuss? Alexa wished she could listen to the interview. What would Lynn have gained by pushing Katrina off the cliff? She couldn't think of a motive except anger, which Alexa believed should have been directed at Quinn.

The server Blair met them on the porch of The Retreat, just as she had this morning, her face pinched and pale. "We saw the helicopter lift off the beach." Her eyes darted toward the cliff path. "That policeman with the blue eyes told us Ms. Flores was dead. Did the edge give way?"

Sergeant Atkins adjusted her police cap so that it covered her orange hair. "We don't know what happened. We need to see her room."

"Is Mr. Amit Gupta still here?" Alexa asked.

"He's in the lounge. Guests gather there for drinks and nibbles. They've got to be talking about what happened. One couple checked out. Said the place was jinxed."

"I need their names and contact info," Sergeant Atkins said.

"Did you ever see Mr. Gupta and Ms. Flores together?" Alexa asked.

"When he checked in."

"Any other time?" she prodded.

"Can't say that I did. Why?"

"Who's in charge of The Retreat now?" Sergeant Atkins asked.

"The owner, Mr. V, will be here tomorrow. My shift was over at two, but I've stayed on to help out."

"Good on ya," Sergeant Atkins said. "Get me those names. No one else leaves until we talk to them. The Detective Inspector will be along. Let's see Ms. Flores's room now."

The orange flowers in the lobby drooped. Blair nodded to the American couple Alexa had seen in the golf cart this morning. "There's wine and cheese in the lounge," she told them.

Alexa waved at them. "Can I have a word?"

The woman nodded pleasantly. She wore a romper outfit that Alexa thought was more suited for a toddler. "We heard your accent. Where are you from?"

"North Carolina." Sergeant Atkins followed Blair toward a hallway. "Don't touch anything," Alexa called.

"We're from Jacksonville. I'm Marge Fleener and this is my husband. We saw you this morning."

The man stuck out his hand. "Al Fleener, North Florida Beer and Beverage Wholesale."

Alexa bumped her fist into his hand. "My name is Alexa Glock. Have you heard about the manager?"

Al looked pained.

"It puts a whole damper on our experience," Marge said.

It put more than a damper on Katrina's experience, Alexa thought. "How was your golfing?"

Al perked up. "I only lost three balls. Spectacular views."

"What time did you start playing?"

"Right after we saw you," Marge said. "Our tee time was ten. We missed the whole thing with the manager. I heard the helicopter, though."

"Was the course crowded?"

"Not at all," Al said. "It's a five-star experience. Never a wait. We barely saw a soul."

"Who *did* you see?"

They looked at each other. "A few other players in the distance," Al came up with.

"Were you on the grounds before you played golf?" Alexa asked. "Maybe for a walk?"

Marge blushed like a guilty teenager. "We slept in. Had room service."

She thanked them for their time and found Katrina's room, which looked more Holiday Inn Express than luxury retreat.

Sergeant Atkins stood between the unmade bed and dresser. "No sign of an altercation."

Katrina's beige dress was draped over an armchair. The open closet was crowded with hanging clothes. The strappy shoes from last night, one upright, and the other on its side, were parked between black pumps and pointy-toed heels.

"No maid service, looks like," Sergeant Atkins said. She pulled on a pair of gloves, as did Alexa.

The bureau top was a jumble of makeup, phone charger, handbag, keys, coffee mug, jewelry box, and a framed photo, which Alexa picked up. She recognized a younger Katrina between a man and woman. "Maybe her parents."

Sergeant Atkins rustled in the jewelry box. A New Zealand passport nestled under a sparkly bracelet and a chunky necklace.

Sergeant Atkins examined it. "She went to Australia two years ago, Italy in 2020." She set it aside and nudged through a few more trinkets. "Nothing the Queen would wear."

The wallet held the usual IDs and a single credit card. "Twenty and change in cash." Sergeant Atkins removed other items from the handbag: a brush, lipstick, scarf, tissues, Tampax. "No love notes."

The small bathroom was a mess, but Alexa didn't see anything that linked Katrina to Harlan Quinn.

Sergeant Atkins said, "Let's hope the techies have luck with her phone. Why don't we visit with Mr. Gupta, seeing how he's here and so are we?"

Alexa took several photos before leaving.

Mr. Gupta was in the lounge, as Blair reported. Alexa scanned the horse paintings, the fireplace, the trio of men seated on leather furniture. To her right, on a sideboard, a charcuterie board of cheese, olives, nuts, and slivered prosciutto set her mouth to watering. Ice buckets held wine and an array of beer and cider.

Amit Gupta and a man in a loud pink shirt had their backs to them. Gupta's head was cocked; he appeared to be listening to the man sitting across from them. "There was more forgiveness on number thirteen than I realized with my uphill chip. A bogey and I was glad for it." He glanced at the women and stopped talking.

"Number sixteen got my heart racing," Pink Shirt said. He began spouting, "dogleg left," "waggle," and "lay up."

They sounded like yoga poses. Alexa rounded the sofa and waved at Mr. Gupta. "We'd like a word."

Pink Shirt took off his cap. Mr. Gupta set his beer on a side table and nodded. "Excuse me, gentlemen."

He led them through the lobby and restaurant—waitstaff were setting tables—and into the empty bar. "Why pay for drinks here when they're free in the lounge," he commented. He pulled out two chairs.

"This is Sergeant Atkins," Alexa said.

He pulled out a third chair and sat. He had changed from jeans and dress shirt to a polo and quick-dry pants—maybe golf attire. "How can I assist you?"

"It's about the manager, Ms. Katrina Flores." Sergeant Atkins flipped open a pad and looked at Mr. Gupta expectantly. "Have you heard what happened?"

"I hear she is dead." His voice was flat.

"Had you met her?" Alexa asked. She straightened her leg under the table to test her knee.

"Miss Flores checked me in when I arrived and showed me to my suite, late as it was." His gaze, through the lenses of his oval glasses, was unwavering. "I saw her talking to you and the other officer in the lobby last night."

Alexa hadn't realized he'd seen her. The notion unsettled her. "Did you see Ms. Flores this morning?"

"No. I conducted business from my suite until after ten."

That slight tic Alexa had seen in the viewing room at the morgue returned to his right cheek. "And then what?"

"I played golf with the two gentlemen you met in the lounge. We teed off at ten thirty."

Sergeant Atkins wrote something on her pad. "Who can confirm your whereabouts between seven thirty and when you played golf?"

He tented his hands and lowered his head so that his nose almost touched his fingertips. "Perhaps the employees on my conference call?"

"I'll need names," Sergeant Atkins said.

He gave her a business card. "My assistant will provide them."

A man in black pants and a Retreat polo hustled past them to behind the bar. "I'll be right with you, Mr. Gupta. Drinks on the house after what happened."

"Ladies?" Mr. Gupta asked.

"Nothing, ta." Sergeant Atkins made notes in her pad and looked up. "We know you had a nip with Mr. Quinn's, uh, companion, Ms. Lockhart, on Saturday night. Shortly after your arrival, eh?"

Gupta stared, his eyes calculating.

"The bunker was broken into that night, just so happens. Did you see or hear anything while you were in the cottage? Or when you left the property?"

"Nothing comes to mind," he said quickly. "I was jet-lagged."

Sergeant Atkins fiddled with an ear stud. "We know you and Mr. Quinn started a business together. He was the boss, right? The CEO?"

Mr. Gupta's nostrils flared. "We were partners, as the name suggests. Q&G Biologics."

"We read an article that said Mr. Quinn was"—the Sergeant made air quotes—"'shown the door.' Don't look back, Jack, so to speak. Why the split?"

"Office politics."

"This is a murder investigation," Alexa broke in. "Be more specific."

"I won't speak ill of Quinn. We parted amicably. He excelled at starting companies and raising capital. It was time for him to move on."

Alexa disliked his flat affect. "Did his new company compete with the old company? Your company?"

He took his glasses off and polished them with a silky cloth from his pocket.

"Competition leads to a more robust market."

Alexa guessed that was true. The drone of a helicopter passed over the inn. She raised her voice. "How is your company doing since Quinn left?"

His eyes, unfocused without the glasses, shifted. "We've begun a new randomized control study. I'd be happy to discuss the biosimilars landscape another time. When will Quinn's body be released?"

"No time soon," Sergeant Atkins said.

"And his personal effects?"

"Same," the Sergeant said.

"What will happen to Quinn's company?" Alexa asked.

"I am not privy to BioMatic's succession plan."

If Quinn's company floundered, Gupta's company might profit. "We know that Mrs. Quinn didn't ask you to represent the family," Alexa said. "You volunteered."

Gupta's nostrils flared. "There is nothing more I can do for the family here." He stood abruptly. "I'm leaving tomorrow. I have a company to run."

"Detective Inspector Horne is on his way here," Sergeant Atkins said. "Don't leave the grounds. He wants to speak with you."

He bowed and pushed in his chair.

"Hold on," Alexa said. She pulled out her ink pad and cards.

He stared at her supplies. "I never share my biometrics."

Chapter Thirty-Nine

"What do you think?" Sergeant Atkins asked after Gupta left.

The bartender hummed something tuneless and turned the faucet on.

"Better check out that conference call."

Sergeant Atkins waved at the bartender. "How's it?"

He wiped his hands on a towel. "Ow, it's devo, what happened. Ms. Flores was spot on. A hard worker."

"We're trying to understand her schedule prior to the accident," Sergeant Atkins said. "When had you last seen her?"

His neatly trimmed goatee almost camouflaged his double chin. "She came in last night after the dinner guests left. Had a nightcap."

"What time?"

"Half past nine, maybe? She sat right here." He patted a spot on the gleaming metallic bar top and then rubbed it with his rag. "I made her a Manhattan with Manuka Smoke Single Malt." He laughed. "You think they're old-fashioned, Manhattans, but they're back. Old-Fashioneds are, too. She told me to go on. She could tend to any late-night customers. That's how she was."

Alexa straightened. "Was Ms. Flores alone?"

"She was when I left." He attacked another spot with his rag. "I found another glass next to hers when I got here today. Someone joined her." He paused. "I do this thing where I take a whiff of an empty glass and can tell you what was in it."

"So what was it?" Sergeant Atkins asked.

"Easy. A white Russian."

An idea popped into Alexa's head. "Have you washed the glasses?"

He twirled his rag. "First thing I did."

Her last copy of *Forensic Science International* included an article on recovering latent fingerprints from glass that had been submerged in water. The best results came from using the fuming chamber. "Did you use soap?" she asked.

"Of course."

Sergeant Atkins noticed her disappointment. "Chur, bro," she told the bartender.

Alexa stared through the restaurant to where Amit Gupta had disappeared. Had he joined Katrina? Or had Lynn Lockhart? Had Katrina shared something that got her killed the next morning?

They questioned another server on their way out, but she'd left at nine p.m. As they stood on the porch, the wind kicked up and carried the rank scent of guano.

"Let's go talk to the rental guy," Alexa suggested. "He doubles as the valet. DI Horne and I spoke with him this morning." Back when she still trusted him. "He might have seen something, or be able to confirm that Katrina used a Can-Am to deliver the picnic basket. His name is Skip or Skippy, like the peanut butter."

"I prefer SunButter," Sergeant Atkins said.

A NewsTalk van pulled into the parking area as they crossed. A reporter climbed out and scurried to the inn. "The bunker body, the gang funeral, and a cliff death," Sergeant Atkins summed. "The press probably doesn't know which way is up."

A note on the door of the rental office and pro shop gave a phone number: CALL TRIPP FOR RESERVATIONS.

Skip, Tripp. She'd been close. Alexa punched the number into her phone. After six rings, a voice slurred, "Retreat rentals?"

"This is Alexa Glock. I need to speak to you."

"We're not letting now. There's been an accident."

"I don't want to rent. I'm with the police. We met earlier."

There was a clatter. She thought maybe Tripp dropped the phone and then picked it up. "I'll be right down."

This morning when she'd been there with Bruce, Tripp had shown them the full fleet of Can-Ams. Alexa walked to the ATV wing; all four were accounted for.

Tripp showed up tucking his Retreat polo into his pants. He had impressions on his left cheek, maybe from a blanket or sheet, and Alexa figured he'd been napping. She introduced Sergeant Atkins.

He skimmed the Sergeant's orange hair, multiple piercings, and black-rimmed eyes. "Don't think you'd be hired here," he blurted.

"Discrimination based on appearance? Might have to complain to the Ministry of Business." Sergeant Atkins kicked into the earth with her stomper boot. "Besides, I don't need a job, do I?"

He blushed. "Sorry, eh? I don't know how Ms. Flores fell off the cliff. Suppose we'll have to put up guardrails now." He turned to Alexa. "You're the bird lady, eh?"

In her mind, Linda Crosby was the bird lady.

"The rescue team said you froze on a ledge with the gannets. They had you surrounded."

"I wasn't frozen. Just…"

"Captain James Cook wanted his Christmas goose pie when he sailed into Hawke's Bay," he said. "We didn't have geese around here, so his crew shot a gannet. Good thing they're protected now, or our guests might want gannet pie."

"Not looking for pie," Sergeant Atkins said. "When did you last see Ms. Flores?"

He rubbed the soft bristles of his cheeks. "I saw her through the entrance doors last night. She greets guests in the lobby. Maybe eight?"

"What was it like working for Ms. Flores?" the sergeant asked.

He rubbed his hands together as if to get the blood flowing. "All business, she is. Well, was. Show up on time, do your job, the guest is king."

"King?" Sergeant Atkins said.

He blushed again. "Or queen. She was fair and all."

A parrot flew overhead, squawking. Alexa saw a flash of its crimson belly. "Did she mingle with the guests?"

"She lived in the inn, so it's possible." Tripp studied the over-hanging trees. "Who else was she going to talk to being stuck out here, all alone? I'd go bonkers if it weren't for my girlfriend in Clifton. Most mornings she went for a walk. Probably the only time she had privacy."

Sergeant Atkins jotted notes on her pad. "We'd like to see your reservation records for the Can-Ams. I'm sure you want to help us." She rubbed her right eye, smearing her eyeliner.

"Nah yeah, glad to." He unlocked the rental shop and led them to a cluttered back room. He straddled a chair behind a desktop computer. "What day are you wondering about?"

"April onward."

He scrolled for a minute. "Here ya go."

Alexa caught the papers as they emerged from the printer. She skimmed each one, but didn't see Katrina Flores's name. "We were wondering if Ms. Flores ever checked out the Can-Ams."

"Sure. She was the boss. She didn't need to fill out paperwork. She would show guests around the property or drop someone off at the golf course."

"What about deliveries?" Alexa asked.

"That, too."

Another name on the list caught Alexa's attention.

Chapter Forty

The sergeant's radio bleeped to life as they walked toward the squad car. Alexa heard Bruce's voice. "Constable Cooper and I are on our way. Anything to report?"

Sergeant Atkins said into her lapel, "Lynn Lockhart rented a Can-Am on Sunday. Katrina Flores delivered it."

Bruce didn't respond.

"What would you like us to do?"

"Did you find anything in Ms. Flores's accommodation?"

"No, sir. It was undisturbed. We believe she had a drink at the bar with someone last night, don't know who."

"Get back to the station. You're second-in-command. I need you to make a statement to the press with Superintendent Parker. I want someone here when Ms. Lockhart's lawyer arrives. She won't speak until so."

"Yes, Senior."

Jealousy niggled at Alexa: Bruce hadn't assigned her a job.

They drove in silence, probably passing Bruce like *wakas* in the night. Sergeant Atkins sped up on the outskirts of Hastings. "Second-in-command. Sweet as."

The station lot was full of press vans, satellite trucks, and cars. "Let's go around back," the sergeant said.

Constable Gavin met them in a hallway. "Superintendent

Parker is looking for you, Sarge. She wants to go over the press release. Thought I was going to have to do it. The lobby is chock-a-block. Everyone wants to know if the terrible accident at the cliffs is related to the bunker murder?"

"The press is calling it murder?" Alexa asked.

"They're on it like bees to manuka flowers." A shadow crossed his earnest face. "You know Ms. Flores's phone? The tech lads say it had an app installed that erased all text messages. You know, like Snapchat?"

"Snapchat?" Alexa let the crime kit slip off her sore shoulder to the floor.

"Still on Instagram, eh? Everything on Snapchat, and this new app that was on Ms. Flores's phone, disappears soon after you hit send? No need to worry about drunxting."

Alexa must have looked clueless.

"Texting while drunk," Constable Gavin explained. "Your message is gone from your phone *and* the recipient's, minutes after sending. Or the other way around. You know. Like 'I miss you' to your ex, or 'Send me a nudie.' Things you regret when you sober up."

Superintendent Parker careened around the corner. "There you are," she said to Sergeant Atkins. She waved a sheet of paper. "The press are all about Ms. Flores. They've forgotten about the weapons debacle. That's to our advantage. Be downstairs in five minutes."

Sergeant Atkins read the paper aloud. "'A woman was fatally injured falling off a twelve-meter ocean cliff at Cape Kidnappers Sunday morning. She has been identified as Katrina Flores, twenty-nine, manager of The Retreat at Cape Kidnappers. Hawke's Bay Rescue Helicopter medic Donna Andrews pronounced Flores dead at the scene.'" Sergeant Atkins stopped reading.

"What else does it say?" Constable Gavin asked.

"'Hastings pathologist Dr. Jennifer Li states cause of death as blunt force trauma. Police are investigating the event as an accident, pending further investigation.'"

Constable Gavin pointed to his eye.

"What are you on about?" Sergeant Atkins asked.

"Know you want to look your best? Your eye stuff is smeared."

"Chur." Sergeant Atkins did an about-face and headed toward the Ladies'.

"What did you find out about Gupta?" Constable Gavin asked Alexa.

She filled him in, ending with, "He wouldn't give his fingerprints. He says he's flying home tomorrow."

"He wasn't in the country when Quinn died, right?"

Alexa shrugged. "No one vouches for his whereabouts except for one meeting. DI Horne asked the California cops to dig into it. What's up with the kid and the gang?"

"There's been some incidents, you know, related to the *tangi*?"

Alexa followed Constable Gavin into the briefing room, where he picked up a report. "Vehicle seizures, traffic offenses, and our young Joe? His father was arrested for breaching his bail conditions. He's locked up. OCU Festinger is grilling him. I wouldn't put it past him to have ordered a kill so he could send his kid in to get those weapons back and double dip."

"But isn't most gang violence internal? And what about Katrina Flores? Why would they kill her?"

"Might be she saw them. Like when she was riding around in one of those Can-Ams. Maybe that's why she called you."

Not returning Katrina's call right away would haunt her forever. "Did you have trouble bringing Ms. Lockhart in?"

"She pitched a fit, eh. She's cooling off in an interview room."

Lynn Lockhart had motive, means, and opportunity to kill Harlan Quinn and Katrina Flores. Was she that unhinged? Alexa told the constable about the Can-Am rental on Sunday and how Katrina Flores had delivered it.

"She asked to speak with you. You're the only one she trusts."

"Me?"

"Nah yeah."

She thought of the night she'd spent at the cottage. Had she slept with a killer? But Lynn had willingly given her fingerprints, and they hadn't matched the duct tape prints. Maybe she was innocent. "What do you think?"

He patted his cowlick. "Only if I go with you."

Alexa looked toward the door, anxious and curious. "Let's do it."

Lynn Lockhart jumped up from the table when Alexa and Constable Gavin entered the room. "Can I leave?"

Her face fell when Constable Gavin said no. She sank back into her chair. Her sleek black turtleneck had lost elasticity at the neck, as if she had burrowed her head into it.

Alexa set the crime kit on the table. "What did you want to see me about?"

"Can you explain why I'm here?"

"It's not for me to say," Alexa answered.

Lynn's eyes flew to the constable. "I'd rather speak to Miss Glock alone."

"Not happening." He folded his arms across his chest and leaned against the closed door. A duress button was on the wall next to him.

Alexa sat on the opposite side of a table and waited.

Lynn bent over to pick something out of the tread of her sneaker and spoke in a soft voice. "This is all a nightmare. I want to leave."

Alexa's stomach growled. She had lost all sense of time, but her stomach hadn't. "What did you want to say?"

"Remember that night I invited Amit Gupta for a drink?" Her dark hair blocked her face. "He insisted on... Well, he said something that concerned me."

Constable Gavin fumbled in his pocket for his notepad.

"I know it's not true." Lynn's jaw set. "Harlan was an honest man."

She is delusional, Alexa thought.

"Amit Gupta said Harlan stole secrets from him."

This sounded like middle school drama. "What kind of secrets?"

"About a drug they had developed. A pharmacological treatment for diabetes. Harlan's daughter has it. The only time I ever saw him emotional was when Audrey called him over some crisis. Candide was hypoglycemic, and Harlan was yelling instructions. Anyway, it's all lies."

The little girl wearing her dad's sweater ran across Alexa's mind. "He would go to the police if it were true." Or somewhere. She had no idea if trade secrets were the domain of the police.

"That's how I knew he was lying." Her eyes hardened. "Speaking ill of the dead. It's slanderous. I asked him to leave."

Alexa went for a switch kick. "Why did you rent a Can-Am on Sunday?"

Lynn's jaw clenched tighter.

Alexa glanced at Constable Gavin, who stood with his pen poised.

She leaned across the table, her eyes drilling into Alexa's. "I suspected that Katrina slut was the one Harlan met in the bunker. I knew she'd deliver the Can-Am. I confronted her and she denied everything. She was lying, wasn't she?"

"Did you kill her?" Alexa asked.

Lynn shot out a hand and gripped Alexa's wrist.

Chapter Forty-One

Bugs attracted to the headlights splattered against her windshield. They reminded her of suspects vying for attention: Lynn Lockhart—splat, the gang—splat, Amit Gupta—splat. At least she could squeegee Bird Lady off the glass.

Constable Gavin had jumped at Lynn Lockhart and pried loose her vise grip on Alexa's wrist. "Do you want an assault charge?" he'd yelled.

Her wrist throbbed. Constable Gavin had said he would tell the team about "the stealing of secrets" and Lockhart's behavior.

She unlocked her room and checked her messages. Bruce had called. She wasn't ready to speak to him and deleted the message without listening to it.

She threw her torn khakis in the trash, took a shower, dressed in tomorrow's work outfit, and headed to the quaint lobby.

"The Flax will do you," the clerk said when Alexa asked about restaurants. "It's a family-friendly bar. Rugby on TV, a patio, and only four blocks away." The clerk looked out the window. The motel was on the edge of town, and the traffic was sparse. "There's no place for grown men who bark like dogs. We're all holding our breath until this funeral gathering is over. The police say they're monitoring the situation and, unless you're a mobster, you're safe, but it doesn't feel safe. You should drive, not walk, young lass all alone."

Young? No. All alone? Yes. A motorcycle passed. The reverberation hurt her ears. "How can the drivers stand the noise?"

The clerk grimaced. "They take the mufflers off to make them louder. My sister was forced off Omahu Road by a convoy of them running red lights, taking up both lanes, revving their bikes. Her Aussiedood was traumatized."

"Her what?"

"Aussiedoodle. Cross between an Australian shepherd and poodle. His name is Wally."

She heeded the woman's advice and drove to the restaurant.

The host thrust a menu in her hand. "Sit anywhere, luv."

Alexa crossed the scuzzy carpet to a tall table with two stools. She opened the menu and breezed over the light offerings—imagine salad for dinner—and ordered lamb shank and mash with a Tui beer. Her phone buzzed as the beer arrived: Unknown Caller. She thought of the last time she'd ignored a call and answered.

"It's Coop. Boss wants to know where you are."

"I'm about to eat dinner." Suddenly she was lonely. "Want to join me?"

The lamb fell off the bone at the touch of her fork. Alexa scarfed it up. By the time Coop arrived, dressed in a black T-shirt, cargo pants, and thong sandals, the bone was bare, and she was ready for a second beer.

Coop eyed Alexa's empty plate. When the server stopped by, she ordered a burger and two beers.

"Did you and DI Horne find out anything at The Retreat?" Alexa asked.

"Senior advised Mr. Gupta to stay in town, but Gupta said he was leaving. We can't hold him without a valid reason. One guest confirmed seeing Ms. Flores leave the inn at seven twenty-five. Nothing else. Boss is at the station, waiting for Ms. Lockhart's solicitor to arrive." She tucked her hair behind her ears and scanned the room. "My auntie just called. She said a little *manu* wants to know more about the evidence that was found in the bunker. Sergeant Atkins told the press about the fingerprints left behind."

Alexa wondered who the little bird was. A gang member? "What's the latest on Joe?"

The server delivered Coop's burger and the beers. "*Tēnā koe,*" she said.

Alexa sipped the beer as Coop ate half her burger and then used a napkin to wipe her hands. "*He waiata whakaaroha tēnei*: a sad story. His father broke his parole to find Joe at the *tangi*. Not smart, since he's on electronic monitoring. He *said* he wanted to warn the kid off gangs. He didn't know Joe was already in custody." She sipped her beer, her eyes downcast. "Joe claimed he joined the Curs and raided the vault as an initiation to make his *pāpā* proud. And now *pāpā* is trying to escape the house of the dog."

Alexa thought of that story about the comb and watch chain. Each person sacrificing their only treasure for love. She was pretty sure a North Carolinian wrote it. Henry Somebody.

Coop attacked the second half of her burger. The jukebox played "All She Wrote." A trio at the bar sang along with gusto.

When the song was over, Alexa asked, "Did Joe say anything about the weapons?"

Coop pushed her plate away. "He wouldn't say where they are or who helped him. He won't rat out the dogs. He heard about the weapons by listening in on his auntie, DI Steele."

"He won't rat on the dogs, but he rats on his aunt? That's messed up."

"You haven't lived his life," Coop said. "When you're cast adrift, you seize the closest *waka*."

"But DI Steele and Kersten are trying to help him."

Coop's eyes took on a faraway look. "I was like Joe. Did you know DI Horne helped me? Kept me from being patched?"

Bruce's face flashed in her mind. "I didn't know the Curs had women members."

"Eh. I was hardly a woman. I was Joe's age. But patching is

different for girls, for *kōtiro*." She lowered her eyes. "It's called blocking. They take turns."

Alexa's stomach dropped.

"I was about to do it. I was an iceberg inside, thought nothing could hurt me." Coop finished her beer and wiped foam from her upper lip. "DI Horne kept me from that."

Alexa scooted closer. She wanted to hug Coop or pat her hand, but refrained.

"DI Horne got me into Taumata Raukura, a police training program. Whenever I got off track, he led me back on." Coop waved the server down and ordered more beers. She laughed. "I was fat. He helped me get fit, even ran with me. Started me with the body building."

Bruce running with Coop. Bruce running on the beach with Sammie. Bruce running around on his wife. Alexa gulped the fresh beer.

Coop made an impressive bicep. "I can bench-press sixty kilos. He was looking for you at the station. I could see worry in his eyes."

Alexa loved Bruce's eyes.

The dusky blue of Coop's facial tattoos faded to shadow. "DI Horne is casting. *Ka pu te ruha ka hao te rangtahi.* As an old net withers, another is remade."

Alexa tried to decipher Coop's words, but her head was woozy.

The door opened with a bang. Three men wearing gang paraphernalia strutted to the bar, sucking the conversation out of the room so quickly that Alexa heard the chain rattling from one's belt.

"You've time for a round, boys," the bartender said jovially. "We close at ten."

Alexa couldn't hear what they said, but the bartender backed up and averted his eyes. "Out back," the tallest of the three said.

All eyes in the tavern followed the men as they headed to the patio. One man paused next to Alexa and Coop.

Alexa froze.

He splayed his hand on their table, his dirty fingernails inches from Coop's mug. *C-U-R* was tatted down his middle finger. He nodded at Coop, closed his hand into a fist, and followed his buds outside.

A whoosh of air escaped Alexa's lungs. She scooped up the check, ready to leave.

Coop pushed her beer away and scanned the room. People gathered their belongings. A woman said loudly, "Pure and simple scum."

"They've a right to be here, like everyone else," Coop said to Alexa. "I'll stay around, make sure everything is okay."

"But what about that guy? Why did he stop at our table?"

"He's a cuz. Text me when you get to your motel."

Alexa paid the bill for both of them and followed a youngish couple into the parking lot. She slipped into the Vitz and crawled under the speed limit back to the Apple. She parked and walked to her room, checking over her shoulder. The pool glistened turquoise and serene, mocking her fear. Inside, she locked up.

Safe, she texted Coop. She flung herself on the bed spread-eagle to gather her thoughts.

They circled around her head like flocks of birds until she heard a buzz. Coop sent her a thumbs-up emoji. She turned off her phone. The last thing she wanted before she burrowed under the covers was a call from Bruce.

TUESDAY

TUESDAY

Chapter Forty-Two

At six she kicked her way out of tangled covers and decided to call her brother. She rubbed her eyes and thought of Charlie's affable face—so much like their father's—and the way they'd grown closer on their hiking trip. He'd helped her understand the scars on her back weren't the fault of her stepmother's negligence. Charlie would commiserate with her about Bruce. She did the math: it was two p.m. yesterday in North Carolina.

Charlie answered after five rings. "Lexi? What's wrong?"

Her head hurt. Her knee hurt. Her heart hurt. "Nothing. Are you at work?"

"I'm on site. We're removing a dam on the Watauga River. You won't believe what will happen over the coming months."

She listened with a slight smile to his ardent speech on fish passage and water temperatures. "Trapped water heats up. Letting it flow helps it cool." He broke off. "Why did you call? Are you okay?"

Tears blurred her vision. "I'm thinking of moving to Scotland."

"Scotland? What the hell? What's wrong with New Zealand?"

Words clumped in her throat; she couldn't speak.

"What about that detective? Are you still seeing him?"

"Bruce is a detective inspector. Yes, I'm still seeing him. Maybe." Alexa remembered when Charlie had told her that Mel had cheated. He'd come to New Zealand to figure things out. "How are things with Mel?"

She heard the rumble of some machine in the background—an excavator or bulldozer—and tried to picture the North Carolina mountains and imprisoned fish. "It's hard," he said. "But we're seeing a therapist."

"Bruce cheated, too," she blurted.

Anger rose in his voice. "Son of a bitch. How did you find out?"

She had never asked Charlie how he learned about Mel's infidelity. "A doctor told me."

"What's that mean? What doctor?"

"A pathologist. We did an autopsy together. Well, she did the autopsy, and I watched, and now there's a second body, but she knows this *other* pathologist in Rotorua. I met her once. Dr. Hill. That's who Bruce cheated with."

"On you?"

"On his wife."

"Wait. The bastard is married?"

She rubbed her eyes. "He *was* married, and that's when he cheated. He's divorced now."

"He didn't cheat on you?"

Charlie was muddying the waters. "Not that I know of."

"Lexi, are you saying Bruce cheated on his wife? When they were married? He didn't cheat on you?"

"I don't even know if it's true. "

"Have you talked with him about it?"

"Not yet. But if it is true, how could I ever trust him?" She should have kept her mouth shut. Implicit was how could Charlie ever trust Mel? "There's this university in Scotland that has an exceptional forensics department."

"You're good at running away," he said flatly.

She blinked to clear tears from her eyes. "What's that mean?"

"You look for an excuse to leave every man you're with. Like Jeb. He was a good guy."

Charlie had liked Alexa's live-in boyfriend in Raleigh. Everyone liked Jeb. Alexa liked Jeb. That was the problem. She liked him but hadn't loved him.

"Give Bruce a chance to explain," Charlie said. "Not that his former marriage is your business."

"Why are you defending him?"

"I'm not defending him, and I'm not condemning him. Grow up. Quit with your righteousness."

"Grow up? You're telling *me*—your older sister—to grow up?"

"Or you'll end up alone."

She looked at the queen-size bed, one side neat. "There's nothing wrong with being alone."

"I've got to go," Charlie said.

Their goodbyes were terse. So much for brotherly consolation. Alexa tossed the phone onto the sheets. The light seeping into the room was gray, like her mood.

Running would help. She downed two ibuprofen—for her knee—and pulled on running clothes. What about the Curs? Was it safe to run? Coop had said they weren't interested in someone her age, and Bruce had said the public had nothing to fear. She'd be damned if she was going to let a few helmet-wearing Neanderthals keep her from running.

Plus she had her phone. She fetched it from the sheets and stuck it in that pocket at the back of her tights, twisting to get it and her ID card situated. She brushed her hair into a tight ponytail, ran Chapstick over her lips, and avoided her eyes in the mirror.

The sun struggled to poke a hole in the heavy clouds as she headed in the opposite direction from The Flax. Out into the countryside. She didn't worry about the goose bumps on her bare arms; she'd warm up quickly. What she couldn't outrun was Charlie's words.

You're good at running away. You'll end up alone.

Charlie was wrong. She always stood her ground. She formed a plan as she increased her pace: play it cool for the rest of the case and then talk with Bruce when it was over. Give him a chance to explain. In a mile, she'd left town behind. She hopped off the road as two cars approached, and then back on, passing acres of solar panels, then the loaded apple trees that spanned both sides of the road, their cheerful appearance and scent proving April was fall in the southern hemisphere. She guessed this was where Apple Motor Lodge got its name. Hazy mountain humps in the distance never enlarged as she crested a long straight hill.

Three squat metal buildings and several planes spread out on the right side of the road below. Alexa flew down and read the sign: WELCOME TO HAWKE'S BAY AERODROME.

This tiny airport was where Quinn's pilot had dropped him off and someone with red hair—probably Katrina—had picked him up. Amit Gupta had landed here, too, and rented a car, although there was no sign of a Hertz or Thrifty.

Two insect-like jets, several smaller planes, and a New Zealand News 6 helicopter were parked beside the tarmac. Alexa walked through an open chain-link fence, breathing hard, and stopped to look at the security cameras. She saw a blinking light indicating she was being recorded. Further in, a man emerged from the Hawke's Bay Aero Club hangar. "Pardon," he said into an earpiece. He nodded to Alexa. "The airport is closed. We open at eight."

"Is the manager around?" Alexa asked.

"I'm the manager."

She wiped her brow as he finished his call. Something about flight lessons. "How can I help you?" he asked.

She awkwardly extracted her ID from the back pocket and showed him. "I'm a forensic investigator."

He eyed her running attire and studied the card.

"I'm jogging and didn't know I'd pass the airport. Have the police spoken with you about the man who died in the bunker? His plane landed here."

"I've talked to a constable. He hasn't been out yet. I have the logbook records ready for him."

"I can deliver them," Alexa said.

"I'd rather wait for the officer."

"Were you here when Mr. Quinn arrived on April first?"

"We don't have many Gulfstream G650s land here, so I remember. It's a beaut. I'm Hamish Aschenbeck." He had a large nose and friendly face. "Cup of coffee or some water?"

"Water, thanks."

He led her to the middle building, through a minimalist waiting area, and into a messy office. He filled a cup at a water cooler and handed it over.

Alexa gulped it down. "Thank you. Did you speak to Mr. Quinn when he arrived?"

"His feet barely touched the ground before someone whisked him away. I received his Passenger Arrival Card from the pilot—he had nothing to declare and entered the country on a visa. I watched the pilot and crew clean and disinfect the plane. Then they fueled and took off for Auckland."

"What's the big deal with the Gulfstream?"

His eyes gleamed. "The range. Thirteen thousand kilometers. Say nonstop from LA to Melbourne."

"Can I see Quinn's Passenger Arrival Card?"

"The PAC is classified information. New Zealand Security and Intelligence Service would have my badge. You'll have to contact them."

"Can a plane land at this airport without authorization?"

"Sure, and the pilot loses his license. It's an offense to fail to notify an airport of your intended arrival."

"Is someone here all the time?"

"We're staffed seven to seven."

Unsure of what she was rooting for, Alexa forged ahead. "Who owns those two jets out there?"

Mr. Aschenbeck followed her gaze. "That's also private information. Is there anything else I can help you with? I've a fuel truck due."

She thought of Gupta, who said he was leaving today. "If I wanted to fly to Auckland today, how would I do so?"

"We've one flight a day to Auckland. It comes in at twelve forty-five and leaves at fourteen hundred."

Gupta might be leaving at two p.m. "Can I see those logbook records?"

He looked down his large nose at her. "What happened to the lass at The Retreat? The owner is due in early afternoon. On a Beechcraft Premier."

"We're working to find out. It'll help with the investigation if I could see those records."

Mr. Aschenbeck led her to a closet-like office and introduced her to Murray Beckett. "She can look at the logbook. Remember the Gulfstream G650?"

Beckett nodded.

"I'll leave you to it," Mr. Aschenbeck said and left.

Beckett blinked as she gave him the date. "All Fools' Day, eh?" He opened a large black book and flipped to the right page. "Everything is computerized, but I still record the comings and goings on paper." He ran his finger down a column. "The G650 landed at fourteen twenty hours."

He was Alexa's height and smelled of cigarette smoke. She tried not to wrinkle her nose. "How do you communicate with the pilots?"

"No radar here. It's all by CTAF. That's the common traffic advisory frequency. Pilots are responsible for monitoring the airspace and broadcasting their intentions."

"Can you show me the Gulfstream on the CCTV?"

"There's no CCTV on the runway. Our cameras are aimed at the driveway gates." He searched for five minutes on his computer. "One way, in and out. That way the camera catches all comings and goings. Here you go. This is the car that came to pick the gentleman up."

Alexa watched in grainy black and white a Mazda compact drive through the gate. She could see one person in the car. Probably Katrina.

Beckett fast-forwarded the tape. She could see the backs of two heads as the Mazda left the airport property. She got goose bumps, knowing the occupants' terrible fate. She cleared her throat and squinted at the columns on the logbook: date, time, aircraft identification numbers, and three-letter airport of origin identifiers. Quinn's point of origin was SFO. He'd flown nonstop from San Francisco.

She checked to see where the other planes on the same page were from. AKL appeared three times. Auckland, Alexa guessed. Planes had also landed from ZQN and NAN. "Where were these planes from?" she asked.

"Queenstown and Nadi International Airport," Beckett said. "I make it a point to know all the codes."

"Nadi? Where's that?"

"Fiji."

Alexa turned the page to April second. There were two planes from Auckland, one from Christchurch, and two others. "What do these stand for?"

Beckett ran a stubby finger down the column. "BNE is Brisbane, and SJC is San Jose."

"Mexico?"

"California."

Goose bumps coated her arms. One day after Quinn arrived, a plane had landed from San Jose. Amit Gupta lived in San Jose. A lot of other Silicon Valley CEOs lived there too. Had Gupta tailed Quinn?

"Can I see the CCTV tape for the time right after this one landed?"

Beckett found it quickly. A Toyota Camry passed through the gate, one head, and left fifteen minutes later, two heads. "Can you zoom in?" Alexa asked.

Beckett froze the frame and zoomed in. The enlargement resulted in two blurry backs of heads. Dark hair. The license plate was blurry, too. "Can I see the Passenger Arrival Card?"

"That's classified, lass."

Looking at the CCTV reminded her of the webcam in the bunker. The camera pointed down—probably from that Norfolk pine—at the Black Reef gannet colony and included a portion of cliff and beach. It probably recorded her climbing down the cliff.

She rubbed her arms. What if it had recorded Katrina's murder? She knew of one case where a murder was recorded by webcam, unbeknownst by the killer. "Do you know anything about webcams?"

Beckett looked startled.

"Like how they work? Is it like CCTV? Does it save footage?"

"I know the basics. It's all about streaming live images, eh? Straight to your internet router, which can make them available on your computer or phone or whatever."

"But is the data saved?"

"All depends." He stroked his chin. "Some will record and store so you can watch it later."

Maybe, maybe not. She was itching to find out.

She photographed the logbook page with her phone and thanked Beckett for his help. She almost dialed Bruce, but settled on Coop and left a message. "A plane landed at Hawke's Bay Aerodrome on April second, from San Jose. Someone needs to look into it."

She'd share her webcam theory when she got to the station.

Chapter Forty-Three

It was just after seven, and traffic into Hastings was picking up. At the crest of the hill, she spotted urban sprawl in the distance and a glint of sea at the horizon.

Excitement fueled her stride; she sensed the case was on the brink of being solved. Maybe by her webcam idea. Bruce would be impressed. She jabbed the air and mentally corralled all the bits and pieces of forensic evidence that she'd gathered the past four days.

First, the horrid bunker. Harlan Quinn's decomposing body. She'd dusted for prints on his laptop and the picnic basket handle. In the morgue she'd discovered the pink tooth gleaming in his mouth and suspected carbon monoxide poisoning, which tests confirmed. Then she had identified Harlan Quinn by comparing his antemortem and postmortem dental radiographs.

A sweetness wafted in the air as she passed rows and rows of apple trees on both sides of the road. She recalled her last case. A bite mark left on an apple had helped her identify a killer. The orchard awakened hunger pangs. Glistening apples lured her off the road and over a fence.

"Go ahead and take a bite," the serpent said.

Hadn't that been the beginning of the fall of mankind? Unless you have a bunker. Then you might survive. Alexa laughed uneasily and plucked a speckled beauty.

Apples in April. It sounded like the title of a song. She dusted her prize on her tank top and bit in. Tartness filled her mouth. She took another bite and continued her recap. The vent of the bunker—a lifeline—had been clogged by a rag and duct-taped. Locard's principle popped into her head: every contact leaves a trace. In the case of the duct tape: fingerprints and hair. She was glad it wasn't the DI's nephew's fingerprints on the tape. Joe was in enough trouble.

The next discovery was the weapons. Here today, gone tomorrow, a fingertip nub left behind.

Joe's nub would grow back because the slice occurred above the edge of the fingernail. She finished the apple and rejoined the road, her pace steady.

Lynn Lockhart let Alexa take her fingerprints. Katrina Flores and Amit Gupta refused. In her book, it made them look suspicious. Dr. Li had helped her take Katrina's prints posthumously. *A-tisket, a-tasket, a green and yellow basket.* Katrina had touched the picnic basket, but not the duct tape.

She realized she didn't have Audrey Quinn's fingerprints. Could the whole yoga retreat be bogus? Had she flown from San Jose on April 2 to track down her cheating husband?

Cheats. The world was full of them. The apple soured in her gut.

The growl of an engine pierced her thoughts. She jumped off the road as a big black motorcycle barreled toward her. Before she could blink, two, three more motorcycles throttled into view, their roar deafening, the riders a blur of red and black and fringe and chain. She froze on a thatch of grass, her veins turned to ice, her ponytail lifting in the fumes and wind of their passing.

She turned and watched. Her mouth dropped as first one, then another, then all, made U-turns.

Holy shit.

She scanned the acres of blank-eyed solar panels. There was no place to hide, no eco-farmer in sight to see her plight. She groped for her phone. What idiot designed rear centered pockets? Her ID fluttered to the ground as she pulled it out. Dammit.

She squeezed her phone and started running. Surely a car would come.

In two seconds a bike was behind her. She felt its breath on her calves.

Another bike kept abreast of her stride, five feet to her right. The throttle of its engine drowned her moan. She thought of Medusa but looked anyway. The rider didn't bother to look back. His black helmet and visor concealed his profile. She thought she would faint when another motorcycle came up on her left, off the road. The final bikes were the coup de grâce. They pulled ahead and wheeled around to face her.

She stopped, took a photo, and then stabbed 111 on her phone.

A car approached and slowed. Alexa waved. The woman driver took a look at her and sped up. She was stranded.

The ear-splitting motors drowned out the operator's voice.

"I need help," Alexa yelled into the phone. "Near the airport."

The driver to her right cut his engine, set his kickstand, and climbed off.

Alexa clutched the phone to her ear. A voice said, "Is your emergency fire or police?"

The man's thick hand slapped her phone into the air before Alexa answered. It hit the pavement and slid to a rider who stomped it with his enormous black boot.

Ways to save herself swirled in Alexa's head: scream, fight, appeal, run.

The man raised a fist, thumb and pinkie extended. The other bikers cut their engines. In the sudden silence, Alexa heard short fast breaths, like the panting of dogs. Then she realized the sound came from her: she was hyperventilating.

Nothing in her life had prepared her for this man stepping toward her, in broad daylight, surrounded by his brethren, flaunting his power. She felt kinship to all women terrorized by men.

The man removed his helmet. Alexa stared: first at his hard eyes and then at the fangs tattooed on his lips. A drop of blood hung from one pointy tip. He looked Māori. She'd seen him before. Was this Coop's cousin?

Fang stepped closer. A rank odor clung to him like a swarm of menace. Alexa hopped back and bumped the fat tire of the bike behind her.

She stepped right and straightened to feign strength. "What do you want?"

The corners of Fang's lips curved upward. The other bikers barked like hungry dogs, like a bloodthirsty pack capable of killing. Then the barks became growls.

She sensed movement and whipped around. The biker behind her set his kickstand and got off his bike. A red bandanna concealed most of his face. His vest swung open and Alexa saw a gun handle poking out of an inner pocket. He brushed her shoulder as he handed a slip of paper to Fang.

Alexa eyed his bike—the empty black saddle—and wondered if she could jump on it and drive off. She edged backwards, closing the gap. In her peripheral vision, she saw the other bikers dismount and form a circle.

She was trapped.

A flutter of white caught her attention. In Fang's hand was her forensic ID card. She saw her proud miniature face. Fang exchanged a long look with Bandanna. A wordless exchange passed between them. Fang made that hand symbol. The growling ceased.

Alexa checked the road. Where the hell were all the cars? She thought of brave Coop standing up to these guys. Her greenstone pendant throbbed against her chest.

She could stand up to them too.

"Wynne Cooper is my friend," she said to Fang. "Isn't she your cousin?"

His eyes stayed still, reptilian.

A fact she'd forgotten about Coop flowed from the pendant to her tongue. "Constable Cooper is named after Dame Whina Cooper, right? Dame Cooper worked for the rights of her people. Coop is too."

Fang blinked. He slipped her ID card in a pocket of his vest and stepped closer so that she could smell his hot breath. "*Kia whakatupato*. Be warned. Joe Rotman was the only one in the bunker." He challenged her with his eyes as his pack howled. "If other fingerprints show up, I know where to find you."

Alexa's knees trembled.

Fang walked to his bike and slid his helmet back on. The riders climbed onto their bikes. Engines roared to life. One by one they turned and whizzed by her.

Then there was silence.

Chapter Forty-Four

Six motorcycles and a pickup truck whizzed by five minutes later. Alexa stood on the side of the road, clutching her smashed phone, watching. Then four cars drove by, followed by a few more cars in either direction.

The Curs had set a blockade. That's why no one had driven by.

She started running. She heard a car coming from behind. She whipped around. A woman leaned out the window. "Everything all right? Do you need a ride?"

A siren wailed in the distance, growing louder. She spotted a white pickup and a patrol car hurtling her way. "I'm okay. Thanks."

The woman rolled up her window and drove off.

Alexa watched Bruce's truck grow larger. The patrol car behind it had its lights and siren going. Bruce swerved to a stop, jumped out, and ran to her. "What happened?"

She couldn't speak. Bruce pulled her close. "You're safe," he said into her hair.

Her pendant pulsed between them. From over his shoulder she watched Coop park and get out of her car. Alexa pushed back from Bruce and held out her phone to Coop. "They smashed it."

Coop nodded. "Did they hurt you?"

Alexa shook her head.

"A woman called the police," Coop said. "She reported a jogger was being harassed. Then you called."

"Why were you out here alone?" Bruce demanded, his eyes sparking.

Fear, anger, and relief bubbled over. "Why shouldn't I be? Why shouldn't any woman go walking or running or whatever? The public has nothing to fear from the gang; isn't that the message?" She turned to Coop. "Can you give me a lift to my motel?"

Bruce just stared at Alexa.

"Go to the airport," she told him. "Check the logbook and CCTV for the day after Quinn arrived."

"Why?"

Did she have to explain everything? "Just do it."

Coop drove Alexa to the Apple Motor Lodge and took her statement in the room.

"They cut me off and surrounded me. Tried to scare me." She had been terrified. She freed her hair of the scrunchie and shook it loose to dislodge the helplessness she'd felt.

Coop swallowed. "But did they hurt you?"

"One of them had a handgun. I dropped my ID card and they figured out who I was. They have my name. Remember the guy with the fangs? From the Indian takeout place? It was him."

"That's Rikki Griffin."

"I mentioned your name, told him we were friends." Her face heated up. Coop probably didn't think of her as a friend.

Coop shrugged. She didn't seem offended.

"He said Joe was the only one in the vault," Alexa continued. "If any other prints surface, he knows where to find me."

"Intimidation tactic," Coop said. "He's worried. Probably he's involved in the break-in. Might even be his prints."

Alexa sat on the edge of the bed. "He has my phone number."

Coop's lips twitched as she looked at the phone still clutched in Alexa's hand. "Don't think he can call."

The bottom half of the glass was shattered. Alexa turned the phone over to examine the frame. It was unscathed. She turned it on and was amazed to see her screen light up. She eyed it like it was a snake. "What if he does?"

"Then we trace the number."

"Wait," Alexa said. "I took a picture." The icons were hard to see through the shattered glass. She tapped where she thought Photos was, and then Today. She could only see the top third of three riders straddling their bike, coming toward her. She held it out to Coop.

"Send it to me," she said.

The phone was too messed up. "We can get it from the cloud."

"The OCU guys need to know about your encounter." She stood up but then sat back down. "Why did you tell DI Horne to go to the airport?"

Alexa filled her in on the logbook and CCTV. "A San Jose plane came in on April second. I think that's key."

"That's where Gupta is from," Coop said.

"He's leaving today," Alexa reminded her.

After Coop left, she splashed cold water on her face, over and over.

Chapter Forty-Five

OCU Festinger met her in the station lobby. The past day or two had added gray shadows under his eyes. He led her into his office. She set her laptop on his stand-up desk. He paced as she located the photo. "Ballsy of you," he said.

She emailed the photo to him and stood by his side as he enlarged it on his computer screen. The image of the three approaching bikers kick-started her heart. She took a deep breath. "One of them had a gun."

"One of these three?"

"No. Another one. He was behind me." She could almost feel him breathing on her neck. "There were six in all."

"If the gun was loaded, that's an offense. If he doesn't have the permit, that's an offense." He leaned closer to the photo. "The helmets make it hard to identify them. Except for this one. The Stahlhelm exposes his face."

He was referring to the half-helmet that made Alexa think of Nazi soldiers. Dark tattoos swirled between it and the red bandanna covering the biker's nose and mouth.

Coop came in and stood by Alexa. Her presence was calming.

OCU Festinger scratched his bald head. "Looks like Bulldog. He's a local. A year ago he was charged with trafficking of firearms and Class A drugs. Thought he was locked away. I'll find out."

Coop nodded. "I think Rikki Griffin was with them."

"I'm not surprised. He's from Havelock North. He slipped out of our clutches when we had a warrant to search his home last month. Someone tipped him off. The search was a bust. We suspect he's importing and selling meth."

"Pull them in for threatening behavior. They surrounded Ms. Glock. Wouldn't let her move," Coop said.

Alexa practiced her yoga breathing.

"DI Horne already has guys tailing them," OCU Festinger said. "Let's see where they lead us." He popped a knuckle. "We've got a confession from the caretaker, Tony Cobb. He used his connections to stock the bunker. Said Quinn asked for a full range of protection and paid him ten thousand dollars, plus costs, no questions asked."

Alexa thought of Lynn buying furniture, clothes, art, fossils. Her payment had been a cottage and false promises. Then she thought of Lynn grabbing her wrist. She had the beginnings of a bruise.

They left OCU Festinger's office. In the hallway, she asked Coop, "Did DI Horne interview Lynn Lockhart last night?"

"He's holding her."

Relief washed over her. "So he thinks she did it?"

"She hasn't been arrested. We can only hold her twelve hours. Time is about up."

Alexa sighed. If Lynn was guilty, she'd sent Bruce on a wild goose chase to the airport. She told Coop about the bunker webcam. "It could have footage of who killed Katrina. Maybe it shows Lynn Lockhart pushing her."

But her fingerprints weren't on the duct tape. This bothered Alexa.

Coop started walking. "Let's tell the team."

As they entered the briefing room, Constable Gavin put his finger to his lips. He pointed at Sergeant Atkins, who had her back to them. "She's talking with the FBI," he whispered.

"The FBI?" Alexa said. "Are you sure?"

Sergeant Atkins turned around and frowned. "Special Agent Jacobs, I'm putting my phone on speaker so the team can hear. My constable will be recording us."

Constable Gavin fumbled about with his phone and then nodded.

Sergeant Atkins spoke toward her phone. "Can you repeat what you said in regards to Harlan Quinn?"

Alexa stepped closer.

"We're investigating whether Mr. Quinn took a patent-pending product from Q&G Biologics with him to BioMatic and engaged in a fraudulent scheme to accelerate the timeline of the product. We are also looking into whether Mr. Quinn defrauded investors. United States Attorney Joyce Waterbury is reviewing the case to decide whether to pursue the indictment posthumously."

Sergeant Atkins met Alexa's eyes. "He stole secrets from Mr. Amit Gupta?"

"It is alleged that Mr. Quinn brought classified documents with him to BioMatic. Mr. Quinn allegedly used the information to cut corners and avoid trial failures, as well as bait to raise capital."

"Did Quinn know he was being investigated?"

"Mr. Quinn's attorneys have been notified and were cooperating."

Sergeant Atkins twirled an ear stud. "What kind of product is it?"

There was a conferring of voices on the other end. After a moment, the agent said, "It's an alleged diabetes treatment."

A treatment for diabetes would be huge, Alexa knew. Someone had said Quinn's daughter had it. Alexa thought of the bewildered little girl, wanting her dad home by her birthday. No wish on a candle could make it true.

"Did Mr. Amit Gupta accuse Quinn?" Sergeant Atkins asked.

"The complaints came from investors."

"We'll need their names."

"That's confidential information," Special Agent Jacobs said.

Sergeant Atkins made eyes at Constable Gavin. "See, we've got Harlan Quinn's murder investigation going on here in New Zealand. His body is at the mortuary, and Mr. Gupta is prancing around at a luxury inn, all the players so to speak, plus another body—one of Mr. Quinn's girlfriends—so please give us the information."

Go girl, Alexa thought.

There was more conferring. "We can't disclose that information."

Sergeant Atkins blew out her mouth. "My senior, DI Mic Steele, I mean, DI Bruce Horne, will be in touch. Meanwhile, send me all documents in regards to your case so that my team can determine if they factor in on Quinn's murder."

Chapter Forty-Six

No one said anything. Finally Sergeant Atkins broke the silence. "Maybe one of the investors killed Quinn."

Constable Gavin said, "But what about Lynn Lockhart?"

"Just because Senior is holding her, doesn't mean she's guilty."

"Doesn't mean she isn't," he said.

"Who found out the FBI was investigating Quinn?" Alexa asked.

"Our Chief Petrie," Sergeant Atkins said. "He…"

Her radio interrupted her. Alexa heard Bruce's voice.

"Ten-ten. OCU has located the weapons. Maraekaho Road and Kirby, past the cemetery. Occupants have barricaded points of entry."

"Ten-three, boss," Sergeant Atkins said. She motioned to Constables Gavin and Coop. "Let's go."

Alexa started to follow.

"Stay here," the sergeant ordered.

The three officers were out of the room before she could lodge a complaint. She was a part of the team until she wasn't.

She pulled out a chair and sank into it. What if something happened to Bruce? She lowered her head below her knees, trying to tamp her panic. Her loose hair created a dark cave in which she imagined a worst case scenario: shots fired, man down. Then she told herself to get a grip. This was New Zealand. Gun violence was rare.

The fax machine buzzed to life. When the printing was finished, she retrieved the papers.

The cover sheet said: FROM: Special Agent Larry Jacobs, FBI Field Office Los Angeles, TO: Sergeant Allison Atkins, Hastings Police Department, New Zealand, Confidential. She glanced at the first page—legalese about Harlan Quinn's pending charges with conspiracy to commit theft of trade secrets. She skimmed the next page: BioMatic's knowledge, research, and development of certain biosimilars had been obtained using misappropriated intellectual property.

Quinn had been a cheater in more ways than one.

The documents were confidential. Alexa had been privy to the phone call and knew Quinn had been in hot water, but her boss, Dan, had said no coloring outside the lines. She tidied the stack and set them on the table. More papers slipped out of the fax machine, but she ignored them and made sure the door locked behind her.

The thirty minutes she spent in the empty lab—Pamela-Not-Pam had the morning off—dragged.

She threw down her Pilot G2 pen and checked her phone. She couldn't see anything through the smashed screen. She decided to drive to the bunker and check out the webcam herself. Catch Lynn, if it was her, red-handed. She licked her chapped lips, gathered the crime kit, and hustled to the parking lot. She thought of telling someone, but remembered a police officer was assigned to guard the Black Reef estate. She'd check in with him or her before entering the bunker.

She focused on the news from the FBI as she drove. Why did Quinn steal secrets from his former partner? Why not stay at Q&G Biologics and develop the drug there? Maybe Gupta had been a rule stickler and Quinn wanted to speed things up, to help his daughter. What did Gupta know about the investigation? Why would he come to New Zealand to assist Quinn's family when Quinn had stolen from him?

Alexa hunched forward in the driver's seat, anxious to pass the slow-driving car ahead of her. Who drives the speed limit?

Gupta said he was leaving today. She decided to stop by The Retreat and ask him about Quinn's betrayal. Before he slipped away.

Movement in her rearview mirror caught her attention. A lime green camper van tailed closely, probably anxious to pass the slowpoke up ahead as well.

She lost them both in Clifton, and now the sea was out her window, gray instead of turquoise, a lone boat plying its waters.

No one greeted Alexa at The Retreat. The vase on the round table was empty. No cheerful voices or clink of glassware came from the dining room. Alexa walked into the restaurant, surprised it was empty. A server backed through the kitchen doors, carrying a tray. She turned. "Oh. *Kia ora*."

Alexa hadn't seen her before.

"It's buffet this morning, in the lounge," the server said. She lifted the tray a few inches. "Fresh cinnamon rolls."

"No one was in the lobby. I'm visiting a guest."

The server looked panicked. "Oh, well, we're short-staffed. We've had a tragedy." Her eyes brimmed and Alexa worried for the pastry. "Which guest are you visiting?"

"Mr. Gupta. He's still here, right?"

She glanced at the rolls. "Is he expecting you?"

"Yes," Alexa lied. She tried to remember the name of Gupta's suite. Tranquility? Serenity? Katrina had said there were only six rooms.

"Just go on, then; it'll be fine."

Alexa tried the opposite wing from Katrina's office and room. She passed Halcyon and stopped in front of the door labeled HARMONY. This was it.

She knocked.

No one answered.

She knocked harder. "Mr. Gupta? It's Alexa Glock."

Still no answer.

Alexa looked down the spacious hallway. At the far end, a large window framed hilly dunes covered in dancing grass. She stepped down the hallway to the last room: Peace. Everything was quiet. Too quiet.

She returned to Harmony, banged at the door, waited, and then turned the knob.

Locked.

Her hand tingled, as if Gupta had morphed into water and slid through her fingers.

Chapter Forty-Seven

She drove the narrow winding lane to Black Reef as fast as she dared. The webcam, not Mr. Gupta, was the reason for her mission. She parked near the big house, surprised there was no patrol car. She guessed the officer had been called away with the team.

She ignored the flutter of panic in her chest.

A slice of cottage porch was visible past the pool. She felt Lynn's fingers squeezing her wrist: a phantom reminder of the woman's strength.

But Lynn Lockhart was still at the station.

Crime kit over her shoulder, she headed past the main entrance of the bunker and up the berm. She wanted to check that the hatch in the shed was open to ensure air flow and a means of escape, should she need one. She ducked under the police tape and looked in. The hatch gaped open in the middle of the floor.

Outside, the air was cold and salty, the sky overcast. No gannets or gulls circled above. The branches of the fake tree were bare. She thought of Linda Crosby's bleak prediction of a land without birds, and her own future, if she left New Zealand: a land without Bruce.

The caution tape flapped across the main entrance of the bunker. She pulled on gloves and a mask and tucked her Maglite into her pocket, mindful of how dark it had been when the lights went out during her first visit. Had that been Joe? The stairs reverberated under her feet. She walked through the first door, glad it was open wide. Weak light illuminated the far end of the concrete corridor. Her feet slowed as she approached the decontamination shower.

Her former boyfriend Jeb had talked her into going to a haunted house in Raleigh a couple years ago, some Halloween fundraiser. Ghouls and ax murderers had hidden in every recess, waiting to jump out.

And then there was *Psycho.*

The shower was empty.

She shouldered the second door open wider. The smell, like a bad dream when you first wake up, lingered. Five days ago Harlan Quinn had been a decomposing John Doe. Now the team was close to finding who had killed him.

She passed the shelves of food and checked the power panel: It was set on Solar. Alexa exhaled. Sun power didn't cause carbon monoxide to build.

The lighting was set to Day. She patted her Maglite through her pocket, just in case, and headed to the webcam monitor. The screen blinked to life when she touched it. Her menu choices were File, View, Camera, and Live View.

She touched Live View. The screen filled with gannets. Chicks hopped back and forth on their ledges. An adult crash-landed, knocking into another adult. They sparred with their long bills. Above, a clear view of the cliff path, empty. Below, a sliver of beach, rock, and waves performing their endless cycle.

Life, Alexa thought. It was precious. It was precarious.

She adjusted the angle of the hidden camera so she could see more beach and then more cliff path. A sound made her freeze. Her eyes flitted around the room. She held her breath.

A whoosh of air blew across her face. Maybe a storm was brewing. The breeze was proof of the open door and freedom.

She touched View on the monitor screen. It took her to a collection folder.

Bingo.

She searched the dates for Monday, 11 April. Katrina Flores was last seen at 7:30 a.m., so Alexa started with 7:45. Her fingers trembled. Gannets. Chicks. Seaweed and feathers. Sparring and loving. The lighting was bright. She increased the playback speed and watched the birds hasten through the minutes.

7:50: No one on the cliff path.

7:55: Nothing.

8:00: A seagull.

8:03: Red hair, pink jacket, walking quickly.

8:04: Dark hair.

She heard footsteps on the stairs.

Chapter Forty-Eight

Instinct told her to ditch the kit and get out of there. She tore into the kitchen and living area, frantic to remember which bedroom had the escape hatch. The webcam drapes were open. She caught a glimpse of someone, a man, walking along the cliff top.

Alexa blinked. It was Amit Gupta.

She ran to the drapes, pressed her back against the screen, jerked them closed.

Over the pounding of her heart, the footsteps grew louder. Control room. Kitchen. Dining area. If Amit Gupta was walking cliffside, who was almost to the drapes? Lynn Lockhart? Had she been released?

"Hallo?" a man called.

Alexa froze.

"Constable Karu, Hastings police. Who's here?"

She let her breath go and opened the curtains.

The constable jumped. "Eh? What are you doing?"

"Hiding from you."

"Nah yeah, you're the CSI lady."

"Alexa Glock. I didn't know who was here. There was no patrol car when I arrived."

He hitched his pants up and stammered. "Drove off to, um, use the facilities like."

She whirled around to check the webcam screen. Gupta was gone. Had she really seen him? "I found some footage," she told Constable Karu. "I think, well, let me show you."

He followed her back into the control room. The recording had continued to play. She was appalled to see herself clambering down the cliff like an ungainly stork. She froze the frame.

"Isn't that you?"

She ignored the constable and rewound the recording to 8:00. She pushed slo-mo and willed her heart to slo-mo. She glued her eyes to the cliff top. "Watch."

The constable hitched his pants again.

"Any second now," she whispered.

Katrina Flores strolled into view, perhaps troubled because she walked head down instead of looking out to sea or at the birds. Her untethered hair lifted in the breeze.

A man sprang into view and shoved her from behind.

"No," Alexa cried.

"Jaysus," Constable Karu said.

Katrina, arms whirling like pink wings that couldn't save her, fell in slow motion.

Constable Karu looked at Alexa in disbelief. His youthful innocence leeched away before her eyes. He'd close his and replay this scene. Over and over.

So would she.

Evil crouches in the recesses of all of us, Alexa thought, *and most of us reined it in, kept it at bay, never let it see light.* Blood pulsed in her ears as she rewound the clip. She froze the frame and studied Amit Gupta about to murder Katrina in cold blood.

Her brain kicked into gear. "This might be the only recording. I'm going to take photos as backup."

She dug the camera out of the crime kit and hung it around her neck. Constable Karu was mute as she photographed the horrifying image. "Forward the frame," she commanded.

His hands shook.

She photographed the next image—Gupta's hands outstretched—and fantasized about rewinding time and saving Katrina. "Forward again," she said.

Gupta was gone in the next frame, jarring her memory, adrenaline flooding her veins. "I just saw him. Walking along the cliff. Go call for backup!"

Constable Karu crashed into a stack of canned soups. "Bollocks."

Progresso barley vegetable rolled to Alexa's foot. She picked it up and noticed the constable's eyes widen. She followed his gaze.

Amit Gupta—the in-the-flesh Amit Gupta—blocked the exit, his face hard, a vein on his forehead pulsing. He raised something metal over his head—a bat, maybe. Alexa hurled the can at him. It struck his cheek. He lurched back, the bat still poised. Constable Karu ducked his head and charged Gupta like a bull. Alexa turned and ran into the bunker, the camera bouncing against her chest. She heard a sickening thwack. A cry of pain. Another thwack.

She dashed through the living area. When the lights went out, she opened her mouth to scream but caught herself. She groped her way into the hallway, feeling doomed that the escape hatch in the bedroom would be shut. Blocked.

Trapped.

She felt her way down the hall, past the theater room and weapons vault. The bedroom she wanted was next. She patted the door, the walls, sensed fresh air. Faint light led her to the walk-in closet. She grabbed the handles of the pull-down stairs and looked up. Crossing into the light meant life, not death.

She climbed two steps at a time, her ankles throbbing at the thought of Gupta grabbing them and yanking her back.

The floor of the shed, knee to wood, was comfort for one second. Then she jumped up. She had to get help. She considered closing the hatch, but couldn't bear the thought it might trap Constable Karu.

Wind lifted her hair outside the shed. Ugly brown clouds

smeared the sky. She started running to her car, her knee protesting. Halfway, she stopped.

The car keys were in the crime kit.

She zeroed in on the patrol car. She galloped toward it, thinking of the radio. The camera thumped against her chest until she trapped it under her armpit.

The patrol car was locked.

She tore up the cottage steps and bashed at the door, tried the knob, thinking there might be a landline inside. It was locked. "Help," she screamed.

The wind whisked her words away.

She looked toward the bunker. Amit Gupta emerged from the stairs. He looked straight at her. Stunned, she jumped off the porch and veered right, toward the big house, the camera banging again. From the corner of her eye, she saw Gupta running too, loping across the grass.

She veered between the pool and the big house. At the edge of the cliff she looked left, then right. Miles of openness in both directions. Gupta would appear any second.

Down was the way to go. Again.

Chapter Forty-Nine

She plopped on the edge, stretching her feet until she made contact with the first ledge. Her hair blew in her face, making it hard to see. She lowered herself to the next ledge. Two gannet chicks hopped out of the way. Another one threw its head back, opened its bill, and screeched. An adult, its pointy wings stretched wide, flew by so closely that Alexa felt a draft.

She looked up.

No Gupta.

She looked down.

Rock. Sea.

She had to face the cliff to reach the next ledge, vaguely aware of the ammonia stench. She lowered down, feeling for traction with her Keds, longing for the thicker tread of her running shoes. The camera caught on a rock. She tugged it free. It hit her chin.

A stab of hope: the bird lady would spot her and send help. Or maybe a tractor would round a bend.

Where was Gupta?

She'd done this before. She scrambled right, sat on the edge, and lowered her legs. One Ked slipped in guano. Her legs flew out, and she landed on her butt. The camera bounced and pain shot up her spine. Chicks krokked and chittered. Fat raindrops agitated them further. She pressed her back against rock. An adult swooped by, its blue eye watching her.

Sweat popped out of her forehead. Her heart pounded.

She groped in her pocket for her phone. Empty. She tried the other pocket. There it was. She yanked it out and swiped. It lit up, but the shattered screen made punching numbers impossible. "Call Bruce," she shouted, hoping to activate the voice control. "Officer down." She pressed the phone to her ear. Nothing. She tried again. "Dial 111."

"Give me the camera," a voice said.

She dropped the phone. Her fingers dug into grit as she watched it bounce to the rocks below, scatter birds, and then launch over the abyss. Like Katrina.

She looked up.

Amit Gupta's face stared down. His cheek dripped blood. His glasses glinted from the edge of his nose and then slipped free. He grabbed for them, but they bounced next to Alexa and then over the side.

Alexa lowered down to the next shelf. Something slick with rain—a shell maybe—sliced her palm. She stepped on a pile of fish bone. Speckled chicks surrounded her. They beat their wings.

She sensed upheaval, a foaming of the sea.

Was Gupta climbing down?

A cascade of pebbles scattered the chicks. The one next to her flapped its wings open, shut, open, shut.

"Why did you kill Quinn?" she yelled up. "Why didn't you just report him?"

More pebbles rolled off the ledge. Gupta was coming. What did he have to lose? Like Bob Dylan sang, "Nothin.'" There's no going back after murder.

"I couldn't," Gupta called.

She heard a thump, a shriek. A chick, trying to flap its wings, hit the rock below, bounced, went limp.

The bastard had kicked a chick.

Alexa's greenstone pendant pulsed and burned against her chest. She scrambled to the edge, slick with guano and rain, turned her body, and lowered, feeling for the next shelf. She toed right. She toed left. Just void. She let go and hit the outcrop below, flinging herself forward. A gannet shook its butter-colored head violently, sharp beak open, and emitted kroks and *ka, ka, kas*. Other gannets joined the cacophony. She turned her body and looked skyward. A snowstorm of gannets, fifty, maybe a hundred, veered, swooped, dove, and hovered.

A pebble bounced off her hand. She looked up. Gupta's foot dangled over the lip. One leather low-top sneaker. Then another. Alexa scrambled to her feet and stretched to reach the closest foot, inches from her fingers. She envisioned yanking Gupta over the ledge.

Something kept her from it. "What about the science?" she called. "How could you forsake science?"

The dangling feet stilled. Gupta didn't answer.

She saw his calves now. He was coming.

The scene played out in her mind: Gupta and her on the same ledge, a duel with one of them falling like the chick. Like Katrina.

Two gannets swept in like dive bombers.

Gupta's feet disappeared. "Christ, shoo," he yelled.

Alexa heard a scuffle, the flap of wings, the clacking of bills. A shower of feathers and seaweed fell from Gupta's ledge.

"Goddamn birds! What the fuck."

More gannets swooped in, swooped by.

The next outcrop was too steep to reach. Alexa sidled along the ledge, keeping a hand on the wall, to a place where it wasn't as precipitous. The rain intensified. The camera scraped as she lowered herself to another ridge. She stuffed it in her shirt. Chicks made room, their gray-blue eyes watching.

Gupta screamed. When she had a vantage point, she looked up. A swarm of white encircled him. His arms flailed.

She lowered herself to the thin lip below and sidled right,

groping cracks and crannies. Her hand landed on something unnatural. She jerked it away. A box was tucked into a nook. A trap, set by the bird lady. Flies swarmed around it. Behind the mesh of the cage she saw a dead stoat, mouth open, its sharp teeth now useless to kill.

The sound of waves grew with each lower shelf. When her feet were planted on wet sand, she looked up. The sky churned with flapping wings. It darkened to mottled brown as one by one, ten by ten, fifty by fifty, the gannet chicks fledged.

Chapter Fifty

A maelstrom of sand blasted her face as a helicopter landed on the thin strip of beach ahead of her. A man jumped out and ran at her with a large yellow slicker, which he wrapped around her. She recognized Graham, the guy who'd accused her of having a panic attack.

She spit out sand. "I'm okay."

"Hurry," he said, gesturing to a breaking wave. "The tide has turned." He ushered her into the waiting copter where the pilot gave her a thumbs-up. Her hands had cramped; she couldn't buckle her harness. Graham did it.

"Wait." She grabbed his wrist. "The birds." She craned her head. The moving cloud was over the bay, like a squall. The chicks were safe. For now.

"Call the police," she yelled.

Graham indicated he couldn't hear and handed her a set of headphones. She brushed her hair out of her eyes and pulled them on. "Call the police. There's a man in the bunker. He needs help."

"He crawled up the steps and radioed for assistance. He's already been medevaced."

She sank back against the seat. Her stomach lurched as the chopper lifted. They circled toward Black Reef.

The camera. She panicked until she felt its form against her chest. "There's another man."

Graham pointed out the window. "They've got him."

Alexa peered down. Through the rain-blotched window, she made out three police cars, flashing lights, and a white pickup truck parked at haphazard angles around her silver Vitz. A gaggle of people, most in blue uniforms, gathered cliffside. She tried to pick out Bruce.

"We're to take you to hospital," Graham said through the headset.

"I don't need a hospital."

Graham glanced at her lap. Alexa unfurled her left hand and looked at her palm. The jagged cut dripped blood. She pressed it to her thigh.

They landed on the hospital roof in fifteen minutes. Graham helped her out, and an orderly met her with a wheelchair. She sank into it gratefully.

She wouldn't let anyone tend to her until a police officer took possession of the camera. Her hand trembled as she filled out the date and time on the chain of custody form. "It's key evidence," she told the unfamiliar officer.

He nodded solemnly.

Then she allowed a nurse to wash and bandage her hand and chin where the camera had taken a divot of skin, and check her for other injuries. She couldn't stop shaking. The nurse wrapped a blanket around her and brought her hot tea. She was on her second cup an hour later when Bruce tore into the waiting area. For a second Alexa wondered who he was so concerned about.

"Alexa."

She dropped the blanket and let herself be crushed against his chest. She closed her eyes and let herself feel safe, feel loved, feel home.

Bruce pulled back but held her arms. He looked her up and down. She was a mess: hair whipped and full of sand, torn and smeared khakis. He met her eyes again. "We got Gupta."

Alexa nodded.

"I've been calling. Why didn't you answer your phone?"

Reasons duked it out on the tip of her tongue: My phone was under the boot of a Cur. The screen was cracked. I dropped it off the cliff. Because you cheated.

She settled for, "How is Constable Karu?"

Bruce squeezed her arms. "They're working on him now. The doc says he has a fractured patella and a nasty scalp wound. Maybe brain swelling. It's too early to tell."

Alexa thought of the brave Constable ramming into Gupta so that she could escape. "I thought he might be dead."

"Gupta used a branch from that metal tree to attack him. Then he beat the webcam to destroy footage."

"I have pictures."

"Good for backup. The tech guys will find out if footage is stored elsewhere."

If not, only she and Constable Karu would hold the moving image of Katrina flying through the air, bouncing off rock, landing on the beach. Maybe it would be better that way.

"You did good," Bruce said.

First Constable Karu helped her, then the birds. "The gannets surrounded Gupta so I could get away."

Bruce raised an eyebrow, which maddened her. She stepped back.

"Gupta was on that plane—a hired private jet—that landed the day after Quinn arrived," Bruce said. "He left ten hours later. Made it back to California and called a meeting the same day. He's here, on the fourth floor. I'm heading up now."

"I want to go with you."

"You aren't a police officer." He watched her mouth open. A flicker crossed his eyes. "Okay. But only from the doorway."

Constable Gavin sat outside Gupta's hospital room. He jumped up when he saw Bruce and Alexa. "The doctor is with him. These are for you." He handed Bruce a stack of papers.

Bruce turned his back to read them.

Constable Gavin smiled shyly at Alexa. "Chur, Ms. Glock. Is it true about the gannets?"

Chapter Fifty-One

Gupta had Frankenstein stitches on his cheek. Alexa was thrilled that the can of soup she'd hurled had hurt him. Without his glasses, his eyes were unfocused. His arms were bandaged, and his right wrist was cuffed to the metal frame of the bed.

The doctor nodded to Bruce. "We've started Mr. Gupta on antibiotics. Bird scratches or bites cause an array of diseases."

Alexa looked at her gull pecks. The area around them was pinkish.

When the doctor left, Bruce motioned for Constable Gavin. He squeezed past Alexa. Then Bruce turned on his phone's recorder. "Mr. Gupta, I am arresting you for the murder of Harlan Quinn and Katrina Flores, and the attempted murder of Constable Reeves Karu." He continued with the rest of New Zealand's version of Miranda Rights.

Gupta didn't appear to be listening. His vague stare settled on Alexa. "You," he said.

She stepped into the room. "I don't understand why you just didn't report Quinn. Why kill him?"

Bruce glared at her. "I'll handle the interrogation."

"I'm not talking until my lawyer arrives," Gupta said.

"That's your right," Bruce said. "I'll answer your question, Ms. Glock." He held up the papers Constable Gavin had given him.

"It wasn't just Quinn. Mr. Gupta was also being investigated by the IRS, the FBI, and the Acting United States Attorney, too. Let me see." Bruce took his time scanning the documents. "Charges include fraud and false statements to a government agency."

Gupta's faced darkened.

Alexa stepped closer to the bed. "Now that you've been charged, an officer will take your fingerprints."

Bruce didn't interrupt.

"I think they'll match the ones I lifted from the duct tape," Alexa said. "And from Katrina Flores's jacket. You left a perfect palm print."

"There's the CCTV at the little airport, too," Constable Gavin threw in. "Shows your comings and goings."

"Physical evidence goes over well with the judge," Bruce said.

Gupta struggled to sit straighter. "It was Quinn who falsified data. He made sure my name was on everything. He dragged me into the gutter. My work, my research was ruined."

Alexa remembered something Gupta had said at the morgue: his work was his family.

Gupta squinted at her. "Quinn couldn't wait out the years drug trials take. Everything was about his daughter." He jerked at the chain tethering him to the bedside. "When I met him at a party, he acted as if he'd done nothing wrong. Slapped me on the back, asked how the old company was doing. He told everyone he was about to cure diabetes. People lined up to write him checks."

Bruce shot Alexa a look. "Quinn must have known you were angry. How did you get in the bunker?" he asked.

Gupta barked a laugh. "The hubris on that man. I told him I bought New Zealand property and wanted to build a bunker. All good, bragging about your Plan B at a dinner party, but the chance to show it off? He couldn't resist."

Bruce kept his face neutral. "Mr. Gupta, we have photos of you pushing Katrina Flores off the cliff."

Gupta shook his head. "She passed me the day I left Quinn's

bunker. Nearly ran me off the road in one of those ATVs. I came back to see if she recognized me."

Alexa couldn't stomach any more. She left the room. She set off for the station. Halfway there she stopped to sit on her park bench.

Harlan Quinn had everything he could have ever wanted and wasn't satisfied. And Amit Gupta committed murder for being wronged by a business partner.

A couple strolled by, holding hands. Alexa studied them. Did the guy with the bad haircut have a wife back home? Did the girl—laughing loudly—harbor evil? Did everyone? Did she?

Constable Karu had risked his life for her. Charlie, with his hazel eyes that looked like hers, showered her—mostly—with wisdom and forgiveness. Coop overcame a hard childhood to do good in the world. Then there was Bruce. His dogged quest for justice. His almost declaration of love. He deserved a chance to explain when she was ready to listen.

She struggled to her feet and trudged to the station. Constable Cooper was in the briefing room. Her face blossomed into a smile at the sight of Alexa. "Couldn't wait for me to get back, could you?"

Alexa returned the smile, just to see if she could. Her face didn't crack. "What happened with the weapons?"

"Your friend Bulldog led the OCU guys right to his house. The weapons were in the garage. A couple shots were fired, but most of the people were hungover and sleeping. I imagine it was like we thought: the Curs double-dipped."

TWO WEEKS

LATER

Chapter Fifty-Two

Alexa relished having the Auckland apartment to herself. Her roommate, Natalie, was still away on canine training; no chance of her overhearing her showdown with Bruce. Alexa cleaned up her dinner dishes, which consisted of throwing away takeout containers, and settled at the kitchen table with a glass of wine to wait for Bruce.

She hadn't seen him since returning from Hastings. When she got around to buying a new phone (she took out insurance this time), she had five texts and three voicemails from him. She imagined how infuriating her ghosting had been, but what if she didn't like what he had to say? She had applied to the university in Scotland as a backup. They had a position open for an associate professor in the forensics department.

Bruce had finally walked over from the police station to the Forensic Service Center and stopped by her cubicle.

"Alexa, what's going on?"

"What do you mean?"

He waited patiently.

"Come over tonight," she'd finally said. "We'll talk."

His eyes lit up. He gazed at her a moment longer, but she turned back to the evidence log she was updating.

Charlie said she owed Bruce a chance to explain. Charlie also said what had gone on in Bruce's marriage wasn't her business. She sipped her wine anxiously.

Then there were the girls, Sammie and Denise. It was one thing dating Bruce, who may or may not be trustworthy, but it was another thing to form a relationship with his daughters.

She ushered him into the kitchen a few minutes after eight. He skirted the enormous dog crate and looked toward the stove. She saw disappointment in his eyes. She handed him a glass of wine, kicked off her Keds, and sat.

He set the glass on the table. His familiar scent was tantalizing. "What's up, Alexa? Why have you been ignoring my calls?"

She was strong. She could do this. Her heart raced. She wasn't ready. "Any news about DI Steele? Is she back at work?"

"You're stalling." Bruce sat across from her. "Mic's taken parental leave. It's her due, being a foster parent. It was Superintendent Parker's idea."

"What about Lynn Lockhart? Does she get to keep the cottage?"

He drummed his fingers on the table. "Chief Petrie said she wasn't mentioned in Quinn's will."

That was a cautionary tale, if she ever heard one. Don't rely on someone else. Alexa studied the worry lines on Bruce's forehead. She hated being responsible. She gulped the last of her wine and pushed the glass away. "Why did you and your wife, I mean ex-wife, get divorced?"

He stilled. "Why are you asking?"

Here goes. "Did you cheat on her? Is that why?"

His shoulders slumped a fraction. "Why the sudden interest in my former marriage?"

"We've never talked about it. Why you got divorced."

"You've been quiet about your past as well."

Alexa didn't respond.

"Sharla wasn't happy." He met Alexa's gaze. "Over the years being married to me took its toll. She didn't like the hours and stress of being a cop's spouse. She didn't like the pay. She wanted me to compartmentalize and never talk about work at home."

Alexa loved talking shop with Bruce.

He shrugged. "She met someone else."

"You mean she…"

He narrowed his eyes. "She what?"

Alexa studied her socks. Scientists estimate only three to five percent of mammal species practiced monogamy. What was the big deal? Then she thought of the gannets. Constable Gavin had said they mate for life.

"Sharla met Riley a couple months ago. She said he completes her. The girls have met him."

Poor Sammie and Denise. Their parents thrusting new people at them. "Do you, did you love her?"

He looked at his left hand. Maybe where his wedding band had been. "I did. It was like not being able to solve a case that dragged on for years. I worked all the angles, but I couldn't solve my marriage." He stood as if the seat were hot and went to the refrigerator. "Do you have any beer?"

"But were you faithful to her? When you were married?"

He kept his back turned. As far as Alexa was concerned, his silence was an answer. She felt a lead weight in her stomach.

He shut the fridge and returned empty-handed. "What's this about?"

"Dr. Li said…" She stood on a precipice and found her footing. "It's about trust and respect."

"I'm listening." He remained standing. His eyes sparked like they did when he was angry.

"I don't know that I'm ready to take our relationship farther. Maybe we need a break."

"What the hell? All of a sudden you don't trust me? Trust what we've been slowly building? I love you, Alexa."

She was not expecting this declaration. For a moment she couldn't breathe. What if Bruce's alleged infidelity was the excuse she needed to follow her love-'em-and-leave-'em pattern? "I have a commitment problem. You can ask Charlie."

His unexpected smile cracked open her heart. "I don't think so. You just hadn't met me." He walked to the door. "It's your choice whether to call me," he said and left.

She sat so still that she could hear the faucet drip. Bruce had gifted her a choice. She felt weightless, as if she had wings and wind.

After a while, she opened her laptop and read an email from Natalie: His name is Kaos. He can't wait to meet you. The attached photo was of a blackish German shepherd with mischievous gold eyes.

Living with a puppy was a choice.

She opened the next email:

> Dear Ms. Glock:
>
> This is to acknowledge that we have received your application for Associate Professor of Applied Forensic Science at Abertay University and are processing it.
>
> On a personal note: Thank you for your comments on retrieving latent prints from bird feathers under lab conditions. I am glad the technique helped you solve a crime.
>
> We have improved on the technique to recover fingerprints from bird feathers that have been left outside and exposed to environmental factors such as wind and rain. Bird crime incidents are difficult to prosecute, so this new technique could be transformative.
>
> The Department secretary will contact you to set up an interview.
>
> Sincerely,
> Ben Odden, PhD

Director, Forensic Science Program
Abertay University
Dundee, Scotland

Alexa closed the laptop on all her choices. Then she closed her eyes. She summoned a sky full of fledging chicks, setting off on their trans-Tasman flight, the spray of the future biting at their faces.

ACKNOWLEDGMENTS

Cape Kidnappers in New Zealand is resplendent with Australasian gannets and Māori myth. The Gannet Beach Adventures tractor tour my husband and I took inspired this book. Thank you for taking me there, Forrest, even if we got stuck in the sand.

Thank you to Kim Lindsay, managing director of Gannet Beach Adventures, for answering my questions about the gannets and the spectacular geology of Cape Kidnappers.

My forensic consultant, Dr. Heidi Eldridge, is helpful and delightful. After reading one scene, Heidi said, "I'm so jealous right now. Vacuum metal deposition is hella cool—also hella expensive. Only about two labs in the U.S. even have one." I think you're hella cool, Heidi.

Forensic pathologist Dr. Leslie Anderson guided me on the death investigation system in New Zealand and read my autopsy scenes for accuracy. Dr. Anderson says it is a privilege to be the last doctor a person sees and to be able to speak on their behalf. She was generous with her time and knowledge.

My writing group is my village. Thank you Nancy Peacock, Lisa Bobst, Denise Cline, Linda Jansen, and Ann Parrent.

Diane DiBiase is my terrific editor at Poisoned Pen Press/ Sourcebooks. She strengthens my books with her guidance and buoys me with her faith in Alexa Glock. Thanks also to Beth

Deveny, assistant content editor extraordinaire, and the rest of the team at Poisoned Pen Press/Sourcebooks.

Thank you to Barbara Peters, my first editor, and to Laura Bradford, my agent.

Some of the places in *The Bone Riddle* are real, and others are made up. Any mistakes are real and mine alone.

ABOUT THE AUTHOR

Sara E. Johnson lives in Durham, NC. She worked as a middle school reading specialist and local newspaper contributor before her husband lured her to New Zealand for a year. *The Bone Riddle* is the fourth Alexa Glock Forensics Mystery.

© Morgan Henderson
Photography